"*Thieves* is a clever,
dissembling, genre-busting
tumult of a novel."
Ottawa Citizen

PRAISE FOR

THIEVES

"The brilliance of *Thieves* lies in the way Kulyk Keefer reveals Mansfield in all her facets. . . . *Thieves* will steal your imagination. It's a love story and a mystery that folds over and over itself, only to deliver finally a most satisfying answer to the questions it poses."   —*Calgary Herald*

"Janice Kulyk Keefer long ago proved that she can hold her own with the best writers in the country. . . . [*Thieves*] is certain to vault her to the very top of that list."
—*Winnipeg Free Press*

"If you were among the many swept by Michael Cunningham's book (and movie) *The Hours* . . . the next logical step is to pick up a copy of Janice Kulyk Keefer's *Thieves*. . . . A truly admirable, engrossing read. The beauty of *Thieves* lies in the way it makes the academic pursuit of a literary icon seem every bit as exciting as crime detection."
—*The Gazette* (Montreal)

"The genius of Keefer's book is that she brings Mansfield's own fiery qualities alive in her pages, proving that the art and soul of this prickly artist has triumphed over time itself."   —*Toronto Star*

OTHER BOOKS BY JANICE KULYK KEEFER

The Paris–Napoli Express

White of the Lesser Angels

Transfigurations

Under Eastern Eyes:
A Critical Reading of Canadian Maritime Fiction

Constellations

Reading Mavis Gallant

Travelling Ladies

Rest Harrow

The Green Library

Marrying the Sea

Honey and Ashes

THIEVES

THIEVES

A Novel of Katherine Mansfield

———

JANICE KULYK KEEFER

Harper*Perennial*Canada
HarperCollins*PublishersLtd*

Published by Harper*Perennial*Canada,
an imprint of HarperCollins Publishers Ltd

First hardcover edition by HarperCollins
Publishers Ltd: 2004
This trade paperback edition: 2004

HarperCollins books may be purchased for
educational, business, or sales promotional
use through our Special Markets Department.

HarperCollins Publishers Ltd
2 Bloor Street East, 20th Floor
Toronto, Ontario, Canada
M4W 1A8

www.harpercollins.ca

The author gratefully acknowledges the
assistance of the Canada Council for the
Arts in the writing of this novel.

Library and Archives Canada Cataloguing
in Publication

Keefer, Janice Kulyk, 1952–
Thieves : a novel of Katherine Mansfield /
Janice Kulyk Keefer. – 1st trade pbk. ed.

ISBN 0-00-639281-4

1. Mansfield, Katherine, 1888–1923 –
Fiction. I. Title.

PS8571.E435T46 2005   C813'.54
C2004-906583-1

RRD 9 8 7 6 5 4 3 2 1

Printed and bound in the United States
Set in Monotype Plantin

Front cover illustration adapted from the
cover of the libretto to the opera Turandot,
by Giacomo Puccini. Ricordi, Milan. Museo
Teatrale alla Scala, Milan, Italy. Courtesy of
Scala/Art Resource, NY.

Front cover image is a photograph of
Katherine Mansfield, taken by Stanley
Polkinghorne Andrew. Making New
Zealand Centennial Collection, courtesy
of The Alexander Turnbull Library,
Wellington, New Zealand (Image reference
MNZ-2632-1/2 – slightly cropped).

I had ceased to ask that terrible question—what is the good of it all? Now it seemed quite plain and simple: the proper object of life was happiness, and I promised myself much happiness ahead.
—Leo Tolstoy, "Family Happiness"

THIEVES

To a woman with as many names as she had masks, as many roles as she had selves, most—perhaps all of them—false. A woman whose face was as expressionless, some said, as a china or a wooden doll's; a woman who some compared to a chameleon, to quicksilver or a divining rod. Who could liken a newborn kitten's paws to unripe raspberries and confess to a desire to put all the people she hated on a toasting fork, to watch them frizzle.

Who knew at nineteen exactly what she wanted out of life: not love or happiness but "power, wealth, freedom," without which, she knew, there could be no love, no happiness worthy of the name. Who, at the age of twenty, put half a globe between herself and her native land, the icy disapproval of her family, wanting, "more even than talking or laughing or being happy," to be a writer.

A writer who could describe, like no one else, the dangerous delight of being alive, "so that you are almost afraid to breathe—as though a butterfly fanned its wings upon your breast." Who, dragged out by illness, compared herself to a fly fallen into a milk jug, a stray, eager dog with a body like "a cage on four wooden pegs." A woman who, within a whisper of dying, could write to her sister for a cream to bleach incipient moustache hairs, pine after Charlie Chaplin films, send a friend a postcard of Blake's Mirth and Her Companions—*dancing figures, naked and alert.*

Who lived, during her thirty-four years, in eight countries and dozens of flats and borrowed houses. Whose characters shared the same transient world as she: not only park benches, public gardens, cafés, and endless city streets, but rooms in cheap or lush hotels, those "permanent railway stations without trains."

Who was satisfied, in her writing, with nothing less than perfection. Who never believed her work achieved anything like perfection, though critics have declared it to have changed the course of the short story in English. Whose best stories have the dance and quickness of a candle, burning up the life they catch as if it were paper.

A woman whose material remains include a blade-shaped bookmark crafted from silver and greenstone; a scrap from a white-and-gold-striped dress. A solid brass pen-wiper, shaped like a pig and given her by her father; the fringed shawl, embroidered with birds and fruit and flowers, that draped the bareness of her coffin. A lock of her hair, so dark and lustrous that it looks alive. And books, journals, reviews, story fragments, letters. Hundreds and hundreds of letters, of which some of the most passionate will cross two oceans, be locked in a cabinet, bequeathed to a library, stolen, and, just as mysteriously, returned, although the thief remains unknown.

BEYOND THE BLUE MOUNTAINS

Remember . . . it is with the eyes open that you must fall—
otherwise it is useless.

Karori, New Zealand, 1898

Three small girls, sitting on the front steps of a large wooden house in the country. They are dressed for a summery day in late November: high-necked, long-sleeved blouses, blue serge pinafores with narrow shoulder straps, scratchy wool stockings, and tightly buckled shoes. Their heads are crowned by straw hats that look like amputated stovepipes.

It is hot, hard work sitting still like this. The older girl has a sweet, pliant face; she is humming a song she learned at Sunday school. The youngest is nearly asleep; her eyelids keep drooping and her mouth goes slack, until she remembers herself and, like a dog shaking water from its coat, jerks awake. But it's the middle sister who steals your attention, the pudgy one bursting out of her tight pinafore, her steel-rimmed glasses glaring in the sun. She sits with her legs wide apart, taking up as much room on the step as she possibly can; her face under the ridiculous hat, with its broad ribbon and upward-poking funnel, is half shadowed, half in light. She looks longingly at a four-year-old boy making mud pies in a sandbox just across from where his sisters sit, so neat, so stiff, and so obedient. The girl is watching how, as her brother lifts his spade from the bucket, thick dark drops fall onto the sand below.

Beyond the sandpit is a mass of garden—not flower beds, but plants blooming just as they please, woolly nightshade and eyebright and angel's trumpet. On any other day, she'd have spent the afternoon exploring that garden, looking for shells curled up beneath the leaves and nestling into the soil. Snail shells like empty houses, pale grey streaked with blue, treasures she'd stuff into the pockets of the pinafore lying now in a heap on her bedroom floor. The girl starts kicking her shoes against the step, each kick a little harder, a little angrier, until the oldest one cries out, "*Don't*, Kass, you're giving me *such* a headache," in a voice copied from a petulant adult's.

Kass gives a few last kicks before replying: "If you've got a headache, Chaddie, it's because you're bored. Why should we have to keep still while Belle's getting ready? We could be sitting here until tomorrow."

Chaddie clasps her hands, anxious in spite of herself: "If she doesn't come soon, we'll be late getting to the docks. We can't be late—Mother and Father would never forgive us." The smallest sister, the one on the step below Kass, starts to whimper, and Chaddie sings out, "Don't fuss, Jeanne. We can't be late and so we won't be late."

Kass reaches out her hand to tickle the back of the small girl's neck. "I tell you what, Jeanne: let's play a game."

"What game?"

"Something I've just invented. I'm calling it 'Beyond the Blue Mountains.'"

Jeanne wriggles free from Kass's hand; she's afraid of mountains, she says. And Chaddie objects that they'll get into trouble—they always do when they listen to Kass. But Kass insists that nothing bad can happen; the game is only pretend.

They'll stay here sitting on the steps exactly the way they've been ordered to do, while in their minds they'll fly off on amazing adventures. This is how the game goes: they're orphans—their house has been destroyed in a fire. They've got nothing now but the clothes on their backs, and the cake and ham and ginger beer they managed to snatch from the kitchen before the timbers came crashing down. Jeanne, who doesn't want her house to burn, and who is puzzling out the word *orphan*, sniffles loudly. Kass shouts over the noise, so that Chummie stops his spadework for a moment and stares at her. "What we've got to do," she yells, "is find a way to get beyond the Blue Mountains. So we can reach our Heart's Desire."

Chaddie objects that there are no mountains in Karori, just hills, and Jeanne, forgetting where she is sitting, begins to wail, "I want to go *hooooome*."

Kass's face flushes a dark red. The game will only work, she insists, if you want to find your heart's desire. And you won't know you even have a heart's desire unless you can imagine something different from where you are right now. That's where the Blue Mountains come in.

But before the game can begin, two women sail out the front door. One is really a girl—Vera, the oldest sister, tall, slender, dressed like the others, but looking much less like a burst sausage. Why, she asks, is Jeanne crying? Chaddie immediately complains that Kass has been trying to make them play pretend. Vera picks her way down the steps, wipes her youngest sister's face with a linen handkerchief, and, in a cold, clear voice, without even looking at Kass, proclaims, "You know very well that 'pretend' is just another word for telling lies. You're in enough trouble at school for lying, Kass. What is Mother going to think when she hears what you've been up to?"

"I don't care what Mother thinks."

"And I'm sure, Kathleen, that your mother doesn't care

3

whether she ever sets eyes on you again. When she finds out how wicked you've been, she'll pack you off to the Home for Waifs and Strays."

It's Aunt Belle speaking in her high, brisk voice—the voice she reserves for family. Turning to look at her, the children see a slightly younger version of their mother, pulling on her gloves, adjusting the veil on her hat, and stepping down the stairs as if her nieces were so many piles of dust to skirt. Belle looks at the happily muddy child in the sandpit and calls out, "Mother, you *must* come and get the boy, he's got filthy again!" She proceeds towards a carriage that is drawing up beside the grassy island in the drive, an island crowned by an aloe plant with soaring sword-like leaves. The sisters follow, Kass at the rear, scowling, looking behind her to see a short stout woman in an aproned dress and white lace cap scurry over to the sandpit.

Suddenly, all Kass wants is to be the child scooped up into the woman's arms; she runs back towards the house as her sisters are climbing into the carriage; she throws her arms around her grandmother's waist.

"There, there," the grandmother murmurs, "don't make a scene, my darling, you'll muss up all your lovely clothes." But she speaks with such kindness that Kass, who would rather have died than betray herself to her aunt or sisters, begins to cry, hot fat tears that drool down her cheeks. Her grandmother stoops, kisses her, and gives her a little push in the direction of the carriage.

———

The road from Karori to Wellington is four miles of dust and bumps and steep inclines, of rakish whistling by Pat the driver, of the horse's clopping hooves and sharp farts that everyone pretends not to hear. Jeanne has fallen asleep; Chaddie is examining the ends of her blond, curling hair. As for Vera and Belle, they are discussing who among the town's elite will be down at the wharf to greet the ship, and speculating on what Annie, the girls' mother, will be wearing—something wonderfully smart from the best shops in London. Only Kass has eyes for the land through which the carriage jolts. She sits with her body twisted away from her companions, her hands grasping the edge of the buggy. Behind their spectacles her eyes eat up the gullies full of karaka and cabbage trees and nikau palms; creamy funnels of arum lilies; clumps of fern and spiky grasses; and rough, bush-covered hills rising up in the distance. Phrases from Belle and Vera's conversation—"nine whole months . . . Father's cousins . . . all the way across Canada!"—are so many beads pierced through by Pat's sharp, clear whistling, looping round and round the carriage.

But they do get to the harbour in time to meet the ship on which Annie and Harold Beauchamp have sailed home all the way from England. Aunt Belle stands waving a lace-edged version of the linen hanky Vera had used to scrub the tears from Jeanne's face. Belle's four nieces are lined up behind her in descending order of height and age. The sky is turquoise, studded with perfectly white sheep-shaped clouds: there's hardly enough wind to rustle the flags hoisted on the posts along the harbour. At the pier everything unfolds as it should, with the first-class passengers being the first down the lowered gangplank. In spite of herself, Kass looks eagerly at the procession, biting her lip so as not to cry out when she sees them, the handsomest couple of all: her sandy-whiskered, strutting father; her mother so elegant and lovely and aloof. Even with her arm wound through her husband's, and the tip of her parasol spiked into the ground, Annie looks as though she could blow away—as though she'd quite like to blow away from the family lined up so solemnly to welcome her.

Suddenly, the girls' parents are looming before them. Father is booming out to a reporter eager for a quote from one of Wellington's leading men of business: "Yes, as our friend of pantomimic fame has so frequently observed, 'Here I am again.' New Zealand, my good man, may be the brightest gem that adorns the Imperial diadem, but we must be vigilant. Markets for our frozen meat are under pressure from Argentine and, more importantly, from Australian producers." He frowns long enough for the reporter to appreciate the seriousness of this pronouncement, then grins, promising him a lengthy interview in a few days' time. At last he turns towards his children.

"Here's a splendid crop, don't you think so, Annie? Just look how they've shot up!" But Mother, embracing her sister, doesn't look; she is whispering, "I almost didn't make it back, Belle—I almost jumped ship and swam all the way to China." But then she, too, turns to her daughters, stooping to kiss the proffered cheeks of Vera, of Chaddie, then stopping before the out-thrust face of her third child. She speaks slowly, clearly, so that her voice carries: "Well, Kathleen. I see you are still as fat as ever." Then she moves on to give a kiss as hard and small as a cough drop to Jeanne.

———

On Taranaki Street, not far from the harbour, the Trowell family is out walking: Thomas Wilberforce, the music master at St. Patrick's; his harried wife, Kate; their ten-year-old twins, Arnold and Garnet; and the youngest child, Dolly. Dolly is decked out in ringlets and bows and laces, but it's the boys who draw the eyes of passersby. Each twin's hair is a cloud of flame, ruddy gold like mediaeval paintings of the Burning Bush. Arnold is carrying a three-quarter-size cello and Garnet a similarly diminished violin in black beaten-up cases. Their mother is explaining to their father that the town's resident phrenologist-cum-psychic has pronounced the boys' organs of artistic genius to be especially well developed. He has predicted that crowds of people, crowned heads among them, will gather to hear the twins perform; that Arnold and Garnet will become the toast of Europe, reaping rewards far, far beyond their parents' fondest dreams.

Thomas Wilberforce harrumphs—they won't accomplish anything unless they work at their rudiments, and because of this foolishness of hers they've lost half a day, as well as a good deal of money better spent on sheet music. His wife is about to reply when a heavily laden carriage, followed by a cart full of trunks, swings by close enough that the Trowells must shift to the edge of the pavement. A big, bluff man with pale blue prominent eyes and sandy whiskers nods genially at them; the beautifully dressed, delicate-looking lady at his side barely inclines her head. The rest of the carriage is bursting with people, including, the Trowell children notice, a troupe of identically dressed girls with their noses in the air. Except for one of them, a dark-haired girl wearing glasses, her face as mask-like as the moon. She twists round to look at them until someone snaps, "Sit straight, Kass, and stop your staring!"

Mrs. Trowell is grateful for the interruption; instead of having to defend her visit to the phrenologist she is able to launch into an attack upon "those Beauchamps." She pronounces it Beechumps instead of Beecham: her husband frowns and the children giggle as Kate Wheeler Trowell trots out her standard harangue. What gives Annie Beauchamp the right to purse her lips at them? Everyone knows that one of Annie's grandfathers kept a pub in Sydney, while the other drowned himself in a cistern. As for Harold, *his* father couldn't keep a job for more than a couple of months at a time. Hadn't he been a storekeeper, prospector, bushwhacker, sawmiller, politician, merchant, and auctioneer before he died a bankrupt? The airs and graces some people put on, scoffs Mrs. Trowell, shaking her head in its made-over hat.

The Trowells' home is on Buller Street. Though it's a modest house, it has stained-glass panels above the door, and the front parlour is crammed with a grand piano, a cello (full size), and shelves overburdened with sheet music. This is the studio in which Mr. Trowell teaches the children of Wellington's well-to-do, and where he drives his children through their musical paces. This includes Dolly, who'd far rather be hanging clothes on the line in a southerly buster than playing scales for her father, given as he is to slapping her head with a ruler after every fumbled note. The Trowells are as respectable a family as any in Wellington, but their clothes are worn and unfashionable. They can barely afford to keep their servant girl, who's far more trouble than she's worth, as Mrs. Trowell often sighs, taking up the rolling pin to rescue the pastry or a duster to spare the cranberry glass. Today, the girl has managed to burn the pie intended for the Trowells' tea; they will all have to sit down to brown bread and cheese instead. There are worse things than brown bread and cheese, they all know this, but philosophy doesn't improve the general temper of the party. The phrenologist's rapturous predictions fade into the steam rising from the teapot. There is work to be done, Mr. Trowell announces, rising abruptly and pointing at his sons, who know better than to ask to be excused from practising.

And a good thing, too, since it's on this night, while he's playing through a Vivaldi sonata, that something overtakes, or overcomes, Arnold. Mr. Trowell makes a motion for Garnet to put down his violin: he stands behind Arnold, registering the sounds pouring from the cello, sounds so limpid they make the pool of light cast by the gas jet seem dirty, clumsy in comparison. It's not that the boy's playing well—

he always plays well, with that proficiency and confidence that so impress people who know nothing about music. What's different tonight is something unpredictable in Arnold's playing, a gleam, an expressive edge to the perfectly correct technique that makes Thomas Wilberforce believe there might, after all, be something in the phrenologist's predictions.

When Arnold finishes, he looks up and grins at Garnet, who grins back at him. Mr. Trowell says nothing other than "Better, rather better—but you've got a ways to go, my boy." It is extravagant praise, and to keep it from going to Arnold's head, his father orders him and his brother to play tone-rows for the next half hour while he goes to the kitchen, where his wife is supervising the washing-up. He grabs her by the shoulders and exclaims, "It's there—tonight for some reason it's there!"

"Arnold?" she asks, and he answers, "Come, woman, you didn't expect it to be Garnet, did you?" He drops his hands and goes off to his desk, where he begins drafting a letter to be delivered to Gerhardi. The world-famous cellist will be performing next week at the Concert Rooms; the letter humbly requests ten minutes of the great man's time to listen to young Arnold Trowell play.

―――――

At the same moment that Thomas Trowell is deciding that his son has the makings of a virtuoso, Harold Beauchamp is holding forth over a dinner table laden with the remains of roast duck and a fine burgundy brought up from the cellar to celebrate his homecoming. Belle has dressed for dinner. Annie, who has a weak heart and must be cosseted, is wearing a sky blue wrapper. Her face is pale and she's let down her fine, crinkly hair as though it, too, hasn't the strength to bear up after the exertions of the day. The children are asleep, even Chummie, who cried so hard when his grandma whisked him away, in his crisp new sailor suit, after his father had tossed him once in the air. If only, Harold jokes, Annie would consent to let him toss her. He needs some physical outlet for the satisfaction that seizes him as he boasts of his plans to move back into town, into a house with a tennis court, rose garden, and wraparound verandah. A house, he says, that will hit you bang in the eye as you walk by, wondering who the lucky devil of an owner could be.

The grandmother shakes her head, but Belle's eyes brighten—she is sick to death of the country, which is no place at all for a pretty woman still of marriageable age. Annie looks at her husband quizzically, as though he's a small boy who has just told a whopper. But when Harold leans towards her and, like a conqueror pouring the riches of the world into her lap, mentions the Christmas present the Premier is preparing for him—directorship of the Bank of New Zealand—pinches of colour print Annie's cheeks. She reaches up to gently tug her husband's whiskers, as if they need straightening.

———

In the room Kass shares with her grandma, no light is burning. The dark is her enemy, unstoppable as spilled ink, sealing her eyes and mouth, stuffing her nostrils till she can't breathe. If you stop breathing, you die: how can something so simple, an accident or game like holding your breath, make you die? It was the dark that got you, killing you in your sleep, the way it killed Baby Gwen. The photographer had come from town with his black hood and box; he'd taken the picture of Grandma in her best frilled cap and apron, holding Gwen in her arms. When you look at the picture, you can't even tell she's not breathing, Baby Gwen. The one who'd come after Kass and always been so good, they said, no trouble at all.

Kass's heart drubs in her chest, like a stick hitting along a picket fence. Stretching out her arm, feeling for her spectacles on the night table, she knocks over the water glass; it rolls across the floorboards, then stops, knocking a little, back and forth, before lying perfectly still. Slowly, Kass hooks her spectacles around her ears, steadies herself. She must get up; if she doesn't, the dark will keep on pressing down until it smothers her. But if she gets up, she'll have to cross the dark between the bed and the door; she can feel it leering at her, ready to pull her into its soft, wet mouth. Somehow, she throws off the bedclothes and stumbles to the door, holding her hands against her mouth, kicking at the hem of her nightdress. At the head of the stairs a gas jet flutters, lighting the way down to the hall outside the dining room.

Sparks and flashes from the chandelier over the littered table; the grown-ups looking so safe, so separate in their brilliant, careless world where she has no place. They've left the front door open to catch the evening breeze; they are laughing, joking; no one so much as lifts an eye to where she stands in her bulky nightdress, watching them. And because all she wants is to be with them, to be like them, and because she knows already that she never can, she looks round for something to take from them, some way to hurt them into understanding. All she finds is a pineapple in a huge crystal dish on the trolley outside the dining room, a pineapple destined for dessert. She smells its warm, ripe sweetness; she hears her father teasing Aunt Belle, her father's great, bursting laugh as Belle says, in a voice like chipped glass: "That isn't funny, Harold." She hears her mother's silence as her grandma, smoothing things over, calls out, "Time for pudding." And then she's rushing out the front door, down the porch steps, and into the garden.

The sky is starless: there's only a fingernail of moon to show the island in the centre of the drive, the swords rising up from the lush banked grass. Kass stops a little way from the aloe, staring at the massive stem that flowers only once every hundred years. Her mother said so that very afternoon; stepping out of the carriage, she walked back to the aloe, stripping off her gloves and stretching out her hand to a leaf all grey and stiff and edged with thorns. Her mother let them just graze her bare palm. And then she told how long the aloe takes to bloom, drawing her hand back and walking past the daughter who is stretching out her own hand, now, towards the ugly edge of the aloe leaf.

"Child, child," sighs a voice behind her. Kass's hand remains outstretched. She has sensed something that she cannot say; she must wait here till words come to her, or until silence slowly fills itself, and falls. But her grandma takes her by the hand, her grandma, saying, "Come now, let's tuck you back into bed. If we're quick, no one will see us." And Kass is being hurried past the wash of yellow lamplight on the flower beds, up the stairs and back into the very dark from which she ran away. But this time a candle is left burning on the washstand, in front of the mirror; as soon as the table's cleared and the house locked up for the night, her grandma promises, she'll come to bed. For a while Kass watches the two candles flickering on the washstand, then closes her eyes, imagining the large warm body of her grandmother sliding under the top-sheet, curving in towards her; how she will sleep all night beside her grandma, like a shell curled under a leaf.

Wellington, 1902

From one of her bedroom windows, fourteen-year-old Kathleen (she's outgrown nicknames and spectacles alike) can see the guests arriving in evening dress: emerald silk, silvery taffeta, rose and saffron chiffon cut by the men's stark black and white, black and white, regular as prison bars. They are all trooping up the stairs of a fashionable house with a wraparound verandah bristling with gingerbread. She watches for a moment, then goes back to her desk, under the window that looks out onto the hills round her native city, hills in sulphurous yellow bloom. Her hands are plump and ink-stained; she is given to waving them wildly when she is talking of something she has a passion for—flowers or swimming or poetry.

Kathleen takes up the open notebook lying on the desk and begins to read from it languidly, self-importantly: "*Shall it always be from my window that I must watch the fire breaking? . . . May I not hold the flames in my hand—if only for a little while—and hold them against my heart and laugh as they fiercely attack it?*" And then, in a deeper, sterner voice: "Karl Mansfield." Unsatisfied with the effect, she practises saying her *nom de plume* in different ways: "*Karl* Mansfield. Karl *Mansfield.*" From the hallway stairs her sister Vera is scolding her—why isn't she downstairs, greeting the guests? Kathleen takes her time rising from her desk, stopping in front of the mirror, sucking in her stomach. It's little use: her body's wedged into its yellow satin as tightly as a cork in a bottle.

Downstairs, the room is packed with people. She knows every one of them, has already eavesdropped on their conversations, settled the stories of their lives. Wellington is a very small city, and the circle of her parents' friends stiflingly select. Still, she goes about the room, fingering the flowers in their silver bowls, her expression one of amused indifference that she's copied from her mother. She doesn't deign to notice the two tall boys in the corner, awkward in their formal clothes, their narrow faces pale and tired-looking. She has already made known her opinions about the quality of music played during her parents' *soirées*: simpering songs about rosebuds and dying swallows; club-footed waltzes on the piano. But when the announcement is made that the Trowell twins are about to perform, Kathleen plunks herself down in an empty chair, sitting in the way she's always being told is far from ladylike—legs crossed and nursing one knee, her fingers interlocked. She stares at the musicians as if daring them to play something that will blow the roof off and the windows out.

Between two giant vases crammed with mimosa, the twins are tuning their instruments, Arnold briskly, Garnet with a dreamy look, as if what he held in his hands were a book instead of a violin. When they start to play, Kathleen fixes her gaze on Arnold; he is playing something so fiendishly intricate it makes her head hurt. He plays perfectly, he plays with total abandon to the music, as if he were on a desert island or rapt up to the seventh heaven, anywhere but the Beauchamps' drawing room, in a fashionable suburb of a colonial capital. Arnold Trowell with his flame red hair, his superb disdain for everything and everyone but his music. She decides to fall madly in love with Arnold Trowell. Before he's stopped playing, she's forgotten it was a decision at all.

The applause for Arnold is exuberant and immediate, Garnet's especially so. He steps back as the ladies rush up, making much of "The Young Virtuoso," "Wellington's Own Gerhardi." Arnold's confidence fascinates Kathleen—that a mere boy could hold the attention of the entire room, could stand there in his too-small evening clothes like a little Caesar suffering the adulation of the crowd.

After the applause dies down, Harold Beauchamp walks over to the grand piano, where he coughs and hems and finally claps his hands to get the room's attention. Kathleen rolls her eyes as her father settles into his speech: it is his great pleasure to announce that the good people of Wellington— from the humblest to the most illustrious, from typists and

stevedores to the city's greatest businessmen—have suc-
ceeded in raising sufficient funds to send the talented twins to
Europe, where they will develop their prodigious musical
gifts at the world's best conservatories.

He is sure, he says, that the Trowell boys fully understand
how many hopes are resting on their shoulders. And now, to
Kathleen's embarrassment, Harold waxes poetic: "You are a
pair of tender, pliant trees, rich with promise. And yet"—he
raises his hands as if bracing for a blow—"the ripe fruit of
your genius has yet to be tasted. Let us pray that your efforts
will be crowned with the roses of success and not the thorns
of failure." At this mention of the latter possibility there's a
sudden checking of spirits, which Annie overcomes by summoning the waiters with their trays of champagne and sug-
ared almonds.

Someone starts laughing; Mr. and Mrs. Trowell, who have
been standing a little stiffly at the back of the room, accept
their champagne and the congratulations of Harold and
Annie Beauchamp with good enough grace, though Thomas
Wilberforce mutters "pompous ass" as the Beauchamps
move away, and Mrs. Trowell clutches his arm, fearful lest
anyone hear.

Kathleen has heard; she smiles brightly as she walks up to
Mr. Trowell, for she shares his opinion of her father. "Mr.
Trowell," she announces, "I've decided I simply *must* learn
the cello. It's the only instrument worth playing, the piano's
nothing compared to it. Will you teach me? I would be
tremendously honoured." But before Mr. Trowell can
respond, she rushes across the room to congratulate Arnold.
He's talking to an elderly lady at a table laden with a huge
bowl of crimson-coloured punch; Garnet is standing off to
one side, watching as Kathleen breaks in, introducing herself
as a daughter of the house, gushing to Arnold about the
beauty of his playing—the passion. He sees how Arnold

pauses, then barely presses the hand Kathleen has offered him before he resumes the conversation she has interrupted. It's Garnet who steps in to the rescue, pouring Kathleen a glass of punch and leading her out to the garden that backs onto the music room.

The garden is full of roses: yellow ones with scarlet edges; deep red bosomy roses blown open to expose their gold centres. Garnet is talking enough for both of them, which is lucky because Kathleen is still stunned at Arnold's snub and can't decide whether she hates or admires him for it. She holds her cup of punch with both hands, gulps it down, spilling a little on her dress, then looks her rescuer full in the face. She registers the disappointing colour of his hair—not fiery like his twin's, but a dull red-brown. For the first time she actually listens to what he's saying, something about Frankfurt, Brussels, the Conservatoire, then cuts him off. The Trowell twins aren't the only ones leaving New Zealand, she declares. Next year she and her older sisters, along with Aunt Belle as chaperone, are escaping to London for three whole years. To a college where they'll read literature and study languages and go to concerts and all the newest plays.

Just then there's a tumble of laughter. Arnold has come out into the garden, leading a young woman, one of Kathleen's friends from school: Maata Mahupuku, a Maori princess, extravagantly beautiful, excessively rich. The Beauchamps invite her to all their parties, especially as there's no danger of her ensnaring their still-small son. Maata is telling Arnold about the American bar that's just opened at the Central Hotel; she's daring him to take her there and order her one of the new drinks: Rock and Rye, Milk Punch, Gin Fizz . . .

Arnold drops Maata's arm to pick a rose from the nearest bush. But instead of presenting it to her, he hides it in his jacket pocket and strides to the bench, where he's caught sight of Garnet sitting with Kathleen. Half as a game, half because he wants to keep Miss Beauchamp's adoration for himself, however little he may value it, he waves his hands around her head and pulls, out of her ear, the perfect rose.

"Magic," she says to him, her voice clear as rinsed glass, her face utterly blank. And then she takes the rose, slips it into her décolletage, and smiles at him, a smile so blind and open that Garnet rises from the bench and walks off with a giggling Maata as Arnold takes his brother's place beside Kathleen.

Later that night, when the maids have carried the dirtied plates and glasses down to the kitchen, and the butler has turned off all the lights—for the Beauchamps' house has, among its many newfangled features, electricity in all its rooms—Kathleen sits up in bed, writing. In her loose, mad-dash way—her handwriting is that of a woman, not a girl of fourteen—she has filled five pages with the glories of the hero she has christened "Caesar." She twists her body so she can watch her face in the mirror as she recites what she's written: "*He drew the melody from the strings as one draws the perfume from a flower, with a kind of slumbrous ecstasy.*" She sighs, then makes a face at the mirror, shutting the book with a little flourish. In all the words she's written down about the evening, not one alludes to Garnet.

London, 1906

Kathleen, eighteen, is at the end of her time at Queen's College, Harley Street. Dressed only in her petticoats and camisole, she's leaning out the window of her room, breathing in the April air, which she pronounces delicious. It's not all jasmine and jonquils, though: in the mews below, men in singlets are swilling carriages with pails of water, horses stamp and neigh, and through all the shouting and joking a baby wails. "Life," she declares, "real life—beneath my very window. How can anyone live anywhere but London?" She turns to look round her room, trying to read it as a stranger would. Vases of lilac and bunches of violets; a cello in the corner; books by Wilde, Whitman, D'Annunzio, prominently displayed; reproductions of paintings by Whistler and by Watts. This is the self she's fashioned, this is what she's made of the raw colonial girl who arrived three years ago in the Great Metropolis that she, like so many of her countrymen, has always called Home.

She's not as confident about the photographs in showy frames crowding the tables and mantelpiece, photos that could as easily have been shot in Wellington: Kathleen playing tennis or cello, taking tea with schoolfriends in a park pavilion. There's a knock at the door; one of the friends from the photograph walks hesitantly in, a large, awkward girl with a round face and pale, vague eyes. Her name is Ida Baker; she's come to help Kathleen dress for the evening she's about to spend with Aunt Belle and the Trowell boys, who are visiting from Brussels.

Ida laces a still-plump Kathleen into her corset; she helps her pull on a long skirt over her petticoats and fastens the buttons of a high-necked blouse, which Kathleen struggles to tuck into the waistband of her skirt, cinching a belt to hold in flesh and fabric. Finally, with a sigh of effort, the fashionably dressed Miss Beauchamp sits down at her dressing table. As Ida takes up a fistful of hairpins, plying her friend's thick, dark, frizzy hair into the pompadour of a Gibson girl, Kathleen tells her that the concert is at the Bechstein Hall. Kreisler will be playing the Franck violin sonata, which she adores. The Bechstein will be the perfect place for Caesar's debut in a year or so: there's not a shadow of a doubt that he's going to pick up the gold medal at the Conservatoire—that's what Garnet's told her. Garnet writes her often. Caesar can't, of course, he's far too busy with his practising.

Ida is putting the last pins into her friend's hair when Kathleen jumps up and seizes her wrists: "We're going to marry as soon as he finishes in Brussels. You mustn't breathe a word to anyone, Ida, but I've written to him—offered myself to him, body and soul."

"Oh, Katie," Ida whispers, all mournful alarm, till Kathleen bursts out laughing.

"I didn't say I actually sent him the letter, you goose. But we'll be married, all the same, I swear we will."

———

Into a night brilliant with streetlamps people stream out of the concert hall onto a road where horse-drawn carriages throng and couples walk decorously arm in arm. Aunt Belle pulls down the veil on her hat, announcing that they'll all go back to Miss Wood's for cocoa and biscuits. Kathleen pulls a face at the twins, who link their arms through hers and invite Aunt Belle to lead the way. Belle is in a sour mood. She hadn't enjoyed the concert: she's been stewing about the likelihood her trousseau may not be ready for her wedding day; about how irritating it is that seamstresses in little garrets in Soho are prone to pleurisy. She calls out to the trio at her heels, "Do be careful not to fall behind—I can't imagine why there's such a crush tonight." She's too preoccupied to glance behind her; she fails to notice Arnold nodding at Garnet and Garnet nodding back before they run with Kathleen down a side street and across a lane. Kathleen is delighted—she tells them of a café she knows where they can smoke and even have a glass of wine without anyone making a fuss.

In a steamy-windowed café off the Marylebone High Street the trio sits at a wooden table so small that their knees are jammed together. The twins, with their big black hats slanted over their narrow faces, smoking cigarettes in extra-long holders, talk music till Kathleen interrupts with a flurry of questions. What are the flowers like in the parks in Brussels—are the women elegant or dowdy—who are their friends at the Conservatoire—have they read any Walter Pater—when will Arnold make his London debut—has he composed anything for her, as he's promised to do? Arnold puts his hand to his heart and swears that he's started on a suite for cello he will dedicate to the incomparable Miss Beauchamp. Before Kathleen can ask any more questions, Garnet warns they'd better get her back to Harley Street, or there'll be Belle's hell to pay. Kathleen takes care of the bill, leaving an extravagant tip. She is quivering with pleasure; it seems her feet have turned into birds and she's skimming over the pavement as the twins link arms with her again to walk her home.

When they reach the front door of Miss Clara Wood's boarding hostel, Kathleen expects Garnet to step back and turn away so that Arnold can pull her close to him and kiss her. But Arnold disengages his arm from hers and merely shakes her hand, while Garnet coaches her on what to say to Aunt Belle—how they fell behind when a very stout gentleman and his equally stout wife and their four stout daughters stepped out of a doorway in front of them. Kathleen is shaking with anger: "Don't you dare to presume to teach *me* how to tell stories, Garnet Trowell!" She rings at the door, where Belle has been waiting for hours. She strides wordlessly past her aunt as the twins doff their hats, bow, then whisk their scarlet-lined scarves round their necks and lope off into the night.

Belle knocks as loudly as she dares at the door of her niece's room, with no result: Kathleen knows that her aunt won't dare to make a scene and rouse the other boarders. Not long after Belle retreats, Ida appears in a dark brown dressing gown buttoned up to her chin. She slips a piece of paper under Kathleen's door and a moment later is whisked inside. From the look on her friend's face, Ida knows better than to say a word.

Kathleen has been lighting candles all around the room. When she finishes, she turns her back to Ida, who undoes the buttons of Kathleen's blouse and the hooks and eyes of the painfully tight skirt. She goes to Kathleen's wardrobe and pulls out a silk kimono, wraps the girl in it, and sits her at the dressing table. And then Ida kneels down beside her, asking, "Are you all right, Katie? You look ill, dearie."

For answer, Kathleen starts yanking the pins out of her hair. Ida rises and helps her, then takes an ivory-backed brush to her friend's hair. Gradually, Kathleen's hands relax; she sighs and leans back in her chair as Ida keeps brushing by candlelight, and the sound of heavy rain fills the room from the open window.

"It was," Kathleen sighs, "marvellous, intoxicating!" She closes her eyes and recites, without a shadow of self-parody: "*Do you not hear the quick beat of my heart? Do you not feel the hot rush of blood through my veins? Your hand can pluck away the thin veil, your eyes can feast upon my shameless beauties.*"

Ida drops the hairbrush. "Katie—you didn't—?"

"I'm not telling, Ida. Keep brushing." And as Ida takes up the brush and begins again, Kathleen announces that she's going to give Ida a completely different name. "Ida Baker—it's as romantic as rice pudding. If you want to make anything of yourself, you're going to need a strong name, something with at least a hint of grandeur."

"I'd have liked to be called Katherine," Ida ventures. "It was my mother's name."

Kathleen straightens her spine, waggling her head so that Ida stops brushing. "You can't be Katherine. That's the name I'm taking for myself. I hate 'Kathleen'—it makes me think of bad Irish tenors. You had better be Lesley. Lesley Moore. Don't you think that's a perfect name for you?" She doesn't wait for Ida's answer but closes her eyes again, settling back in her chair. "When I give my first concert—or when I publish my first book, whichever comes sooner—it will be as Katherine Mansfield. Mansfield's my middle name, my grandmother's married name. I loathe Beauchamp, it's a name fit only for bankers. And butchers—did I ever tell you that my father started out in the frozen meat business?"

Reverently, Ida brushes her Katie's hair while Kathleen talks of how unjust it is that her parents will be arriving any day now to drag her back to New Zealand. "They don't understand me, they never have. How could they? My father's idea of art is a well-roasted duck, and my mother—she can be *ice*." Staring into the dressing-table mirror, Kathleen addresses her reflection: "I want to live, not just go to silly parties and dance with even sillier boys, one of whom they'll make me marry. The way Aunt Belle's going to be married off to her Surrey shipping magnate." She screws up her face, intoning, "Surely she shall know money and leisure all the days of her life, and she shall worship at the Holy Green and the Temple of the Tennis Court, forever and ever, Amen."

Ida can't help being shocked at the blasphemy, but then she starts to shudder. It has finally come home to her that her friend will be going off to the farthest place Ida can imagine; that she may never, ever see her again. Gathering up a great hank of Kathleen's hair, she winds it round and round her hand. "Will you write to me, Katie? I promise I'll write to you every day." And then—she can't help herself—she buries her face in Kathleen's hair, half sobbing: "You are so beautiful! You don't know how beautiful you are—beautiful, beautiful!"

Kathleen pulls away, stands up from her chair, her face like wood, her voice no less icy than her mother's. "That's enough. That's quite enough. Thank you. You've brushed my hair beautifully. Goodnight."

Ida can feel the repulsion in Kathleen's voice; she stumbles, in her ugly brown dressing gown, to the door, then stands there, gathering her courage. At last she speaks, very softly, her eyes cast down. "You will let me write, won't you, Katie?"

Wellington, 1907

In the drawing room of another, grander Beauchamp residence, this time on Fitzherbert Terrace, Vera and Chaddie are talking lace and ribbons while Kathleen pretends to read a volume of Chekhov stories. Her sisters are accustomed to Kassie's blue funks, her inability to reconcile herself to what she has called the "suitable appropriate existence" of a marriageable girl of good family. What they don't understand is that Kassie's are no ordinary blues: behind the boredom and sullenness lies a sense of despair, like the pits of shadow under the fuchsias when she walks through the garden at night. It tells her that she is no one and nothing; that for all her dreams of returning to London, of making something rich and gorgeous of her life, she will fail to find even a fraction of her heart's desire.

When Chaddie makes the mistake of offering her sister the latest Marie Corelli instead of that dreary Russian stuff she's poring over, Kassie flings the Corelli against the wall and runs from the house, grabbing a coat and tam as she goes.

Behind her, someone's shouting her name: only when she realizes it's her young brother does she stop and let him catch up with her. He's grown to be as tall as she is now; of all her siblings he is her sole confidant and confederate. Linking arms, the two head off towards the sea. Sand and dust whirl up from the road. Wellington's winds are ferocious, and most people try to avoid them if they can, so there's no one for sister and brother to have to greet or hide from as they reach the stone embankment by the water's edge, leaning as close as they can to the waves smashing below.

Spray drenches their faces; Kathleen snatches off her tam, letting her hair blow wild and loose. Suddenly, she jumps up on the ledge of the embankment, holding her arms outstretched as if daring the wind to hurl her into the sea. She is shouting, laughing, shaking the spray from her face and hair as the boy tugs at her coat and begs her to come down. She would jump into the waves if she were on her own: she is a strong, passionate swimmer. But she has her brother to look out for, and so she scrambles down at last, pointing to a ship far out from harbour. "Look—that's our boat! We're on board, you and I, steaming away from Wellington and Fitzherbert Terrace forever. We're on our way beyond the Blue Mountains and we don't bloody care what anyone in this stupid, ugly, stuffy city says or thinks!" She grabs her brother's hand: Leslie, the only boy and baby of them all, the one they call, adoringly, Chummie. Zigzagging crazily, the two of them race across the pavement as the wind tries its best to shove them down.

———

What is it like, this "stupid, ugly" city that so suffocates the Londonized Kathleen? Turn-of-the-century Wellington is a combination of the raw and respectable: squat tin-roofed houses and zealous imitations of the great monuments of "Home," whether parliament buildings or concert hall. Streets of poky little shops: Chinese groceries with pineapples, oranges, cabbages crowding the windows, a mess of straw and torn newspaper on the pavement. Laden clotheslines strung across asphalted yards, gullies choked with refuse, lumber yards giving off the sharp, sweet smell of new-cut wood. The weather's far too often wet and windy, foghorns blowing over a sea snot grey as Joyce's own. Yet unlike Ireland, this colony to which Kathleen has been consigned flames beneath the thickest mist. Gorgeousness is incorrigible here: kowhais strung with chains of golden flowers, pohutukawas flaring scarlet at Christmastime, cannonball bursts of green from the fern trees.

If the natural world is voluptuous, society is as prim and narrow as you'd find in any of England's cathedral towns. In 1907, the population is barely sixty thousand. The city's self-congratulatory dullness infuriates Kathleen, who's made a patron saint of Oscar Wilde. She is quoting him right now as she copies his epigrams into her journal: *"Never,"* she recites, *"relight an old cigarette or an old passion."* It's twilight, her favourite time of day; she is sitting in her bedroom, where she's been locked by her father as punishment for one of her frequent breaches of family harmony. Between Kathleen and her parents a war of attrition is going on; in the spirit of *à la guerre comme à la guerre*, Kathleen has let her old schoolfriend Maata know of the ladder hanging from her bedroom window, one of the wooden house's many fire escapes. Maata is knocking at the glass this very moment; Kathleen looks up from her desk and helps her inside, where Maata sits down as coolly as if fire escapes were the usual means of entry to 47 Fitzherbert Terrace.

Outside, the foghorn wails; inside, candles flicker. Maata accepts a cigarette from a silver box, her favourite brand:

Abdullahs. Their richness gives the room an air of luxury, even decadence. Kathleen has transplanted the Watts and Whistler reproductions, the crowds of photographs from her quarters at Queen's College; her cello gleams darkly in a corner. An entire wall of this room is lined with bookshelves, from floor to ceiling. But today the girls choose to ignore the books: Kathleen winds up the gramophone so they can listen to the Venezuelan pianist Teresa Carreño playing Liszt. Flinging herself back into an overstuffed chair, Kathleen sighs, "Doesn't it give you *such* pleasure, sitting in the gloom, smoking purloined cigarettes, and listening to a *magnificent* artist? Doesn't it make you positively *languid* with delight?"

"No," answers Maata, matter-of-factly, holding up her arms to admire the way the antique lace drapes at her elbows. "I'd much rather be at a ball with hordes of marriageable young men telling me how gloriously, unforgettably beautiful I am."

Kathleen leans back, cigarette in hand. "Then let me tell you, my dear, how ravishing—how bewitchingly beautiful you look this night."

"Do I?" Maata asks, inviting more outrageous compliments. For answer, Kathleen stubs out her cigarette, then walks over to where her friend is settled on an ottoman. She pulls her to her feet, takes her into her arms, and kisses Maata slowly, sensuously on the lips.

Heavy footsteps in the passageway; Harold Beauchamp pounds at the door, which he's forgotten he's locked. The girls break their embrace, but remain standing, side by side, as he fiddles with the key and bursts inside. For a moment, Kathleen's father can't seem to see either of them; then he switches on the light and stares at Maata. "What in blazes are you doing here?" he barks.

Kathleen speaks before her friend can venture an answer.

"Maata is performing an act of Christian Charity, Father. Visiting the Imprisoned."

Harold brings his fist down on the table, making the cigarettes jump out of their box. "It's dark!" he shouts. "You two—are standing—together—in the dark!" The girls nod at him. He blusters on in the High Paternal mode. "Now see here, Kathleen. Your sisters are playing cribbage downstairs. Your mother insists that you join them. *I* insist. We all want you downstairs. This moment. At once!"

Kathleen says nothing; she goes to fetch her cello, while her friend declares that she must be getting home.

Standing so that he blocks the window, waiting till Maata's swept down the stairs, Harold continues to harangue his wayward daughter: "If you think your family is going to stand by while you sully our good name—"

Kathleen draws her bow across her cello and replies: "I could do far worse than smoke cigarettes with a princess, Father."

Harold has been waiting for just this cue: his face looks as if it's been boiled, his chest heaves. In spite of herself, Kathleen is impressed, though she keeps her head unbowed as her father rages. "There will be no smoking in my house, do you hear? No smoking by young ladies. Let me remind you that you *are* a young lady. I didn't pay a fortune to educate you so that you could behave like an actress in your own home!"

Reluctantly, his daughter puts down her bow. "Don't you think," she begins, "that our expensive education allows us just a bit of freedom from the Ten Deadly Conventions?"

Harold's face goes white; he takes a step towards Kathleen, his hand raised, then catches himself and steps back again. Kathleen is holding her breath: she's frightened, but she's also wildly curious as to what will happen next.

Harold hangs fire, then pounces on an exit line: "And don't you think I'm letting you go on stage with that—that cello of yours! No daughter of mine will be allowed to make a public spectacle of herself!" He slams out of the room and thumps down the stairs.

Kathleen waits until the noise diminishes, then picks up her bow and plays a few bars of a Bach sonata, not at all badly. But she stops, abruptly. Locking her cello into its stiff black case, she walks over to the full-length mirror on its rosewood stand. She tilts the glass so that her reflection greets her at an angle. And then, making a low bow, she addresses her image in the manner of a Teresa Carreño, world-famous Venezuelan pianist. "Very well, Father. I renounce my ambition to be a professional musician, performing to riotous applause on the concert stages of Europe. I'll become a writer, instead. A student of Life, with an appetite so big I'll eat up everything that comes my way. Bring on the public spectacle!"

———

At a ball in the Drill Hall, Kathleen is dancing with a young naval officer while her mother tries to appear as though she isn't spying on their every move. There's something more than a little mocking, something brazen, frankly uncontrollable about this daughter of hers. Everyone in the room is aware of it—the gossips are at full gallop on the track of Kathleen Beauchamp, so sadly different from her sisters, so unfortunate for poor Annie. Annie herself will have no truck with anyone's pity. Yet what can she do to prevent it? Look there, right before the cream of Wellington society, Kathleen and that officer, waltzing through instead of past the archway at the end of the hall. And all Annie can do is signal to Vera—as placidly perfect a daughter as Kathleen is impossible—to go after them.

In her spangled gauze, Vera runs down a dimly lit hallway. She stops suddenly, relieved to smell the smoke of cigarettes.

What she overhears from the couple in the alcove is both better and worse than she expected.

"Of course I will," her sister is saying. "I've had two pieces published already in an Australian paper, and the *Native Companion* has just accepted a vignette. Not that the people who set themselves up as critics here have the least idea of what I'm trying to do. The editor of the *New Zealand Mail* thinks I'm obsessed with the 'sex-problem.' And my father's secretary—she's lovely, she types out all my stories—she *is* a little shocked. Actually, she's aghast at some of what I've shown her. But then, I'm not writing for my father's secretary."

Kathleen traces her partner's lips with her finger and whispers, "Listen." A waltz from *Eugene Onegin* is being played in the ballroom; ribbons of sound flutter towards them. "It cannot be possible to go through all the abandonment of Music," Kathleen intones, "and care humanly for anything human afterwards."

By the time Vera's realized why the talking has stopped, the damage has been done. Sharply, she calls out her sister's name, waiting long enough for the lieutenant to flee down the rest of the corridor and out a back door. Kathleen, her eyes brilliant, her face and neck flushed, allows Vera to seize her arm and lead her back to the ballroom.

Annie is aware of the eyebrows raised at her daughters' entrance; when Kathleen breaks into loud, helpless laughter, belly laughs as they're vulgarly called, Annie can feel the whole room recoil at the child who was born, it seems, to cause her family nothing but shame.

That night Annie sits propped up in bed on lace-edged pillows while Harold struggles out of the prison of his evening dress. She's determined not to lift a finger to help him; she needs to prove her point. She addresses the subject of their problem daughter as simply as if Kathleen were a spill of gravy on a damask tablecloth: "We simply have to wash our hands of her and let her leave for England. She's doing everything in her power to cause a scandal here. If we try to keep her, she'll ruin Vera's and Chaddie's chances, and Jeanne's, too. The gossip is intolerable, Harold. Give her a steamship ticket and a hundred pounds a year and let her 'make her way as a writer' as she insists she wants to do. And if she does succeed in getting anything published, I think the best course by far is not to read it. We'll just paddle along in decent ignorance, as long as we can."

Annie sighs and closes her eyes: she looks so young, still, her brown hair crisping over her forehead, her skin perfectly smooth except for little creases between her brows. Is she sleeping already, or simply off in that imaginary world of hers, a world in which she's sailing along the rivers of China, ecstatically alone, without a thought for husband or children? Harold could swear she's utterly forgotten him, standing helplessly buttoned-up beside her; forgotten Kathleen, too, the plan for her disposal. But Harold is wrong. As he finally shakes off his boiled shirt and dives under the quilt beside her, Annie brings out her trump card.

"So it's settled, then. She goes. I can't take any more of this, my dear—as you know very well, my heart won't stand it."

MONTY

Come, my unseen, my unknown,
let us talk together.

Wellington, New Zealand, January 1987

You've asked me to write to you; you asked for my story.
Here it is at last, the letter I promised. A story that starts with
one theft and ends with another, though they seem to me to
now to be something quite different: gifts I'm only beginning
to unwrap. I've tried again and again to write this story down
as simply as possible, to be perfectly open and straightfor-
ward. But the only way I can tell it is the way you find it written here. We are, after all, as good as strangers to each other,
you and I; sometimes masks show more than mirrors do.

My story begins some four months ago, with a young man
walking briskly along Jervois Quay, his head down and a
parcel stuck like a large thermometer under his arm. This
was a spring day in mid September, hardly three months
ago; the sky was a hard, bright blue, with cirrus clouds raked
by the wind. Wellington is famous for its winds; it is one of
those rare cities in which rain can be observed falling hori-
zontally. Years ago a demon gale blew up from nowhere and
smashed a ferry boat into the harbour walls; the harbour

itself was created by an earthquake pushing up the hills that circle the city. Whirlwinds, earthquakes, brute upheavals—the odds for apocalypse in Wellington work out as fair to strong. This suited our young man striding along Jervois Quay, suited his frame of mind, which would have done justice to Revelations, especially the parts about the tortures of scorpions' stings and names—his was Montgomery, shortened to Monty—being blotted from the Book of Life.

Monty was walking so forcefully along the quay because he had a boat to catch. Not the ferry across Cook Strait to the South Island, the entranceway to sombre Lindis Pass, the glories of the Southern Alps, the fogged fjords of Milford Sound. But the East by West ferry, a little boat that travels between Wellington and Day's Bay, a beach resort popular with day-trippers. The happiest times of Monty's childhood had been spent at Day's Bay, perfect summer afternoons when, under his father's watchful eye, he'd leapt in and out of the breakers with a bunch of Maori kids, tossing a ball and laughing wildly whenever a wave or elbow knocked him down. But the day of which I'm speaking now was some twenty years on from those afternoons of diamond sun and somersaulting waves.

There weren't many people waiting to board the ferry—it was a working day, as Monty well knew, having just left his desk at the Alexander Turnbull Library. The dead weight of filing cabinets and microfilms and index cards hadn't made him up and run but, instead, a sudden awareness of the uselessness, the hatefulness of the work and world into which he'd been boxed for so long. It hadn't struck him like lightning or bullets; rather, it was as if the countless grains of sand creeping over him for the past four years had finally reached his head. To clear that head he clambered to the ferry's upper deck, throwing himself onto a bench screwed into the planking, clutching his parcel in his arms. As the boat pulled away, the wind, once cold, turned icy. It bruised his ears and snaked under his coat—he'd forgotten his scarf, so that his neck was exposed, along with the large green pendant he wore on a piece of waxed cord.

The boat pulled into harbour at its first stop: not Day's Bay but a small, melancholy island named after—who else?—a successful colonial entrepreneur. Monty rushed to get off. He was followed by a pack of teenaged boys who'd skipped school for the day and were pummelling each other, shrieking and swearing for joy. He'd hoped to have the island to himself, but it was big enough, he reasoned, that they weren't likely to bump into each other till the boat returned. He had had more than enough, by then, of the company of boys.

Somes Island boasts a government weather station and experimental farm, the daisy-chained ruins of a tennis court, and five-hundred-year-old rubbish dumps in which Maori had chucked the detritus of shellfish feasts and trading ventures. During the two world wars, the island had been a detention centre for enemy aliens; the century before, it had served as a quarantine station for boatloads of settlers arriving from the British Isles. Many survived the appalling voyage only to succumb to typhus or smallpox on Somes Island. Whenever Monty had come home from his school in Christchurch, he and his father would visit the island, always stopping by a monument to the perished. Most of them were women and children, sometimes mothers and newborns wrapped in the same shawl before being dug into earth. Annie Smith, died March 26, 1874, aged 4 years; William Palmer, died March 28, 1874, aged 1 year; Clara Lee, died October 16, 1874, aged 12 days.

Roger would read out the names and dates in his fine, strong voice, conjuring them up for the moment he spoke them: Annie, William, Clara. And then the dead would disappear again into the blasting wind, while Roger and Monty continued their pilgrimage to the northwestern side of the island. There they would stop at a place on the cliff edge, where a large rock thrusts up from the sea. It, too, is a monument, though you won't find any inscription chiselled into it. Eighty-two years ago, a would-be immigrant from China died on that upthrust rock, where he'd been deposited with his scant belongings and some rough tools with which to build a shelter. He was suspected of having leprosy, you see; every day, for the rest of his life, food and the bare necessities of life were sent out to him by a system of wires and cables and pulleys called a flying fox.

Annie, William, and Clara. Kim Lee, whose name Roger managed to unearth from the archives. The fate of these unwilling residents of Somes Island had fascinated the adolescent Monty, had put a sharper edge on *failure*, a word he'd come to connect with the sad stagnation of his father's life. Failure was something Monty had vowed to escape at any price. Five years ago he'd abandoned New Zealand for the splendours of London, or as many of those splendours as could be had on a British Council scholarship. Now, back in New Zealand, making his solitary way around Somes Island, the salt- and iodine-thick air gusting towards him, Monty realized that failure was far more complex and varied an achievement than he'd ever suspected. From the vantage point of his present situation, the fates of Clara or Kim Lee appeared almost enviable. For their names, carved on rock or locked in a library, had not been blotted from the Book of Life. Pathos confers its own immortality on us, if our situation is extreme enough and someone's around to notice we've gone under.

Wind bullied the purple flax; small pale flowers clutched at their flailing stems as Monty headed by. Thousands of waxy leaves clacked as he gained the headland directly above that jut of rock where Kim Lee had endured unthinkable loneliness. The sea was a glassy turquoise, streaked with violet: it shoved crazily against the rocks below. For what might have been a moment or an hour Monty stared into the salty lace churned up by the pounding of the waves. And then he reached for the package wedged so tightly under his arm. Unsealing the envelope, he drew out a thick sheaf of paper. One sheet flew off before he could stop it, whirling like the abstraction of a bird before the wind punched it over the headland and down to the sea. It gave him fierce satisfaction to think of the page getting torn on the rocks, the page whose contents he knew by heart:

> Dear Mr. Mills,
>
> I have read the current version of your dissertation with considerable care, and regret to inform you that serious problems remain. To be blunt, Mr. Mills, you are flogging a dead horse—a hobby horse, to call a spade a spade. While you have, indeed, unearthed a great deal of unexpected biographical detail, it adds up to nothing that can be called a viable argument, or even a persuasive hypothesis. I really haven't any more time to waste on this project. If you will not or cannot, in the next six months, turn it into a thesis that will meet the requirements of this institution, I shall have to wash my hands of you.
>
> Yours *etc. etc. etc.*

Monty held the manuscript firmly in his hands. He was sick to death of thesis, institution, and the hands of his supervisor, scrubbed or dirty. Crawling into a corpse was a more attractive prospect to him than yet another version of his doctoral thesis. Yet how could he let it all go, concede the colossal failure of the past five years of his life, roll up his sleeves like some senile boy scout and get on with his life, as his father had been urging him—ever so gently—to do? So there Monty stood, on the lip of a cliff, wind tearing at his coat, arms raised, ears ringing with his supervisor's weary words. If it hadn't been for a scrambling and shouting breaking out behind him—the group of schoolboys from the ferry—he might have stood there, frozen, forever.

The boys were laughing wildly at some joke they'd made among them; they paid no attention to Montgomery Mills, who could have been a cabbage tree or small grey stone for all they cared. But their presence turned the moment into a matter of pride, or showmanship, or panic—Monty couldn't decide which as he unclenched his hands. In a great white rush the papers flew up over the cliff to Kim Lee's rock below. The boys stopped their shouting and stared at him with something like awe. It was a novel experience: he was far more used to scoffing and practical jokes from boys of that age. Half desolate, half resolute, he strode back to the dock to wait out the hours till the boat returned.

There was a small structure by the dock, the remains of a fumigation shed containing table and chairs and a grandly named but grotty "Public Convenience." The interior of the shed had been scrawled with graffiti; someone had tried to cover the worst of it by hanging up calendars, the kind given away by grocers and garages and adorned with photos of pretty girls or kittens or flowers. This one was a hybrid: roses arranged in a garland around the faces of two angora kittens, black and white.

Monty wasn't overfond of cats or flowers; roses inspired in him a nausea that he traced back to the ceiling of a certain seminar room at the University of London. It was, in fact, the very room that once had been the bedroom of the alarmingly intelligent young woman who became Virginia Woolf. In this room, during the first year of his doctoral studies, Monty had delivered a seminar in praise not of Woolf but of her colonial rival, Katherine Mansfield, from whom, he'd proceeded to argue, Woolf had stolen the bones of her best fiction.

That seminar had been Monty's academic crown. Bear with me now as I sketch it out for you—it is, for better or worse, a part of this story you've asked for. Monty had begun with a remark on the imperial double standard. Both Woolf and Mansfield, he'd pointed out, were known as flagrant exaggerators and habitual dissemblers. They were both guilty of malicious gossip and cruel witticisms about people they professed to admire, or at least to like. Nevertheless, most critics merely scolded the Englishwoman as a mischief-maker, while roasting the colonial as a liar.

Monty had then observed that Woolf's modernist masterpiece, *Mrs Dalloway*—in which Death crashes a party, giving a socialite a visionary glimpse of the mystery at the heart of life—is an expanded version of Katherine Mansfield's "The Garden Party." As for *To the Lighthouse*, much of what distinguishes that novel—the way it portrays the blood sacrifice of marriage, the battles and conspiracies of family life—appears in embryo form in Mansfield's "Prelude," which the Woolfs had printed on their own Hogarth Press. These same themes figure large as life in the New Zealand writer's later story "At the Bay," published six years before that famous voyage to a lighthouse in the Hebrides.

But Woolf hadn't borrowed mere themes or subject matter. And here Monty had risen to his challenge, his voice getting stronger and more confident the riskier his argument became. No, what Woolf had stolen from Mansfield had been a technique for singling out and intensifying the small, seemingly shallow things in life—a woman combing her hair, a child playing with a bowl of porridge. Everyday existence becomes luminous, not just with significance, but with the kind of perception made possible only by an intense, disinterested form of love. This fusion of vision and technique, Monty had observed, had been described by Mansfield as early as 1908, when Woolf was still toiling away at reviews for the *Times Literary Supplement* and had barely begun to sketch out her first work of fiction.

Someone had asked a question about Woolf's famous essay on the bankruptcy of the traditional novel, "Mr Bennett and Mrs Brown." Monty intercepted the query as easily as if he'd been tossed a rose instead of the academic version of a grenade. Mansfield, he'd pointed out, had anticipated Woolf's complaints about the plodding so-called realism of the Arnold Bennett school a good five years earlier. She'd expressed her disgust with safe and formulaic fiction in a review of three minor novels; he'd memorized a paragraph from the review and quoted it to great effect:

> The citizens of Reality are "tied to town" and very content to be so tied, thankful to look out of the window on to a good substantial wall, plastered over with facts and topped with a generous sprinkle of broken bottle glass. Nevertheless, they are forever sighing to travel. Not that they are prepared for long and difficult journeys. On the contrary. What they cannot have enough of is the small excursion, the timid flight just half-way to somewhere, just so far that Reality and its wall are out of sight while they picnic in the unfamiliar landscape, which distracts, but does not disturb.

Compare, he'd urged his listeners, Woolf's often stilted sentences and cumbrous similes with her rival's fresh, arresting images and fluid prose. Surely these differing styles have something to do with the writers' differing perceptions of their bodies? Woolf's dismissal of her own sexuality was widely known; why not read in that context her remark about Mansfield smelling like a civet cat that had taken to street-walking? For his *coup de théâtre*, he'd produced for the class's benefit a bottle of Genêt Fleuri, the expensive scent

Mansfield would order from Paris to remind her of flowering broom on the hills of her native Wellington.

In a letter to her sister Vanessa, Monty had concluded, Virginia wrote that Katherine had gone every kind of hog in her salad days; fellow-hog Vanessa, she'd implied, would hit it off with the wild colonial girl. Woolf's envy of Manfield's sexual adventures and allure fuelled an insistent case of professional jealousy: Katherine Mansfield, as everyone knew, was the one writer Woolf acknowledged as a rival. Had Mansfield chosen to link her life with a man who was her equal, and not with males she could easily dominate and manipulate—a cowardly boy; a puffed-up, pink-cheeked tenor; the husband she immortalized as a man without a temperament—had she found the equivalent of Virginia's brusque and steady, incorruptible Leonard, surely she might have lived long and written truthfully enough to have produced the major works that eluded her.

Yet this pugnacious display below a chaste garland of plaster roses became the engine of Monty's misfortunes in the world of academe. He had planned to write his doctoral dissertation on a friend and collaborator of Joseph Conrad's, a man who'd been the editor of an important literary journal as well as the author of novels, not mere short stories. But after the triumph of his seminar, Monty threw over Ford Madox Ford for Katherine Mansfield. To his academic adviser, who'd warned him against this change of subject, he quoted the adolescent Mansfield: "To acknowledge the presence of fear is to give birth to failure." And he might have been able to carry it off if he hadn't allowed himself to explore all kinds of minor roads in Mansfield's life: roads that exposed the dark, subversive—even cruel—side of her character. Her treatment, for example, of little Charlie Walter, the sick, half-starved boy from the London slums whom she'd "adopted" for a summer, whisking him away to the mountains, lavishing milk and eggs and attention on him, then shipping him back to his mews off Welbeck Street without a word of explanation or regret. Monty had wasted a good chunk of time trying to discover the fate of poor Charlie Walter.

All these minor roads, needless to say, turned out to be dead ends. Ignoring his supervisor's warnings, postponing their meetings, and failing to send her anything resembling a thesis chapter, he found his scholarship withdrawn and himself shipped home from school like the young Kathleen Beauchamp, eighty years before. And not even to Wellington, but to Invercargill, at the southernmost tip of the South Island. He'd scrounged up a teaching post, you see, at an establishment that has the distinction of being the boys' school nearest the South Pole. The boys at this school are, for the most part, the ones who can't get into the more demanding establishments, no matter how wealthy their parents might be; it is also the place where "problem" boys are sent, in the hope that the bracing air of Te Waewae Bay will rescue them from the delinquencies that have driven their parents to the breaking point. As for the effect of this splendid air on Monty, it was supposed to have inspired him to complete his thesis while introducing his students to New Zealand history and the challenges of modern English literature, for which they cared far less than for the colonies of albatross and the slow-breeding, toe-tagged tuatara lizards he'd take them out to see on half-holidays.

All of which was, Monty's father had conceded, a disappointment, but hardly a disaster. Monty could easily write his way out of the dark and clammy cold of Invercargill winters; with his doctorate in his pocket, he could apply for a more congenial post at a university closer to the temperate than the subantarctic zone. Encouragement from his father—what greater proof of failure could Monty have received? What else was that father guilty of, or at least plagued by, if not the failure to finish any project he'd undertaken, other than a few slender books of poems published by small presses named after New Zealand's indigenous birds and flowers?

Ashamed and resentful, Monty had kept his distance from his father since coming back to New Zealand. Over the past year he'd confined his contact with Roger to short visits paid at half-term and in the long holidays, when he'd come up to Wellington to consult the Turnbull Library's abundant Mansfield holdings. He could have rented a room close to campus, but he was saving every penny for his eventual return to London. Which explains why, after his excursion to Somes Island, Monty headed west, to the hilly suburb in which he'd grown up, and where Roger had arrived forty years ago after committing his own great act of defiance: running away from home.

───

Roger has owned the same house in Hataitai ever since he arrived in Wellington from the wilds of Mayfair. He settled himself, his typewriter, and an ever-growing multitude of books in a bungalow on a steep hill, with an open-air elevator to take him from the street to his front door and a magnificent view of Evans Bay. The house has a large terraced garden full of plants that many New Zealanders class as weeds but which Roger has always encouraged: arum lilies, fennel, *Clematis foetida*.

As I have already mentioned, Monty's father had a watchful eye. And like most watchful people, he gave very little of himself away. You couldn't have described him as a secretive man, but he'd always found it painful, almost paralyzing, to talk about himself, even to his son. From what that son had been able to piece together, it appeared that Roger was the only child of a London banker infuriated by his offspring's attachment to the wrong kind of printed paper; if he'd had anything like a heart, it would have been broken by Roger's decision, at age eighteen, to become a writer. Unlike another banker-father of a stubbornly rebellious child, Mr. Mills refused to provide the means for his son to follow his calling. Roger might have spent his life calculating debits and credits if it hadn't been for the death of his Uncle Montgomery, who left him a sizable inheritance. Not out of love, it seems, but to spite his banker-brother, with whom he'd quarrelled soon after the birth of his namesake. In gratitude for this deliverance, the writer-in-waiting—who'd grown up called by his middle name, Roger—resurrected "Montgomery" as his *nom de plume* and, later, as the name of his only child.

New Zealand was Roger's land of heart's desire, or, at least, the farthest remove from his father's sphere of influence. It was also the birthplace of Katherine Mansfield, as Roger discovered while buying as much New Zealand literature as he could find in the Wellington bookshops. He had never embarked on a university degree of any kind, and so he came to Mansfield's work without prejudice or preconceptions. Freed by his uncle's bequest from any need to earn a living, he happily fed his obsession, reading every word of Mansfield's he could lay his hands on, including notebooks and letters and the scraps of stories she'd left behind at her death. He devoured biographies, scholarly articles, and critical studies, becoming an amateur expert on the life of New Zealand's most famous writer. In the process, he came to forsake poetry, believing it his vocation to write a novel about Mansfield's life, an enormous, unwieldy novel which kept changing shape and direction, and which, whenever it came close to completion, Roger would decide was worthless, an insult to the memory of the writer with whom he'd fallen hopelessly in love.

It was this novel-in-eternal-progress, Monty believed, that had driven his mother away from husband, child, and home. Or, rather, it had been Roger's failure to complete the novel, to stop rewriting it year after year, to let it—and Katherine—go, that had done the damage. That, at least, had been Aunt Estelle's complaint. When he was ten years old, Monty had overheard an argument between her and his father. She, at least, was shouting—Roger never raised his voice, which infuriated Aunt Estelle all the more. "I can't wait forever, Roger. You have to let her go. You're a grown man, you have to face the facts—she is dead and gone." Estelle was, of course, an honorary aunt, a pretty, youngish widow who lived three houses down from them. She had left innumerable casseroles for Roger in the first months after the accident; she had helped look after the infant Monty when Roger had needed to deal with mewling and puking as well as the rules of literary revision.

———

Roger was cooking supper when Monty came home from Somes Island; they sat down to tinned peas and bangers and mash, each of them, as usual, with his own book propped up by his plate. It was another of Roger's peculiarities that, as a man who spent most of his life reading and writing, he had almost nothing to say that didn't concern literature. Small talk was a torture to him; big talk defeated him utterly. At each crisis in Monty's life—when, for example, Roger had shipped him off, aged eleven, to boarding school—Monty's father made only the briefest, most oblique attempt to explain. Roger had been honest enough not to try to hoodwink Monty about this earthquake of his expectations; there had been no speeches about how good it would be for him to have the company of boys his own age, to have access to the larger possibilities that would open up to him at Falconbridge. In fact, Roger had been unable to say anything to his son at all until an hour after their arrival in Picton for what Monty had believed to be an impromptu holiday tour of the South Island. On the train to Christchurch, Roger had blurted it out, looking so ill that Monty had been torn between rage at his father's treachery and fear that Roger would drop dead of a heart attack, as Aunt Estelle's father had done at the news that Singapore had fallen to the Japanese.

And here was that same shy, silent Roger, spooning in soggy potato and devouring *The County of Cornwall* as Monty jabbed at the food on his plate, not even pretending to read. His mind was stuck, like a broken projector, at that moment on Somes Island, his manuscript a whirl of blind white birds in the wind, his future a prison cell: teaching exiled, miserable adolescents at a school that was a poor cousin of the one he'd so loathed during his own miserable, exiled adolescence. The grandeur of his gesture at Kim Lee's rock had shrunk to the size of the peas he was mashing with his fork. Glancing up at his mother's portrait, Monty confirmed this sense of diminishment. The photo stood, as it always had, on a corner cupboard in the kitchen; as a boy he'd been able to imagine Tui watching him eat fried bread for breakfast or fried fish for supper (Roger's two specialties).

But what, you ask, of the portrait of the woman who'd made the fatal mistake of becoming Monty's mother? A woman named for the tui, the feisty, happy, honey-eating nightingale of New Zealand. In her photograph, Tui seems nothing like her namesake. The only way you could describe her expression was to compare it to a candle the moment after you've pinched the wick, the smoke rising sketchily over the still-warm wax. Her dark hair was cut short; it made her look very young. Below her eyes the skin appeared shadowed. If you looked carefully, you could see the mole, like a single inky tear, under her left eye. Barely visible around her neck was the waxed cord holding the greenstone tiki Monty now wore—the pendant about which you've been so curious.

Curiosity was never Monty's strong suit. Whatever he knew about his mother he'd learned from Aunt Estelle. That Tui was the foster child of a born-again couple up in Auckland. That she was a mix of Maori and Irish and English. That she'd been killed in a road accident while Monty was still a baby. That she'd been very young—barely nineteen—when Monty was born, and had found it difficult to cope with all his illnesses: not just croup and colic but jaundice and eczema, too. He'd been a difficult child, Estelle had informed him: weak and pale and sickly. She had tried to help Tui with building him up, but—and here Aunt Estelle always sighed—Tui was only a girl, a girl who'd needed a mother far more than a husband.

The one time Roger had become angry in Monty's hearing, it had been over a remark Estelle had made about Tui. Monty had woken one night, hearing noises; he'd crept to the hallway and hidden there while the voices jumped back and forth. It was much, much worse than Estelle's "dead and gone" speech, the "I can't wait forever" one. There had been the sound of something breaking, a pause, and then Estelle blurted out, "You know very well why she did it. You know and you haven't got the courage to tell him—"

Roger had interrupted in a voice Monty had never heard from him before, a cold, tight voice more frightening than any shouting could have been: "Get out of my house and don't ever come back. And stay away from my son!"

Monty sat looking at his mother's photo now, wondering if he'd dreamt that scene between his father and Estelle, or whether it had happened as he remembered it. It was certainly true that, shortly afterwards, Aunt Estelle had gone to visit her sister in Gisborne and hadn't returned, even when her house had been sold. Roger never mentioned her again, and Monty had been packed off to Christchurch shortly afterwards. His wretchedness there had had nothing to do with missing Aunt Estelle; he'd been well behaved with her, but only to get her to speak of his mother, to tell him the things excised from Roger's one and only story: how he'd met Tui while walking in the Botanical Gardens one summer afternoon; how they'd sat together under the pohutukawa trees, their branches fiery with blossom, and simply, silently, fallen in love.

Monty could imagine a destitute runaway girl taking refuge in the Botanical Gardens and permitting a shy older man to sit by her side. What he could never imagine was Roger's getting up the courage to speak to Tui in the first place, never mind invite her back to his house and into his life. His only explanation was that life and art had collided in that charged moment; that whatever Tui had been thinking as she saw, walking towards her, a thin, tall man with a paperback stuffed in his pocket, Roger's head had been full of a Mansfield story—and not even a very good one, at that. In it, a society woman, as plain as she is wealthy, acts on a whim, taking home with her a young girl begging on the street. The woman gets rid of her "pick-up" when her indulgent, if not passionate, husband admits how very pretty he finds the girl to be—how astonishingly lovely.

Roger, on the other hand, had married his waif, who'd borne him a child, as the saying goes, and then, if Aunt Estelle were to be trusted, had left the house without a coat one winter morning, walked down the hill, and thrown herself under a passing van. An accident, Roger had insisted when Monty finally ventured the question. For Roger's was a story of rare and perfect happiness cut short by one of the freak accidents that happen rather more often in life than they do in fiction. Tui's death, he'd sworn, had made her son's life all the more precious to him.

Ultimately, Monty had rejected both versions of Tui's end: death by accident or by design. To him, Tui was neither the loving, girlish wife-and-mother nor the burdened, despairing child-with-child but the defiant victim of Roger's confusion of art and life. Tired of serving as a stand-in for a character in a short story, refusing to play permanent second fiddle to the author of that story, she'd performed the only action she could to assert her own self, leaving her son behind as a footnote of sorts, no more and no less.

Of his mother Monty had only invented memories, stitched together from a few photographs of Tui pushing him in a pram or holding him in her lap, his small hands bound in white mittens to keep him from scratching the rash on his face. To tell you the truth, he'd always felt alarmed at the thought of his mother's life, her failed rebelliousness, her lethal instability. From the picture on the kitchen cupboard he knew how much he resembled Tui: the dark hair and skin, even the small mole under the left eye. The few photos she'd left behind were his only evidence that she'd ever existed; there was no grave for him to visit, the way orphaned children do in fairy tales, pouring out their grief and asking for assistance. Roger had had Tui's body cremated, her ashes scattered in the garden.

Monty looked up at his father. Did he relish his loneliness? Had the death of his over-young, under-educated wife come as a release? The few collections of poems Roger had published clarified nothing; they'd all been written before his marriage. No extracts from his novel had ever been printed; as far as Monty knew, the text was nothing but notes, quotations, and questions jotted down in his father's near-illegible handwriting on countless spiral-bound stenographer's pads. Monty had long since given up waiting for the novel to appear, along with whatever clues it might offer him. By the time he'd reached adolescence, his relations with his father had been skewed by resentment, not just at his Christchurch captivity, but also at Roger's loyalty to Tui on the one hand and his obsession with Katherine Mansfield on the other. Instead of having one dead mother to deal with, it seemed to Monty that Roger had given him two.

There were times when Monty would have preferred his father to have raged at or beaten him, so that he could have done what Tui had to her foster parents, or what Roger had done to his own, and run off forever. From school, from the house in Hataitai, from any contact with his father and reminder of his mother. But Roger's love had been as stubborn as it was strong; it had survived the cool contempt with which his son had treated him on his visits home from school, and it had weathered Monty's supreme act of defiance on completing his undergraduate degree in Wellington: reversing Roger's trajectory by escaping to London to work on a writer as little like Mansfield as possible.

Roger was reading as intently, as obliviously, about the county of Cornwall as if he'd been transported to Fowey or Bude and his son were a mere rock or tree helping to make up the view. Until Roger suddenly looked up at him with such helpless concern in his eyes that Monty had to turn his head away. This visit had been awkward to the point of pain: Monty's testiness and brooding, Roger's mute and dogged tenderness, had burdened the very air between them. If Monty had been expecting his father's look to translate into meaningful speech, there was no cause for fear, or for hopefulness, either. "I've got that new biography of Ottoline I was telling you about" was all Roger offered, as if promising a bag of sweets to charm away a tantrum or skinned knee. "It's in the study, if you want to take a boo at it."

The study was the one windowless room in the house; it was where Roger kept his most valuable books, his typewriter, and the minimal correspondence that came his way—

telephone and electricity bills, bank statements that piled up on his desk unread, even unlooked at, until they finally toppled. Monty found the book on Ottoline Morrell and sat down at the desk, ignoring the framed photograph that had stood there for as long as he could remember. It was an enlargement of the famous passport photo of 1918. Mansfield had been thirty when it was taken; her face looked as expectant as that of a girl of eighteen. Yet what she was waiting for wasn't the start of her life, a life of her own, but the final aloneness of death. The caved eyes, the dense shadow staining one side of her face, had terrified him when he was a child; he used to force himself to go to his father's study and stare at the photo, which seemed a mirror of his mother's portrait on the kitchen cupboard. It had been the one consolation of boarding school: the end of these showdowns with the images of long-dead, dying women.

Roger had marked a section of the biography dealing with Ottoline's daughter Julian, her memories of how kind Katherine had been to her at Garsington, how well she'd understood the plight of children. He shut the book and let it fall to the desk, knocking over the pile of neglected correspondence in the process. As he gathered up the envelopes, one of them caught his eye. It was the same shape, size, and colour as the others, but whoever had typed it had been using an old-fashioned machine that bit through the paper whenever it printed an *O*. The envelope was postmarked Chicago and addressed, unlike all the others, not to "Mr. Roger Mills," but to "Montgomery Mills, Author."

It was no business of Monty's that his father had a literary correspondent in America. Roger had never mentioned any friend or acquaintance living abroad; he wasn't the sort of person to have more than a very few friends and acquaintances. For him to receive a letter, as opposed to a bill or circular, was something of an occasion. Monty held the letter in his hands, wondering, idly, what it might contain. He could have taken it into the kitchen and shown it to his father, asking him to open it and share its contents. But any such show of interest would have diminished the distance he'd worked so hard to keep between them. He could also, of course, have put the letter back on the desk for Roger to discover for himself, a week or month later. Instead, more out of pique than curiosity, he picked up a paperknife. The letter might just as well, he told himself, have been addressed to him. How could it hurt to open it—carefully, so that it could be sealed again, invisibly?

THE AUGUSTUS GRIFFITHS FOUNDATION
FOR COLONIAL AMERICANA

To Mr. Montgomery Mills:

I've spent close to forty years and big sums of money collecting material on the life and work of Katherine Mansfield, and it's time to decide where my collection should go when I die. I was thinking of the Turnbull Library, in Mansfield's hometown. I guess you know they lost out on Jane Dick's collection of Mansfield manuscripts some years ago. But it's occurred to me that the Mansfield Trust might be a better place for my collection. It may be smaller than Mrs. Dick's, but it's got things no one's ever laid eyes on before. And it tells a different story about Miss Pure-and-Innocent than the one we've been spoon-fed all these years. I'm betting it'll be worth your while to take a look at my collection. In exchange, all you've got to do is give me your honest opinion of a piece I've written on Mansfield's early years in London.

I saw an ad in the *Journal of the Mansfield Trust* about some kind of biography you're writing about her. I see you're also on the advisory board of the Trust. Look here, Mr. Mills, I'm not a person to waste time or opportunities. The deal I've got in mind works best face to face and hand to hand. So if you're interested, come to Chicago and see my collection for yourself. I'm not letting it out of my sight.

Yours,

C. Baby

The letter was typed on heavy watermarked paper, but it might as well have been scratched on a jumbo scribbler. It was a hoax, of course; it had to be. No serious collector would be so rude or peremptory. Nor would he malign, with that Pure-and-Innocent remark, the very subject of his obsession. And what possible connection could there be between a foundation specializing in early Americana and the life of Katherine Mansfield? As for the reference to an ad in the Trust's glossy quarterly (which Monty routinely ignored as the work of amateurs), it was absurd. Roger was writing a novel, not a biography; if Mr. Baby wanted a scholar's opinion on his collection, he'd applied to the wrong address.

Roger was calling out from the kitchen. Monty slipped the letter back into the envelope. There was no time to reseal it, so he stashed it for the moment in his jacket pocket and returned to the kitchen. His father was standing by the fridge, a bottle of milk in his hands. "Shall we go and do the usual?" he asked. "Would you mind bringing the bread along?"

The moon was almost full, but even had it been pitch dark, Roger would have gone out as he had most nights for as long as he'd lived in Hataitai. When he reached the flat, grassy stretch at the top of the garden, he set down the saucers he was carrying; into each he poured milk, while Monty tore the bread into pieces and scattered them round. And then the two men sat on a small wooden bench, waiting in silence for however long it took until half a dozen hedgehogs moved from the edges of the garden to the saucers. The animals were tame enough that you could hold them, curled tightly, in the palm of your hand, their rubbery bristles just prickling your skin. Monty had held them like that as a child, when this nightly ritual had been as good as magic. Long past the time when the magic had stopped for his son, Roger had gone on summoning these small armed creatures, with no one for company but moon or stars or cloud, and the ghost—if you believe in such things—of a sad-eyed girl.

The hedgehogs appeared, at last. Single-mindedly, they lapped up the milk, ate the scattered bread, and returned to their burrows. It was time for father and son to say good-night, to go inside to their separate rooms and islands of sleep. Yet Roger made no move to rise. Instead, he took out his pipe, lit it, and, after a long, agonizing moment, began to speak in his low, soft voice, a voice so quiet that you always had to lean in to hear it.

"I've been thinking, Monty, that it's time I made a trip back to England. And I was thinking—I was hoping—you might come with me."

Monty's mouth fell open; he felt as though he'd been punched in the gut. He knew, of course, that Roger meant to make his peace with the country he'd run from all those years ago. The plan had been for him to fly out for Monty's defence of his thesis and the granting of his degree. What it meant, his extraordinary invitation, was that he'd given up all hope there would ever be a thesis to defend, a degree to confer.

Roger relit his pipe—a faulty one that Monty had given him years ago—and pressed on, speaking quickly now, almost defensively. "It's for the book, you see. I think it's time I finished it. As a matter of fact, I have to finish it, whether I feel it's ready or not. The Trust keeps asking for the manuscript, they want to have it in plenty of time for the centenary. They don't want my novel, of course—they want something short, snappy, a sort of scenic biography. So that's what I've got to give them. I've even signed a contract," he added apologetically.

I saw an ad in the Journal of the Mansfield Trust *about some kind of biography you're writing* . . . Surreptitiously, Monty felt for the letter stashed in his jacket pocket. He knew there were a number of projects being planned to mark Mansfield's birth, among them a life-sized statue of the writer to be placed in the Botanical Gardens. He was astonished that the Trust had given Roger a contract; surely they knew that moss would fur that statue in the Botanical Gardens long before the short and snappy biography ever appeared. And then he recalled the substantial sums his father had donated over the years to the Kathcrine Mansfield Trust; what else was this contract but a long-overdue receipt? This wasn't a very charitable thought, it's true, but Monty felt too bitter to be generous. That Roger should be preparing to launch his Mansfield book at the very moment that he, Monty, had thrown his own away . . .

"We might," Roger was saying, "go to some of the places where she lived. Menton, Sierre, Looe—even Fontainebleau. It's the end of the book that's giving me so much trouble, you see." He tried again to light his pipe: it kept going out, and finally he put it down. "We've nearly a fortnight before you have to be back in Invercargill. We could leave tomorrow—fly to Paris, mooch around France, hop a ferry to London. My treat, of course."

"Of course." It was all Monty could trust himself to say. Since winning his scholarship, he'd never taken a penny from his father. Roger had never been able to believe in this attitude of independence; he was always trying to break it down. And now he'd found the perfect way. This talk of a contract, a flight to London, a research tour on which his son would tag along like some junior assistant—it was all meant to force

Monty to admit the utter failure of the past five years of his life, that period when he'd been free, at last, from Roger's chequebook, solicitude, preoccupations.

"Splendid! There's a flight we can take tomorrow—I'll pay for the seats first thing tomorrow. I can't tell you how glad I am—"

But Monty dashed whatever gladness his father had been about to express; he felt a surge of the recklessness that had taken him to Somes Island that afternoon. "As a matter of fact," he blurted out, "I'll be doing some travelling of my own. In the opposite direction. I need to go to Chicago—I need to do some work at the Newberry."

"Chicago," Roger said, laying his large thin hands on his bony knees. "Yes, of course." After a moment he stooped to gather up the bottle of milk and the saucers. Then he rose and turned to face his son. "If you need help with the fare—"

"I can manage." Monty's voice sounded harsher than he'd intended. He was about to add, "Thank you," when he found himself shouting at his father, standing there so meekly with the milk bottle in his hand. Shouting at Roger, and at the sullen boys he taught in Invercargill, and the rowdy ones who'd witnessed the suicide of a useless sheaf of typescript. "I said I can manage. In spite of everything you've done to trip me up, I can manage on my own. I'm a grown man, for Christ's sake. Can't you get it into your head that I'm not your child any more?"

Roger looked down at the grass and then up at the moon. He was squinting, as if it were printed with words too small for him to read. When he spoke at last, all he said was, "Well, then. Goodnight. I suppose we both ought to get a proper sleep."

Monty waited till he heard the closing of the kitchen door. He took a swing at the air, then sat with his head in his hands. He felt neither shame nor relief at his outburst; it seemed to have come from someone else, some stranger who'd blundered into the garden. As for Roger, he would simply pretend that nothing angry or ugly had been said; it would be like all the other times when Monty had thrown childhood tantrums, or spouted adolescent tirades about how stifling and boring and dead Hataitai was, Wellington was, and every square inch of the New Zealand Roger clung to so blindly. It would be best to forget the outburst, it would be best to do as Roger always did—go on as if nothing had happened.

Except that, absurd as it might seem, he'd committed himself to flying off to Chicago. The cost of the ticket alone would ruin him, never mind the price of a hotel, meals, the books he would certainly buy. But then he felt the low glow of fatalism warming him; wasn't he ruined already?

Monty found himself reaching, not for the letter in his pocket but for the pendant round his neck, the one that had belonged to his mother. The same tiki he fastened round your neck three months ago, gave to your safekeeping. A small carved figure made of pounamu, a stone the green of seas churned up by storms. The figure is human in the way an embryo is human, crouched and coiled with gaping mouth and bulging eyes. It's female, your tiki, a birth goddess with a large open vulva. Open to daring, open to risk, open to seizing the heart's desire.

Was it waiting for him in Chicago, his heart's desire? The possibility, however slight, that he might discover something important about or by a long-dead writer—something he could use to clean up the mess he'd made of his chances? If it seems a poor thing to call success your heart's desire, remember that success was Monty's food and drink, his sleeping and waking. It was his freedom from the burden of his father's failures and his mother's absence, his only way of getting his own back on academe and supervisors and everything else that had gone so disastrously wrong for him in London.

It would be crazy to go to Chicago. Even if the letter wasn't a hoax, the mysterious Mansfield collection would doubtlessly turn out to be facsimiles or blurred photos, the usual mix of odds and sods. And if by some slight chance it contained something worth seeing, the journey would still be long, costly, and difficult: no small excursion and no timid flight.

He drew the letter out of his pocket, turning it over and over in his hands. He could reseal it, place it back on Roger's desk; pretend to fly off to Chicago and back while Roger was away. He could try to undo his day's work at Somes Island, returning to his notes and files, labouring to turn a diatribe into an argument, drudging at the library for the next two weeks before term began again in Invercargill.

Crazy, risky, ruinous, any trip to Chicago. As much of a trap as the one Roger had sprung for him that night. Of course he couldn't just fly off to Chicago.

Of course he would.

BEYOND THE BLUE MOUNTAINS

London, October 1908

Porters whistling, pigeons thumping, people shouting, waving, shoving, and in the midst of it all, Ida Baker, trying to
look as much as possible like Lesley Moore. In her shabby
grey coat and mushroom hat, she is, however, only the same
shy, clumsy Ida left behind a year ago. But Katie! Ida
devours the sight of the figure stepping off the boat train in a
brown travelling suit and daisy-trimmed hat, under which
her face shines with a self-possession rare in a girl of twenty.
It all happens too quickly for Ida. At first there'd been a huge
hole in her world when Kathleen left—and then her whole
world had become that huge hole, with only the thin plank of
a letter a week to keep her from falling in. And now here's
Katie without a mark on her of their year of separation, as if
she's popped up to London from Brighton instead of New
Zealand. Kathleen, it's clear, has the power to make time
stop, fly back, erase itself; she has the power, too, of taking
people by storm, making at least some of them love her, as
Ida does, with a saint's unquestioning devotion.

There's a fuss about getting all of Katie's trunks into a second cab. She insists on bringing her cello in the hansom she and Ida take; the instrument sits on the seat across from them like a mystery guest or mournful chaperone as they set off for Beauchamp Lodge. There's no connection—thank heaven—with her family, Kathleen explains. Built as a residence for the Puerto Rican ambassador, Beauchamp Lodge is now a perfectly respectable hostel for female musicians. Whether there are any respectable male musicians, Kathleen jokes, she really can't say. They are going up the Edgware Road now. Ida puts her hand on Kathleen's solid, tweedy arm; she has some awkward news for her friend about Arnold Trowell.

Katie shakes her arm free from Ida's touch. "Arnold's expecting me—they're all expecting me at Carlton Hill," she says, defiantly.

Ida is used to Kathleen's rages and queenly fits; she proceeds, meekly, but stubbornly, too. "Katie, dearest—since the Trowells have settled in London . . . Well, it's just that . . . Arnold has been seeing rather a lot of a friend of yours from Queen's College."

There's a long silence that Ida finally blunders in to fill. "It seems . . . he may have got her in the family way."

Kathleen is far too calm. She puts the little twist of violets she purchased on the platform up to her face, addressing them instead of Ida. "You are not to repeat vile gossip to me, now or ever. You haven't the right to even mention his name—you wouldn't know genius if it punched you in the eye!"

Ida's face crumples. "Katie," she whispers, "I only wanted to prepare you."

Suddenly Kathleen notices that Ida looks exhausted, as if it were she who'd spent the last seven weeks on tossing seas. Being Ida, she'd have been up since five that morning and at the station by seven to meet the ten o'clock train from Dover.

Kathleen puts her arm around her friend, though her words are anything but tender: "Not another word against Arnold, ever. Do you understand? The subject is closed."

In its scraped and battered case, the cello looks on, perfectly indifferent.

———

Beauchamp Lodge is a handsome Regency building only a little worse for wear, its cream-coloured stucco peeling in places, its woodwork chipped. An attractive young woman named Margaret Wishart introduces herself as a fellow lodger and musician; she shows Kathleen upstairs, with Ida bearing the cello behind them, followed by the cabby and the hostel porter trundling the Beauchamp luggage up to a large room on the second floor. Kathleen sweeps inside and runs to the French doors that look out onto the canal and a small island full of willow trees, beyond.

"That's Browning's Island," Margaret explains to Ida, smiling warmly, trying to bring the stolid Miss Baker into the conversation. "Robert Browning—the poet—lived right down the road."

Kathleen unpins her hat and flings it across the room, jubilant. The omens are perfect, she declares: she will write a masterpiece here, sell a million copies, buy a house in St. John's Wood and a villa somewhere in Italy, with a view of the violet sea, and nightingales in the umbrella pines. Grudgingly, Ida watches Margaret kindle in Katie's presence, revel in her impetuous style, her gusto for life, her sheer bravado.

Just after Margaret leaves, a maid brings in a telegram. Ripping it open, Kathleen crows, "It's from the Trowells. They've asked me for tea, if I'm not too tired—tea at Carlton Hill!" She throws her arms round Ida and dances her across the room, then starts unbuttoning the brown travelling suit in a frenzy. "Come on, Lesley, fetch me some hot water and soap and towels, there's a darling. And could you open that small trunk over there—the one with the gold stickers all over it?"

What can Ida do but obey, though she permits herself to say, wistfully, "I'd thought we'd have tea together at home. I've ordered in a special meal—everything you like best, Katie."

But Kathleen isn't to be moved by wistfulness. "How perfectly sweet of you, Lesley." And then, with a warmth that Ida could almost put out her hands to, "Dear old Faithful One. I'll come to tea tomorrow—I promise. But today, I must see the Trowells, I can't keep them waiting after a whole year away."

———

The Trowells are all living together again in a house near Regent's Park. It has none of the trappings of Beauchamp Lodge—no urn-filled niches or delicate plaster friezes with subjects such as Charity and Victory—but it's a pleasant house all the same: three storeys with a small garden at the back. Mrs. Trowell is in the cellar making apple pies with the maid-of-all-work and Dolly—now a very young thirteen—when Kathleen comes running down the stairs. She is at least an hour early. Throwing her arms around her future husband's mother, the wife of her dear, marvellous cello teacher, she squeezes her till Mrs. Trowell has to beg her to let go. Her pleasure at seeing this robust ghost from their Wellington days is tempered by embarrassment at being caught making pastry, in her apron, by a guest dressed far too splendidly for tea. But Kathleen is oblivious. She dances from object to object in the warm and steamy kitchen: the big black stove with the fire glowing red behind its open bars, the rolling pin and paring knives and earthenware bowl, the sky blue plates displayed on the white-painted dresser. "It's all so wonderful," she cries, "it's all so real and simple and—human."

From upstairs, flamboyant welcoming noises: crashing piano chords and a voice imitating a trumpet. Kathleen abandons real, simple, human Mrs. Trowell with her floury hands and heat-frizzed hair. She dashes up to the drawing room, where Arnold will be waiting for her. Except that it's Garnet making the trumpet sounds, the crashing chords. Tall, spindly Garnet with his stooped shoulders, unruly hair, and smile warm as burnished copper. As for the figure entering the parlour behind her, it's only Thomas Wilberforce, grumpy about all the noise. He smiles, just a little, at the sight of Kathleen—Kass, they can't help calling her—holding out her arms to him.

High tea in the dining room, its red velvet curtains drawn against the night, the lamps lit, the air smelling of ham and cheese, apple and cinnamon, and the wine Garnet's insisted on opening in Miss Beauchamp's honour. It isn't until the maid begins to clear the table that Arnold is heard at the front door. Kathleen has kept herself from asking about him; none of the Trowells has volunteered to tell her where he might be. When he enters the dining room, everyone tenses; it's clear they are all in Arnold's bad books, and he in theirs. "Rehearsal?" Mr. Trowell barks, and Arnold replies, just as abruptly, "Teaching." Whereupon Mrs. Trowell shushes Dolly, who's begun to say, "But I thought—"

Kathleen, to whom Arnold has nodded without saying a single word, is rising from her chair. Her eyes are suspiciously bright, her hands shaking. She is about to rush from the table when Garnet grabs her wine glass, the last of his parents' crystal. He wets his finger with the dregs of wine and rubs it round and round the goblet's rim. A ringing fills the room, delicate and teasing at first, then loud, almost raucous. Kathleen gives something between a sob and a laugh, Dolly claps her hands over her head, and Mrs. Trowell orders them all out to the parlour before the constable comes to haul them off for causing a ruckus.

Later, when Garnet insists on walking her back to Beauchamp Lodge, Kathleen, who feels perfectly safe on her own in the well-lit streets, announces herself delighted to have his company. And so they set out, Dolly between them, holding a hand of each. Garnet talks about the job he's going to start next month with a travelling opera orchestra— engagements in Birmingham, Liverpool, Glasgow. "The Moody-Manners," Dolly breaks in. "It's the finest orchestra of its kind." Garnet tweaks Dolly's hair; Kathleen congratulates him with all her fraught and volatile heart. For by the time they reach Beauchamp Lodge, she has convinced herself that it was never Arnold that she loved, but only, always, Garnet. She is already composing the passionate letters she will send to him care of the opera halls and theatres of Birmingham, Liverpool, Glasgow, where he will make his musical name, returning in triumph to her and showing brotherly tolerance, of course, for poor ordinary Arnold.

———

Here is how Kathleen spends her new life in London. Waking before sunrise, standing wrapped up in a brilliantly patterned shawl at the French doors, watching willows emerge from the mist on Browning's Island. Writing in her journal in a room filled with huge bouquets of flowers, embroidered cushions, and a rented grand piano. Going shopping for a whole new wardrobe, having decided that the clothes she's brought from New Zealand are hopelessly provincial. Drinking cocoa in Margaret Wishart's far more spartan room, Kathleen curled up like a cat before the fire and the two of them discussing Walt

Whitman, for whom they share a passion. Selling her cello at a dingy shop near the Albert Hall for the derisory sum of three pounds—the amount she happens to owe her milliner. Walking with Garnet and Dolly on Primrose Hill, delighting in the green, open space, sending Dolly off to pat various small dogs so that Garnet and she can hold hands unobserved.

Going with the Trowells to see Garnet off to Birmingham and passing him, from its hiding place in her muff, a note which he reads as soon as the train begins to move, a note of one underscored word: "Husband!" Going to a studio to have her picture taken; enclosing it in an envelope on which she writes her lover's stage name: "Carrington Garnet, Esq., Moody-Manners, Theatre Royal, Glasgow." Being helped by Ida into evening dress, with Ida risking a "Must you go, Katie—is it really wise?" Kathleen doesn't respond except to look more intently at a newspaper clipping pinned up on a spare bit of wall:

Grand Theatre and Opera House, George Street,
Hull
Moody-Manners Opera Company Tonight at 7:30
"AIDA"

Mesdames de Vere Sapio, Toni Seiter
Messrs. Philip Brozel, Lewys James, Charles
Magrath, Charles Manners
Conductor: Signor Romualdo Sapio
Chorus of Sixty. Orchestra of Forty-Five
Full Company: One Hundred and Forty Artistes
Saturday Matinee & Evening Performance.
Private Boxes 2 pounds 2 shillings—6d for Gallery

And at the bottom of the page, an ad for the Hull Trades Exhibition:

"Look Out for Mr. Fidmont's Magnificent Show
of Artificial Teeth."
Diploma 1906–7. Stand 48 (In the Gun Room)

Ida repeats her warning, and Kathleen pulls away from the
hands trying to pin a bunch of roses on her shoulder. "If
Garnet can bear it, Ida, so can I. Mayfair is preferable to
Hull. Besides, I need the money." It's impossible, she adds,
to live on the anaemic allowance her father sends her; performing parodies of Salvation Army songs at posh parties is
as good a way as any to keep body and soul together.

Stammering, Ida offers Katie all the interest on her small
principal, so that her friend can devote herself to her writing.

Moved, contrite, Kathleen cups Ida's face in her hands.
She is about to apologize to her good and faithful servant, or
at least confess how little she deserves all Ida's done for her,
when she hears a rustling down the hallway. "Quick, the
roses! That's better. They're lovely—they must have cost a
pretty penny. Really, Lesley, you're the extravagant one.
That astrakhan coat you gave me for my birthday must have
ruined you—though it's absolutely gorgeous. I feel I could
lead the retreat from Moscow in it!"

Margaret knocks at the door and the two young women, in
their silky dresses, dyed feathers in their hair, and the best
imitation pearls swinging from their throats, rush down the
stairs, leaving Ida to tidy Kathleen's mess of clothes and
kicked-off shoes, which she does in her dogged, loving way.
As if she were happy to be Kathleen's lady's maid or impoverished spinster cousin; as if, perching on the edge of Katie's
life, she can protect her from whatever harm goes on at Mayfair parties and other places Ida can only wonder about.

Margaret and Kathleen have climbed into a cab; as they
rattle along, Margaret reaches into her evening bag and
takes out a thin gold ring set with the smallest diamond

imaginable. She is secretly engaged, she announces, to a pianist, a man whom her father the Admiral would sooner keelhaul than permit to so much as smile at his daughter. Kathleen grabs her friend's hand, admires the ring, then pulls off her gloves with a flourish. On the fourth finger of her right hand, she wears a thin gold ring set with the smallest imaginable diamond.

━━━━━━

A month later: deep November, the trees skeletal, Virginia creeper crimson over stained brick walls. At the front window of the Trowells' house Kathleen and Dolly watch as a cab pulls up. When Garnet, violin case, and valise tumble out of it, they run to embrace him, shivering and laughing as they pull him up the steps and through the front door. Unwrapping the scarf round Garnet's throat, trying to straighten his shaggy hair with both her hands, Kathleen tells him that his parents are away at a wedding for the weekend. Garnet is bending his face towards Kathleen's when Dolly grabs his hand. She tugs him into the parlour, offering him roast chestnuts, planning what they'll do to celebrate his being home for a whole week's holiday.

Not long afterwards, Dolly is sent to bed, protesting. When she's settled for the night, Garnet and Kathleen sit on the floor in front of the fire, Kathleen hugging her knees, Garnet with his arms tightly crossed. Neither says a word or looks at the other. When only a few red coals are left in the grate, they reach out their hands to one another, locking their fingers tight. That night they become lovers.

Very early the next morning, Kathleen wakes in Garnet's bed. She pulls a sheet around her and walks over to the window, through which she sees, to her delighted disbelief, a flock of sheep being herded down Prince Albert Road. She's been told that shepherds are still to be found moving their flocks through London, but she hasn't believed it until now. It reminds her of New Zealand, of the sheep grazing near the bay where her family would rent a bungalow for the summer. In sheer happiness she cries out to Garnet, who joins her at the window, kissing her shoulders where the sheet has slipped away. For a moment they stand together, skin against skin, looking out the window—a moment long enough for Dolly, who's been woken by Kathleen's cry and who has opened the door of their room, to see them. Her mouth forms a perfect *O*. Gently, she closes the door; she has crept back to her bed by the time Kathleen says, "I must go, love, before Dolly wakes." She pulls on her clothes, not bothering to fasten her corset or do more than tug at the laces of her boots. "I'll write as soon as I get home, I promise you." She kisses the top of Garnet's head, then tiptoes down the stairs, running out of the house while Dolly stands at her window, watching Kass make her way down the road, in the wake of the all-too-innocent sheep.

Kathleen visits Carlton Hill the next day, pitching in with the cooking and even helping Mrs. Trowell—very badly—with the darning, while Garnet practises upstairs. Dolly keeps her distance, refusing the chestnuts Kass has roasted for her, stomping out of the room when her mother tells her to mind her manners. Kathleen is about to go after her when Mrs. Trowell tells her to stay right where she is—she needs Kass's help, and Dolly has to learn that the earth doesn't turn round her curly little head. Later that week, when they all go to see Garnet off at the station—he is heading north to tour again—all seems pleasant and calm, except for the way Dolly clings to Garnet when he tries to board his train.

Passionate letters arrive daily from Garnet, triggering equally passionate responses from Kathleen: letters in which the two lovers—he the finest violinist of his time, she a world-famous writer—sweep all before them. Over onions boiled on a gas plate and served in *bols de mariage* purchased on a brief jaunt to Paris, Margaret and Kathleen talk of how they'll live on love and a shilling a week, and damn their families. But there must always, Kathleen insists, be flowers on the table; far better to go without milk for one's tea than to scrimp on flowers.

There is nothing at all to warn Kathleen when she runs up the steps of the house at Carlton Hill, her arms laden with Christmas presents. That the door will be opened by a stony-faced Mrs. Trowell, with Dolly looking on beside her; that the whole street will ring with Mrs. Trowell's words: "We are respectable people here, Miss Beauchamp. Our son is a decent young man who deserves far better than to be corrupted by the likes of you!"

As the door slams in her face, Kathleen's parcels tumble from her arms; she turns, walks with exaggerated care down the steps, and forces herself to walk, proudly, down the road. A trio of neighbourhood children have been watching the scene; before Kathleen has disappeared round the corner of the street, they have snatched up the gold-and-crimson-wrapped packages and run off in the opposite direction.

———

In the foyer of Beauchamp Lodge languish the parched remains of a Christmas tree. Kathleen has moved to a different, smaller room; the piano has vanished, but the bed still has its dark blue coverlet embroidered with golden domes and a border of leopards. Curtains of a matching blue-black are drawn dramatically across the windows; the only light comes from a desk lamp, its shade painted with small red apples. In her usual tearaway handwriting, Kathleen is scribbling a letter to Garnet, which she seals in an envelope and then, with a little cry of impatience, tears up. Margaret knocks at the door; when there's no response, she lets herself in. She doesn't put her arm round Kathleen's shoulder as she intended: she can sense how jumpy her friend is, how explosive her mood. Instead of an embrace, Margaret offers an invitation to a musical evening at the house of a writer she is acquainted with, a man who knows several London publishers. Kathleen keeps staring at the floor; Margaret bends down, taking her friend's hands in her own. "You can't go on like this, Kassie. It will be all right—as soon as he comes back, he'll make things right. He adores you—he'd do anything rather than hurt you."

Kathleen shakes off Margaret's hands and walks to the fire; into it she throws the halves of the letter she's been writing. When she looks at Margaret again, her face is hard and bright. She grabs a huge black-and-silver shawl patterned with what she describes as Maori designs; she puts on long greenstone earrings and rouges her face. "The wild colonial girl!" she cries, racing down the stairs, with Margaret barely able to keep up with her.

The writer lives in Chelsea, in a flat furnished with crammed Globe Wernickes and a good upright piano. There are many hard chairs and one minimally upholstered sofa, on which Kathleen settles, lighting a cigarette and reclining like a Madame Récamier from New Zealand's back blocks. One of the guests keeps walking about the room, finding new angles from which to observe this extraordinary young woman, so outlandish and assured, so watchful and so silent. Finally their eyes meet, and the man goes up to introduce himself: his name is George Bowden, he's a singer, vocal coach, and elocutionist, and he is delighted to make her acquaintance. Kathleen's face remains utterly blank, but she makes no objection to his sitting down beside her in one of the terribly straight chairs, this blond, pink-cheeked fellow in his well-brushed suit, his hair parted scrupulously down the middle, his little moustache clipped.

Later, Margaret notices that the two are talking, and though Kathleen still wears her poker face, Bowden looks amused, attentive, and happy in a way that seems almost indecent for a party of this elevated sort. He insists on seeing both women home; he calls a cab and, all through the ride, beams silently as Margaret and Kathleen discuss the evening, Kathleen giving vivid imitations of their host, his butler, and some of the guests who, unluckily for them, drew her caustic attention. While Margaret thanks Bowden as they pull up at Beauchamp, Kathleen barely nods; this doesn't prevent him from stopping the cab a block farther on, jumping down, and lingering on the Ha'penny Bridge. He could spend the whole night there, he tells himself, looking over the canal at the back of Beauchamp Lodge and wondering which window, lighted or dark, belongs to the woman he's already calling his Miss Beauchamp.

———

Early March. Purple and yellow primulas bloom in the window boxes; along the canals countless buds thicken on the trees. And along the road toils Ida Baker, trying to think of herself not as the obedient daughter of a cantankerous doctor but as that fine, free creature hatched from candlelight and hairbrushing less than two years ago: Lesley Moore. Making her way to Kathleen's room, she can hear her friend reciting something to squeals of laughter. She stops, as though she has a stitch in her side; her face darkens for a moment, then resumes its milky mildness. She hasn't come here to share Katie with anyone—she's sure Margaret Wishart is in the room with her, clever, handsome Margaret who got Katie mixed up in that business of making pin money at Mayfair parties. Instead of knocking at the door, Ida retreats. She will come back later, she will come at tea time, bringing some penny buns and a bunch of the Parma violets Katie loves so much.

Kathleen isn't reciting one of her stories about young women who reject romantic love to become the Vestal Virgins of Art, or about seduced seamstresses expiring of botched abortions, the stench of rotten bananas wafting up to their garrets from the street below. To Margaret Wishart and a group of other lodgers, Kassie is reading out a love letter, one of the many love letters she's been sent by George Bowden. Before she can finish, Margaret, the only one who isn't laughing, seizes the letter. "How can you be so unfeeling, Kass? He's mad about you." Kathleen snatches the letter back. She crumples it furiously, which all the other girls except Margaret take as a signal to leave the room.

Once they're alone, Kathleen cries out, "What else can I do if he chooses to make an ass of himself—and chooses me of all people for an audience? If he'd come to sing below my window, I could at least have thrown a flower pot at his head. But these letters—the absurdity, the conceit of the man! A tailor's dummy could write better love letters. I know what a love letter should be—" She breaks off and walks blindly to the window.

Gently, Margaret asks, "You've still not heard from him?"

Kathleen's fury has condensed into despair. "There's never any answer when I write care of the theatres, and anything I send to Carlton Hill comes straight back. They hate me there, Margaret—how can anyone hate me so?" Kathleen leans her forehead against the glass.

Margaret comes up to her, placing her hands very gently on her friend's rigid shoulders. "They're afraid of you. They know how much Garnet loves you. There's been some terrible mistake, some misunderstanding. He's just a boy, Kassie—

he's barely twenty. Why don't you go to him? As soon as he sees you, he'll—"

Kathleen wheels round, snapping, "Take me back?" She laughs then, and her whole face shifts: she looks detached, remote. It's the look her mother so often wears, as if the people, the objects, closest to her simply don't exist. She takes her coat down from the hook on the door, pulls on her gloves. "I'm off. I have shopping to do." She leaves Margaret stranded by the window, puzzled and angry.

At a milliner's on Bond Street, the lady asks to see hats: black hats, only. The assistant brings out a row of them—feathers, velvet, fur—but this customer reaches for a hat on a stand in the corner, jet-black straw with a narrow brim, a hat not unlike the one she wore as a child of ten the day she drove in a carriage to Wellington Harbour to meet her parents' ship. "Wouldn't madam rather—?" the assistant begins, but Kathleen cuts her off. She pays for the hat—it's not cheap, though it's only straw—and leaves clutching the hatbox in her arms.

She is next to be seen, wearing the hat and dressed entirely in black, walking to the Paddington Registry Office. Ida is with her, clutching her arm. They enter a dingy room in which George Bowden is waiting in an impeccably tailored suit, with the writer friend at whose flat he first met Miss Beauchamp.

It's not much of a wedding, though the bride and groom go off to a decent restaurant in the Strand and take in a play before checking into their room at one of the better, though not specially grand, hotels. The room is lit by lamps with pink satin shades to match the shiny pink satin of the bedspread. Kathleen stands by the door her husband has shut and locked; she makes no move to take off even her hat, so Bowden unpins it, laying it carefully on the dresser. He takes his wife by the arm and sits her down on the bed. She looks up at him as if he were a perfect stranger; he pushes her back, gently, so that she's lying stretched out on the bed as he leans over her. Her face is white and closed, her body a log. "I can't," she whispers. "I just can't."

Bowden shakes his head, bends to kiss her, then pulls back, in a blur of indecision. Kathleen doesn't see the hurt on his face, only the perfect parting of his hair. He switches off the pink-shaded lamps and lies down beside his bride on the satin bedspread.

For the longest time, there's only the sound of their tight, separate breathing, but at last Bowden shudders into sleep. Kathleen moves carefully off the bed, opens the curtains to let the street light in, picks up her hat, her bag, the small dressing case she's borrowed from Ida, and walks away.

———

As the London express pulls into Glasgow Central Station, a pale, reedy young man with a mop of plain brown hair and a stricken look on his face is pacing up and down the platform. When the passengers start to emerge, he crumples the telegram in his hand. Her letters he'd sent back, unread; he'd promised his parents that much. But a telegram is different, a telegram's an emergency you can't refuse to meet.

When Kathleen descends from the first-class carriage, he freezes for a moment, then rushes towards her. She looks as though she hasn't slept in weeks; her eyes are dry and bright. Holding him at arm's length, she speaks with strict intensity. "We won't say a word about your parents. We won't let anyone spoil this for us. Not a single question, promise me, Garnie."

These last three words are spoken out of pain that makes him think of blood on the blade of a knife; they cut straight through the tangle of Garnet's loyalties. He throws his arms

around her, she drops her suitcase, and they kiss passionately, scandalizing passersby.

━━━━━

Kathleen in a silk kimono, a towel round her freshly washed
hair; Garnet in trousers, frayed suspenders, and an under-
shirt, fiddling bits of the overture from Balfe's *The Bohemian
Girl*. They're in the small bedroom of a Glasgow tenement
house—not a slum but a superior building made of soot-
blackened sandstone, with a porcelain-tiled entrance hall.
Their landlady, a Miss Muckle, is a seamstress who blames
the fall-off in her trade on her failing eyes; to make up for lost
income she lets her bedroom to respectable travellers and
sleeps in a tomb-like cupboard bed off the parlour. In Miss
Muckle's eyes, anyone from the Moody-Manners is as
respectable as travellers come. Charles Manners is a gentleman; his wife, Fanny Moody, is a lady. The fact that they
sing for a living is beside the point. As for the newlyweds in
her spare room, she is happy to have them as long as they
don't splash in the bath or make noises other than music.

"You could easily get a part as a super," Garnet's telling
Kathleen, who is trying to towel her hair dry while reading
Little Dorrit. The window's open; it's late afternoon, a Fri-
day. Half of Glasgow is plying the curling tongs; whole
streets smell of singed hair. Now Garnet's wrapping his violin in a white silk handkerchief and putting it carefully back
into its case. "You wouldn't need to sing," he says. "You'd
just have to stand about the stage looking gypsy-like."

Kathleen puts down her book and turns her towel into a
shawl around her soft, full body. In the floor space available,
she attempts a bosom-shaking gypsy dance. "They'd really
pay me?" she asks. "Pay me for not singing, not dancing, just
standing round looking like a fortune-teller?"

Her lover grabs her and sits her on his knee, kissing her wet, dark head. "Not a king's ransom, but enough for kippers and brown bread for tea. And Miss Muckle's superior roof over our heads. What more do we need?"

"It sounds like something out of Dickens," Kathleen says, laughing. "The simple, easy lies of the theatre. Simple and easy sound like heaven, just now." She kisses Garnet, hard, and he kisses her back; where she's said *lies*, he's heard *life*, and all he can think of is how much brighter and richer, how altogether delightful his life has become with Kassie here to share it.

———

Kathleen flounces into the Theatre Royal through the Performers' Entrance; she is called into the office and asked to sit down at a plain wooden table to read the contract she must sign before she can appear on stage. She will have her rail fare (third class) paid for by the Company, likewise her costumes, "with the exception of shoes, feathers, ornaments, and all *basso vestiario*"—the latter term, she's told, translates as "underwear." If she is ill and unable to perform, or when Public Calamity or Royal Demise causes theatres to close, she will receive no salary. She begins to read aloud, in mounting disbelief, the rules and regulations. "All Members of the Operatic Company shall, on their arrival in each town, send notice to the Hallkeeper of the place of their abode." "Every Member of the Operatic Company must remain with the Company in each town where the Company is performing, even when not engaged in the performance, and any Members absenting themselves without the written permission of the management will be fined half a week's salary." Then comes the worst of all: "Fines of a week's salary will be levied for writing to the papers, without written permission of the Company, respecting any business to do with the Moody-Manners."

Shaking her head at the pettiness of it all, she lights a cigarette, which the office manager whips from her fingers, squashing it as if it were a black beetle. "Smoking in any part of the Theatre is strictly prohibited," he says in an acid voice. "No intoxication before or behind the curtain, either." Kathleen looks daggers at the man, but contains herself; she does, after all, need the job, however ludicrous its conditions.

When she enters the actual theatre, however, she forgets the office manager and succumbs to the beauty of illusion. In the upper tiers of Glasgow's Theatre Royal, amidst the gilded cream of plaster decorations, under lamps shaped like closed buds, white and amber, the audience sits hushed before the stage. Knights in armour, hunters in brown leather, gypsies flashing green and red ribbons, wearing brilliantly embroidered shawls and straw hats huge as cartwheels. A castle with battlements and turrets, a glen both flowery and wooded, chandeliers and moonlight, blazing fires, crowned and cowled heads—it's no wonder that no one has eyes for the orchestra pit sunk between the stage, with its plush maroon curtain, and the dress circle.

No one but Kathleen, who's been given a free ticket to study just what degree of smiling and scowling is expected from the silent gypsies before she joins their ranks tomorrow. Her eyes are fixed on the crescent of darkness in which musicians and conductor perform, barely visible in the hot jets of light by the music stands or flaring by the podium. Garnet's told her how, when they're not required to play a given passage, the musicians tell jokes, read betting forms, write letters, play chess or cards, yet somehow manage to take up their instruments again exactly when needed. He seems proud of the skill, the impeccable timing required. All Kassie can think, peering down into the darkness of the pit, leaning as far over the balcony rail as she can, is that Garnet should be on centre stage with his violin, a soloist playing music for its own sake, not to keep the gypsies hopping. Soon, she tells herself, soon he'll be done with these stunts in the dark, finished with being invisible, obscure.

———

They spend nearly two weeks together in Glasgow, breathing in spring with the smoky air. Theatre life proves more strenuous and difficult than Kathleen anticipated. There is much to get used to—the foul air, the cramped space, the icy drafts on the one hand and the lamps' sickening heat on the other, blocked and overflowing toilets, and, most intolerable of all, the pittance earned by the pit musicians. There's never any money for decent meals at proper restaurants, only pub fare of mince and potatoes or sausage and potatoes, with a dish of rabbit or a bowl of vegetable soup if one's lucky. Garnet's friends drink far too much, though he sticks to a pint of ale most nights. She dislikes one of the cellists: his cough sounds too much like consumption, and she worries that Garnet sits too close to him in the orchestra pit.

When they're not rehearsing or performing, punching in or out at the huge time clock just inside the stage door, they wander about the city, playing tag in Kelvingrove Park or sauntering through the Garnethill district, behaving as if all its fine and stately homes are Garnet's to inherit. Underneath the coal dust, Garnet tells her, the stone is the colour of creamed honey. Kathleen doesn't hear; she's watching a woman coming up the street, a woman bundled in a plaid shawl out of which a baby's face is peeking. "Look, Garnie— just like a kangaroo!" Kathleen exclaims, delightedly. It's an image she will fix on later when the gypsies are killing time, telling stories in the dressing room, and Dorrie recounts how a man moving into one of the tenement flats in a nice enough part of the city traced a nasty smell to a tin box left behind by the previous tenant, a woman of twenty-two. Opening the box, he found the remains of a baby. "It's true," Dorrie will shriek. "My landlady told me, and she lives right next door."

What Kathleen likes best, however, is fortune-telling, at which she outdoes Dorrie or any gypsy in *The Bohemian Girl*. Sitting on the bed in their room at Miss Muckle's, taking Garnet's outspread hand, turning it this way and that, she makes her prediction. After a short period of penury, spent in a cottage on a moor or a bedsit in Chelsea, Garnet will be acclaimed a genius by a German or Italian guest conductor of the Moody-Manners. He will be plucked from the pit and put on centre stage at the Bechstein Hall, where he'll be acclaimed by critics and bravoed by rapturous audiences. Instead of a coin to cross her palm, Garnet gives her a kiss and then another and another, until they fall back together on the horsehair mattress, laughing so hard that Miss Muckle removes herself from the parlour to the kitchen, hoping the gas boiler will drown out the sound of the brass headboard hitting the wall just under the sampler that reads "Rest in the Lord."

Afterwards, when they lie naked in each other's arms, Kassie spins her own future, how she'll pull herself together and, instead of the little scraps and splutters she's been working on, write a novel that will astonish the world. They'll have pots of money, they will live as they should: in freedom, in comfort, in style. In London and Paris, Garnet offers; never, Kathleen adds, in a Surrey mansion like golfing Aunt Belle with her shipping magnate. Or in a stone house in the snowy wastes of Quebec, like Vera and her precious Canadian.

Towards the end of their stay in Glasgow, Kathleen insists they have a decent meal. She leads her lover down to

Sauchiehall Street, past alleyways strung with laundry—sheets, shirts, nappies puffed up like bladders in the wind. Lounging in the Willow Tea Rooms designed by Charles Rennie Macintosh, Garnet teases Kathleen about the joy she takes in the absurdly high-backed chairs, the rose and white and grey decor; he's had teas just as good, he declares, at a London A.B.C. Then he's a dolt, Kathleen retorts. It's not about the tea in the pot, she says—though she adores a really good cup of Darjeeling, with lemon, of course, and no sugar, or Lapsang suchong, with its smoky taste of grey November skies. Garnet laughs again, and this time Kassie's expression changes from indulgence to impatience. She quotes to him from *Little Dorrit*, the description of the uncle who, after his fall from financial grace, resorts to "playing a clarinet as dirty as himself in a small theatre orchestra."

Garnet wiggles his little fingers inside his ears and brings them out with a pop, as if to show her that they couldn't be cleaner, at which Kathleen rises—with some difficulty—from her high-backed chair and storms from the tea rooms. Garnet chases after her, but by the time he reaches Miss Muckle's, Kathleen has barricaded herself in the bathroom. Sounds of splashing answer Garnet's frantic knocks at the door, until suddenly it opens. A naked Kathleen throws her arms around her lover, oblivious to who might be watching, and to the neatly printed warnings about water damage and the need for prompt mopping-up posted over the small tin tub.

———

Tell-tale tit
Yer mammy canny knit
Yer daddy canny go tae bed
Without a dummy tit!

Children are playing beneath their window as Mr. and Mrs. Trowell prepare to leave Miss Muckle. She knocks at their door with the morning's post: a letter for Garnet; his father's stilted writing on the envelope is unmistakable. Garnet stands for a moment, weighing the letter in his hand. This is the moment for a grand gesture, something ringing and superb. He could rip up the letter unread, toss it into the waste-paper basket—better still, burn it on what's left of the fire. But what if something's gone wrong at home, what if one of them should be ill? The breakfast tray is still on the dresser, plates littered with toast crumbs, smears of marmalade, and the shells of boiled eggs. What makes up his mind about the letter is nothing more than this: how Kass looked at him that morning as he grabbed the egg from its cup, smacked it on the table, ripped off the small pieces of shell, and gulped down the meat. She sat there, her knife poised at the tip of her egg, ready to slice off the top and then to delicately hollow the shell; she sat and looked at him as if he were a Visigoth pillaging Rome.

Ma knickers are clean
So they're fit tae be seen

Taking the very knife that Kathleen had aimed at the tip of her egg, Garnet slits open the envelope Miss Muckle has given him. The part of it in his father's tight hand he disregards; what catches his attention is the enclosure, a clipping from *The Morning Post* announcing the marriage on March 2 of George Bowden with Kathleen Mansfield Beauchamp, of Wellington, New Zealand. He drops the knife. It falls on the little hooked rug with its design of chocolate-coloured roses, so Kathleen doesn't look up but keeps packing her satchel with the books and journal she's brought with her from

London and is lugging to Birmingham, the next city on the Moody-Manners' tour. When she happens to turn round, when she registers the shock on his face, she takes the newspaper clipping from his outstretched hand. She doesn't have to read it; she bends to the few coals left in the grate and watches the scrap of paper slowly, imperfectly, burn.

Of course there's a fight, a short, bitter one, with attempts at explanation turning into accusations. Garnet keeps saying, "They were right about you, they were right to warn me."

"You'll never be an artist," Kathleen shouts back. "You'll spend your whole life as sweated labour in a grimy tux—a pit musician, the Invisible Man!"

"What do you know about the pit?" Garnet roars. "Who do you think rescues the soloists when they start on a wrong note and the whole piece has to be transposed, half a step down, just like that? Covering up for the conductor, the tenor—preventing train wrecks. It's all in a night's work, and a damn hard night at that, if you want to know."

Kathleen's face is dark with rage, almost green. "Is that the height of your ambition? Is that your heart's desire—covering up for seedy tenors? What a coward you are! You're afraid, Garnet. You've always been afraid. Of your parents, of living up to your brother's talent, of taking risks—"

"And you?" he hisses. "You marry a man you hardly know and say you don't love, then run to me here, saying nothing, not a single word. Where's the risk in that? Where's the courage?"

"You'll never understand," Kathleen cries, grabbing her coat and suitcase and satchel, rushing down the stairs and scattering the children with their skipping ropes. Jumping into a cab that has just drawn up, she orders it to the station. She strides past the Moody-Manners people gathered at the entrance; ignores their questions about what's happened to Garnet. Her purse contains just enough coins to purchase a third-class ticket to London. To the one person she can trust to take her in without questions or conditions: her slave, Ida; her closest friend and dauntless confidante, a trusty fiction by the name of Lesley Moore.

———

Eight weeks later; a hot morning in the middle of May. Another railway station, in London this time. A flushed Kathleen, in a loose summer dress and the same black straw hat in which she was married, has come to meet the boat train from which she emerged so joyfully eight months before. Joy is not what's called for, now. Her mother is on that train; her mother, who, for all her delicate heart, has steamed up from New Zealand on receipt, from some interfering English relative, of the very clipping from *The Morning Post* that made such a mess in Miss Muckle's bedroom. To Annie Beauchamp it was the reddest of flags, that announcement of a marriage that means nothing to Kathleen but the convenience of being able to sign herself into hotels as Mrs. Bowden. She's done her fair share of travelling since Glasgow: temporary, runaway travel to France, Belgium. Nothing like the itinerary her mother has in store for her.

The wife of the Director of the Bank of New Zealand emerges from the carriage oblivious to the steam-bath heat of the station; she is perfectly dressed, and she receives the crush of relatives who've come to greet her as an empress might her loyal retainers on her return from some benighted colony. Annie embraces her sister Belle, lavishly dressed and accompanied by her much older husband; she touches the ringlets of their little daughter, dressed up as Belle-in-miniature. No one pays the slightest attention to Kathleen, in her mismatched dress and hat, until Annie finally detaches herself from the crowd and walks, slowly, gracefully, towards her still refractory, plumper-than-ever daughter. It could be ten years ago, on Wellington wharf, for what Annie offers by way of greeting is this: "Heavens, child, what an awful hat—it makes you look a hundred years old—it makes you look just like a charwoman."

———

In the luxurious bathroom of the expensive hotel suite to which Annie has swept her, Kathleen is throwing up her breakfast. She is trying to be discreet about this: her mother is writing letters in the room next door. As Kathleen splashes cold water on her face, Annie calls out, with poisonous emphasis, "Your *friend* is here to see you, Kathleen. *Again.*" The friend in question is, of course, the eternally faithful Ida, whose frumpy clothes and awkward manners have not endeared her to Mrs. Beauchamp, though they hardly account for the raw dislike Annie shows her. Kathleen looks impatiently at Ida, who can only stare vaguely back until the telephone rings in an adjoining room and Annie is obliged to leave them to answer it. There's time for only a few scant whisperings.

"Does she know?"

"I don't think so—I've been as careful as I can. Has there been any word? You can't have been trying hard enough!"

"The company's in Dublin now. I've found that out, at least. But he's not replying to the telegrams. Katie, dearest, you really will have to tell your mother."

"No!" It's the only word Kathleen has time for before Annie returns, gloved and hatted and holding out her daughter's coat.

"Goodbye, Miss Baker. I have an appointment that won't wait, and Kathleen is having lunch with her aunt." Annie says this without even looking at Ida, and without waiting for any response from her before walking over to the door and holding it pointedly open.

Mrs. Beauchamp's appointment, it turns out, is with Ida's father, a former doctor with Britain's Indian Army, a disgruntled-looking man with stained white moustaches and a red-veined nose. They meet in an office belonging to Mr. Kay, who runs the London branch of the Bank of New Zealand, and who is responsible for paying out Kathleen's allowance. Mr. Kay has had his suspicions about Kathleen; he'd even begun to flirt with her in a desultory way when she came to the bank each month to collect her cheque. But he is the soul of propriety now, showing Colonel Baker into the room where Mrs. Beauchamp sits waiting, then leaving the two in the strictest privacy.

Though Colonel Baker is a dab hand at tyrannizing his daughters, one glance at the steely pose of Annie Burnell Beauchamp shows him he's hopelessly outclassed. Her argument is, after all, unanswerable: the friendship between their daughters is as unwise as it is unwholesome, given the deterrence it poses to his daughter's finding a husband, and to her own daughter's actually living with the husband she's so foolishly chosen. It is, in fact, that husband's considered opinion that Kathleen's refusal to take up her conjugal responsibilities has to do with the unfortunate attachment she has formed with Colonel Baker's daughter. If the Colonel promises to send Ida off on a cruise somewhere sufficiently remote, the Beauchamps will dispatch Kathleen to a continental spa that offers cures for this unthinkable disposition.

Colonel Baker proposes the Canaries as the farthest destination he can afford; Mrs. Beauchamp would prefer someplace far less accessible—Rhodesia would be ideal—but makes the best of his offer. They both agree to believe that once the separation has been effected, and the change of scene has done its work, all will be well—they will, at least, have lived up to their parental obligations.

Mrs. Beauchamp nods but does not offer her hand to Colonel Baker, who nods back at her and leaves the room. On her way out of the bank, Mrs. Beauchamp turns to Mr. Kay, who is escorting her and has asked what steps she is taking to have the marriage annulled.

"None," says Annie. "She's no longer a Beauchamp. What she does as Bowden needn't concern us. As long, that is, as he takes her back, once she returns from Bavaria."

Mr. Kay raises his eyebrows.

"Bavaria, Mr. Kay. For this kind of situation, Scarborough or the Lake District won't do. Bavaria isn't the most inviting spot, but then this isn't a holiday she's setting out on, is it?" She shakes his hand, then turns her back on him as the cab he's called pulls up. She slips inside it like a coin into a purse, then vanishes from Mr. Kay's admiring gaze.

———

In yet another expensive hotel, this one filled with stout but ailing Germans, Annie oversees the packing of her trunks. Kathleen has her back turned to her mother and is staring out the window. There's a fountain in the square below where a benchful of Bavarian nannies gossip with one another and fuss over the babies in their charge. A small boy is being made to sit still beside his nursemaid; he can't keep himself from swinging his feet, scuffing the leather of his shoetips in the sandy dirt below. Katherine feels a little pleat in the skin of her heart; she's remembering her young brother making mud pies that afternoon when she and her sisters were trotted out to Wellington to mark their parents' homecoming. She thinks of the game she wanted to play that day, the game of imagining herself elsewhere, imagining her heart's desire. Gently, she puts her hand to her belly, trying to feel or coax into being any signal Garnet might send through this child of his she's carrying. Hand on her belly, eyes fixed on the boy on the bench below.

When the packing is done and the maid has left the room, Annie goes over to her daughter. She puts her hands on Kathleen's shoulders, but it is not an embrace. "My poor child," she says. "You will simply have to learn how to behave in this world. There is no other world to run away to, however much you—and I—might wish there to be." Then she drops her hands and walks to the door, where her travelling cloak and hat are hung.

Kathleen turns to watch her take them from the hook; watches with those sharp dark eyes of hers.

"I've come this once to straighten things out, Kathleen—I will not come again." With this pronouncement, Annie abandons the room and her daughter.

It's not the last time Kathleen will see her mother; the Beauchamps will make another of their trips "home" to England on the occasion of George V's coronation, two years later. And Kathleen will greet her family wearing the kind of hat of which her mother approves; will try to please them as hard as she earlier tried to outrage them. She will not have discovered that the first thing Annie Beauchamp did on quitting Bavaria and regaining New Zealand was to send for a lawyer and arrange to cut her middle daughter out of her will.

———

Kathleen has stayed on in the small spa town of Wörishofen; she's rented a clean, sparsely furnished room over a pharmacist's shop, which offers postcards for sale and booklets on Father Kneipp's famous Water Hose Cure, by which Mrs.

Beauchamp has set such store. Although Father Kneipp's treatment extends to many areas besides dubious sexual desire, it has never been advertised as a cure for pregnancy, and this may explain why Kathleen has, after all, submitted to the icy hosings and barefoot walks in mountain meadows for which her mother has paid in advance. She has given the town's other attractions a miss—the casino and tennis club. She's as determined to have Garnet Trowell's baby as she was determined never to spend a single night with George Bowden.

The various treatments have failed to restore her health and spirits; all they seem to have done is give her a bad cold and a worse fever. And yet she can't sleep; she sits in a long white nightdress at an undersized table that does duty as a desk, reading through Garnet's old love letters. They are too precious to leave on the table, with the maid waltzing in and out of the room as she pleases. Kathleen stores them in a trunk on top of the wardrobe; that trunk is now lying open on her bed. Fever makes the bed look higher than it really is, makes the wardrobe look shorter. She puts the letters back, then, despite her being four months pregnant, hoists the small, brass-bound trunk.

There's no sound but grunts and puffing as Kathleen struggles to take control of this one small matter, tidying up the traces of anything that could give her away. What happens next makes no noise at all. From under her nightdress what look like dark red coins spill onto the floor. First one, then three: delicate, tentative. And then a gush of blood over the scrubbed white boards.

ROGER

. . . Who could do better than marry a problem?
Misunderstanding keepeth Love alive.

Menton, September 1986

This is as good a place as any to begin, this small café looking out onto the Mediterranean under a sky so blue it seems naked in its cloudlessness. I have abandoned the bathers on the public beach to the balm of coconut oil and the icy showers that scrape the salt off their skins; it is autumn here, and I am of an age, now, to prefer seasonable pleasures.

I'm not the oldest patron of the Café Bon Vent; there's a couple here in their seventies, at least, tucking into pan-fried trout and endive salad at one of the tables inside. I asked for a table on the terrace—that's the limit of my sprightliness. Jet-lag—our modern equivalent to your generation's *mal de mer*. You were a good traveller, of necessity—all those trains and boats and carriages you had to take, all those taxis and, when you could afford it, motor cars. Had you lived another ten years you'd have flown, no doubt, at least across the Channel.

If you had found the cure for your disease, it's not inconceivable that you would be alive today, fast approaching your ninety-eighth birthday. After all, your father and your sisters

87

lived to a ripe old age. To look at the photos of you as a child, a girl, a woman of twenty, who could have predicted anything but a long and healthy life for you? On the last day of your nineteenth year you wrote to your lover, "Just think, when we are both *over thirty*. I think we will be very young indeed." And then you added, "I must work," as if you knew how very few years over thirty you would have.

But this is a sorry start to my journal: I bought it at a *librairie* this afternoon, choosing one with a cheerful orange cover, the colour of your favourite flowers. And I have done much besides making a purchase or two. I have walked through the old town and prowled round the Villa Flora, peeking through the bars of the gate and hoisting myself up to get a view of the garden over the fence. It was not a successful visit, though I placed myself as close as possible to where you would have stood watching lizards crawl along the wall, or looking at the sea to the south, the hills to the north. I'd thought that if I looked long and hard enough, I would be able to feel as well as see, feel what you must have lived through here. Not just the misery of illness and loneliness, but the joy there must have been as well, the perfect happiness when, sitting down to work one morning, you wrote for twelve hours straight, creating nothing short of a masterpiece, with hardly a word to be changed or line crossed out.

I can't expect anything remotely like that rage of inspiration, and yet I hope that in this journal I will be able to speak with you as if face to face, to tell you, for the first time, something of myself. I have brought no books with me on this journey; I have nothing to tide me over through the solitary meals and train rides and endless evenings in hotel rooms but these blank pages in which I note, not other people's thoughts and words, but my own. "I shall be obliged," you wrote in one of your diaries, "if the contents of this book are regarded as my private property." I hardly need to pencil in such warnings: no one will read this journal once I've returned to Wellington, unpacked my case, and settled back into the old life. No one—not even me. My son may find and thumb through it one day, but then he's far too strict a keeper of secrets to feel right about stealing mine.

I am drinking your health at the Café Bon Vent, Katherine, not because of the fare—*aïoli* and *bouillabaisse* and any number of fine burgundies and bordeaux—but because it feels so familiar. It reminds me, you see, of the small café in Wellington where I used to take all my bachelor meals, when I didn't make do with beans on toast or egg and chips. A view of the sea across a road lined with trees offering shade and the illusion of something like freshness in air thick with the stench of diesel fumes. There was no terrace at the Oriental Bay Café, but my table was positioned right against the glass of the large bay window, so that if I tired of the book I'd brought along, I could look at the people passing by.

I don't know how many meals I ate at the Oriental Bay before that evening I first saw her—twelve years' worth of midweek specials and Sunday dinners. And it was a Sunday when I noticed her huddled under one of the pohutukawa trees lining the promenade. A young woman, only a girl, really. She was obviously waiting for someone who, just as obviously, was not going to appear. I ate a bowl of soup, watching her as the mist thickened and the sea got greyer and rougher behind her. And then I stopped watching. For the second time in my life, I did something completely out of character. I left the café and returned ten minutes later with the cold, wet, hungry girl, whom I sat at my table, and for whom I ordered soup and cutlets and strong, sweet tea. I let the girl eat her fill; I made no mention of the look on her face, the look, I thought, of someone who's drowning. I didn't ask her a single question. She made no objection when I offered to drive her home; nor did I, when it turned out "home" would have to be my house in Hataitai. I made up the bed in the spare room, ran her a bath, and then left the house for a stroll in the rain, so that she could wash and go to sleep, in a pair of my pyjamas, as quietly as possible.

Her name, she revealed, was Tui: you would appreciate that. Her foster parents had tried to call her Terry, but she'd refused to answer to anything but Tui. She never told me anything more about her past than this one story of how she'd kept her name. That and the soaked-through clothes on her back, the tiki round her neck, were her sole possessions, not counting, of course, the child she was carrying. Of the father, all Tui would say was that he was a tourist, backpacking round New Zealand. She was, for those last four months of her pregnancy, in a state of shock that took the form of silent fury, though she must have loved him even more after the failed rendezvous at Oriental Bay than before. This is what I failed to understand. I wanted to believe she would settle for what I had to offer her: a home, a name for her child, comfort if not joy. I did believe this, when she agreed to marry me, when we went through the motions at the registry office. She wore for the occasion the first maternity clothes she'd consented to put on. Afterwards, we went for a walk in the Botanical Gardens and had something to eat in the restaurant there. She said she would like to see a film, I can remember every minute of the hours that we sat side by side in the cinema, though I have no recollection at all of what film we were watching. And when we got home that night, I took my wife by the hand and led her not into my bedroom but out into the quiet of the garden, bearing bread and milk.

Up until the day of our marriage I had been, as they say, a perfect gentleman, my head full of what you'd had to go through in that first, false marriage of yours. For when I'd first noticed that small, soaked, shivering girl, her belly both empty and full, it wasn't one of your characters I saw, one of your sad *dames seules*, but you. It was you I went to rescue, Katherine; you I brought home with me. As for me—who was I but the ungainly rescuer, transformed by Tui's need into someone she had to trust, to use as she saw fit? I fancied myself, you see, a better Bowden, coming to the rescue of a woman trapped by a man who clearly wasn't fit to tie her shoelaces, never mind able to keep her out of the rain. Where Bowden had been greedy, I would be selfless; there would be no helplessness, no misery in a hotel room with pink satin shades on the lamps. All would be honest and open and free.

If I had taken Tui into my room instead of the garden, would everything have turned out differently? Or is the truth I'm so afraid to face just another lie, as well as the worst kind of self-deception? Tell me, Katherine, give me the benefit of your vast experience. You lay like a doll on that slippery pink counterpane while Bowden tried to embrace you; you didn't burst out laughing or shrieking but stared at him with a mix of shock and chagrin. You had wanted a marriage of pure convenience; Miss Beauchamp's transformation into Mrs. Bowden was going to turn you, at long last, into a bachelor, with all the freedom of bachelor habits. In place of Beauchamp Lodge, with its maidenly rules and restrictions, you would have a flat and a latchkey and no one at all to answer to. You would come and go as you pleased, and Bowden would treat you with the same casual good fellowship he showed to his flatmate. But everything changed once that ring was on your finger, your black straw hat unpinned from your hair, Ida's note in your hands, the note she'd stuffed into the dressing case she'd lent you: "Bear Up!"

I did not want this girl I had rescued to have to bear up on my account; she had enough to bear already. She was, as my neighbour Estelle kept telling me, very young. If I had listened to Estelle, I would have understood how foolish I'd been with this reckless, ridiculous marriage; how careful I'd have to be with a girl like Tui, a girl who'd seen a good deal too much of life and who, she warned, had picked up a lifetime's bad habits. I didn't listen to my neighbour. I am glad of that. What gnaws at me is that I didn't listen to Tui, to what her fits of temper and steep silences were telling me. That what she needed most then was to feel herself loved; that what I'd meant as generosity she took as proof of what her lover's absence had driven her into believing: that she had no worth any more, no power, no future. That no one, not even a balding middle-aged poet, could desire her.

I never told her what I'd begun to feel for her even before the child was born. There would be time, I thought, all the time in the world for that kind of talk between us. But then all my time and attention were taken up with the son who looked so much like his mother, the same dark skin and hair, the same birthmark, too, like a small sooty fingerprint under the left eye. The morning Tui left—I had been up all night with the baby, I had thrown myself back into bed for whatever sleep I could catch—she came into my room. She leaned down beside me and, very gently, kissed my face. Her mouth was soft and small as a child's. She looked different somehow, but I couldn't put my finger on what had changed except that she seemed calmer than she'd been for months. She was going for a walk, she said; she needed to walk by the sea. And then she was gone.

I lay there between waking and sleeping, feeling that first, unexpected kiss on my skin. How can I describe the radiant and simple happiness it gave me? I fell asleep, and I woke in a panic. For it had come to me, why Tui had looked so different when she'd kissed me. She'd been wearing a shirt that was far too big for her, the man's shirt she'd had on the night

I first saw her. The shirt was buttoned low and loose; the tiki she always wore around her neck was gone. I found it, later, on my desk, where the note should have been. Beside that photograph of you I'd had copied, enlarged, and framed, the passport photo of a woman with a mouth as small as a child's and eyes raw from too much looking at the truth.

It keeps coming back to truth, somehow, and what we do with it. If I could get that right, would everything else fall into place? So that I could write my book and be done—not with you but with the need to live my life through yours, to feel myself alive only through your words, as though I were a mere translation, the original lost or forgotten.

Honesty (why?) is the only thing one seems to prize beyond life, love, death, everything. It alone remaineth. O those that come after me, will you believe it? At the end, truth *is the one thing* worth *having; it's more thrilling than love, more joyful and more passionate. It simply* cannot *fail. All else fails. I, at any rate, give the remainder of my life to it and it alone.*

You who lied almost as you breathed—lied to yourself as much as to others. When you came to choose truth over love, which kind did you mean? The love we receive, or the love we give, asking for nothing—or as close to nothing as possible—in return?

MONTY

Jean Genet, dazed by what he called the "gigantism" of Chicago, longed for a version of the city that would fit in the hollow of his hand. Here, after one week's residence, was Monty's handful of Chicago: the Theodore Dreiser Hotel; the Newberry Library; Apartment #3, 15 Crilly Court; and the Manuka Café on North Dearborn Street.

The hotel he found after much tramping round the city's North Side, rejecting it at first, but returning when he realized it was all he could afford. The Dreiser was a dim, dank place, crammed between a MoneyMart and a pizza/convenience store; it might have been better named after Upton Sinclair. The desk clerk couldn't make out Monty's accent when he asked for a room, but then, Monty couldn't understand hers, though it was clear to both of them that they were speaking English. After paying for his stay in advance, the room was his: small, dirt cheap, and frankly dirty. Its walls were painted a dispiriting brown, unless it was a patina they'd acquired over the seventy-odd years the Dreiser had

been standing. Yet it must once have been a desirable
address, judging from the ornamental brickwork and the
moulded window frames on the facade. It seemed to him an
entirely appropriate setting for a Mansfield scholar, given
how much of her life had been spent in temporary rooms,
some of them as desolate as this.

Monty swam in and out of sleep for the next twenty-four
hours. He left the TV on to drown out the noise of his neighbours, and whenever he woke, thoughts about contacting
Mr. C. Baby played themselves out against the same ads for
luxury cars and stain eradicators. Before leaving Wellington,
he'd gone to the Turnbull Library, searching its data banks
for all known names of Mansfield collectors. He'd found no
Baby but hadn't been discouraged; it's well known that
eccentrics are fiercely suspicious people, jealous of their privacy. When he could locate no Baby, C. (Charles? Chester?)
in the Chicago telephone directory, Monty resolved to present himself at the address scrawled on the letter he'd intercepted on its way to his father and take whatever
consequences came his way.

The Crilly Court apartments were built by a local architect
in the 1890s, in subdued Queen Anne style; they are one of
Chicago's more desirable downtown addresses, if you don't
go in for palaces, that is. Compared to the Dreiser, of course,
genially time-worn Crilly Court was Buckingham Palace:
Monty half expected a bogus English butler's voice to come
crackling back to him through the intercom at number 15.
When no one answered, Monty buzzed up again, this time
shouting into the grille: "It's Mr. Mills, for Mr. Baby. Mr.
Montgomery Mills from New Zealand." There was still no
answer, but this time he heard the click of the front door
unlatching itself; he pushed inside and started up the stairs
to apartment 3. Its door was open the merest crack. He
knocked, waited, stepped inside, and came face to face not

with Charles, not with Chester, but, as it turned out, with Miss Cassandra Baby.

She must have been a good six feet in her prime; even now, leaning on a cane, she seemed to tower over him. Her thin grey hair was scraped back in a bun from a large, plain, rubbery face that made him think of the paleness of ashes. She wore a boxy tweed skirt and a dark, crumpled shirt; in place of the sensible shoes you might have expected, she wore on her long, narrow feet a pair of alligator pumps. Her voice, when she spoke, was blunt and gravelly, not unlike the voice of Professor Winnifred Grandby, Monty's supervisor at the University of London. Except that Miss Baby's voice was as American as the professor's had been English. She was far more formidable-looking than Dr. Grandby, and yet, in his relief that she actually existed, he could have thrown his arms around her and kissed her. Luckily, he merely held out his hand, which she ignored.

"You're too young," she barked, by way of greeting. The remark seemed to express a general vote of censure, not suspicion, for she ordered him in, shut and bolted the door behind him, then lurched down the hall, which he took as an invitation to follow. They entered a room full of leather-bound books, fine, worn furniture, and windows where dust had grown like moss. She pointed with her cane to a chair pulled up to a mahogany dining table, then seated herself in a huge wing chair at its head. When she spoke again, it was a variation on her opening remarks.

"Montgomery. That's a ridiculous name."

After a moment's hesitation, he replied in kind. "Baby is just as ridiculous."

She pursed her lips and shrugged. "It's pronounced 'Babby.' It's French, an old French name. My first name's Greek: Cassandra. I call myself Cassie—not that you can."

She took her stick and pointed to a tantalus in the corner. "You can have bourbon or gin," she said, "but if you want coffee, you're out of luck. It's poison. Tea's just as bad." Though he would have killed, just then, for tea or coffee, Monty's chief feeling was one of relief that his gamble had paid off, that this paranoid, wealthy eccentric, this Cassandra or Cassie or Miss Baby, preferred rudeness to civility or, to look at it in another way, truth to tact.

"You're a writer," she declared. "Not that you've written anything much—I've checked you out, Mr. Mills. As for that biography thing you're working on, you ought to know that biography's worse than useless. Stealing people's privacy from them, and giving what in return? Pinning people down to being this, doing that, feeling and thinking maybe a hundred things when they've thought and felt hundreds of thousands. Making you believe you can know somebody else just by turning a page—when the person you're reading about probably didn't even know himself."

As she spoke, Miss Baby's face became even grimmer, if that were possible. "Just what kind of justice does your biography do to all the little people, the ordinary joes mashed up in the lives of the famous ones? It makes them look blind or stupid or plain nasty. Or else it ignores them, it makes out they never existed. When without those common, ordinary people, Mr. Mills, there wouldn't have been anyone to love or care for the famous ones, or remember them as they really were."

She spoke with vehemence; she startled Monty with the passion of her conviction. What she was saying about biography was, of course, absurd; did she expect him to pick a quarrel with her, to give her an excuse to throw him out now that she'd so grudgingly admitted him? He was about to make some remark about how difficult it was to write the life of someone as secretive as Mansfield, how all he could hope to do with his writing was to make his readers search out Mansfield's own, when Miss Baby addressed him in a tone like iced vinegar.

"I don't want biography from you, Mr. Mills, I want work. Hard, plain, honest work. If you're willing to tackle it, then I'll live up to my part of the bargain. I happen to own documents that you biographers would kill for. So here's the deal: you look over my manuscript and give me your honest opinion, and I let you see my collection."

Monty thought for a moment of what it had cost him to be sitting here, across from a stranger who'd revealed herself, in the past few moments, to be rude, belligerently opinionated, and possibly delusional. He reminded himself, as well, that he was here under false pretences, and for desperate purposes. "When would you like me to start?" he asked.

"Nine o'clock sharp, tomorrow morning. You can see yourself out."

He was nearly at the door when she called out behind him. She had changed her mind about seeing him out. She came forward, leaning on her cane, and stood close to him in the strong light of the hallway, so that he noticed for the first time a bluish cast to her lips. A phrase of Roger's came back to him: she had *a dicky heart*, Cassandra Baby. The sooner he could examine her papers, the better.

"I've lived without upsets or accidents in this apartment for thirty years, Mr. Mills. I don't intend to start having them now. There's nothing in this place worth stealing, except my Mansfield collection, and that's under lock and key. Lock and key, Mr. Mills, and my dead body. Now get out and stay out till tomorrow morning."

Monty couldn't tell whether he felt more intrigued or insulted by this send-off. But, given the airlessness of the apartment, the smell of dust burning on lightbulbs, and the sharp point of the cane wielded by Cassandra Baby, he had no difficulty in shutting her door behind him and heading out into the mild September afternoon.

———

He approached the Newberry Library from a little park named for George Washington but called Bughouse Square, after its popularity with soapbox speakers. Monty felt no need to declaim anything just yet; he sat on a bench in front of the fountain, quietly eating a submarine sandwich and rehearsing what he knew of the Alexander Turnbull's chief rival. For example, that it housed an extraordinary cache of Mansfield manuscripts collected over a period of fifty-odd years by a Mrs. Edison Dick. Jane Dick had acquired her collection through the agency of Misses Hamill and Barker, Chicago dealers with a special line through to Mansfield's husband, John Middleton Murry. Katherine had left him her papers and manuscripts, with the request that he destroy all but the small amount of work worth publishing. Murry— whom one of his wife's friends described as boiling Katherine's bones to make his soup—kept, and published, a small fortune's worth. Once he'd left London and his job as editor of a literary journal, he took up farming in Norfolk; every time he needed a new piece of machinery, the story goes, he would place a call to Chicago, offering this or that letter, notebook, photo. The bulk of these sales had ended up in cardboard boxes on the third floor of a purpose-built literary gentleman's club at 60 West Walton Street, across from Bughouse Square.

Not that the Turnbull hadn't wooed Jane Dick for her collection; she and her husband had been treated as visiting royalty eight years ago when they'd come to New Zealand to see the library for themselves. Roger had been at one of the dinners given to charm them into transferring their Mansfield manuscripts from America's Midwest to the Land of the Long White Cloud. He'd told Monty that Mrs. Dick, whom he'd always thought of as "the American Huntress," was, in fact, a charming woman; it especially pleased him that she'd begun her collection not as an investment but because, at the age of twenty, she'd been "touched to the heart" by a selection of Mansfield's *Letters*. She'd been given the book as a Christmas present just three years after Mansfield's death.

Others who'd attended those lavish Wellington dinner parties spoke wryly, once Mrs. Dick had decided to leave her collection to the Newberry, of how Mansfield's papers would be lying side by side with Louis Hennepin's maps of the Great Lakes; of how first editions of *Bliss* and *The Garden Party* would be rubbing shoulders with those of *The Pit* or *The Jungle* in the Newberry's Special Collections. But Roger had demurred. He'd pointed out that it wouldn't have been unthinkable for a young writer to have run away to Chicago instead of London back in 1908. Mansfield could have published her first poems and sketches in Harriet Monroe's *Poetry* (for money) or Margaret Anderson's *The Little Review* (for glory). She would have been in good company, too, along with T. S. Eliot (whom she admired), Ezra Pound (whom she loathed), and later, James Joyce (who thought she had a better grasp on *Ulysses* than her husband did). Besides, Roger had reminded them, Katherine had always wanted to run away to America, and now, in a way, she had.

Despite its origins, the Newberry is a friendly library, one that, like the Turnbull, aims to be helpful to the general public. It was easy for Monty to obtain a reader's ticket and head up the grey marble stairs, past the ivy-hung padlocked windows to the Special Collections. He wanted to remind himself of exactly what the Newberry had in the way of

Mansfield documents and, thus, what Cassandra Baby might just be keeping under lock and key, as she'd proclaimed. Something throwing a less than lovely light on Katherine's character, it would seem. Perhaps those letters Kathleen sent to Ida from Wellington in 1907—the ones Ida declared she'd burned eight years later at Katherine's insistence. Or those "big, complaining notebooks" from 1908 to 1913 that Katherine (who kept every other journal she'd written, through dozens of moves) supposedly destroyed herself. Perhaps one of those "lost" stories she mentioned in her correspondence towards the end of her life, a story that had escaped the notice of the tractor-hungry Murry.

What Monty found at the Newberry were most of the known manuscripts, letters, and notebooks belonging to Mansfield; there was also a stash of ephemera. A piece of sheet music for a sentimental little song called "Sealed Orders," Katherine's handwritten inventory of two dozen heterogeneous handkerchiefs, a sheaf of undistinguished, unsigned pencil sketches, and a sprinkling of photographs. In them he recognized a grumpy late-adolescent Kathleen in evening dress and a proudly egotistical Miss Beauchamp in her room at Queen's College. A photo postcard sent from Wellington revealed a scowlingly reluctant repatriate; a faded snapshot showed a much thinner convalescent Katherine at Rottingdean, leaning on a walking stick and posed by a drainpipe. Finally, he found a badly scarred late snap of the emaciated consumptive, Mrs. John Middleton Murry, an image far too close to the photograph in his father's study.

He couldn't help thinking how easy it would be—the librarians on the other side of the partition, his fellow readers absorbed in their work, senses dulled by the buzzing of electric lights—to palm one of these photographs. Or else to slip into his notebook one of the more dubious items—for example, the backing to a photo that had been torn off, leaving only a dark strip at the top, with a florid inscription to Ida on the back. Who but a Chicago millionairess would have paid good money for that? But for Monty, theft—if you could call his lifting of Miss Baby's letter to Roger by so weighty a name—was a thing of the past. Besides, he was rummaging for traces not of Mansfield, now, but of the woman who'd collected her. He'd hoped there might be a photograph, even a portrait in oils, of Mrs. Dick somewhere on the Newberry's fourth floor, but there were only reproductions of ancient locomotives and one studio portrait of a small boy, unidentified, in cowboy gear. He wanted to compare Jane Dick's expression (modest? complacent?) with the defensive scowl of Cassandra Baby. He did at last find photographs of Jane Edison (née Warner) Dick—kind-faced, generous, smiling—in a simply bound volume of *Recollections* he pulled from the stacks and devoured in a sitting.

In these *Recollections* Mrs. Dick mentions almost everything in her life—parents and siblings, husband and children, political work for Adlai Stevenson and the United Nations, her dairy farm furnished with rustic Swedish furniture, her winter home in Jamaica—before the name of Katherine Mansfield ever appears, fourth on a list of hobbies, after 1) gambling—"only for fun," 2) the Chicago Symphony and Fine Arts Institute, and 3) reading. Only then does Mrs. Dick describe what she defines as both a treasure hunt and a pastime that have expanded her mind and given her valuable contacts over the years: collecting anything she could find of Katherine Mansfield's. Not just papers but objects that would bring her closer to the writer by virtue of having belonged to, having been touched by, her. It struck him as ironic, or perhaps predictable, this urge for the original and authentic in a woman married to the son of the man who'd invented the mimeograph.

Edison Dick, however, was one of a kind, as far as husbands go. Not only did he applaud his wife's political work in
Illinois and at the UN, but he supported it by stepping in to
sew buttons onto the children's clothing and preparing
meals for them when his wife was away. What's more, he had
the endearing habit of buying Jane this or that Mansfield
item for her birthday, wedding anniversary, or Christmas—a
sensible choice since, as Mrs. Dick so candidly confessed, in
the late 1920s and the 1930s you could pick up first editions
of Mansfield's works for scarcely more than the publisher's
price. As a collector, then, Jane Dick had advantages with
which Miss Baby couldn't compete; as a person, she played
Snow White to Miss Baby's Evil Queen. A perfectly lovely,
decent, ordinary person, Jane Dick was in the extraordinary
position of being rich enough to satisfy her heart's desire, or
at least that part of desire untapped by forays into gambling,
opera, travel, and fine art.

In a volume on Chicago's museums, Monty found mention
of the Augustus Griffiths Foundation; he assumed that Miss
Baby had worked for the Foundation in some capacity, no
doubt as a volunteer. From what he'd seen of her apartment,
she had to have plenty of money, even if she'd grown averse to
spending it. But he failed to find any clues in works like
Chicago and Its Makers as to how Cassandra Baby had come
by this wealth, or even to the contacts that had allowed her to
become a collector in the first place. The only reassurance he
had on that point was something he couldn't find a trace of in
Jane Dick's *Recollections*: the passion, the possessiveness, the
urgency he'd detected in Miss Baby's connection with a
woman who was, to most people, a name on the spine of a few
thin volumes—if that.

As you can see, Monty was flying blind as he made his
second approach to Cassandra Baby. On his way to Crilly
Court the next morning, he recalled how Mansfield's first

independent biographer had sought out Ida Baker as a source: an elderly version of the Ida who'd driven Katherine mad with her slow, slight intelligence, and who'd proved surprisingly canny at skewering her rivals for Katherine's affections. The biographer had managed to charm Ida not only into talking freely about her long-dead friend, but also into giving the Turnbull Library the first draft of what Mansfield knew to be her finest story. To his credit, he'd seen to it that the Turnbull paid Miss Baker a decent sum for the manuscript of "The Daughters of the Late Colonel," but what a coup! It had launched his long career as *the* Mansfield man. He'd even got Ida to show him an extract from Katherine's journal that no one—not even her husband—had known to exist. Why shouldn't Monty pull off a similar coup with Cassandra Baby? Why shouldn't she be just as generous with him?

Alas, Monty put his foot in it the moment he stepped back inside Miss Baby's apartment. He'd meant her to be impressed by his allusions to the Newberry; instead, she was clearly insulted. Sitting at opposite ends of the mahogany table, he without coffee, she with the remains of her breakfast in front of her (a crust of toast, a smear of marmalade, a finger of bourbon), they resembled enemies loath to declare a truce.

"So you've gone to see the Dick collection at the Newberry. Jane Dick is a hobbyist!" Miss Baby hissed, pronouncing "hobbyist" as though it were "harlot." "Get out, then. Go and talk to Jamaica Jane if you're so interested. That's where you'll find her when it gets too cold for her in Lake Forest—Jamaica!"

Monty assured Cassandra Baby that his sole purpose in coming to Chicago was to see her own collection; he judged this hostility towards Jane Dick to be the permanent ugly duckling's resentment of the lifelong swan. After glaring at him for another long moment, Miss Baby rose stiffly from the table, staggering off to what Monty conjectured to be her bedroom. She was gone for what seemed an awfully long time. He grew tired of staring at her breakfast plate and got up to stretch his legs. He was examining her bookshelves—not the leather-bound editions of Hawthorne and Fenimore Cooper, but a section of humbler publications he hadn't noticed before. There was a small shelf of Mansfield's works, all first American editions, except for a Canadian copy of *Bliss*, inscribed to "Cassie" by a J. B. in 1936, with the words, "making for the open gate between the pointed rocks that leads to . . ." Next to it was a volume published in 1924 by one Oscar Cremer, *How to Become a Professional Violinist*. Monty was just reading a tip on page 54—"In applying for an engagement, remember that a good appearance (dress, clean linen, well-polished boots, etc.) goes a long way. The man who has a 'soiled' appearance stands far less chance of an engagement than one who is neat and clean"—when Miss Baby called out:

"Didn't anyone ever tell you not to touch what doesn't belong to you?"

Guiltily, he put the book back. Guiltily? How could Miss Baby know anything about the letter he'd purloined from his father's desk? He turned to her as if she had seen straight through him. But she merely lowered the cane she was holding out in his direction; onto the dining table she dropped a string-tied bundle of papers, the same expensive stock on which her letter to his father had been typed. With a gesture that struck Monty first as stagy and later as superb, she shot the papers the full length of the table, so abruptly that he had to scramble to catch them. And then she went back to the book she'd propped up against a small heavy-looking sculpture of a young boy's head, leaving him to sit down and read, as best he could, what turned out to be a piece of detective fiction, dealing not so much with Katherine Mansfield as with that minor figure and quasi-fatal lover in her life, Garnet Trowell.

MISS BABY

*You do not necessarily get to your destination
by taking the right turning at the beginning of your journey.*

What Really Happened During Those Six Months Between Katherine Mansfield's Return to England and Her Departure for That Bavarian Spa

*A Vindication by C. Baby,
Assistant Director, Augustus Griffiths Foundation*

1. Mischief in Montevideo

On July 6, 1908, Kathleen Beauchamp boarded the *Papanui* at Lyttelton Harbour in southern New Zealand, bound for London. Her parents took the trouble to escort their nearly twenty-year-old daughter all the way from Wellington. They even drank tea with the *Papanui*'s captain in his private cabin, and you can bet they warned him what a pain in the ass Kathleen could be. Years later the captain still remembered his famous passenger: "Couldn't stand the woman," he'd say to anyone who bothered to ask.

The *Papanui*'s first stop on that voyage was Montevideo, the capital and largest city of Uruguay. In 1908, Montevideo was famous for the luxury hotels along its sugar-sand beaches and for its meat-packing plants. After the storms and icebergs south of Cape Horn, the passengers of the *Papanui* must have been glad of both attractions. They poured off the ship, among them Miss Beauchamp, arm in arm with an unnamed male passenger.

You can be sure this particular couple didn't take tea with Uruguay's bigwigs in any luxury hotel. Maybe they strolled through the botanical gardens of the Prado, maybe they visited the cathedral on the main square, but sometime that day they must have stopped at some drinking hole or cheap hotel. Supposedly the bartender was bribed to slip our heroine a Mickey Finn. Whatever happened, she could never remember how or when she got back on board the *Papanui*. And by the time she got to London, Kathleen was scared to death she'd been knocked up. At least her journal says she had to go see a Mrs. Charley Boyd to set her mind at rest.

I don't believe that Mickey Finn. Think of what would be involved in violating, never mind impregnating, a banker's daughter in 1908. A heavily drugged woman who could give you no help in removing any of the following:

a hat made from a mountain of feathers
a heavy tweed "tailor-made": close-fitting jacket and
    ankle-length skirt
a shirtwaist fastened with hooks and eyes or else micro-
    scopic buttons
a corset, with firm busks, tightly laced and extending
    from just below the collarbones to just below the
    hips
a camisole beneath the corset
petticoats, heavy and plenty of them

the kind of elaborate underpants called drawers
woollen stockings and assorted fasteners.

Possible weight of clothing discarded for ease of copulation:
sixteen pounds. Bear in mind that the clothes horse here was
no frail and fragile maiden. At nearly twenty, Kathleen
weighed in at forty pounds more than she did at the end of
her life. Fully dressed, she could have matched her seducer
pound for pound.

You could argue that all he had to do was lift her skirt, tug
down her drawers, and hit home. But where would be the fun
in that? And think a little more. She was hankering after new
experience, she was a fan of Oscar Wilde's. Why would a girl
like that want to miss out on the spectacle of her deflowering?
It's my belief that Kathleen Beauchamp fulfilled her parents'
worst fears by losing her virginity—such as it was—in a
Uruguayan dive en route to England.

2. A Bride for Two Brothers

In *Maata*, a fragment written after her cooling-off time in
Bavaria, Katherine Mansfield recounts—you could say rein-
vents—her arrival on the boat train at Charing Cross Station. Because where Kathleen Beauchamp was met by Ida
Baker, her heroine Maata walks off on the arm of Philip, the
dashing violinist whose "furious unbearable expectation" at
being reunited with his New Zealand pal isn't furious and
unbearable enough to stop him looking up at the smoke
thinning out overhead: "That's the way the high note on a
fiddle played *pianissimo* ought to sound," he tells us as
Maata's train draws near.

It's tea time when Maata gets to London, but she doesn't
go to Philip/Garnet's for a spot of the national beverage.
Instead, she orders her hansom cab to that "dusky" room in
a high white house in Little Venice, her base of operations.

Half undressed, she watches the streetlights paint the walls, then "lolls & stretches & flings out her arms . . . laughing & chuckling."

There you have the triumphal entry of New Zealand's Best Bad Girl into the Great Metropolis! This sketch of a novel, a handful of letters, and a few cryptic notebook entries are all we've got to help us judge what happened in the next few months—the most important and disastrous months of Mansfield's short existence. Critics, biographers, they'll all have you believe that what follows is tragedy: a naive, eager, innocent girl falling madly in love, betrayed by the heartless seducer who knocks her up and then abandons her. What I'm going to show you is that the shoe is on the other foot. It's a naive, eager, innocent boy who falls madly in love and is heartlessly abandoned by an actress playing many roles, taking on different selves, and keeping her friends and lovers in separate compartments.

But first you need to know something about that boy— how he got to know Kathleen Beauchamp, how he happened to be in London when Kathleen steamed in, and how he fell victim to her affections in the first place.

3. Children of the Sun God

There was a first-born son, Lyndley, who died of pneumonia at the age of ten. There was a daughter, Dolly, a consolation prize to the long-suffering Mrs. Trowell. And in between, born one year before Annie Beauchamp presented Harold with Kathleen, come the twins, Arnold and Garnet.

They grew up to be musical prodigies, two small boys with fire-engine hair, hounded to practise by their father, a music teacher at a boys' school in Wellington. What kind of a father was Thomas Wilberforce Trowell? Dolly remembered him smacking her on the head when she played a wrong note at the piano.

There's an indication that he took his young sons on tour. At least, they told an English journalist they were "kidnapped by Maoris" while visiting the small rough towns in the gumfields north of Auckland. Sure, they were probably pulling some gullible imperial legs, but there's got to be more to this story. Why couldn't the kidnapping have really taken place, at least in the fantasies of two small, overworked boys, lugging their pint-sized violin and cello through a wilderness of lousy roads, scrubland, and godawful plains?

Those northern bush towns were all the same. First the sawmill, next to the lumber camp, then a general store and hotel, then the baker's, butcher's, shoemaker's, and the shanties where their customers lived. Think of the dullness and dirt of life in those towns. Think of the welcome people there would give any visiting ventriloquists, magicians, clairvoyants. Think of the entertainment value they'd get, sitting in the lobby of the one hotel or on the hard benches of the schoolhouse, hearing two tiny boys play Goltermann's *Concerto in A Minor for Violin and Cello.*

And think of the boys themselves, lying in their beds after their concerts, feeding the bedbugs left there by the previous tenants, dreading another full day's slog to one more bushtown. Of course they'd spin stories of miraculous escape or daring rescue. Of course they'd tell those stories again, years later, on tours that were just as much of a slog:

Arnold Trowell, who has won fame all over Europe, is to make his debut before a London audience in April. The sensation-loving public will find him interesting because of the remarkable adventures he has had in his short career. He is one of twins, his brother Garnet being also a musician. When about nine years old, the boys, while touring the bush towns of the North Island, were kidnapped by superstitious Maoris and worshipped as children of the

Sun God. The extraordinary heads of golden-auburn hair with which the twins are blessed were the attraction which led the New Zealand natives to depute certain of their warriors to enter at night the hotel where the boys were sleeping, and carry them from their beds. The twins were borne off to the native village in the bush, and placed in a specially prepared hut. The whole tribe was summoned for worship, and during the several days the boys remained in state in the hut, they were loaded with attentions and worshipped day and night. So well were they cared for that when a search party discovered them the twins could not hide their disappointment.

—*New Zealand Freelance*, April 27, 1907

I've got a hunch that Garnet told Kathleen that story—it's just the kind of fairy tale she was hooked on, the lonely, loveless kid who runs away to Paradise. I believe she stole that story and reworked it into her early pieces about a good-as-motherless child named Pearl Button who is "kidnapped" from her picket-fence-and-best-behaviour house by a group of Maori women. They pet her and hold her on their laps while she eats mangos and pears, laughing as juice squirts down her starched white dress. They take her down to the water's edge and introduce her to the ocean. When the cops come running after her, she screams, the kind of scream you give when you wake from the good kind of dream into a dark worse than any nightmare.

4. *Happy Families*
Arnold, Garnet, Dolly. Their father was born in Birmingham in 1858 and died in 1945 in some British backwater called Berkhansted. New Zealand was just an interlude in Thomas Trowell's life, though he moved up from teaching hymns to tone-deaf boys to being conductor at the Wellington Opera

House when touring companies came to town. When he was twenty-two, he married Kate Wheeler and set up house on Buller Street. It was the same house where eighteen-year-old Kass Beauchamp came for lessons. If I'd been Kate Trowell, I would have gagged at the sight of her—a rich man's daughter putting on airs, dressing all in brown to match her cello. If I'd been Kate Trowell, I'd have heaved a sigh of relief once I'd packed off my teenaged boys to that conservatory in Brussels, especially the favourite son. Not Garnet but Arnold, the brilliant, handsome, ambitious one.

Across the oceans separating the banker's daughter from the musical twins, letters flew from Kass to Arnold. Letters calling him the first real artist she'd ever known, the first person she could show her true self to. At school in England she kept his photo on her dressing table; she even visited him in Brussels, chaperoned by Aunt Belle and her older sisters. She says she slept with his letters (how many, nobody knows) under her nightie. In her journal she pledged herself to him, body and soul: "Whenever you want me, with both my hands I say—unashamedly, fiercely proud, exultant, triumphant, satisfied at last—'take me.'" In return, Arnold published *Six Morceaux* for violin, "Dedicated to my dear friend Kathleen M. Beauchamp."

That very year, 1908, Arnold met and fell in love with a South African cello student at the Royal Academy. Her family were wealthy and they nixed her marrying a mere musician. By 1918, the couple had managed to convince them otherwise, and two children were born of what seems like a happy marriage, or at least no more unhappy a marriage than most.

Arnold never did become the greatest cellist in the world. He ended up accompanying the likes of Mischa Elman, John McCormack, and Nellie Melba. He taught at the Guildhall School, where his students nicknamed him "Toothies." By the time he died, in 1966, there wasn't a single mention of him in *Grove's Dictionary of Music and Musicians*. Earlier volumes mention how "Trowell plays upon a cello made by Domenico Montagnana (1710), an instrument with a delicate and most agreeable tone." All we know of Arnold's later life is that he took up collecting minor Dutch paintings and blue-and-white china. Like his brother, he's become nothing but a footnote in the life of Katherine Mansfield.

Garnet? He must have been aware of the stream of steamy letters from Kass to Arnold. At least, he seems to have accepted his brother's better luck in love and music. He's remembered by one of Kathleen's friends at Beauchamp Lodge as dreamy and nervous, a tall, thin boy who loved books almost better than his violin. One thing's sure, he wasn't any kind of he-man. Katherine's tastes ran to calves, not bulls, in that department. Ida Baker says Garnet was less of a looker than Arnold—quiet, gentle, even-tempered, and without a lot to say for himself.

In all the information we have on the Trowell twins, there's not one piece of evidence that Garnet ever envied his brother his talent or his role as Prodigy and Genius, the One Who Was Going to Make Good, which means Make Money. Consider this article from the *New Zealand Mail*, October 29, 1902, five years on from the Kidnapping tour:

Youthful Musicians—
The Masters Trowell—a remarkable 'cellist

At this very moment the fair city of Wellington harbours a boy who is destined to become a great artist. This is Master Arnold Trowell, whose performances as a 'cellist have led to only one conclusion in the minds of musical judges: that he ought to have the fullest opportunity for the development of his genius in the great musical centres of Europe. Mr. Alfred Mistowski, a recognized authority on stringed instruments, heard Master Trowell and his brother—Garnet Trowell, a violinist—while he was in Wellington.

On the 23rd, at the invitation of Mr. and Mrs. Dean, a large number of the musical public of Wellington assembled at the Sydney Street hall to hear the Masters Trowell. Arnold Trowell is undoubtedly a boy with a great future before him. Garnet, who has also been carefully trained, plays with remarkable accuracy, but seems to lack the full inward feeling and poetic temperament of his brother.

It's the same story in all the newspaper articles, including the one that prints the twins' praises next door to a report on the "Protector" submarine, launched at Bridgeport, Connecticut, and able to wheel along the ocean floor. Next to a drawing of the "Protector" comes a large photo of the Trowell twins, Arnold seated with his cello while Garnet lounges in the background. After telling us all about Arnold's amazing talent, the writer states that "Garnet, likewise, makes wonderful progress on the violin." Poor Garnet. He must have felt that "Likewise" was his middle name. He must have felt grateful for any mention at all, among the ads for Mason's Finest Non-Intoxicating Herb Beer and Towles' Still Pills for Females— Woman's Unfailing Friend. For all the hoopla and fanfare, and the public subscription that sent him off with Arnold to Frankfurt and Brussels, Garnet ended up playing violin with the Moody-Manners, a travelling opera company.

Long after Kathleen Beauchamp sprang in and out of his life, Garnet, like his brother, fell in love with a young music student in London. Marion Smith's disapproving family were Canadian, not South African. The engagement was only a little shorter than Arnold's ten-year wonder. Like Arnold, Garnet fathered two children. Unlike Arnold,

Garnet kept on the hoof. In 1921 he hopped a boat for Durban, South Africa, where he married his Canadian sweetheart and became concert master of the city's brand-new symphony orchestra. Eight years later the Trowells hopped another boat, landing in Windsor, Ontario, on their way to make their musical fortunes in the United States.

They'd planned to spend a month in Windsor visiting Marion's father, an Essex County judge. He was a man of means and position, by all accounts, but he couldn't even help them cross the Detroit River to the Promised Land. Why? Because of a trifle no one expected to happen, a piece of bad luck that hit while Mr. and Mrs. Garnet Trowell were crossing the Equator. The Great Depression. That month in Windsor became twenty years. Garnet and Marion opened a music studio on Ouellette Avenue, founded a chamber group, and played with local musicians in benefit concerts that were supposed to inspire the citizens of Windsor with the desire for a symphony orchestra of their own. So much for inspiration on demand. After 1939, Garnet did war work for a Windsor branch of the Ford Motor Company. He stayed there till his death in 1947, surviving his father by two years and Katherine Mansfield by almost a quarter of a century.

During all those moves, across all those oceans, through two world wars, until his dying day, Garnet kept the love letters Kathleen sent to him that autumn of 1908. He kept them as his secret, not as a trophy. I ask you, is this the action of a deep-dyed villain?

5. *The Case Against Garnet*

What do we do with Ida Baker's famous description of how the fragile, pregnant Kathleen, in her rickety flat in Maida Vale, writes a stream of heart-wringing letters to Garnet, begging him to get in touch with her? How could a man with any heart in him be deaf to this weeping violin? But consider—if he did receive those letters, why didn't he keep them, along with the others that sleep in the bosom of the University of Windsor library? Because they were so incriminating? Or because Kass never sent them in the first place?

When Ida got around to publishing her memoirs, guess who wrote to her out of the blue? Who but Dolly Trowell, now a Mrs. Richards. Just one old gal to another, after all those years of separation and forgetting.

Dolly swore it just wasn't possible that her "dear gentle Garnet" could have been cruel to Kathleen, never mind dishonourable! Dolly was shrewd enough to point out that other men had caught Kathleen's interest before Garnie came along, though she doesn't mention the *Papanui*. She reminds Ida that Kass's first choice was Arnold, and she hints that the flirtation with Garnet was some kind of smokescreen for a constant, hopeless crush on Caesar. But here's the point Dolly keeps hammering home: it would be foreign to Garnet's nature, getting a girl pregnant and then running out on her, especially when he'd know she had no one else to turn to.

Dolly loved Garnet with all her heart, but she wasn't blind and she wasn't stupid. If she says it was foreign to Garnet's nature to be a villain, then I believe her, a hundred times more than I believe that dimwit Ida Baker. Ida claims Garnet drove Katie to drugs. She'd be swallowing veronal just to get a few hours' sleep each lonely night, so Ida says.

Did Garnet ever find out about that baby? If Kathleen did write those letters and they went to Carlton Hill, his parents would have ripped them up instead of forwarding them to their prodigal son. If the letters were sent to the theatres where he was playing, at least some of them could have arrived long after the Moody-Manners had cleared out. And supposing— just supposing—Garnet knew about the baby. Why on earth would he preserve the evidence of what he and Kass

Beauchamp had been up to—the evidence of those love letters he lugged around from one hemisphere to another? No. The fact that Garnet held onto those reckless, passionate letters proves just how tender and faithful a lover he was, and how badly treated he's been. Not just by Miss Beauchamp, but by all those biographers of Katherine Mansfield, too.

Let's go back to that August day when Kathleen, newly arrived in London, hell-bent to set the Thames on fire, switches her affections from Arnold to Garnet, quicker than a magician can pull hankies from his sleeve. Let's try and find out what really happened next, and who's to blame. Take a look at the only written source—Mansfield's letters of late 1908, early 1909, mostly to Garnet, far away in Birmingham, Leeds, and Glasgow. And the reminiscences of friends who knew her in those better-forgotten, distant days.

We can start with Kathleen in her big, expensive room at Beauchamp Lodge, handing out cups of cocoa to the other lodgers and talking about everything from dress reform to free love—a topic she'd already dared to raise, aged fourteen, at Miss Swainson's School in Wellington. Here she is on September 9 attending a concert at Queen's Hall while Garnet rehearses for his upcoming tour of the provinces. Queen's Hall is packed, yet "Garnie's" absence, she writes him, makes the hall seem as good as empty. The very next night she sleeps for the first time at the Trowells' house in Carlton Hill—or at least it's her first sleepover when Garnet's under the same roof, though not in the same bed. On September 11 she plans a pre-breakfast walk with him, maybe up to the top of Primrose Hill, where they'll huddle under his big fur coat and take in the panorama of London. By the sixteenth, Garnet's off to Birmingham with the Moody-Manners, with a ring on his finger, an opal that one of Kathleen's New Zealand aunts gave her as a going-away gift. By September 17 Kathleen's been given a present in return—three studio portraits of Garnie. She arranges them in her room so that the moment she wakes his face will hit her, smack in the eye.

On the evening of the day our heroine receives Garnet's photos, she attends a meeting of the Women's Suffrage Movement in Baker Street. But she's not ready to chain herself to any lampposts, our Kathleen. Instead she runs out into the street, buys a huge beef sandwich, and eats it in a hansom cab heading back to Beauchamp Lodge. Once there she dashes off a note to Garnet, calling him "Husband" for the first time. Now, in previous letters, she's made up a honeymoon scenario (Kass and Garnie leaning out of windows, looking up at the "mystical" night sky while puffing away on pricey cigarettes). Does this calling Garnet "Husband" mean they've already slept together, or that they're secretly engaged, with ceremony and honeymoon to follow? Kathleen promises to send him the few pieces she's managed to write since coming to London: namely, the poem later titled "October," dedicated to her oldest sister Vera. The poem, by the way, is filled with fog, dead leaves, dull streets, mutilated men, and Virginia creeper bleeding down the house fronts.

Returning from a stay in Surrey with her golf-aholic Aunt Belle—never one of her bosom pals—Kathleen goes off to the Palace Music Hall on Shaftesbury Avenue to see Maud Allen dance *Salome* in a scrap of gauze and a rope of pearls. A senior member of the Conservative government would write an article about this same Maud Allen ten years later, under the title "The Cult of the Clitoris," but that's another story, as they say. Maud Allen is far more entertaining to Kathleen than any Suffragette. That night she writes to Garnet, sawing away in Halifax, that she aims to do for the art of recitation what Maud Allen has done for modern dance. And what about what Maud Allen has done for her bank account? That couldn't have left Miss Beauchamp cold. The American dancer made a killing with her take on Oscar Wilde. She wowed everyone from Edward VII to bankers' daughters by inventing the shimmy, single-handed.

Yet all the time that Kathleen's pouring out her lonely love and colossal ambition to Garnet Trowell, she's having nightmares about huge black birds beating over her head, suffocating her. They come as warnings she'll die young, she says—that she'd better not waste the little daylight she's got left. There's something else, too. In her notebooks she confesses to hankering after the carnal and sensual, what she calls the "sea cry." Translation: "the desire of a more abundant life, of unlimited freedom, of an unknown ecstasy." This at the same time she's out to clip Garnet's wings. I quote: "Oh I would lock you in a prison of my arms and hold you there until you killed me, then, perhaps, I would be satisfied." She writes that to Garnet—dreamy, gentle Garnet. She writes as though she'd got him mixed up with one of those "undesirable men" Ida talks about in her memoirs, the ones who couldn't keep away from Katie. The ones Katie couldn't stop meeting, or writing to, accepting their invitations to appointments she was supposedly too scared to keep.

Being young, Ida says, her friend made a lot of mistakes. From the written evidence, it seems these mistakes had a lot to do with sheep. In one of the fifty-three notebooks Mansfield kept during her thirty-four years, writing in them any old how, entries jumping about between the years like fleas on a dog, there's an undated passage which repays your attention:

Night. *J'attends pour la première fois dans ma vie la crise de ma vie.* As I wait, a flock of sheep pass down the street in the moonlight. I hear the cracking of the whip *&* behind the dark heavy cart—like a death cart, *il me semble*. And all in this sacrificial light. I look lovely. I do not fear, I only feel. I pray the dear Lord I have not waited too long for my soul hungers as my body all day has hungered & cried for him. Ah come now—soon. Each moment, *il me semble*, is a moment of supreme danger, but this man I love with all my heart. The other I do not even care about. It comes. I go to bed.

Skip the phoney French, the "I look lovely." You can even skip the fact that the writer of this passage is a woman with at least two lovers on a string. Let's concentrate on one question: where on God's earth is she, and what is she doing with all those sheep supplying the background music? She's not in New Zealand, even if it is one of those countries where sheep outnumber people.

Remember, during that year of her return to Wellington, Kathleen's love affairs involved girls and women: Maata Mahupuku, the "bewitching" Maori millionairess and princess; Edie Bendall, a children's book illustrator ten years older than Kathleen—mother love that never turned into sex with all the trimmings, thanks to Edie being conventional or plain clued out. No, the man our heroine loves with all her heart in this passage (in contrast to the "other" guy, the one she dismisses) has to be Garnet Trowell, and the setting for this grand sacrifice has to be London. I've seen a photograph to prove it: six hundred sheep being herded along Piccadilly from Hyde Park to Green Park, at six o'clock one fine morning in nineteen hundred and twenty-four. Who says they couldn't be herded at nighttime, too?

Night or morning, you find sheep in every one of Kass's descriptions of happy love—not that you find all that many. Take the poem she wrote for Garnet, "Sleeping Together." It's one of the few poems of hers that doesn't make you feel you're on an IV drip full of corn syrup. It's about lovers sharing a bed, falling asleep in each other's arms. One of them wakes up, watches the other sleep, then walks over to a window, only to find a flock of sheep passing by. Sheep—not always to the slaughter, but sheep mixed up with the heart, when the heart's no valentine but a mess of blood and muscle. "You're young and you're innocent," says one of her early characters to the woman he loves. "Why, you don't know any more about real Life than a lamb in Spring." Those sheep that Kathleen connects with love instead of lust—those sheep are her way of showing a virginity that survived the *Papanui* and Montevideo. When she writes of facing that first-time, all-important crisis, what else is she talking about but the very first opening of her heart? Her secret, double-dealing heart.

Visiting the Trowells at Carlton Hill, taking Dolly off to the Victoria and Albert to look at Venetian glass and the Vienna Café for hot chocolate, writing every day to Garnet—"My Dearest One," "Beloved," "Heart's Dearest"—this is the way she wants to see herself, the way she sets herself up to be seen. Naive, loving Kass about to have her heart cracked by a Heel. But what about the other men in Little Katie's life? Gentleman callers like Sidney Hislop, a "rather charming man," Ida tells us. Was he a passenger on the *Papanui*? Did he take our heroine ashore at Montevideo? Ida says Sidney fell in love with Katie, she says he ended up being "a good friend" who encouraged her to keep on writing. So it's got to be Sidney, not Garnie, who'll be pleased by her working away at that "happy story" she mentions in her journal.

Or maybe it's Mysterious Martin. All we know about this character is what Miss Beauchamp gives us in writing—that she's had an "awful, shocking, terrible" meeting with "Martin." And there he is again in a list of gifts or purchases scribbled in her notebook, next to this entry: "I wonder if I will ever be happy again . . . It seems my brain is dead. My soul numbed with horrid grief. A man in the bus is blushing—a vivid purple hue. This hand on my heart again. <u>The Shadow of the Hand</u>." All this on a day she spends having lunch with Ida and supper with the Trowells, at least so says her letter to Garnet. So young and so untrue? So much in love, and crooked as a dog's hind leg? Was she having an affair with Martin all the time she was pining for Garnie? Is Martin the original for Max in *Maata*? Max, who lures the heroine away from her innocent, happy love into the Toils of Passion?

Sidney Hislop from Montevideo. "Awful, shocking, terrible" Martin. When she declares she must "more definitely arrange" her life, what does she mean? Keeping Lover A separate from Lovers B and C? Why are her notebooks from this time in London filled with story fragments about love triangles, women fighting off respectable suitors and falling for evil seducers? Miriam and Tim and Howard, for example. Howard's the kind of man who catches a Miriam in his arms, moaning, "So much beauty—my God, I could kill you!" Tim's the kind who catches her *by* the arm, warning her about the Dangers threatening her Innocent Self when it goes off into the Far, Wide World. Tim drives Miriam crazy with his "good sense, his innate spirit of gentleness, his unfailing patience and self-sacrifice." Does Garnet play Tim to Martin's Howard?

Think of the poems she sends Garnet—about a widow watching a "bride" wearing a chaplet of ivy leaves instead of a wedding ring. About a seabird screaming to a woman waiting at the shore that her lover is drowned. About a lilac tree that used to shelter a pair of lovers, and now is stripped and bare—true poor love grown rich, old, and empty. You'd think Garnet would wake up and smell the coffee. Maybe he had second thoughts about this grand passion and whether he could live up to what Kass expected from him as an artist and lover. Or maybe he kept reading the lines of her dashed-off letters instead of between them: "Garnet—when I say your name—I almost *tremble*—I love you & you & you—"

On the night of November 23, 1908, Garnet comes home for a holiday before heading off with the Moody-Manners on a Christmas tour of Ireland. According to *Maata*, there's nobody home but the kid sister—the field is finally clear for the lovers to sleep together. Only Sis happens to spy on them; she spills the beans to the outraged parents, who hurl the fallen woman from the house where she'd once been so welcome. You're probably asking yourself why the bankrupt Trowells were so shocked at hanky-panky between their unbankable son and the banker's daughter. Ida Baker says it's because of the big gap in wealth and social class between the Trowells and the Beauchamps. But why wouldn't Garnet's parents push their son to marry Kathleen right away, betting the Beauchamps would come round to the union, even throw a bunch of the boodle their way? After all, they weren't going to be marrying her off to a handy-dandy Canadian geologist or Indian Army colonel the way they did with Vera and Chaddie.

I have a hunch that the Trowells were sick of Kathleen's high-and-mighty ways, her tantrums and gushing and plain old lies. Nobody knows for sure why they blew up at her, but one thing's clear—it all happened after Garnet shipped off to Ireland. It's not a pretty picture, I admit, Garnet keeping his distance in Dublin, safe from his parents' fury and the misery of his humiliated fiancée. Why didn't he fly to Katherine's rescue? Why didn't he send for her? Did his fear of being a bad boy keep him from acting like a man? Was his passion for Kassie so fly-by-night? Listen to Lady Ottoline Morrell stating the case for the prosecution: "She was not hard, but obviously from some painful and bitter experiences in her early youth she had become frightened, suspicious and antagonistic, where she might have been affectionate and trusting." Hey presto!—Garnet's responsible for turning Dorothy into the Wicked Witch of the West.

Or is there another possibility, where the Crisis isn't suffered by the Abandoned Woman but scripted by the Fickle Artist, who decides that the guy she's supposed to have fallen for hasn't got the "necessary impetus of character" to "achieve a great deal of greatness"? That was the reason she gave a year earlier for ditching Edie Bendall. Why shouldn't her "marriage" to Garnet Trowell have gone on the skids for just the same reason? After all, what were her choices? Living happily ever after with her Beloved Husband on cheap meat pies and bunches of violets—or achieving Artistic Greatness? The kind of greatness that gives you the good life, as a bonus. Think about that visit Kathleen paid to the celebrated pianist Mme. Carreño, who gave a London concert the first October of Miss Beauchamp's return to England. For two hours the women talked of Music and Life and the Splendours of Being an Artist in a luxury suite full of flowers and photos of Carreño's famous friends. Was Kassie remembering that type of hotel room when she went on tour with Garnet five months later, staying in rooming houses stinking of unwashed socks and kippers cooked over gas lamps?

In her last recorded letter to Garnet, Katherine describes a dream of being with him at a concert when a flock of big black birds fly screaming over the orchestra. Then she tops that off with another dream about wandering through a castle where the doors are locked and the windows barred—except that Garnet has opened the gates and is waiting for her to clue in. But it turns out Kassie's had the keys in her pocket all the time, and so she hands them over to Garnet. In the dream he owns the castle, and he's decided he wants to give her the whole shebang, keys included. Whatever's his is hers, he tells her: he belongs to her.

It's all there: next to the horrible discovery by the big black birds of family, the fantasy that Garnet will always be there for her, whatever she does, no matter who she's seeing in secret, and no matter how much noise the gang at Carlton Hill are making. A man's heart is his castle, and Garnet has not just opened it up, he's given away the keys. What a hero, brave, courageous, and bold, not to mention self-sacrificing, at least to Kass Beauchamp's tune. But there's one small catch. Garnet—sweet, dreamy, bookish Garnet—ain't no hero. You can guess what he made of those lines in her letter: "Why is it we so love the strong emotions? I think because they give us such a keen sense of *Life*—a violent belief in our Existence." Especially when she rubs it in by declaring how the one thing she can't stand is mediocrity. Now, a violent belief in his existence would have scared the pants off twenty-year-old Garnet Trowell. You remember his tyrant-father's temper? You can guess that strong emotions were something he'd want to avoid, or talk down into something manageable, comfortable—mediocre, which, by the way, the dictionary defines this way: "of middling quality, neither bad nor good."

6. *The Marriage Game*

Late December of 1908, early January of 1909. Garnet seems gone for good, and Kathleen's sulking in Beauchamp Lodge. If they exchange any letters, not a scrap of them survives. What we do know is that right after Valentine's Day, Kathleen meets a singing teacher named George Bowden at a dinner party given by Dr. Caleb Saleeby, a popular-science writer. Events move quickly. Kathleen visits Bowden's studio flat that he shares with a friend and an over-the-hill servant named Charles. A few days later, Kathleen picks George up from hospital, where he's had his tonsils out. The next thing you know, they're announcing their engagement at another Saleeby dinner party.

All the way through this whirlwind engagement Kathleen doesn't seemed choked up by anything: she sheds no tears George Bowden can see, even at the Paddington Registry Office. Bowden is one of those perfect English gentlemen you read about in magazines, but he gets his digs in all the same. He says he experienced enough of Katherine's dark and light moods to know her for a born performer. He doesn't say whether he shed any tears of his own when she left him on their snow-white wedding night. Later, he told his mother-in-law that lesbian impulses towards Ida drove Kathleen from his arms. Ida swears Katie walked out on her marriage because she "couldn't bear the pink satin bedspread at the hotel, or the lampshade with pink tassels. She hated pink tassels."

And then there's the mysterious note Katherine wrote, sometime in 1909, a note pitched to some anonymous "You" and folded inside another piece of paper serving as an envelope, inscribed "Never to be read on your honour as my friend, while I am still alive. K. Mansfield." The note is vintage Kathleen, flirting with suicide and full of dark hints about Oscar Wilde's unspeakable influence on her during her teenage years in New Zealand. The "fits of madness" leading to ruin and mental decay that he drove her to then, and that hit her now, whenever she's down in the dumps. Her fears that this secret terror—vice, you could say—will drive her insane, paralytic, and dead. And all of it she's kept a secret from this "You" who's supposed to understand why.

No biographer that I know is putting any money on who the "You" could be. Ida? Garnet? Margaret Wishart? Maybe it's Arnold Trowell, or the supersap, George Bowden. There are those who believe the whole thing's a confession of what Virginia Woolf & Co. called "Sapphism"—why else the reference to Oscar's "exact decadence"? To me it smacks of those sermons about self-abuse delivered to teenagers the moment they start asking for locks on their doors. In my humble opinion, the reason no one can figure out who this trumped-up letter is supposed to be for is that Kathleen Beauchamp wrote it to herself. She was an actress writing for another actress, both of them herself, or parts of all those selves she claimed were hers.

All her life long she was acting. Everyone who knew her tells you that—her schoolfriends, her sisters, her literary pals—story after story. About how she impersonated the mother of a future student of Queen's College, grilling the principal. How she played the role of shopgirl for a day, or pretended, in the drawing rooms of the stinking rich, that she was a prostitute come in out of the rain to gawk at paintings and fine furniture. And how sometimes she couldn't tell when she was barefaced and when she was wearing greasepaint. Then why not believe she wrote this little piece of theatre for the drama value of the very last line: "I think my mind is morally unhinged and that is the reason—I know it is a degradation so unspeakable that—one perceives the dignity in pistols." This isn't the voice of a desperate woman. It's the note of a stylist, the style of an actor, or, if you want to call a spade a spade, the style of a compulsive liar who can't even write an honest suicide note.

If Katherine married George Bowden because she had a bun in the oven and needed a legal father for the child, then why didn't she sleep with Bowden at least once before leaving him? If Katherine was pregnant by Garnet when she ran away to him in Glasgow, why did she leave him two weeks later? No, the only possible explanation is this: during the two weeks Mrs. Bowden spent with Garnet Trowell in Glasgow, she happened to conceive a child.

No one in her family was informed when Katherine miscarried the baby, probably in June of 1909; you can bet

Garnet was never told. How could he know she'd left England for Bavaria? The only letter Garnet got from his former lover after her waterhose cure was written and signed by Ida. It tells him that the woman he knew as Kass or Kathleen Beauchamp is now Katherine Mansfield. As divorce papers go, Ida's letter does the job a lot quicker than the ones Katherine finally got from George Bowden, nine years later.

7. Let Us Imagine Garnet Carrington Trowell in Scotland, March 1909

Or "Carrington Garnet," as his stage name went—not the best camouflage, but what I'm trying to show is how bad he was at disguises. Just what was he doing in Glasgow? How did he live? What were his prospects on that fateful day Kathleen Beauchamp Bowden steamed up (she had her mother's habit of steaming) to the Theatre Royal, Glasgow?

I'll bet you've got the wrong idea about the Moody-Manners. You probably think Garnet was employed in some low-life, amateur outfit. So let me correct that impression right now. "What a fine company was Moody-Manners," proclaims the 1966 *Limerick Chronicle*, "with the very best of British singers as well as many overseas artistes!" In its heyday, not long before Garnet Trowell joined the company, the Moody-Manners had a repertoire of fifty operas: "By this time the company numbered 175, and travelled by special train, carrying their own scenery and costumes in ten 45-foot trucks. They were known as 'The Sunday School on Tour' as the choristers, male and female, were not allowed to mix, nor were the principals permitted to fraternize with the chorus. The chorus gentlemen were in the front coaches, principals in the middle and chorus ladies in the rear. Needless to say the corridor doors were locked." As if this weren't enough to protect the virtue of the company, the Manners kept them busy in the off-hours with hockey and football games, fencing lessons, and readings from Shakespeare.

Orchestral players weren't expected or allowed to have temperaments. Garnet was a model musician, keeping his bow well rosined and his dinner jacket brushed and sponged for performances. I'll bet he was mindful of his conductor but no "smoodge," as the saying went. When he felt like celebrating, he'd buy a beer or two, or maybe a book of poems from a bookseller's stall. An upstanding, honourable fellow, true to the Sunday school code of the Moody-Manners. So you can guess the courage it took for him to take her into his arms, smack out of the blue, that wild-eyed girl who rushed up to him at the Theatre Royal, or wherever they met on her rebound from her wedding night.

Garnet had to pretend Kass was his wife. Since he was being paid next to nothing, he had to find this wife a job with the company. He did—she became an extra in Balfe's *Bohemian Girl*, a show as popular in Garnet's youth as *Oklahoma!* was in mine. Talk about dreams-come-true! *The Bohemian Girl* is about a duke's daughter kidnapped and raised by gypsies. She has the time of her life with them before they hand her back to her wealthy father. And what does her hard-nosed daddy do when she introduces him to the penniless exile who's the love of her life? Why, he showers blessings on their heads and happily supports the two of them forever after. You can bet *The Bohemian Girl* wasn't on Harold Beauchamp's list of the greatest operas of all time.

8. *The Facts of the Matter*

It was Kathleen who ran out on Garnet while the company was on tour in the north of England. Ida says it was because of the sloppy way the poor guy ate his boiled egg. Some believe that when Garnet found out about the marriage to

Bowden, his mood turned so ugly that Kathleen couldn't have stayed with him even if she'd wanted to. But why should easygoing Garnet, born playing second fiddle, turn on his lover for marrying an almost-stranger, a stranger she never even slept with? Look at it this way. After her fling as a Moody-Manners artiste, Mrs. Bowden wakes up to the fact that she's not a Bohemian girl after all. Life would be a whole lot sweeter in London, where she could live with the freedom of a married woman, but without the burden of a husband. That freedom comes crashing down on her when something happens that couldn't have been any bolt from the blue—remember her fears after Montevideo and her visit to Mrs. Charley Boyd?

It's only now that Kassie sends off those desperate letters to Garnet, or at least that Maata sends to Philip in the manuscript of *Maata*. And if Garnet did receive and ignore those letters, is it really a sign of "moral cowardice," as one biographer claims? How can we know it was Garnet's "betrayal" at this most vulnerable moment of her life that hardened our Kassie, making her cynical, even cruel? Consider this: if Garnet had coldly, cruelly refused to fess up to being the father of Kathleen's child, why would she write him all those unsent letters from Bavaria, letters more genuinely loving, as far as I'm concerned, than those drum-beating ones she sent him before they were lovers? Sundays, she writes him, are "full of sweetness and anguish. Glasgow—Liverpool—Carlton Hill—Our Home." Don't you find it strange that in her journals, where her writing is about as open and honest as it ever gets, she never once speaks bitterly of Garnet Trowell, this woman so clear on her power to hate? Years and years after sending him back that engagement ring, she could write that the shape of a man's head, the cut of his hair, reminded her of "Garnie." Do we use pet names for dogs who've bitten us?

What about the baby? you say. Why haven't I given Kathleen credit for courage? Sure, she could have gone back to Mrs. Charley Boyd, or someone else who'd have got rid of it for her. And yes, to the end of her life she grieved over losing Garnet's child. But why did she lift that heavy trunk in the first place? And why did she run out on little Charlie Walter, her temporary substitute for Garnie's bundle of joy? Did she ask herself what she'd do with that son she dreamed of having, how she'd bring him up all on her own? Would she unload him on Ida when she couldn't or wouldn't take care of him, when there were trips to take to Paris or the south of France or Switzerland, when she was searching for a place to write, and then a place to keep alive, and then a place to die? Or would she have ditched Ida and turned to her child for love and support? How much love and support could a fourteen-year-old child give to a dying woman? A woman so helpless she often couldn't walk, or speak, or lift her head?

9. *The Case for Garnet Trowell*

Of all the people mixed up with crazy Kassie Beauchamp, Garnet Trowell gets the rawest deal. One of the biographers says George Bowden played rabbit to Mansfield's ferret, but at least Bowden finally got a chance to spill his plate of beans. Likewise Ida Baker, who played workhorse to Katherine's bareback rider. True, Ida was Little Miss Lonely in her passion for Katie. According to the letters and journals, Mansfield despaired, all right, at the mess of Ida's mind, but she was downright disgusted by her body. Still, Ida slaved willingly for her darling Katie, and as far as I can see, the willing forfeit their status as victims. It's different with Garnet Trowell, whether or not he had a clue that baby existed. Two years after Garnet's death, a friend who knew them both spoke of her "indignation" at Kass's treatment of the "heartbroken" Garnet. Given all this, it doesn't hurt to remember just what a constant, brazen liar Katherine Mansfield was, from start to finish. Or, if you prefer the diagnosis given by one of her schoolteachers, how Kassie Beauchamp was "imaginative to the point of untruth."

She was also a thief. That first book of hers, the one she refused to have republished during World War I on account of the cheap and easy shots it took at the Germans? She'd play no part in any hate-mongering, she said. But is it that simple, that noble? Let's go back to those busy biographers. Some of them have pointed out that one of the stories in that first book is a copy of a Chekhov tale. They speculate it was because of this "borrowing" that Mansfield was black-mailed years later by a shifty Polish journalist. She instructed her husband to pony up, and they never heard from Floryan the Extortionist again. But she wasn't finished with stealing plots—towards the end of her life she took another Chekhov story and changed it into "Marriage à la Mode." She was at death's door, she had big doctors' bills, and the glossy magazines paid good money for such stories. Even so, the word "plagiarism" comes to mind, in spite of the opinion of one of her contemporaries that great writers don't borrow; they steal.

Thieves, liars, traitors, truehearts—does it matter after all this time? Put the question another way. How should we live, what do we want from this life we never asked for, that we're so terrified to leave? Of this pair of one-time lovers—musician and writer, mediocrity and celebrity—which is the success and which the failure? Now, Katherine did manage immortality, at least in the eyes of her readers. But Garnet? His reward was 99 percent obscurity.

But what if obscurity is the price we pay for happiness? Garnet, from all we know, had a good marriage to a woman who was his equal, musically and otherwise. He had two sons, and when he died the people he loved were gathered round him. Katherine died alone, or at least tortured by doctors, her husband shut out of the room. She'd had to learn to live alone, too, without husband or child to keep her company in the worst of the worst of times. Speaking of husbands—and what a prize he was—Jack Murry called it one of her "deepest and most secret griefs that she had no child—perhaps indeed, the deepest of all."

10. *The Fable of the Green Tree*

I'll conclude my case with a fairy story written by Katherine Mansfield, though it's really a revenge story dressed up as a fairy tale. The revenge of a sensitive, musical boy against the parents who jeer at his dreams to achieve Something Extraordinary. Revenge against the young, beautiful woman who hears the songs composed by the boy, now a lonely man, and comes to live with him. It doesn't take her all that long to get tired of his love for the magical tree he planted, the tree he writes his songs to and refuses to leave. But the young woman doesn't abandon the Musician. He's the one who turns her out for spoiling his songs. Who does she go to for consolation but a neighbour who marries her so that she can live happily ever after. As for the Musician, the Lover of the Green Tree, when he cottons on to what he's lost, he's struck to the heart. The tree refuses to bear fruit, people chop it down, and he dies, probably with ashes in his mouth.

I put it to you that this story—undated, found in Mansfield's unbound papers—was written after the break with Garnet. I put it to you that the young musician is Katherine Mansfield, and the music-lover turned musician's lover is Garnet. So that what we have here is Katherine's confession of the huge mistake she made when she ran out on Garnet, and her acknowledgment of Garnet's good fortune in finding that neighbour to console him. How can anyone fail to read in "The Green Tree" a vindication of the long, happy, middling life of Garnet Trowell, husband, father, and all round good guy?

It's Katherine's peace with him—her blessing. In fact, it's the last piece of writing she ever sent him, for this little fable of the Green Tree was found with those letters of hers that Garnet kept till his dying day.

BEYOND THE BLUE MOUNTAINS

London, February 1910

Into the cluttered office of *The New Age* journal off Chancery Lane walks a white-faced young woman, asking for the editor. She gives her name as Katherine Mansfield and refuses to take a seat, though she's told that she may have to wait for some time. Mr. Orage is a very busy man. The busy man's secretary looks this terribly impatient author up and down, taking in her thick, dark hair parted down the middle and pinned up at the back, the brown eyes glowering under black brows, the hand clutching her side. When she asks the young woman if she feels unwell, the reply is almost a wail—"No!" and then, "Thank you"—but she does consent to sit down.

At last Alfred Richard—A. R.—Orage appears. An older man, direct and powerfully intelligent, he leans against the doorframe and in his dry voice asks how many of these Miss Mansfield might have. "These" refers to the typescript in his hand. She tells him she has a dozen or more stories—she worked on them when she was convalescing in Germany, a few months ago. Orage raises his hand, as if to forestall anything in the way of details. "We'll take this," he says. "And the others, if they're as good." Katherine shakes hands with him quickly and flees the office. "She must be afraid I'll change my mind," Orage says. His secretary shrugs; she is thinking how large a presence this little Miss Mansfield seems to have. She walks to the grimy window, peers outside, and sees the young woman, her hand pressed to her side again, getting into a cab.

It takes her, via Ida's father's flat in Harley Street, to a private clinic just around the corner. Katherine ends up in a hospital bed, being talked to by a doctor who is closely—rather too closely—examining the bandages covering her abdomen while she clenches her fists, not because of the pain so much as the indignity.

"Miss Bowden, is it?—Ah, Mrs. Bowden, of course. The incision seems to be taking its time to heal. It's a tricky thing, peritonitis—I'd rather not have had to operate, but I'd also rather not have had a corpse on my hands."

Katherine stares at him, her eyes glittering. "You can keep your hands to yourself," she says, as distantly as she can in the circumstances.

The doctor only smiles; he looks down at her body as if it had nothing to do with her words or the tone of her voice. "You ought to have said that to someone else before me, surely."

Katherine refuses to lower her eyes from his face, to turn her head away. She is about to order him out of her room when the doctor pre-empts her.

His tone is caustically professional. "Surgical procedures on female patients harbouring dormant *gonococci* almost always result in the infection of the bloodstream, *Mrs.* Bowden. As a result, the disease becomes systemic, producing a number of rather nasty consequences—"

"The consequences," Katherine interrupts, "are *my*

affair." But she is wrong; they turn out to be the business of the next important man in her life. Not a second-rate violinist, this time, or the legal fiction of a husband who's gone off to America, to her relief. Not the emigré Polish journalist who consoled her in Bavaria for the loss of her baby, giving her gonorrhea in the process. Certainly not this doctor with the slippery hands who has diagnosed it. But a penniless student from Oxford, a diffident man a year younger than she, with the vocation, though not the talent, of a poet.

A year after Katherine discharges herself from the private clinic in Harley Street, she is introduced at a dinner party to the twenty-two-year-old editor of *Rhythm* magazine, John Middleton Murry. The party is in Katherine's honour, to mark the publication of her first book, a collection of sketches and stories set in a spa town in Bavaria and dealing, among other things, with attempted rape, the mess of childbirth, and the killing of one child by another. In a few years' time she will be deeply ashamed of this first book, but now she is drinking in the honours, this dark, slender woman in plum-coloured velvet, with startlingly short hair that she's cropped herself, well ahead of the fashion that will take another eight years or so to sweep London.

And Jack Murry? One of the many other women who fell in love with him has described his dark curly hair and abstracted hazel eyes, the broken nose offsetting the fine, almost delicate, poet's head. A man with the rolling gait of a sailor, yet nervous and shy as a girl at her first ball. A friend takes him aside, warning: "Keep away from Mansfield. She's a New Zealand savage, man—she'll eat you for breakfast and not even bother spitting out your bones." But later that night, over cigarettes and coffee in an alcove, he finds himself pouring out everything about himself to Katherine's beautifully made-up face. How his father was a clerk who barely reached the lowest edge of the lower middle class;

how he was taught, by that same father, to read and do sums by the age of three. How he went to Christ's Hospital on a scholarship and then on to Oxford, in order to become his father's dream: a moderately well-salaried member of the civil service. When all Jack wants is to write, to read—Dostoevsky, for example, and Baudelaire. He spent last summer in Paris, listening to Bergson lecture; he was at Heidelberg before that, and now he's back at Oxford, feeling like a rank imposter, a poor man's son burdened with a poor man's narrow ambitions. Katherine listens in perfect silence, then invites him to take tea with her the next day in her flat at Clovelly Mansions.

What does Jack Murry make of Katherine's bare rooms with their skull candleholders, Japanese matting, and the little mantelpiece Buddha (borrowed forever from Ida) installed, perhaps, as a charm against the ceaseless noise of passing trams? He must have been entranced, because he ends up becoming first Katherine's lodger, and then, at her invitation, though apprehensively, her lover. For he is, erotically speaking, an innocent. Indeed, they often seem more like children than lovers, parading down the Strand in cowboy shirts, pulling faces at one another on the top of double-decker buses, calling each other by nicknames—Jag and Wig. For a while they live off boiled eggs for breakfast and suppers of beer and cheap meat pies at the local pub; they put lavish amounts of time into Jack's magazine, *Rhythm*, while it loses lavish amounts of money. They go off to Paris for Christmas, meeting up with Jack's painter and writer friends there. Katherine is in her element, sweeping into cafés and restaurants in her dramatic black turbans or white fezzes, sporting brilliantly coloured clothes and trading confidences with another exile, the American painter Anne Estelle Rice. But things alter radically when, on their return to London, Katherine starts getting letters from her married sisters, describing their manorial homes. Mac, Vera's husband, was the head of the New Zealand Geological Survey before going on to Greater Glories in Canada; Chaddie's groom is Auditor-General of Military Accounts for the Western Circle at India, headquartered at Poona. He has, she tells Jack, something to do with polo ponies. As for Mac, his only redeeming feature is the maple syrup he brings along on his visits to England.

To the astonishment of their urban friends, the Murrys decamp to the country, renting a handsome Georgian cottage at Runcton, near Chichester. Lorries arrive with masses of pay-on-the-installment-plan furniture, including a baby grand; Jack puts up bookshelves and paints the kitchen chairs black, while Katherine measures the windows for crimson curtains. Crimson curtains and black-painted chairs make their living-together, finally, a marriage, though Katherine is still Mrs. George Bowden and won't take steps to relinquish that status for several years. This is marriage with an escape hatch: a recognition of independence, and a provision, perhaps, for sudden, final separation.

But all through this honeymoon time at Runcton, the Murrys, or "Two Tigers" as they're called by their friends, are staging a play called The Admirable Couple. Here are Jack and Katherine in evening dress, being served dinner at a mahogany table (incompetently, by a servant they'll later dismiss for theft and drunkenness). Here is Jack at the same table, going over proofs as Katherine creeps up behind him, kissing the crown of his head, teasing him about his incipient need of Gro-More Hair Tonic. Here's Katherine standing by Ida's Buddha, to whom she's given a place of honour in the flower garden, and giving the gardener directions about bulbs and perennials in a flawless, unconscious imitation of her mother's manner. Here are the Murrys making love in their moonlit room, with a fire burning in the grate. And here, too, is Katherine, coming in from the garden with a bouquet of turnips and saying—trying to be as offhand as she can—"I may be wrong, of course, but I think it's really happening this time. I'm at least three weeks overdue," while Jack crows his delight.

It's not entirely a paradise for two. Some of the Murrys' London friends come down for weekends: patrons of letters, like Eddie Marsh; poets, like Rupert Brooke; old friends from Jack's Oxford days, like Frederick Goodyear. Witty, learned, exceedingly handsome, Goodyear is everything Jack is, only better. And he has something Jack Murry will never acquire: an ease of manner, a sharp-eyed assurance that leads him not only to hold his own with his hostess but sometimes to get the better of her. One evening, after Katherine's performed a wicked imitation of Goodyear telling off his Oxford tutors, showing them up for the deathly old farts they are, Goodyear applauds louder than all the rest, then launches into his own take on Katherine Mansfield queening it in the Café Royal. He has her dismissing her mentor at *The New Age* as an ass and a bore until, when Orage walks into the café, she switches her tune and praises him above the skies, addressing him as "Master." When Goodyear finishes his turn, the room is silent. Jack is watching Katherine with open alarm. She looks like a lamp about to explode. And then she starts to laugh, huge belly laughs; she runs up to Goodyear and kisses him straight on the lips as Brooke and Marsh and Murry, too, applaud.

One evening Jack returns from a day trip to London to find the cottage cold and unlit. He calls out Katherine's name again and again, finding her, at last, sitting in the dark, staring out a window into an equally dark garden. When she looks up at him, he sees that her face is a plate of misery. "I was wrong. I'm always wrong. I'll never be able to have what I want most of all. And I'll always have to pay, just for wanting it." Jack attempts to console her, to tell her that there is all the time in the world for them to have a baby—as many babies as they like—but she shakes her head, unable even to put her arms around him. And then he tells her, as gently as he can, that his business trip to London has turned out rather badly. In fact, there's been a catastrophe. *Rhythm*'s publisher has gone bankrupt and skived off to the continent, leaving him to pay the printer's bill—a terrifyingly large printer's bill. Drenched in her own grief, Katherine is still able to croon, "Oh, my love, my poor, poor love," drawing Jack down into her arms. He can have her whole allowance, she tells him—he can have her hundred pounds a year. *That* will make a dent in the printer's bill.

Jack kisses Katherine's face, her hair and throat, feeling the pulse beating below the slip of skin. "You're so alive," he tells her. "I sometimes think you've got more life in an eyelash than I have in my whole body." Katherine pushes him away, then holds out her hands to him. "Don't you go playing dead on me, Jack Murry. I should think we're both alive, alive and roaring. We have courage, we have faith in our work. We love each other. Of course we'll come out of this on top—two tigers like us!"

MONTY

After reading Miss Baby's *Vindication*, Monty struck out for the Lakeshore. To his surprise and relief, she hadn't pumped him for a response to her manuscript. She'd told him to keep his thoughts to himself for now; he should return ready to talk at nine the next morning.

He'd been alarmed, at first, by the possibility that Miss Baby could actually read his thoughts—though if she'd been able to, she wouldn't have found what she was looking for. Monty couldn't stand the idea of taking these thoughts to his cheerless hotel; what he needed, he told himself, was to walk them off. So he made his way down West Eugenie Street to Lincoln Park.

What was going through Monty's mind as he stumbled through the park, his bare hands shoved deep in his pockets? Instead of wondering why a Mansfield collector would have spent such time and effort roughing up the writer's reputation, he was undergoing a shocked sense of recognition. You could compare it to the feelings of a man in a funhouse for the first time, looking into mirrors that contort his face, revealing the reflection of a monster. As for the voice he heard in his head, it wasn't the harsh, gritty voice of Miss Baby, advancing her arguments and tossing out her accusations. It was, instead, a charming voice, that of a young woman speaking fluent English with a faint French accent. A woman he'd had to school himself, over the past four years, to forget.

The young woman's name was Edwige, though she went by Eddie. He'd met her his first year in London, in his seminar class on Modernist Fiction. At the beginning, all he'd known about her was that she was enrolled at the Sorbonne and spending a year in London. And that she was brilliant, as well as cuttingly beautiful. She'd given a formidable seminar on *Ulysses*, which he'd followed with his bravura piece on Woolf and Mansfield—a piece he'd freely adapted, if truth be told, from his father's musings out loud on the subject. He should have done something on Ford Madox Ford, but nothing he'd tried to prepare had satisfied him. And so he'd relied on Roger's theories, dressing them up to the nines.

He'd expected Eddie to tear his argument to pieces in the discussion that followed his paper, but what happened was far worse: she hadn't said a word. Of course she'd known it for showmanship instead of scholarship; she hadn't thought it worth her while to prove that she'd been listening—if indeed she had. Except that when the session was over and he was standing by the building's front doors, waiting for the deluge outside to lessen, she had come up to him, taken him by the arm, and declared that they both deserved at least two stiff drinks each.

They headed out into rain bright as tinsel under the street-lamps. At a nearby pub, over a single malt—Eddie drank nothing but scotch or red wine—she congratulated him on his courage. "They all despise your Katherine here," she said.

"They call her slight, limited—or, and this is the one I love—a perfect writer. For adolescents. The English—they are such dumb fuckers." The words sounded strange coming from a woman with hair the straw-blond of a child's and skin so luminously pale it seemed translucent.

She herself, she said, was working on Mansfield's relationship with a minor French writer, Francis Carco. "He specialized in low life, tales about pimps and thugs and prostitutes. Katherine abandoned Murry for Carco in 1915. She had a fling with him behind the French lines, then decided Murry had his good points after all. The next year Carco drew her portrait, viciously, in a novel called *Les Innocents*. She goes by the name of Winnie, she's an English writer—ruthless, amoral, unwholesomely curious—who uses the life and people around her as copy. A *poule de luxe*, Carco calls her.

"You should read the novel. Carco appears in it as a petty crook—Milord, he's called—who fucks her silly on a brocaded sofa in her Paris apartment. When she's had enough of him, she sets off for a provincial town where Milord pursues her, bringing along a little piece of ass named Savonette. Yes, it does mean 'little bar of soap,' but it's also slang for bald tire, in case you didn't know. It turns out that Winnie's as mad for sex with women as with men—she snubs Milord and disappears into her bedroom with Savonette. Now, wait for this— here's where it goes totally outré. At the climactic moment, Savonette wraps her legs round Winnie's neck, strangling her with her thighs. I agree, exaggerated and probably physically impossible. Never mind, Katherine gave as good as she got. She set him up as the literary pimp-and-narrator—"

"Of 'Je Ne Parle Pas Français,'" Monty finished the sentence. "A story her father found so filthy that he threw it into the fire—stupid sod."

"Why stupid?" Eddie asked coolly. "It *is* filthy—that's the whole point. And that's what's so perfect about the way Carco treats Mansfield in his novel. What a relief after all the tripe about Katherine as saint and martyr, Our Lady of the Scented Sorrows. Or are you of Murry's persuasion, a True Believer?"

She didn't wait for his response but launched into a string of anecdotes to prove her point. Some of them Monty was familiar with, though Roger had given them a very different slant; others were new to him, and so extreme he found himself trying to believe they were Eddie's inventions.

As she talked, Monty felt his whole world turning and twisting. From childhood he'd been under the sway of his father's image of Katherine Mansfield, a creature of rare beauty and courage whose writing was as strong as her life was tragic. And while Roger hadn't taken Katherine for a saint of any sort, he'd never hinted at her having such a seamy side. But here was Eddie telling him of Katherine's erotic fantasy of being beaten and thrown across a room by her lover—even strangled. She recounted Mansfield's affair with a writer named Beatrice Hastings; during one of her stays in Paris she'd ensnared and then abandoned less-than-Beata Beatrice, who'd then gone on to seduce and dump Modigliani, just as Katherine had done to her. Vile Beatrice, who wrote poisoned parodies of Mansfield's style and who figured in *Les Innocents* as one of the many lovers cast off by cold-blooded Winnie.

It was through this odd, illicit, and seductive litany that Monty fell head over heels and hopelessly hard for his Scheherazade. Eddie's beauty and brains, her sheer sophistication, would have been enough to entice him; what sealed his fate was the opportunity she offered him to pull the rug of Roger's obsession from under his feet.

That night, in Monty's bedsit in the Redcliffe Road, they

became lovers, talking for hours afterwards as rain lashed against the windows and the chill November damp filled the room. They talked of the countries they came from, where it would be close to summer now. They named the trees and flowers that would be in bloom, the beaches where far luckier people than they were running barefoot over scalding sand into green, glassy seas. For it turned out that Eddie had been born not in France but in New Caledonia, from which her businessman-father had uprooted the family to Paris.

"I was twelve," Eddie said. "I will never forgive him. If he'd waited till I was fifteen, I would probably have been begging him to take us away to France. But I was still a child, and children don't forgive their parents for wounds like that." This was all she ever mentioned of her family; it was as if, becoming homeless, she'd been orphaned as well. Monty was just as glad. He had no desire to tell her of Roger, or Tui. It was easier being an orphan—easier to hide.

Eddie refused his suggestion that they pool their resources and find a flat where they could live together. She had a horror, she said, of domesticity. In this, as in so many other things, she was utterly unlike the girls Monty had known during his undergraduate days in Wellington, the ones who, when he'd brought them home to meet his family—and they'd always wanted to meet his family—had invariably fallen in love with his father. Roger's courtliness proved irresistible to them; his air of gentle helplessness did not irritate but charmed them. They never tried to seduce him: you could no more flirt with Roger than fight with him. But once they'd seen Monty next to Roger, Monty always fell in their estimation, leading, inevitably, to a parting of the ways. Nothing to worry about; his interest in Rose and Brenda and Clare had always been skin-deep, pure and simple.

So it was only justice, pure and simple, that when he did

fall in love, it was with someone like Eddie. Though she ate like a bird and carried herself like a dancer, she proved a glutton for pleasure. She introduced him to a host of bad habits. With Eddie he drank too much, smoked too much, and spent more time in bed than in the library. They went on the academic lam, the two of them: it was their cure for the dark and damp of an English winter. They missed most of their classes and postponed the writing of papers until the last moment, washing down Wideawake pills with shots of espresso. They combed London looking for Mansfield haunts in Chelsea, St. John's Wood, and Hampstead. They found Alastair Crowley's flat, where Mansfield had smoked hashish for the first time and experienced visions of shelves of boxes each marked "Jesus Wept." They located the site of the Cave of the Golden Calf, a reputedly lesbian nightclub run by one of Strindberg's wives, where Mansfield was said to have performed. And they talked, incessantly, about Katherine's courting of shock and scandal.

Once, over dinner in one of Eddie's favourite haunts, an Italian café close to the British Museum, she propounded the theory that all this rebelliousness on Mansfield's part had, at its root, a sad, defeated sexuality. "I don't mean anything as false as orgasm equalling happiness. But fulfillment, wholeness—even if only for a moment. And escape. Yes, escape through the body from the body. You know, like Bertha in 'Bliss.' What is that story about if not—"

"Desire," Monty cut in. "Unsatisfied desire."

Eddie pushed aside her barely touched plate and lit a Gitane. "No—not desire," she declared. "Bliss— *jouissance*—which comes, dear boy, from the verb *jouir*, to play, to enjoy. I'm not talking about happiness, nothing so tame and common as happiness. Remember how the story goes? For the first time in her marriage, on this perfectly ordinary day of her perfectly ordinary dinner party, Bertha is ambushed by bliss. Pleasure invading every pore of her skin, lapping through her body. She is suddenly, deliciously, newly in love: with her child, her house, her husband—with life itself. And when she looks for someone to share this feeling with, because she thinks she will die, that her pleasure will drown her if she doesn't give at least some of it away, who does she find? Not a man but a woman, Pearl Fulton. Who is this Pearl? Just a guest invited to Bertha's dinner party—until the two of them look out the window onto the garden, at the pear tree all silver in the moonlight. Pear. Pearl. A pale radiance . . . You idiot, it's with Pearl that Bertha shares her bliss, to Pearl she gives the overflow of her pleasure, so she can achieve complete fulfillment."

Monty signalled for another bottle of wine from the moody waitress. "Rubbish," he objected, reasonably enough, "it's her *husband* Bertha wants—she can't wait till all the guests go home so she can be alone with what's his name, the one who goes on about pistachio ices and the eyelids of Egyptian girls. The one who's made Pearl Fulton his mistress, though poor little Bertha doesn't find that out until the next-to-last minute."

Eddie lifted her chin aggressively towards him. "Bertha's husband is totally unimportant. The end of the story is a complete lie, of course. Bertha isn't interested in having sex with her husband—his name is Harry, by the way. She wants Pearl for her partner-in-bliss. Harry hasn't let her down by falling in love with Pearl—it's Pearl who's betrayed Bertha by being Harry's lover.

"Don't you see, Monty? Katherine's life is starred by mad affairs with girls, with women. A Maori princess, a schoolmate with whom she reads *Dorian Gray*, an older woman, and who knows how many girls in Wellington. I grant you, the arrangement with Ida is a marriage of convenience, and sexless, much to Ida's disappointment, no doubt. But I'll bet you anything that if we had those journals Mansfield destroyed, the ones from her wild days, when she was sleeping with every Tom, Dick, and Harriet, you'd see it in black and white. That she could experience ecstasy only with women. And that some terrible weight of guilt or shame finally made her turn away from the bliss of a Pearl Fulton to the slam-bam of a Middleton Murry, God help her. You know that story, don't you—about Murry being so ignorant of foreplay that until he happened across a letter from one of Katherine's former lovers he had no inkling you could actually kiss a woman's breasts? If Katherine wanted to wash herself clean after her whole-hog days, who better to use as soap than Jack-be-quick Murry?"

Monty had to defer. Eddie seemed to have access to letters and journals that Roger had never mentioned and that Monty had never discovered. Access to material that went far beyond the secrets revealed in a new, revised biography, the first to tell the truths that Mansfield's father, sisters, and most of her friends, enemies, husbands, and lovers had hoped to bury.

This secret knowledge of Eddie's led Monty astray mentally as well as physically; by the time he was called on to nail down his thesis topic, the subject on which he was expected to slave away for the next few years, he'd scuppered Ford and seized on Mansfield, as I've already told you. He would produce a detailed study of her relationship with Mrs. Woolf; he would investigate the contrasts between the madcap Katherine and the cloistered Virginia, and in so doing chart the ways in which each writer had influenced the other and, in the process, transformed the possibilities of modern fiction.

Despite all the missed classes and last-minute papers, Monty managed this radical shift of subject; he even persuaded one of the university's top scholars to act as his supervisor. In the very few letters he wrote to Roger he barely mentioned his change of focus, the book he would make out of the thesis, the book that would launch his career. He wanted to present it to his father as a *fait accompli*, a sign that he'd been able to achieve, in a mere five years or so, what had eluded Roger for the past twenty-five. Once Eddie and he had landed teaching posts in London or Paris or even New York, he would fly back to New Zealand for a reckoning—a triumphant one—with his father.

Just picture Monty, self-assured, spoiled (for Eddie had taken his wardrobe in hand, lavishing cashmere sweaters and Italian silk shirts on him), and sitting in that Italian café near the British Museum where he and Eddie had become regulars. It is one in the afternoon; he is being served a macchiato (she had taught him about coffee, too) by their customary waitress, a brooding, dark-haired, handsome girl from Bergamo. Monty was a few minutes early; he leafed through a guidebook he'd picked up at a secondhand bookshop down the road. He wasn't worried that Eddie was late; she didn't believe in punctuality, or in giving excuses or explanations when she did at last turn up for meals or plays or lectures. They had planned a trip to the south of Spain to celebrate their first anniversary: Cordoba, Granada, Rhonda, Sevilla. They were to leave in three days' time; he'd bought the tickets and reserved the hotels. It had cleaned him out, but along with a share of her self-confidence Eddie had given him the gift of nonchalance vis à vis bank balances. Monty had finished three coffees and was signalling for another when the waitress came by with a letter she dropped on the table, a letter addressed to him in Eddie's handwriting.

Monty felt his face burn, his lips tighten. Never in all their time together had Eddie written him a letter—telephones were for fun, she'd always said, letters for funerals. He didn't need to open the letter to know what it said; he was already

ambushed by the imagination of disaster. And when the waitress picked up his cup, murmuring, "I got one, too," the
penny dropped with a vengeance. From the doleful, angry
expression on the girl's face Monty knew that he hadn't been
Eddie's only lover over the past twelve months.

But that wasn't the worst of it. The worst came when,
having mastered his shock at Eddie's curt declaration of
farewell, having finally handed in the first chapter of his
thesis on Woolf and Mansfield—an expanded version of
the seminar he'd given—his supervisor returned it to him
with a Xerox of an article that had just appeared in *Modernist Fiction*. This article made, in far more elegant style
and with far more convincing evidence, an argument iden-
tical to the one he'd advanced in his own first chapter. Its
author, one Edwige Vollard, gratefully acknowledged
Montgomery Mills for his helpful comments on numerous
drafts of her paper.

After a week in which he did nothing but stare at the walls
of his bedsit, he decided he'd cure himself of Eddie just as he
would cure himself of smoking: cold turkey. He managed
both, by writing. Out went the comparison of Woolf and
Mansfield; in swept Katherine the Terrible, the very opposite of the sorrowful, suffering woman whose photograph sat
on his father's desk. Monty's Katherine was the woman
who'd impressed Dora Carrington as having the mouth of a
Wapping fishwife; the woman whom T. S. Eliot described as
a "thick-skinned toady" and Lytton Strachey as a "virulent,
brazen-faced broomstick of a creature." She was the
Katherine whose power of hate was at least as strong as her
love of life, who'd once written, after tearing living strips off
her devoted Ida, "Christ, to hate as I do!" This Katherine
had become Edwige, and Roger, too. Especially Roger,
whose devotion to Mansfield had been the source, the start,
of Monty's avalanche of ruin. He imagined handing Roger

his thesis—printed, bound, and acclaimed by his examiners—just like one of those neatly parcelled packets of hate that Mansfield's Linda hands to her doting, oppressive husband in "At the Bay."

Instead, he'd sent it all flying into wind and water, those four years of scrabbling for references to Mansfield's hateful side, of manipulative readings of that side into her stories, of manic note-taking, endless writing and rewriting. And now he'd discovered that a cantankerous old woman without a university degree of any kind had scooped him. Written his book in embryo form, without footnotes or cross-references; without a bibliography or, more important still, a list of sources. Some of those sources he knew; others—the most important ones—didn't exist except in the imagination of Miss Baby. Unless, of course—

It was dark and getting late. In his distress, Monty had walked miles out of his way, ending up nowhere near the Lakeshore. Coming to himself on East Goethe Street, cold, desolate, and hungry, he walked into the first diner he saw. And thus he discovered the Manuka Café.

———

After the brown sludge of the Dreiser, the dust-stiff decor of Miss Baby's, the chill darkness of Lincoln Park, the Manuka was an open jewel box. Lime green and orange walls, a cerulean ceiling, and, at the back, a screen of what looked like paper cut-outs that made him think of Maori carvings. All the spiralling, sinuous lines were there, and yet an openness, too, as if the brilliant screen were a stained-glass window where the lead and even the glass itself had all dissolved into colour. But while some might patronize the Manuka for its brilliant decor, and others for the cheap, plentiful, passable food, any wandering New Zealander would be seduced inside just by the name of the place. For the flowers of the manuka tree, native to New Zealand, make an extraordinarily flavourful honey with the magical property of preventing, not making, holes in your teeth. A description that perfectly described the waitress who took Monty's order.

She couldn't have been more than twenty. She was short and sturdily built; her face made him think of a daisy, or a freshly washed window. But the first thing you noticed about her was a mass of ruddy-gold hair. However hard she tried to tug it back into a knot, that exuberantly coloured hair corkscrewed from its clips, thumbing its nose at anything like the idea of a strict straight line. When she asked him where he was from, and he answered New Zealand, she whooped her delight. She was going to hike the islands, top to toe, one day. She wanted to know everything he could tell her about his country, what she absolutely had to see, and all the places tourists never went to but that she was sure must be the best of all. She'd read tons of books, of course, but to hear it from a native!

Eating his rice and beans, Monty watched his waitress weaving among the tables, balancing glassware and bowls of hot soup on overladen trays, chatting with the customers, her laughter bright as her coppery hair. He left a large tip and waited for a moment at the door, hoping to catch a glimpse of her before he left. But she must have been off in the kitchen, for the only brightness in the room that he could see came from the carved and painted screen. Still, he carried the image of the waitress's hair, her laugh, and her eager questions back with him to the Dreiser. A talisman of sorts, a defence against the scrawl of memory over the long, slow hours until day.

―――――

In the dense and perfect dark, he feels his way across the room, past the tantalus and the mahogany table till he reaches the bedroom, where a lantern is burning, giving off a curiously bright, almost orange light. Shelves line every wall, on them a jumble of objects: a large Japanese doll, a travelling clock, a pistol, an assortment of small boxes, some of them made of Florentine leather or crusted with mother-of-pearl. First editions of Mansfield's books make a neat little row, but of the writer's manuscripts, letters, sketches, even blotting paper he sees no trace.

He starts with the first editions, holding them upside down, shaking them to see if any slips of paper work themselves loose. He searches the Japanese doll to see if something's concealed under the sash of its kimono; he finds nothing in the boxes or crammed in the travelling clock. The other shelves are lined with multiple copies of Oscar Cremer's How to Become a Professional Violinist—*his arms sag just at the thought of leafing through them, looking for the papers that must be hidden somewhere in the room. The only unburdened bit of wall holds a chest of drawers and a small convex mirror; when he peers into the glass, the image it gives back to him is chopped into cubes that scramble his features, so that his eyes are where his ears should be, his mouth and nose confused. Hands shaking, he frees the mirror from the wall, turns it over, and finds, taped to the back, an envelope with the words "Not To Be Opened Till My Death, On Your Honour As My Friend." Something is inside the envelope, a sheet of paper folded over. He is reaching inside the envelope, fishing out the paper when—*

Monty woke unforgivably late for his appointment at Crilly Court.

He was conscious of the disadvantage as he sat at the mahogany table facing Miss Baby. She didn't upbraid him or complain of the inconvenience he'd put her to; she seemed to have expected something of the sort and to revel in the advantage it gave her. When he began by telling her how interesting and unusual a document she'd created in the *Vindication*, she cut him short:

"I don't want compliments. I want to know when you're going to publish it."

Monty stared at her. "When I'm going to publish—?"

"Not you, Mr. Mills, the outfit you work for. *The Mansfield Trust Gazette* or whatever you call it."

Monty swallowed hard. Finally, he found his voice. "Of course I can't speak for the editor, but—"

"Who *can* you speak for, Mr. Mills?"

Remembering that dragons are usually found where treasure's to be had, Monty plunged in. "I'm sure we can arrange for expeditious publication of your monograph, Miss Baby. In two parts, since it's rather lengthy. And, of course, there are technicalities to be taken care of: proper footnotes, checking of quotations, listing of sources. Perhaps it would be better to show your essay to the Trust after all that's been taken care of."

Cassandra Baby gave Monty the kind of smile with which cats are said to swallow canaries.

"That's your ballpark, Mr. Mills—footnotes, accreditation. I guess you know how to type?"

Monty nodded, faintly.

"Good," said Miss Baby. "Just remember what I said before—that manuscript doesn't leave this table. You can make notes here of everything that needs to be checked, and you can find all the sources you want at the Newberry, since you're so crazy about the place. You can use my machine and set to work night and day, as long as it takes to make a fair copy. I'd say five days, tops."

"And then?"

"And then we'll get round to the gold stars for your fore-head. My Mansfield collection, Mr. Mills."

For the next week, Monty made notes, ran back and forth from the Newberry, and recovered his typing skills at Miss Baby's apartment. In spite of himself he felt a strong degree of satisfaction in shaping the mess of manuscript into something clear and cogent, while keeping, as much as possible, the pithy vernacular of the Baby style. He thought of his father, from time to time, but made no attempt to contact him. Roger had given him a schedule of his whereabouts: names of hotels, telephone numbers, urgings to fly over and join him should he finish his own research early. Evidently, Roger had been planning his trip for some time. Judging from the schedule, he would be in London now or moving on to Cornwall. He was saving Fontainebleau for last.

Monty was kept under strict surveillance as he worked at one end of the dining table and Miss Baby sat brooding at the other. Gradually, however, she relaxed her guard, interrupting Monty's work from time to time and holding forth on various subjects: Garnet's time in South Africa, about which she knew very little, or the Moody-Manners Company, concerning which she'd become a minor expert.

Once, over coffee she'd actually ordered in for him, and bourbon she'd let him pour out for her, she retailed the reminiscences of a man named Godfrey Harding, whose father had joined the Moody-Manners after being rejected for the Guards. Harding might have been on the short side, Miss Baby reflected, but it hadn't stopped him playing the Devil in *Faust*, coping with the curtains bursting into flame in the first act, burning his hands but going on with the show so successfully that the audience had thought it was all a special effect. When the Moody-Manners had sung in Dublin back in 1925, he'd had to crawl on hands and knees through the bullets to get to the theatre, with IRA men stationed on one side of the street and the Black and Tans on the other.

And when she spoke of Charles Manners himself, her grey face almost glowed. Manners had been a man after her own heart, she confessed, flying into rages during even the smoothest rehearsals, but handling his musicians with velvet gloves on opening nights.

"He was six-foot-two with a bass voice like Chaliapin's. His wife was something else, though—a rosewater dictator. Fanny Moody hated with a passion—hated jazz and booze. No wonder Manners was a teetotaller. When he was offered a drink, he'd always take it, then pour it into the nearest geranium or sink when no one was looking. But if any man had cause to drink, it was Charles Manners. He was always heading off disasters—the wrong singers falling through trap doors, or swords swung hard enough to bang down the helmet on a singer's head. Then there were the tenors who burst into English in Italian operas. And the Italian hired to play Mephistopheles—he stomped back to Lucca without a word of warning, all because he couldn't stand the English weather."

Monty was intrigued by the mellowing of Miss Baby as she shared these tales. He began to believe that, for all her fits of ill temper, she looked forward to his arrival each morning, to the sharing of what would otherwise have been another day of solitary imprisonment. She was cagey when he ventured any question about her family. "Dead and gone" was all she'd say. "I'm the last of the lot, thank God!" As for friends, she'd point to the books crowding her shelves, tap the papers overflowing her table. "Take a hint from me, Montgomery Mills. These are the best friends, the only friends, a body needs." And when he ventured to ask her something about herself—how, for instance, she'd got interested in collecting Mansfield—the scowl on her face seemed etched on the bones beneath her skin.

"You want me to babble away like Jane Dick in her *Recollections*, is that it? Jane Dick could have been collecting teaspoons for all she cared, all she knew about Katherine Mansfield. Now get back to your work, Mr. Mills. You just mind your own business and let me attend to mine."

Every night without fail, he ate at the Manuka. It turned out that his waitress—her name was Edna—was working the evening shift that week. They quickly became friends; given Monty's isolation and Edna's interest in her customers, her generous good nature, her sheer youthful trust of the world, it couldn't have happened otherwise. Monty always sat at the counter; when things were slow, Edna would come over and talk with him. He didn't know why he enjoyed her company so much. She was like a kid sister, he decided: what people meant by the term "kid sister."

Bright, clear, happily open Edna. Not just innocence but insouciance shone out from her, a sense of being utterly at home inside her own skin. She seemed to believe that happiness was everyone's birthright, and that we needed no justification for our time on earth. She was a perfect countercharm to Miss Baby, and that was all the excuse Monty needed to seek out her company. And while Edna's curiosity could be exhausting—she wanted to know everything about him, what he did and why he'd come to Chicago, and where he was travelling next—it was a sign of generosity, the lack of anything like egotism. When, for simplicity's sake, he told her he was a writer, she asked for the names of his books so she could find them and read them and ask him all about them. She wanted to know his name, of course, and when he told her, she declared it suited him. He replied that he couldn't think of her as an Edna, but she disagreed. She'd been named after a great-grandmother who'd lived to be a hundred and three, a real fighter. Like Montgomery.

Monty had smiled. He'd been surprised Edna knew the name of a British general from a war that had finished nearly a quarter of a century before her birth. He was surprised, too, at how comfortable he felt with her, as if, to use another unaccustomed term, she were family. It wasn't a word he'd ever connected with anything like lightness of heart. But that was exactly what he felt in Edna's company. Once, he stayed on at the Manuka till Edna's shift was over. It was eleven o'clock, but when he asked if he could walk her home, she said she'd rather go for a walk, show him the city lights. She took him to the Hancock Center, where they rode the lightning elevator up to the observatory on the ninety-fourth floor. From the skywalk they could look out on a vast brocade of neon, a panorama, Edna confessed, that she must have seen twenty times before. If she could, she'd come up here every night, it made her feel so happy. Didn't he ever feel like that? Wasn't there some place he went to, if only by closing his eyes, a place where he could forget himself and be perfectly happy?

Perhaps because it was night, and because she was someone he expected never to see again once he left Chicago, Monty gave her an answer. Yet as he spoke, it seemed to him that someone he barely knew was speaking, a self hidden deep inside him, secret and suddenly insistent.

"I suppose there is a place—in New Zealand, in the South Island. I went to school there, boarding school, until I was nearly eighteen. I hated it—I spent six years hating it—but the only time I ever ran away was the day I discovered this place along the coast. I hitchhiked there. I got a ride from a woman who lived in Diamond Harbour. She was nice enough—she didn't ask any questions, though she must have known what I was up to. I'd taken off my jacket and tie, but I still looked exactly like a boy from Falconbridge School skiving off for the day.

"It was springtime, hot and sunny. We drove over twisty roads through the hills, we drove for about an hour, and then she pulled up to a house by the edge of the road. 'That's where I live,' she said. 'If you need help, just knock at the back door.' And then she let me go. I walked along the road—there were a few houses, and a dairy where I bought sandwiches and juice. I stumbled upon a path through a grove of trees and followed it to a slope covered with pines and daisies, huge mounds of white daisies on these feathery stalks, moving in the wind.

"There's nothing more to tell, really. I made my way down the slope onto a deserted beach. It was full of boulders: volcanic-looking, dark grey with some red streaks to them. And there were shells everywhere, mostly broken ones, purple and cream, and tiny spiralling ones like unicorn horns. The sea was the sea—I rolled up my trousers and stood on a sandy bottom while the waves washed in gently, so very gently. I could feel the sand giving way under the soles of my feet and then building back up again. And I felt—not happiness—I just felt that I wanted nothing and needed nothing, that I could stay there forever."

Edna didn't inquire, as he'd expected, how he'd got back to his school, what the repercussions of his running off had been. Instead she asked, "You never went back?"

Monty waited for a moment, then spoke. "I knew if I did that I'd never feel the way I had that day. You know what they say."

"No, I don't," she answered, fiercely. "At least, I don't believe it. And if it wasn't happiness you were feeling then, standing in those waves, what was it? I'm going to get you to take me there, when I get to New Zealand. I want to see that place, I want you to see it with me." Her voice was earnest, almost pained.

He laughed, trying to make light of it. "You'll have better places to visit. No one goes sightseeing to Diamond Harbour."

"Exactly," Edna said, grabbing his hand and tugging him back to the elevator.

They rode down in silence. But by the time they were on the street again, she was laughing. She insisted on walking him home, dropping him off at the Dreiser and striding into the night, part of the brilliant weave of lights to be observed from the observatory of the Hancock Center.

BEYOND THE BLUE MOUNTAINS

London, March 1914

Katherine's come back to London. A far less elegant Katherine, frankly down-at-heel, and taking leave of Lesley Moore. Lesley—or rather Ida—has been summoned to Rhodesia by her foul-tempered father, now trying to make a living by farming instead of doctoring. Ida should be taking her last look at everything that's familiar and comforting to her—the station, the vendors, even the pigeons wheeling under the roof—but all she sees is the shabbiness of her darling's coat and hat. However strapped for money Katherine is, she's found pennies enough to buy Ida a handful of marigolds to take on the journey: flowers are as essential for travel, she declares, as rugs and biscuits. Ida, who is on the verge of tears, takes the marigolds, crushing them against her heart. Just before she climbs into the train, she presses the money she was supposed to have saved for meals and porters into Katie's hand.

After the train has pulled out, Katherine stops at the station florist's, blowing Ida's gift on a huge bouquet of anemones, which she brings back to the bug-infested, cabbage-water-smelling flat she shares with Jack. In the gorgeous blare of the anemones, and the much less showy flowers that replace them as the weeks and months go by, Katherine keeps her journal and writes letters—all that she has the energy or concentration for.

By a weak kerosene lamp, wearing a nightdress and shawl, with her hair in braids wrapped like bandages around her head, Ida opens her week's mail. Her father has tramped off to bed; pale, sad-looking moths cling to the screens, and a few night birds call in voices that hold no beauty for Ida, only foreignness. At first, she barely registers the words; it's the look of the writing she savours, the tilt and dash and scrawl that give her the sense of Katie right there in the room with her, Katie's voice and eyes, her quick, graceful way of moving her head and hands. When Ida does attend to what her friend has actually written, she doesn't know what to make of it. This friendship the Murrys have formed with that new, brash novelist, the miner's son, Lawrence, and his lover, Frieda, the daughter of a German baron and the wife—still—of an English university professor! A wife with three young children in the rigid custody of their ultra-conventional father. The Murrys being witnesses at the Lawrences' wedding, and Frieda giving Katherine her old wedding ring to keep. Jack's being declared unfit for military service, on account of his dicey lungs; Katie's young brother Chummie rushing up from New Zealand to embark on an officers' training course in Oxfordshire. For, on the heels of a perfect summer, war has begun, a war that Ida, and Katie, too, imagine as only briefly shadowing their lives.

Katie's account of their cost-cutting move to a damp, ugly cottage near the Lawrences' at Chesham is comical enough, but her misery comes flooding through the letters that follow. She quarrels constantly with Jack, who spends far too much time talking God with his university friends. Ida shivers at the thought of Katie—who left New Zealand ignorant of how to peel a potato—preparing meals and doing all the washing-up with lukewarm water and scant supplies of soap. Katie makes her see everything to the last detail, even the layers of mutton fat that seem to congeal round not just pots and pans but the very lamps and flowers on the table, too. But there are far more serious things to worry over, such as the attacks of rheumatism from which Katie has started to suffer, forcing her to hobble about like an old woman for weeks at a time. Her plans to go to France and write there, in the flat of a writer, one Francis Carco whom she met the Christmas she and Murry spent in Paris. The violent case of pleurisy that leaves her feeling as though her lungs have turned to sieves. The even more violent case of boredom, despair, and recklessness that drives Katie to run off to France, to bluff her way behind the army lines in Burgundy for a weekend with Carco. Her return, disillusioned, chastened, to a passively accepting Jack and the eternally damp cottage. And, at long last, a reprieve. Jack gets a job with the War Office in London, relieving their money worries. Even better, twenty-year-old Chummie pays them a visit on his way to the Front, a gloriously happy visit, restoring a vision of family love, a reachable Land of Heart's Desire, to his good-as-orphaned sister.

And then, after weeks of silence, weeks Ida spends in a panic of worry and secret preparations to go to Katie's rescue, a note, saying only this: "Chummie blown to bits in France."

In a small, oddly charming villa that overlooks the sea near Bandol in southern France, Jack and Katherine are mending whatever love remains between them. Chummie's death, or rather Katherine's grief at her brother's death, has knocked it to pieces. Excessive, morbid grief, Jack thinks; self-aggrandizing, some of Katherine's circle believe. But the grief has been as disabling, as difficult to dislodge, as a sliver in an eye.

The eye and the love recover, thanks to the idyll offered by the Villa Pauline. Katherine delights in its pink walls and blue-grey shutters, the almond tree brushing against the window, the stone verandah with the round table she can work at all day—happily, the villa faces south. It is private, lovely, and equipped with such luxuries as electric light and indoor plumbing. The sea below them, the sky above, remind Katherine of the childhood she has begun to fish up from memory, that has started to shape itself into words, as well as images.

While the Murrys live their agreeably spartan life in the Villa Pauline, rising at six to do the morning's shopping, working at opposite sides of the verandah table, breaking for lunches of dates and bread and honey, the French are engaged in the immense, useless slaughter that is the Battle of Verdun. Of the millions upon millions of shells fired, the clouds of phosgene gas released, the almost million men, French and German, killed, wounded, or missing at Verdun, not a word is written in this secret and untroubled place. The ghosts and graves of the dead have been locked out, and as for the soon-to-die, they make only occasional intrusions into the charmed life at the Villa Pauline. Thus Frederick Goodyear sends letters from England, declaring himself bored to death working for the Royal Meteorological Survey, pleading with Katherine to answer his letters on the subjects of whores and hedgehogs. Katherine's responses are amusing, teasing, and utterly secretive about her present state of bliss.

For the Murrys' time at Bandol will be the happiest of their life together. The beauty of the Mediterranean, its flowering grasses and herbs, the silkiness of sea and sky, become a bank draft to be drawn on with no questions asked by any Paternal Provider or his delegates. At night, at the dining-room table, Jack works on a study of Dostoevsky while Katherine writes fiction in a fury of joy. She is fashioning something out of the shock of what she's lost, something that gathers up in its arms the people and places she comes from, the belated love that translates them from memory into being—here, now, in the ink scratched over each page. The warm, ample body of the grandmother who cares for them all; the lovely, capricious mother who never holds or nurses her children, who is always off exploring some imaginary elsewhere, even when sitting beside them; the burly businessman-father, as nervous as he is brash in the ways he performs his power over them all. And the odd, observant child, the difficult middle daughter who sees and feels and thinks in ways that punch holes through the prosperous, tidy household, its illusions of permanence and safety. The child of her pen, Kezia, Katherine's guide down to the roots of her painfully split self.

When Jack looks up from his work, when his gaze returns from St. Petersburg or Moscow and becomes the eyes that register a small dark head bending over a sheet of paper, he sees for the first time the naked face of the woman he's lived with all these years. This Katherine, writing in a way that takes the full measure of her heart, is a Katherine unmasked, freed of her heavy jewellery of secrets.

Jack and Katherine are packing up at the Villa Pauline: they've received a summons from the Lawrences in Cornwall, a summons Katherine bitterly resents but that Jack is determined to obey. As she shoves scarves and dresses into a trunk, he repeats all the reasons why they must rush back to England: Lawrence is impoverished, isolated, under suspicion by the Authorities who think his German wife is a spy signalling to submarines off the Cornish coast. Lawrence and Frieda are their dearest friends—they need support, they need a show of solidarity.

For answer, Katherine takes the chiffon scarf in her hands and rips it in two. "What do *we* need, Jack? Let me remind you that since we started living together, we have moved fifteen—no, sixteen—times in four years. This makes seventeen. You know very well by now what Lawrence and Frieda are like. This Cornish idyll can't last more than six months, if that. Which means, since you've never been good at arithmetic, that we'll be on to move number *eighteen* before the year is out."

Jack makes no reply other than shrugging his shoulders and finding an excuse to leave the room.

When the cart comes to fetch the Murrys and their belongings to the station, Katherine keeps the driver waiting as she walks from room to room in the villa, touching, with her whole hand, the surfaces of tables, chairs, lamps that have become as dear to her, in this short time, as family. When Jack calls for her, she marches past him without a word, as if he were less valuable, less memorable, than a table, chair, or lamp.

There are no furnishings at all in the place where we find Katherine next. She is sitting on the floor of a bare, damp, cold room at the top of the cottage the Lawrences have found for them, a stone's throw from their own. She is wearing a Russian blouse and skirt sent her by Kotelian-sky, an emigré writer friend in London. The book in her hands is the *Oxford Book of English Verse*, but the page she has turned to is the fly-leaf, with its affectionate inscription from Frederick Goodyear. A notebook lies beside her; a pen has rolled several feet away, across the dusty floor-boards. Jack comes running up the stairs with a bouquet of wildflowers he's picked for her. She takes them in her hand, puts them halfway to her face, then drops them onto the floor.

"Why flowers? Why not be honest and give me a pocketful of stones?" she asks. "Stones are what Cornwall produces best—at least for me. Five months, Jack, five *months* in this wretched place and I haven't written a line—a word worth keeping. Everything I've tried is either pretty-pretty or so savage I might as well be writing with a carving knife. Maybe I'm catching a case of the horrors from Lawrence. Or of melancholy from big, fat Frieda. I can't bear her any more. Except that I feel sorry for her about the children. And she presumes on it, she keeps reminding me of how I used to help her back in London, visiting the children for her, taking them her letters. And then she'll sit weeping all day for her lost babies till Lawrence is ready to strangle her with a tea towel."

Jack is about to respond when a horrendous noise bursts out—the sounds of a woman screeching at the top of her lungs and a man's mad roaring. Jack rushes down the stairs with Katherine trailing after him, across a patch of rough grass, past an outdoor privy, to the Lawrences' cottage. The door has been thrown open, as if to make it easier for the world to hear and see the following spectacle: a large, fair, plump woman throwing a cast-iron skillet across the room at a small, dark, dangerously thin man clutching a hank of blond hair in his fist. The skillet misses its mark, but as it clangs into the wall, Lawrence lunges towards Frieda, shouting, "I'll cut your bloody throat, you bitch!" Jack leaps in to separate the two. Katherine runs to the dresser, where the knives are kept. She bundles them up in her skirt and races to the privy into which she hurls the lot of them.

The next we see of Katherine, she is, once again, packing. Murry appears, his hands in his pockets, a sheepish expression on his face. "It's over," he announces. "Frieda's eating chocolates and reading a novel in bed. Lawrence is trimming a hat for her—he's actually sewing on roses. The ridiculous thing is that it started over Shelley. The 'Ode to a Skylark,' no less. Frieda apparently dismissed it as schoolboy prattle, and Lawrence called her a bloody fool, which led Frieda to accuse him of playing God-Almighty. Of course Lawrence blazed up—just blazed up like a chimney fire."

Katherine doesn't even look at Jack. "You can stay if you like and keep putting out fires, but I'm walking to town and getting on the first train to London. I'll write with an address where you can send my trunk."

Murry watches her for a long moment, his hands still in his pockets, then sighs and goes over to the dresser, pulling out his socks and jerseys and piling them on the bed, to be packed.

In the moonlit gardens of Garsington, the country estate where so many artists and intellectuals have found shelter from the war, Katherine is walking up and down, breathing in the scent of nicotiana and fanning herself with a transparent fan as black as the sky above her. It's the same small muslin fan she will keep on a night table six years later with volumes of Chaucer and Shakespeare and an automatic pistol—her whole little world, she will confide in a letter to

Ottoline Morrell. It's Ottoline who owns Garsington Manor, along with her politician husband, Philip, who is as eclipsed by his wife as Jack Murry is by his.

From the manor's stone terrace, Ottoline strides towards her wayward guest. Magnificently, theatrically dressed, with an enormous head of mahogany-coloured hair, Lady Ottoline is a woman you could describe as either glorious or hideous, with her huge, staring eyes, prodigious nose, and out-thrust jaw that seems to drag her whole body in its wake. To Katherine, she is as splendid as any of the peacocks that roam her estate and that sometimes end up on her dinner table, rather the worse for wear. And like a peacock, she is alarming to have at close quarters. Katherine, whose social credentials have been diminished by penury and her colonial origins, braces herself when she sees her hostess coming. The disproportion in their incomes is as glaring as that in their height: Ottoline, nearly six feet tall, has, in addition to her husband's salary, an allowance of fifteen hundred pounds a year to spend as she pleases; Katherine, all of five-foot four, is making do with her original hundred pounds a year, topped up by her father via the eternal Mr. Kay.

Clasping Katherine's arm in her own, drawing her close, and addressing her in low tones that can't be described as anything but thrilling, Ottoline begins her barrage. Katherine, she says, is the only one of all her guests with any feeling for the loveliness of Garsington, its poetry. "You are, you know," Ottoline purrs. "Every shade, every shadow and glint in this garden—you've noted it down to be used in one of your stories. You can't deny it. Ah, and people, too—don't think I'm unaware of how you study us all. Artists, as I know to my cost, are ruthless. One evening they are eating at one's table, drinking one's wine, laughing with tears in their eyes at the beauty, the pleasure—the sheer relief Garsington has given them in the middle of this ugly, stupid war. And the next day? There they are, laughing still, but this time there are no tears in their eyes. Oh, no, their eyes are dry and hard, and their pens are full of the most hateful lies about the people who've given them all this!" She waves to the flowers drowsing on their stalks, the vaguely sighing trees, the crooked moon overhead.

Ever so gently and slowly, Katherine disengages her arm. "Darling Ottoline," she croons. "You're right, of course— you see through us as if we were no thicker, in our disguises, than this." Between their faces, she flicks her muslin fan. Her voice becomes sombre. "We *are* ruthless, we're cruel and crude—we're as ungrateful as the bees are to the flowers they pollinate. It sickens me—even in all this enchantment you've made for us here, I'm sick to death of the world and every one of us making it sordid and corrupt. Turning all this beauty to ugliness, and worse. Under every perfect leaf, under every petal, there's a fat, hungry snail, devouring."

The women look at one another over the wall of the fan, then resume their walk, side by side.

Ottoline murmurs, "Yes, yes, I see—I see precisely what you mean."

Katherine begins to speak again, passionately, yet strangely aloof.

"Have you ever lived by the sea—really lived there, made it your home? I have. I grew up in a town on the sea, and what I've lost from that time, what I'm always looking for—it isn't Garsington Manor, it isn't all your marvellous guests with their adorable clothes and adoring eyes, sniggering at you behind your back. In fact, it's nothing more than a quality of light, something random, hovering here and there, so quick that you can never catch it. But oh, Ottoline, sometimes— never when you will it or expect it—that light appears, and it catches something dazzling and fine, something you never knew you wanted. And then it's gone. We called it Jack-on-the-wall back home, that light. Not deep, not a steady glow, but a brilliance making you feel alive, fully alive for just that moment you stand where it's shining."

Ottoline is enraptured: at last she is hearing the kind of speech artists hold amongst themselves. At last she is being let inside, welcomed into the tumbledown but gloriously select House of Imagination. But just as she's about to lean towards her guest and embrace her, Katherine sprints away, calling out, "I simply have to get to my room and cut my corns. Dear Ottoline, if you knew what an affliction my feet are these days!"

———

Ida comes off shift in an aeroplane factory at Putney, a guilty smile on her face. Because, in spite of how endless and murderous this war has become, it has given her the only possible excuse for abandoning her father to his failing Rhodesian farm, for living, for the first time in her life, on her own terms, in a community of women friends and fellow workers. Her hands are as capable as theirs on the machinery; her largeness, looseness, vagueness are contained, corrected, by the overalls she wears, the handkerchief she fastens round her head in place of the braids once wound so tightly there. To keep her head from falling off, she used to think, when she was exiled to Rhodesia; to keep it from cracking, missing Katie so.

Even though she doesn't see nearly as much of Katie as she'd hoped, it's enough to know they're in the same city, under the same Zeppelin-haunted skies. Sometimes they get together in the evenings; once, Ida called for Katie at a house in Richmond, the house of a publisher and his wife, who are going to print that long, happy story Katie began in Bandol.

The wife—she had an odd name that made Ida think of bears and tigers before she got it right, Mrs. Woolf—seemed alarmed at Ida's showing up on her doorstep to fetch her dinner guest; did not seem, Ida felt, to value Katie, the beauty of her in her jewel-coloured stockings, her gold-and-cream-striped silk, her sleek cap of hair.

Tonight Ida will have nothing to do with Richmond. She takes the Tube, the smelly, oddly silent, clattering Tube to Chelsea, where Katherine is renting a studio. She and Jack are living apart, despite the fact that a divorce is finally going through. George Bowden has come back from America with the intention of marrying a woman he met in San Francisco. His obvious happiness both relieves and disturbs her, Katie has confessed: she keeps comparing it with Jack's carelessness about Bandol, his having thrown away its joys and the work they accomplished there for the rude, black-rocked Cornish coast, where Lawrence and Frieda are still chasing each other round the kitchen, throwing skillets, yanking out each other's hair.

Ida can't quite believe they're real, the Lawrences, real as she and her fellow machinists are. It's a different kind of real, an ordinary-real that Katie needs and takes from her. Ida knows this: whatever she can give of herself to Katie she will, however little praise or gratitude she receives in return. It's enough to drink cocoa and eat biscuits together; to tell Katie all about the factory floor; to hear of Katie's visits with her sisters who've settled in England. She can't help but think of them as stepsisters—evil because of how comfortably they're rocked in the family's arms while Katie is seen as nothing but a black sheep, a black eye. Katie, who doesn't have a spare sixpence to spend on an egg timer.

The studio in Chelsea is dark. When Ida lets herself in, she discovers that the kettle hasn't been boiled since breakfast, if then. Alarmed, she calls out for Katie, who doesn't answer, but lies on her bed, slack, unseeing. Her face is flushed, and as she coughs she makes a sound like a spade scraping against stone. Ida lights a lamp, bathes Katherine's face, forces her to take a sip of water. And though Katherine begs her not to leave, Ida rushes out to fetch a doctor. He's a kind man with an exhausted face; he notices how threadbare the studio is and refuses to take any money for the visit. Perhaps this charity stems from his diagnosis. There's a suspicious sound in the lady's left lung; she's at risk of becoming dangerously ill, he warns. She must scrape up every penny she can find and, war or no war, head south, where she can be healed in the sun and warmth of a Mediterranean winter.

A few days later, while Jack wrings his hands and Ida clumsily packs up Katie's things, dropping papers and tipping over medicine bottles, Katherine insists that she will travel to Bandol alone. She is not really ill, only threatened with a disease she'll outrun, outwit. She's not, after all, spitting blood—she's come through pleurisy before, and doctors always exaggerate. Besides, she's an experienced traveller, she's at home in French, and she won't hear of anyone uprooting himself for her sake. Jack has his war work here, and so, too, does Lesley; this illness is nobody's business but her own. When Ida interrupts, Katherine turns on her. Lesley's company will only make her worse—she won't be able to write or even read with her near.

Jack walks off to the kitchen, picks up a book lying on the table, and pretends to examine it. Is Katherine saying all this to let him off the hook, or to twist in the knife? Should he have rushed to Katherine when Ida first came with the news, bundled her in his arms, and carried her off to the boat train? But he has no money, no freedom, no assurance that Katherine wants him in her life right now. And what if she's not really ill, as ill as the doctor says? All doctors exaggerate.

The French trains are icy, chaotic, filled with rowdy soldiers; when they stop, erratically, at stations along the route, furious crowds surge against the carriages, in one of which Katherine has been lucky enough to squeeze, along with a dozen Serbian officers. When she finally arrives at the hotel in Bandol, she collapses into bed, feverish, coughing, crippled with her now habitual rheumatism. The hotel is run by a skeleton staff; there is barely enough wood to make fires in the few inhabited rooms. But Katherine possesses a desperate courage—or perhaps it's the same power of will that enabled her delicate mother with her delicate heart to travel thousands of miles to blot out, at top speed, an impossibly scandalous daughter.

Several weeks of bed and broth loosen Katherine's cough and quell her fever. So that waking one calm, bright morning, after a week of storms, feeling stripes of sun on her face from the slatted shutters, she feels well enough to jump up and fling open the window that looks onto the sea.

It's not enough to jump, to run, to lean out into the clean day's light; she starts to recite Shakespeare's sonnet, "Lo, how the lark at break of day," projecting her voice the way she did years ago, earning pin money at Mayfair parties. It's with the jubilant bread of these words in her mouth that she starts coughing and coughing, her whole body shuddering as she staggers to the washstand and, into the chipped white basin, spits a bead of blood.

Ida had arrived a few days before, enraging Katherine—*I am not an invalid!*—until that first spurt of blood into the sink. Now Ida helps her to pack for their return to England and English doctors—clumsy, loving, indispensable Ida. And, just as in the Beauchamp Lodge days, Ida helps Katie put on a party dress to perform in. For Katherine must convince the local doctor that her unscheduled return to England is a matter of necessity. It's not enough to be gravely ill—she must be seductive, too, playing the sly and odious doctor for all she's worth, flirting, winking, letting him lay his oily head against her breasts as he professes to listen to her heartbeat. Finally, he signs the chit that will permit her to board a train heading north. After he leaves the room, Katherine literally tears off her dress. "If I weren't ill already, I'd be sick from his touching me." Ida picks up the dress, looking regretfully at the fine embroidery across the bodice, the costliness of the fabric, before she drops it into a wastepaper basket.

In Paris, they are forced to stop over, first for a few days, then for weeks, while the authorities make difficulties about their papers. Bombs are falling on the city; in its springtime streets Katherine sees no one but lipsticked mourners with violently made-up eyes. Desperate to get back to England for her long-delayed wedding to Murry, growing sicker every day, she gets through the time by minding the chambermaid's two-year-old son. To distract him from missing his mother, she gives him the last of her last bar of chocolate; she holds him up to the mirror and watches him feed a taste of chocolate to the child reflected in the glass.

That one moment makes the war stop. It erases the shameful episode with the French doctor in Bandol, rescues the marriage that is to redeem all the miseries, all the mistakes she has made in her thirty years on earth. Watching the child share a sliver of chocolate, even with his own reflection, gives her a moment's grace, a moment's reprieve: no more. Enough—yes, everything.

━━━━━

At a photographer's studio off the Marloes Road in Kensington, wedding photographs are being taken. But there is no wedding party, and no discernible bride and groom, just a grim-looking young man with a receding hairline and a hollow-eyed young woman, skeleton-thin. The pictures take longer to stage than usual; several times the woman has interrupted the pose with fits of coughing, during which the man has winced, or surreptitiously wiped his lips and turned his head away. There is no shot of husband and wife kissing or even embracing one another, just the man's arm sloping behind his wife's back at a tense angle. Their eyes are enormous and their lips clamped shut. What is there to say? Legally, respectably, they are finally man and wife; healthy man, dying wife.

They should be leaving together on their honeymoon, but Jack stays in London while Katherine, clutching the thermos of hot tea he's given her as a going-away gift, takes the train to Cornwall. At the station in Plymouth an American friend from her Paris days is there to greet her, Anne Estelle Rice, now Drey, married to a well-to-do London solicitor. Anne of the bronzed skin and periwinkle blue eyes settles her into the Headland Hotel on the west edge of the town of Looe. The hotel is built on a cliff overlooking the sea. Anne takes her friend for excursions among foxgloves and poppies, posing her *à la* Monet, holding a Japanese parasol against the turquoise sea, her body so frail a breeze could carry her off, like the ghost-seeds of a dandelion.

When she is up to walking, physically able to walk, Katherine goes down to the surgery to be weighed, to make sure that all the cream and sugar buns are having some effect. There is a young Irish doctor there whom she likes to tease. She goes to the circulating library, which owns a copy of her first book; she walks out on the beach, leaning against conveniently placed rocks to scribble in her notebook, though all she'll take back with her from Looe are four scanty poems on butterflies and bathers. Most of all, she walks to the post office with letters, endless letters, complaining, enchanting, scalding, morose, to Jack, hunched over German documents at the War Office, ruining his eyes and turning his brains, he says, to turnip.

And when she isn't well enough to walk? When what she calls "rheumatiz of the spine" keeps her a prisoner of her bed, unable to wash her face, change her nightdress, unless helped by an elderly chambermaid blessed with the name of Mrs. Honey? Once out of bed, Mrs. Murry reads Dorothy Wordsworth's *Journals* while smoking "grenades," strong Spanish cigarettes that Ida sends down from London. She sits on her balcony overlooking the green-and-violet sea, under a parasol coloured red and the intense pink of campion flowers. And, like J. Alfred Prufrock, she poses what she calls her "Eternal Question": why it is that with all the stories she has in her head, the images, the ideas, the very words ready to pour themselves onto the page, she cannot bring herself to sit down and write? Though now, more than ever, she perceives the richness, the poignancy of all the life around her, the gate in her head is swollen shut. What makes it a hundred times worse is the pressure of memory, the flurry of detailed impressions filling her mind. The puffed-up purple hands of the lecturer on Bible History at Queen's College—she can see them inches away from her, as well as the images they inspire: an invalid wife atop a donkey in a basket chair; daughters in sand shoes, smelling of mosquito repellent. But she hasn't the energy, the will, to do anything with these images, to try to see through them to their heart.

Instead of sitting down to write, she sits for her portrait to Anne, who brings the blue-green sea into her sitter's face and throat and hands, the meaty red of that parasol into her dress. The Katherine that Anne paints has the face of a wooden doll; her hands are putty-coloured sticks, holding a small orange box containing the cigarettes to which she's addicted. There is no portrait of that girl with burning eyes, sitting staring at the carpet of the room in which her lungs have locked her, staring through all the hours of late night and early morning at a carpet patterned with the fact of her dying. If she is still a girl: that summer in Looe, she has turned thirty.

ROGER

When the Tourist Office opened, which it did between 2:00 and 4:00 p.m., I purchased the *Looe Trail Walkabout*, which kindly informs all visitors that they've missed the town's heyday (during the Hundred Years War) and decline (when its silted harbour collapsed as a naval supply base) by some six hundred years. Looe had the distinction of being one of Cornwall's rotten boroughs, the ten eligible voters dutifully returning four representatives to every session of Parliament. After it lost the pilchard market, Looe recovered through exporting granite from the Cheesewring Quarry. If the guidebook had an index, "Cheesewring" would get honourable mention, but not you, Katherine. At my lodgings, I could have given my name as Mansfield, Karl, and no one would have batted an eye. But then, the owners of the Banjo Pier Hotel are not the literary kind, judging from the lack of books, or even shelves for books, in their establishment.

Once more, through this sad pilgrimage, no trace of you. In Runcton and Rottingdean, in all the London streets in which you lodged, from which you flitted, nothing but blind signs and whispers too faint to hear. Yet I have booked myself into the Banjo Pier, I have tracked down the Tourist Office and even purchased the guidebook to Looe in spite of its grave omissions. For it mentions, at the very back of town, a footpath winding to the top of Mount Ararat. Given the constant, blinding rain that's been falling since the hour I arrived, this is worth knowing.

———

Dodging puddles into town I pass karaoke bars, tattoo studios, Tom Sawyer's Tavern with a Mississippi steamboat winking in neon—even in the narrow streets of East Looe, Thai food and Tex-Mex restaurants compete with ploughman's lunch or fish and chips. When you were here, the fare was just as questionable, though in a different way. Another six months of war to get through; Londoners licking their ration books, while you drowned in fish cutlets and mutton chops, porridge and grilled mackerel, gooseberry and wintercrack jam, not to mention that bane of the bacilli, cream, a whole Sargasso Sea of it. Cornish cream teas brought up to you on trays by pink-cheeked, one-toothed Mrs. Honey, who would have been born about the time Victoria married Albert.

It was the Victorians who discovered Looe as a holiday spot, shortly after the Liskeard-to-Looe railway opened to passenger traffic in 1871. The local council must be trying to appease their stilted spirits, judging by all the "No Rowdyism" signs in the car park. Even the toy poodles in their plastic coats are under surveillance: "Bag It & Bin It" signs are everywhere, red Xs through iconic steaming turds. Seagulls are another favourite target, although their droppings cannot be disposed of in so orderly a fashion. I have lost count of how many posters I have seen of prison bars with bald heads and yellow beaks pushing through: *Public Enemy Number One*. You had very little to say on the subject of gulls, though you teased your husband with accounts of a ferryman "especially handsome and fine" who did not look "in the least mutilated though he has only one eye, & only one good arm, thumbless." You said you would be very much in love with that ferryman if you had any love to spare.

Edgar Rice Burroughs spent his summers here, courtesy of *Tarzan*, I suppose. Nothing less like Lord Greystoke than these holidaymakers in plimsolls and wellies, crooning to their dogs or grandchildren, the pushchairs plasticked over, as if there were chocolates or roses instead of babies inside. Fattish older women in pastel jogging suits; lean, leathery geezers like me in anoraks and polyester pants. When you were here, the tourists sported fake panama hats, heavy ankle-length skirts, and inelastic trousers. From your balcony you listened to newlyweds walking on the sands below, discussing the constipating powers of tinned meat. Now, inside the local Burger King, they are eating their saturated fats with a defensively jolly air. But it was no mere intolerance of vulgarity that set you railing against sweet nothings on the subject of corned beef. Judging from your letters, Katherine, you would have been over the moon to have had your own bridegroom at your side. Reading between the lines of those letters, you were grievously disappointed with him when he did, at last, come down on holiday instead of honeymoon.

You lived with Jack Murry for years before you married him; you left him many times for other lovers, or simply for a room of your own. He failed you in every possible way; you seemed to go out of your way for him to fail you, expecting ardour, joy, courage from a man who reminded you, you said, of a mole hung out to dry. When you claimed to keep an

iron shutter over your heart, were you thinking of his mani-
fold deficiencies, or of those times when he had seemed to
you the most desirable of lovers? A year before you came to
Looe, you recalled how, one night, he had stood, undressed,
talking by your bed. You were overwhelmed, not by passion,
but by tenderness for his youth, his beauty, his very nakedness. You wrote of all the things you loved about his body:
the warmth of his skin, the coldness of his ears, "cold like
shells are cold," his long legs and feet that you would clasp
with your own when you lay down together.

At the very end he left you utterly alone, he let the doctors
push him from the room in which you were dying. Six
months earlier, he'd let himself be pushed away to a moun-
taintop while you were marooned with Ida in the flatland of
your Swiss hotel. On your way to yet another hopeless cure,
you'd sent a letter to him at his snowbound chalet: in it you
wrote that no two lovers could have walked the earth more
joyously together. Imaginative to the point of untruth,
Katherine? Or to the point of transformation?

*Bogey darling, King of the Turnip Heads, Dearest of All, My
own Darling Heart.*

———

A back lane leads from my hotel in suburban West Looe,
down a steep hill, past the Jolly Sailor pub, and into the
mediaeval eastern part of town. Back in 1918, Looe's pretty
little lanes were clogged, you complained, with turds more
human than canine. You kept hearing housewives shriek at
their children, threatening to beat them with a rope's end.
There are no housewives now, or dogs, as far as I can see, just
tastefully renovated cottages, roofed with slate. It's a stone
that comes into its own in pouring rain, its green and orange
lichen glowing phosphorescent.

Most walls in this part of Cornwall are whitewashed; some of them have ribs like an old-fashioned washboard. "No signs of skeletonism yet," you confessed to your mother, long before you learned words like *sputum* or *sanitorium*. In Looe you were "naught but a frame" according to old Mrs. Honey, who fussed over you as if you were a cross between a china doll and a pet canary. The only Honey I have been able to track down here is a woman who, when a schoolgirl, supposedly stabbed the boy sitting next to her with a broken milk bottle. That boy now owns the town's one secondhand bookstore, where I at last unearthed a trace of Looe's most illustrious guest, *pace* the creator of *Tarzan*. It's the copy of your *Collected Stories* sporting a purple cover and that ghastly early photograph of you—or is it only the hair that seems so awful, as if you'd rasped it off with a file? You would still have been a dumpy girl when that picture was taken—"portly" was how you described yourself to your mother. The volume of your stories was mildewed; the bookseller had to search for it in a back room, where he keeps the unsellables. He tried hard to answer my questions about the Headland Hotel. Burnt down, he told me; burnt down years ago, when he was a boy.

I bought that book with its ugly purple cover. I also bought a volume of Tolstoy, because it contained your favourite among his stories, "Family Happiness." Why did you love it so, Katherine? While you lived under your parents' rigid roof, you summed up family life in one fierce word: "damnable." Once you'd lost it forever, family was almost all you dreamed of. Is that why you favoured Tolstoy's heroine, who, after abandoning husband and children, does not die of shame, despair, or disease, mentionable or unmentionable? Who lives to become a loving wife, a mother in more than name and body? Your mother never did. She endured you inside her for nine months, then tossed you into her own mother's arms. She refused to hold any of her babies, to feed them from her breasts, to play with them in house or garden. And yet, it appears that her children, once grown up, adored her. You wrote that you worshipped her spirit, her courage, her love of life; the news of her death, far too soon, far too far away from you, was a blow second only to the death of your brother.

My son knows almost nothing of his mother, except for the story I've made up for him, and the bits and pieces he learned from Estelle. Officious, interfering Estelle, who was generous enough—let me set this down—not to let her honesty get the better of her. For she never told my son the one thing that would have made it impossible for him to have loved me as he once did. He must know, of course; he must at least have guessed. And yet it's the one thing he's never thrown in my face when he has all too rightly found fault with me. But then, he's been incurious, or cautious, from the very start. Born premature, he spent the first two months of his life in hospital. He was one of those babies who can't decide, when they slide into this world, whether or not they want to stay. He had trouble breathing; trouble, too, keeping his heart beating. He had to be kept in an incubator, fed his mother's milk through a dropper. He had to be crooned and whispered to, his minute body fitting into one of my gloved and antiseptic hands.

You believed that having a child to hold in your arms, to kiss and dance into laughter, would protect you from your deepest griefs and bitterness. Had my wife been able to nurse her son, hold him, sleep with him in her arms, might she have been saved from that bitterness of grief? By the time it was safe for her to hold and kiss and dance her baby in her lap, she had lost all desire to do so, she had already started on a journey where no one could follow her, that journey you once described as a train disappearing into a tunnel that never ends.

My wife's inability to love her child was a great sorrow to me. But I would be a liar if I did not say that it was also part of a miracle of luck. It gave me the chance, you see, to turn this scrap of flesh in an incubator, this perfect, perfect stranger, into my son. And though I had nothing to do with giving him life, I helped, in this after-the-fact way, to bring him into the world and keep him there, giving him love just as the respirator gave him oxygen. When he came home, it was I who fed him his bottle, who bathed him and comforted him when he woke in the middle of the night. I, who had never in my whole life trusted my body to dance, danced with my son up and down the room that overlooks the harbour, holding him up to the window to see the stars, the moon, the lights dreaming in the water.

I thought I was doing all that I could to help his mother love him as much as I did. What I have come to understand is that I stole from her the one thing that might have turned her away from the man who'd betrayed her and towards the gift he'd given her. I have consoled myself by thinking that, had I not taken her son from her as I did, she might have taken him with her when she went down to the shore that afternoon, walking, without any warning, straight into the hurtling traffic. Through all the shock and remorse that followed my wife's death, I had my son to hold in my arms, to protect me from the truth. In that respect, you were right to believe what you did. Except, except—oh, Katherine, how quickly our children outgrow our arms. What I hold onto now is the memory of the child who was my son, a shadow of happiness that was never careless or complete, but that still, I swear, was happiness.

———

In *The Looe Guide, 1923*, dug up for me by the obliging owner of the bookstore, I find an ad for the Headland Hotel, run by a Mr. and Mrs. Rock. The hotel boasts: *Sun-Lounge, Drawing Room, Smoking Room, Separate Dining Tables, Central Heating, and Running Water in all rooms.* As I have discovered, the building did not burn down in the 1960s; it was merged with its next-door neighbour, the Hannafore Point Hotel, and butchered in the process. Off went the slanting roof and the steep chimneys—on went another layer to the cake, full of double windows snarling on either side of pointed gables once half-timbered, now stuccoed a pale banana. In place of the latticed verandahs where you and Anne would have taken tea is the Indian Bar, with its logo of palm trees and a scarlet sun. These days, invalids convalescing there can take advantage of aerobics classes and Tropical Island nights. In this Land of Tradition the first law is that no one can ever leave Well Enough Alone.

But I am not being fair to Mr. and Mrs. Rock. The photo in the 1923 guidebook shows an Edwardian pile perched on the edge of a cliff. Between 1918 and 1986, someone has done major shoring-up and anti-erosion work. Where there used to be sheltered gardens or discreet parking places fronting the hotel, there is now a major road, the Hannafore, and at its edge, thick rounded hedges, then grass sloping to the sea. Where the grass ends, rocks begin, brutal-looking rocks even when loosely covered at high tide. There is also an observation platform from which one can look out at low tide to greyish-yellow ribs jutting through sand and assorted debris. You said that Cornwall reminded you of New Zealand. Through the Headland's fuchsia and roses, the pale yellow globes of ornamental ivy, and the rubbery gleam of the laurel hedge, you breathed into your rotting lungs the thick smell of home, the salt stink of sea.

Writers are supposed to be able to undo the past, redeem themselves, the way you, Katherine, altered the casual cruelty of your younger self, home from three years of London, postponing your visit to the grandmother who'd taken care of you as a child. Thinking you had all the time in the world to pay this duty call to an old housebound woman who, without a word of warning, vanished inside her stopped heart on New Year's Eve. The grandmother you draw with such love in your stories of childhood, and from whom the child Kezia tries to force a promise that she will never, never die. I am no such writer, I have no such powers—to raise the dead to life, to transform shows of kindness into acts of love. The most I've been able to do is to try to enter your life, become the one lover who did not betray, deceive, or abandon you.

———

Four days and it has not stopped raining. You who thrived in warmth and sun, in gardens splashed with "great spots of light like white wine," had wonderful weather here. I have had nothing but grey sky and muddy water on England's Riviera. Muddy at high tide, at least, where the river collides with the tidal rush. Out to sea the waves are slate: austere and thus beautiful. When, for a few moments, it fails to rain, when a weak sun manages to squint through, the sea gleams, azure and turquoise.

It must be a consolation prize for the sogginess of the Cornish coast, all this greenery on hedges and fences, rocks and roof tiles, on retaining walls and the sides of bridges. I asked the hotel-keeper the name of a small mauve flower with a bright yellow seed at its centre and intricate leaves, a flower that sprouts from the wall and feeds on grit blown up from the road. He could not say, he apologized—he came from the city. I did not ask which city. When I made the mistake of telling him why I had come to Cornwall all the way from New Zealand, he looked as if he wanted to commit me. He failed to understand, his wife told me later, why anyone would come to Looe on account of Jayne Mansfield.

. You would have relished that. You who could joke about having only one life, and no belief in immortality. What a delight it would be, you wrote, to reach the gates of Heaven and hear some grim old angel cry, " 'Consumptives to the right—up the airy mountain, past the flower fields and the bronia trees—sufferers from gravel, stone & fatty degeneration to the left, to the Eternal Restaurant smelling of Beef Eternal.' " You could not believe in an afterlife, but you could swing in the blink of an eye from crazy optimism to an equally insane despair. Thus you would fantasize, even as your snow white hanky turned to crimson lake, about The Heron, that house you longed for in the country. Gardens full of flowers, paddocks with cows and horses, rooms full of books, and the children you would have by Jack. And thus you would accuse yourself of being a fraudulent wife, miserable and old before your time, diseased and soiled and barren.

From the dining room the radio shrieks into the sunroom, where I sit writing my journal. The radio is never turned off; this morning, over poached eggs on leather passing for toast, I heard it going on about Measures Against Mildew; now it is telling me that a Conference on The Environment has gone down like a damp squib. A squib is an underpowered firework; squibbish is the adjective, if you care to use it. I wonder you failed to, in connection with your husband. All those letters you wrote him, one for every day of your Cornish convalescence, not counting telegrams. Letters urging him to bolt from the War Office and join you now, yesterday, at once. Letters imploring him not to despair at the grime of London, to be cheerful for your sake, since you cannot bear to think of him made miserable by your illness and absence. Letters written in venom, lashing out at him for being cheerful, for smiling at the flower woman from whom he bought roses while you are lying helpless here, in a hell of pain and loneliness.

You had a way of gesturing that people remarked on: you would hold a hand up in the air as if it were a cup, fingers and thumb together. Signifying what, Katherine? Your earliest writings are full of sick and dying children, of orphans and absent mothers, of premature death presented as fulfillment instead of robbery. A cracked cup, a beggar's bowl, that hand cupping the empty air? Fat people, someone has said, are those deprived of early love. Sugar becomes a substitute for maternal milk. Pining for a "sweet toothful" you wrote from Looe to the damp squib, urgently requesting half a pound of good chocolates, which you thought your sister might be able to provide, if he could not or would not.

You ought to have known better. He was never very good at meeting your expectations for letter-writing, never mind sending packages through the post—all that trouble with brown paper and string and printing unfamiliar addresses in block capitals. He was physically and mentally wanting, incapable of reading your heart or mind. That photograph of you he sent your publisher for the dust jacket of *Bliss* in 1921—it made you look like an ox, you cried, and you were not an ox but ill and starved, with bones like broken glass. If he hadn't the heart or stomach to see you as you really were, then so be it, but he was, at any cost, to retrieve that photo of the ox with beastly eyes and burn it. You might have asked him to send the publishers the photo you had taken in Switzerland, just before you left it forever. A postcard in sepia, a brownish ghost-print. In it you wear the face of a keeper of secrets, a shuffler of selves: the eyes alert but guarded, the mouth, by some trick of shadow, both open and shut. Shut up in those snowbound Swiss mountains, you inscribed it, "Dreaming of Paris and Anne."

Like you, Anne was another "permanent movable." Having convinced a Philadelphia department store to send her as a fashion correspondent to the Paris of Worth and Poiret, she paid the rent with columns on the latest in tailor-mades and the kimono sleeve all the rage in France during the Russo-Japanese war. She wrote for money but painted for love; she took a painter for her lover, a renegade Glaswegian named Fergusson. He painted a portrait of her called *The White Ruff*. No haemorrhage red here: Anne's face is the colour of cream-of-mushroom soup. Cream suit with leg-of-mutton sleeves stuffed into elbow-length cream gloves, and, just to make herself visible, a flowery scarf tied at her throat—pink and green and brown so dark it looks black.

When this portrait was finished and exhibited in a Paris salon, you, only nineteen, were languishing in Wellington playing your cello in the dark for Edie Bendall, drinking in the year-old scent of Maata Mahupuku's glove, scribbling soulful unsent letters to the red-headed boy you called Caesar. And all that time, Anne Estelle Rice—ten years your senior, an independent woman, a classic example of the American Girl Who Makes Good, not on an allowance from her father but on sheer nerve and talent—was waiting for you with an unbreachable self-assurance, a sound body and healthy mind that cut a swagger on the canvas. She could be your older sister in that white ruff, her dark brown hair cut in a fringe, her face giving nothing away, since for Anne there is nothing to hide, nothing in the world to keep secret.

All the time you were drinking tea together at the Headland Hotel, picnicking on strawberries at Polperro, or burning on the gridiron sands of a sheltered cove, Anne must have tormented you, having everything you lacked: having her health, practising her art, having her husband nearby, and certainly no worse a husband than yours. For Anne had traded in the champagne and oysters of Paris for marriage and maternity: she was pregnant, that summer in Looe, with the baby you'd become godmother to. Anne had it all— Anne had never been had. While you paid for every inch that you stepped over the line of the ladylike, the line your three sisters toed their whole lives long.

Perhaps it is not the purple-and-violet colour of the sea that Anne paints on your face; perhaps it is the sealed fury, the fuming despair you once described to Jack: "I simply go dark as though I were a sort of landscape & the sun did not send on beams to me—only immense dark rolling clouds that I am sure will never lift."

———

Wonder of wonders: the sun shines and my fellow tourists frisk on the rocks below. The sea looks like quilted silk, the wind raising slubs on its milky blue. A small stream of fishing boats is heading out along the pier to open water. Keeping them company, a sweep of garbaging gulls, fighting it out with cormorants like sawed-off shotguns that have sprouted wings.

Well after lunch and two cups of tea that I made with my miniature kettle, in my miniature teapot, I decided to take advantage of the weather after all and walk along the river to Kilminorth Woods. You and Anne drove through those woods to get from Plymouth to Looe, and on excursions ordered by that young Irish doctor, who thought the banks of bluebells and wild yellow iris would do you good. In the woods it was green as spring: oak trees, mainly, with tortured trunks, leaning over the water. On the hills across the river, though, I could see leaves the colour of a rusty knife. I sent a postcard of those hills to the neighbour looking in on my house, feeding the hedgehogs for me.

I took the footpath everyone else was tootling along—

perfectly pleasant people with perfectly behaved dogs, little ones, on those retractable leads that always seem to me crueller than the ordinary kind, giving the animals the illusion that they can run as far and freely as they want. Like that sickroom game you would play on sleepless nights, summoning up places you had lived, people you had known, reliving them in a state of near-hallucination. You had such precise, such sensuous recall that decades after the fact you could describe the exact combination of smells—Worcestershire sauce and mustard?—in your family's dining room on Tinakori Road. Indelible as blood or ink, your memory of everything you saw, felt, heard, touched, smelled. We become artists, you believed, through intensifying memory and then by exposing "the nerve of feeling," jumping into the bounding outline of things. When you wrote that story of an orphaned child crossing the water to her new home, you were not, you insisted, remembering an experience you had once undergone on just that sort of boat. You were not remembering that voyage until you possessed it, you said; you were becoming it until it possessed you.

Exposing the nerve of feeling, yes, but what of those times when what you felt was not delight but terror? Of the dark, of the absence, even the lessening of light. That summer evening, alone in your studio, the one with the enormous window looking into the garden, where you could see your white silk stockings drying on a "biblical" fig tree. You dropped the pot of coffee you were holding in your hands; you rushed out into the street, carrying a handbag, a block of writing paper, and a pen. You walked all night; you could not bear to be locked in with the dark, alone and comfortless. Or in Italy, shut up in an icy villa with Ida, half mad with fever, loneliness, and hate, you would lie awake while storms banged the shutters and the moon shone, corrosive as salt.

Over and over, you mourned the child you lost when you were only twenty, "the baby of Garnet's love."

Did you ever think it would have been far better to have married him, feckless, easygoing Garnet? Married him, borne his children, led an ordinary life in which you might have had some honest measure of happiness? Or was the most important thing, ever and always, your work? "Oh to be a <u>writer</u>, a real writer given up to it and to it alone!" Did you ever become that real writer, did you achieve anything real, anything true, anything you could show, as you said, to God? Your work, you confessed, was flawed, forced, shallow, scant—you were your own harshest critic.

Does it come back to the same question every time—art or life? Art that is no mask or distraction from truth but a door into what we can't help knowing? Is there no way of having both? Could you have had the happiness of being a loved wife, a loving mother, and still retained the power to wring our hearts? With that sadness you discovered at the core of life—not sorrow, which passes, but sadness, "deep down, deep down, part of one, like one's breathing." It's what has proved so painful for me in reading your work, your life; what's kept me from finishing the book which I'd meant to pay tribute to your life as something fine and true and lasting. You risked all, Katherine; you lost everything. And for what? A handful of stories. Little birds bred in cages, you called them. False alarms.

There are times when I think it monstrous that I should know so much about you; monstrous that anyone who picks up the volumes of your letters or notebooks, anyone who flips through the work of your biographers, can steal into your short, no-longer-secret life. Oh, there are pieces missing, whole years that we can only speculate on, but the fact remains: we know far, far more about you than we will ever know about ourselves. We groan, in our superior way, at the wee, twee side of you, the Katherine who fussed over cats and a large Japanese doll, that surrogate child or stand-in for your increasingly delinquent mate. But it's not just the warts and tarnish we discover; it's also everything that makes us fall headlong in love with your appetite for life, the enormity of your desire.

Those white gloves we pull on in order to handle a scrap of striped silk from a dress you once wore, a lock of your hair—those gloves are there to protect us, not you. To protect us from the life still folded in the silk, still coiled in that bright brown hair. What else can explain what your husband did, just after your death, fleeing to a cottage in the Sussex Downs?

Monstrous, that I should know this. That there should be a letter in the Turnbull Collection from one of your London neighbours, a Mrs. Prudence Maufe. It was she who lent the devastated widower, Jack Murry, the use of her Ditchling cottage; she who found, after his departure, that bright, burning lock of your hair. She wrote to Murry asking if he had left anything behind that she could send on to him. Nothing that he wanted, he replied. She waited for him to write back to her, she waited for years and years, and then, hearing her own death at her heels, she sent the lock of hair, with an explanatory note, to the Turnbull Library. So that people like me could don white gloves and, opening a fold of tissue paper, conjure you up under our greedy eyes and fingers.

Monstrous that paper and ink, hair and silk should survive while your flesh, my darling, is long, long dead.

———

In the oldest inn of East Looe, among assorted horse brasses and scores of blue-and-white china plates tacked up on a wall, I put away a meal of "beef eternal," tinned peas, and treacle roly-poly wrapped up in custard tasting of flannel. In spite of the toughness of that slice of beef, the overboiling of the greens, the gloop of the custard, I ate every scrap of that underpriced dinner by means of which the Golden Guinea is trying to woo away the patrons of Tex-Mex & Thai. You would have hated to see me—you would have lumped me together with the guzzlers in the dining room of the Headland Hotel, the "blowflies" ploughing into their puddings. And yet ten years before you'd had an appetite you would not sell, you swore, for a hundred pounds.

You would have hated to see me, but to tell the truth, I would not have cared a straw for your hate or love just then. For as I drank my coffee and signalled for the bill a trio came into the restaurant, taking the table next to mine. Older husband, young wife, and small dark-haired son. I could not take my eyes off them; I prayed for the waitress to take forever to bring me my bill, to take their order, so that I could listen for as long as possible to the talk at that table. Talk of the hike they might try tomorrow if only the sun would shine, of the fisherman who had offered to run them upriver on his boat. The boy kicking his feet against the table leg, the mother saying, "Don't," and the father drawing something on his napkin to amuse the boy, to charm his feet still.

I, sitting there in the Golden Guinea, would have given every story you ever wrote to be that man eating dinner with his wife and child. Every word of yours I have ever read that has taken such scenes and held them, shining and precise as crystal, up to the light, I would have blotted, then and there, in exchange for that moment of ordinary, unspecial happiness.

So, I am no different from your other lovers, after all.

———

I have learned a little about the aloneness of absence, of unfilled spaces beside me, in my bed, at my table. But in your illness you learned something more extreme—a line cut round your body, shutting you in. Locked in the sea of your lungs, in a desert of bone, your only compass was your pain— wherever it was, you found true north. Or else your body became a huge house left in your sole care; you sat locked up in the attic, listening to thieves rummaging through the rooms below. No tenants, no neighbours, no police to call. Until the thieves decided it was a comfortable place; they set up house in your left lung, in a gland of your neck, or used the delicate nerves threading your spine as bell ropes to summon the servants who fled long ago—the servant you have had to become.

I watch you lying awake in the night. I watch you stare at those three open windows in that vast and empty room at the Headland Hotel, curtains blowing in and out, like breath made visible. I listen to the tassels on the blinds ticking off the hours and minutes and seconds you have left to live. I know that you cannot turn in your bed without feeling that your joints are splintering; I know that for years, now, you have never lived more than an hour without pain.

The sea is shoving clumsily below, hissing and fuming; the gulls, for once, are mute. And for you, no light outside, no halogen lamps with their yellow glare, just darkness, the same darkness in which the body lies, under its mask of skin. Waiting for day to come, which only comes once dark has wrung you dry.

I want to comfort you in this dark, like that man in the train, the man of whom you spoke, once, to a friend. It was during the war, it was in France: the whole train was blacked out; the world had become one narrow, endless tunnel. Until a sailor entered your carriage. He sat down beside you and in the thick dark took your hand and held it, without a word.

He played with your hand, slipping your ring from one finger onto another. You never spoke to him, but kept your hand in his. Until the train drew up at the next station, where he left you in the dark again, alone, silent, unafraid.

MONTY

Chicago, September 1986

Just before noon, on a mild and sunny day a full week on from his arrival in Chicago, Monty typed out the last words of Miss Baby's edited *Vindication*. She didn't thank him when he gave it to her. She asked him to return the next day, by which time she'd have read it through properly, she said. At which time, too, he'd get his reward—just like in the fairy tales. And then she smiled. For the first time in all the hours he'd spent with her, Cassandra Baby smiled. Not that it changed her features to a fount of glee or gentleness, but, for a fraction of a second, Monty believed he saw in her face something like the quick of her, a self she kept fiercely hidden. That brief opening of her heart played out on her face, and for Monty it transformed her grudging words into a blessing.

"Go on, get out into the air—I won't call it fresh, but it's better than what you're breathing in here. Leave me be and come back tomorrow afternoon." She seemed to be reading his thoughts, for she shook her cane in the direction of the door. "I said go," she rasped. "Get out and let me get going."

Monty felt buoyant, light-headed; he wanted to celebrate, and there was only one person in all of Chicago who could help him do so. Edna had the day off. She was supposed to be packing for a canoe trip to Wisconsin with a couple of friends; they were leaving first thing the next morning. But it was such a gorgeous day, and she *had* promised to show him the city. It was so gorgeous, in fact—real Indian summer—that it would be crazy to spend it downtown. She could borrow a car, they could head off into the country.

Edna was in her element behind the wheel, speeding along the Lakeshore with a thousand other drivers. She took an exit leading out of the city into harvested fields and meadows full of black-and-brown cows with white clown faces. The flatness of it all was a shock to Monty; he kept looking for hills covered with yellow gorse, speckled with sheep and the odd hiker. He missed the sight of trees he'd grown up with, karakas and red-flowering ratas. Most of all, he missed the sea, the smell of it in the wind, miles inland. Even the vastness of Lake Michigan couldn't make up to him for the rough tang of salt water. But he gave no sign of this to Edna, wanting to seem to share her pleasure in the tame, level fields, the indistinguishable trees by the roadside.

When he asked Edna where they were headed, all she would say was "Home." Home turned out to be a town called Mundelein, named for the first cardinal of the Roman Catholic Church west of the Alleghenies. Did Monty know that Cardinal Mundelein was a member of the Royal Academy of Arcady? It was an honour awarded him for his defence of Pope Pius X's Condemnation of Modernism—or so the nuns had taught her. Her sister was a nun, in Madison; her parents were visiting her there right now, or they'd have had supper ready at the house. Was he okay with takeout? They could picnic by the lake, if he liked.

Monty said he'd be happy with bread and water, and he

meant it. Nothing could have pleased him more at that moment than to drive with Edna down the main street of Mundelein, past plazas and bowling alleys, the office of the resident psychic, and a dental office with a billboard saying "*Call 24-SMILE.*" The restaurant where they stopped was in the Mexican part of town, after Santa Maria del Popolo Church and Parochial Centre, the Manzana Verde Discoteca, and various Salons de Belleza. This was the part of Mundelein that she liked best, Edna said—this and the small lake where they were headed.

They left the car in the parking lot at the public part of Diamond Lake; Monty carried the plastic bags of takeout food and tins of beer down to the water. Around them the trees stretched out bare branches, like ribs of enormous fans with the silk starting to rip away. Still, there were picnic tables; at one of them a man was drawing—not the exploded milkweed at the verge of the lake, but Buddhist temples and Roman ruins from the pages of a travel magazine he'd propped up next to his sketchbook. It was too early to eat, but they spread out their dinner on the picnic table, over the lovers' hearts and initials scarred into the wood. It seemed to give them a claim to the table, even if they didn't touch the food congealing in its foil wrap and snowy Styrofoam.

They sat drinking beer and talking as they looked out over the water. Or at least Edna talked, and Monty gladly listened. She told him stories of her family: bog Irish, she declared, brought in to work on the canals. Bog Irish turned slum Irish, then respectable working class, and finally teachers, nurses, accountants. Except for her, the black sheep. She hadn't gone to college, though she'd had the grades. She'd broken her mother's heart—her mother was the teacher, a wonderful teacher, which was the rarest thing in the world, didn't he think so? Monty agreed, guiltily. It wasn't, Edna went on, that she didn't want to learn: she was always reading, in a mishmash kind of way, anything and everything she could get her hands on. It was just that college didn't seem to be the place to learn what she needed to know. When Monty said that he understood, Edna cried, "I knew you would. You're a writer—you understand everything." Monty smiled at her. He had to keep himself from reaching out and touching her hair, as if to catch from it some spark he could hold in his hands.

"What about your family? Do you have brothers and sisters? Are you close to your parents?" Edna asked.

"No," he said, far too quickly. "No on both counts."

Edna reached for his hand and squeezed it. The man with the sketchbook had disappeared without their noticing; they had the lake to themselves. It was chilly now that the sun was nearly down—it was time, Monty thought, to head back to the city. But Edna said no, she wanted to show him something first.

He followed her to a section of the chain-link fence that was lower than the others; she clambered over it and again he followed, taking the hand she offered as they walked along a path through a still-leafy grove. They stopped at the door of a cabin boarded up for the winter, its blind eyes looking onto the lake. It had been standing for some sixty years, Edna told him. A pair of spinsters, retired schoolteachers had built it— roof, walls, windows, doors; they'd done everything but chop down the trees and skin the logs. They'd spent a summer and autumn and winter there, till one of them had fallen sick, and they'd had to leave. They never came back. Someone from Libertyville owned the cabin now, somebody on Appletree or Cherryblossom Lane, who would probably tear it down and sell the land.

The front window was boarded up; Edna asked him to help her remove the sheet of plywood. It was fixed by a simple latch and came off easily enough. They peered through the glass, sniffing the scent of resin from the logs below. At first, Monty could see nothing, but then he made out a table and chair, a bed built into the wall, a wood-burning stove, odd bits of crockery. It should have been a melancholy place, but it wasn't. He told Edna this, and she nodded, gravely. "It's the place I love best in the world. If I ever needed to run away, this is where I'd come." They sat down together on the doorstep; Monty draped his jacket over her shoulders. Neither wanted to talk—they were happy just to watch the stars filling the darkening sky. To Monty, the constellations looked tipsy, stars clustered in all the wrong places, and yet perfectly right in their orbits. Slowly, he realized that he, too, felt perfectly right—that this just was what he'd experienced all those years ago at the little bay off Diamond Harbour. A clear, full suspension in the moment. No thought for the future; perfect freedom from the past.

Edna put her hands up to her head, twisting the coil of her hair, trying to tuck in the wiry strands. "It's a place where people have been happy," she said. "It doesn't matter for how long. It's a place where people have lived out their heart's desire." She turned her face to his; she lifted her finger and touched, delicately, the mole under his eye. "What's yours, Monty—what's your heart's desire?"

He pulled away, just a fraction of an inch, but enough that she let her hand drop. He was suddenly angry, not at her, but at how quickly he'd lost that moment of pure happiness, looking up at the stars. She waited for him to speak, but he couldn't trust himself to do so without sounding like a fool or a beggar. He could have told her what had suddenly come back to him, after years of forgetting: how as a child he would wake in the middle of the night in a dark so profound that he knew the world had fallen away, that he'd been left behind with nothing to touch or feel or see or smell, nothing to show him that he even existed. How he'd been unable to move, to

reach out his hand and turn on the lamp beside his bed—
because he had no hand; because there was no lamp. It was
only when he'd cried out, when his father had come stum-
bling from his own dreams into his room, switching on the
lamp, sitting down by his bed, that Monty had been able to
fall asleep again.

"We should go" was all he said. Edna was about to speak,
it seemed, but held back, slipping his jacket off her shoulders, handing it to him. He helped her board up the window,
and they walked in prickly silence back to the car. Monty
offered to drive, and she let him; they spoke only about
which turnoffs to take, and by the time they reached Edna's
street, she had fallen asleep, her hair loose over her shoulders, hair the absurd, gorgeous shade of marigolds.

He reached out and touched her hair then, gently, so as
not to wake her. He felt ashamed, both at the memory of his
night terrors and at his inability to speak of them to her. She
had given him this gift, taking him to the place she loved
most in the world, and when she'd asked him for something
in return, he'd refused her. He'd been refusing gifts all his
life, he'd boarded up his heart far more carefully than the
windows of that cabin. Why was he so afraid? *Perfect love
casteth out fear.* If what he'd felt for Edwige had been love,
then he didn't love Edna Maguire. Why, then, should he be
so afraid of showing her a little of who and what he really
was? In a week's time he'd be boarding a plane back to New
Zealand. Likely enough, they would never meet, even if she
did hike the islands, tip to toe. And yet he wanted to give her
something, something as much a part of him as she'd given
him of herself.

All this time, Monty had been tapping with his thumb on
the tiki hanging from his neck, Tui's gift to him or, at least, her
leavings. He was thinking, now, of how ironic a name his
mother's had been, the name of a noisy, spirited, nectar-eating

bird prone to picking fights with its treetop neighbours. He was thinking this and watching Edna as she frowned in her sleep, then opened her eyes. They were green flecked with gold—he'd never noticed the gold before.

"Sorry," she said. "Have you been sitting there waiting for me to wake up?"

"Not long," he answered. And then he pulled the tiki from around his neck. The stone was still warm from his skin. He put the little figure into her hands; she looked at it for a long time, tracing its sinuous lines with her finger.

"It's beautiful, Monty. What is it?"

"A charm for good luck," he said. "I want you to have it." She told him she couldn't take it, she put it back in his hand, but when he slipped the pendant round her neck she made no move to stop him.

"I want you to have it," he repeated. "It's called a tiki. It suits you—it matches your eyes." Embarrassed, he looked away. "You can give it back when you come to New Zealand."

"Then you'd better tell me where I can find you," Edna said. "Write and tell me all about the tiki. Tell me about yourself, Monty, write and tell me anything you like. Tell me a story."

"All right, then," he answered, giving her back the keys to the car. But after he walked her to her door, she didn't take the hand he offered. Instead, she reached up and kissed him on the mouth, a kiss like a spoonful of hot honey.

Monty noticed nothing but good omens on his way to Miss
Baby's the next afternoon. He felt confident, even light-
hearted, with the tiki gone from his neck and the print of
Edna's kiss still on his mouth. It was as if that kiss had given
him the best part of her to take away with him. He didn't
know what he was going to discover in Miss Baby's collection; it didn't really matter. Whatever it was, he knew he'd be
able to use it to his advantage. He'd be able to fly back to
Wellington and show his father that he'd made good, after
all. That he'd shaken free of Roger's shadow, and the shadows beyond it, of Tui and Edwige, of Falconbridge and the
University of London, of the ghost of Kim Lee, and every
sorry and mistaken thing that had ever touched him.

As usual, he called up over the intercom when he got to
Miss Baby's building. This time, however, there was no
answering buzz from an opening door. He rang again.
Silence. He looked at his watch, in case he'd come too late or
early, but this time he'd arrived at exactly the hour she'd
asked him for. Impatience turned to worry, even panic. She
had a weak heart; she might have had an attack; she might be
lying on the floor of her apartment, helpless or beyond help.
He buzzed the superintendent's bell again and again; finally,
a thin woman with magenta hair came to the door, holding
the lapels of her housedress together over her bony chest. She
stared at him out of the palest eyes he'd ever seen, while he
exclaimed: "I need to see Miss Baby. I'm afraid she may have
had an accident. She was expecting me—she doesn't
answer."

The woman simply shut the door again, on which he
started pounding, frantically. She returned a few moments
later with a large, thick manila envelope, which she shoved
into his hands.

"I take it you're Mr. Mills. She left this for you."

"Left?"

"*El-ee-eff-tee*, left. She's gone outta town for a spell. No, she didn't say where she was going. And no, I can't let you into her apartment, no matter what. And if you keep on bugging me, I'm gonna call the cops."

Inside the large envelope was a typescript, and a letter. In it Miss Baby announced her satisfaction with the work he'd done on her manuscript. He could type, she'd grant him that. The footnotes and sources looked to be in order; she figured the people at the Mansfield Trust would have nothing to complain about. She'd sent them the whole shebang. In exchange for his help, she'd typed up a little something to answer all those questions he kept asking her. A little *Recollections* of her own.

He stuffed the letter back into the envelope. And then he shook off the dust of Crilly Court, feeling the bleached gaze of the superintendent on his back as he walked away.

———

Monty spent the next hour trudging along the lake, staring at the sombre shapes of skyscrapers across the bay. More than once he was tempted to throw Miss Baby's unread reminiscences into the water, a reprise of his little ritual at Somes Island. He ended by stuffing the envelope into the inner pocket of his coat, where it lay like a packet of small explosives against his chest.

It was too cold to stay by the water—he made his way inland and mechanically boarded a bus heading into a part of Chicago that didn't appear in his glossy tourist book under the section *Ethnic Neighbourhoods*. When he'd warmed up sufficiently, he disembarked, walking through streets where almost all the shops except the MoneyMarts were boarded up. Once he saw a group of men in winter jackets sitting on chairs on the sidewalk, gathered round a TV connected to a long extension cord fitted through the mail slot of someone's front door. Edna had warned him how dangerous the city could be, but all he felt, taking in the larger misery around him, was shame at how small his own pain was. How small and useless and insistent.

He caught another bus that took him to Grant Park, and from there he followed the crowd as it moved along, letting his mind and heart go as numb as his ungloved hands. He stopped, at last, on West Wacker Drive, at number 333. The convex glass of the tower held a scramble of reflected lights—crimson, emerald, silver, gold. Looking at the Wacker's beautifully bent glass, he allowed himself to think of the equally bent mind of Cassandra Baby. Was it all a lie, then, the secret collection? Or if she did have important papers in her possession, where had she got them from? Dealers like the canny Misses Hamill and Barker, or family sources—people who'd peel off strips of their own skin and flog them to the highest bidder? Mansfield's sisters, for example, selling off family photos and letters, though they could hardly have needed the money. Spendthrift Murry, hawking the contents of his dead wife's vanity table. She must have writhed in her grave each time a stranger handled one of her letters or photographs, or even the inlaid boxes where she'd kept her cigarettes. Strangers searching for traces of her body—the prints of her fingers, the cells of her skin.

Strangers, Monty thought—and lovers, too. What else was his father? Where was his father right now, if not on the trail of a woman dead for over sixty years, but whom he couldn't bear to consign to the grave? And Cassandra Baby, obsessed with a man whose life had been utterly ordinary, except for its brief intersection with that of the same dead woman

Roger pursued? Secrets, puzzles, mysteries, or just the usual human failure to open the heart, to speak its depths? Staring at the blue-glass walls before him, he seemed to see an image of Cassandra Baby merge with that of his father, their tall, awkward bodies becoming one. They would be, he conjectured, the same age, more or less.

Monty felt his heart contract. For the first time, he understood that Roger wasn't just his father but a man verging on elderly, a man who, for all his refusal to set foot in graveyards, was as mortal as anyone else. At the thought of Roger stepping into the dark without any warning, disappearing with all his secrets clenched tight inside him, Monty shivered. He dug his fists into his pockets, fighting a mix of remorse and resentment. Whose fault was it that he knew almost nothing of his father—and even less of his mother? Whose fault but Roger's and Tui's? Whose fault but his own?

From force of habit he went to the Manuka for a meal, the first he'd eaten since breakfast. It was a mistake—the place seemed dark and miserable without Edna there. He sat not at his usual place, the counter, but at a table that gave him a full view of the carved screen he'd never properly seen before. Toying with his soup, he stared at it, realizing why it looked so familiar. It was telling a story from the book of Maori legends that Roger had given him long before he'd taught him to read. The story of the seventy children born all at once to Earth and Sky, and pressed in a mass between them. Until the strongest of the children, desperate for air, light, and an outline of his own, shoved up his legs and kicked so hard he forced the bodies of his parents wide apart.

Only when the Manuka closed did Monty return to his hotel, the unread typescript still in his pocket. Once locked into his room, he turned on the television, keeping his back to it, wanting only to drown out the grunts and laughter and shouts of his neighbours. No chase sequence or vodka ad would be loud enough, he knew, to shut out the sound of crashing in his head. Everything he'd accomplished in the past seven days, all of his hopes and expectations—he'd been robbed of them by a cranky old woman who'd manipulated him as easily as if he'd been a child. He couldn't get her face out of his mind, the smile she'd given him, which he'd been witless enough to take for a blessing. He couldn't sleep, he couldn't think, and the bottle of whisky he'd bought on the way home—whisky, not bourbon—wasn't helping in the slightest. He might as well, he thought, take his beating; he had all the time in the world to read her farewell, or whatever it was she'd saddled him with, thanks to the superintendent's help. Reaching for his coat, he drew from it the thick envelope and the thirteen closely typed pages stuffed inside.

MISS BABY

Rewards and Recollections

You'll want me to play by the rules, I suppose, so we'll start with where and when I was born. The city of Windsor, Ontario, Canada: 25 March, 1921. You'd never believe it, looking at me, but my mother, Delia Dunstan, was considered a beauty. There are those who called my father, Joseph Baby, "one of a kind," whatever that's supposed to mean. But before Delia and Joseph there were Delia's parents, George and Henrietta—who Joseph Baby's parents were, nobody cared to remember.

Henrietta's father owned a varnish works—most of the city's carriage and motorboat manufacturers relied on that varnish. George went down in local history as the handsomest man in Windsor, and a charmer, too, by all accounts. Henrietta had ice-blue eyes, a wasp waist, and the expression of a Pilgrim Father. George's father must have thought a woman like Henrietta would settle his son down, dampen those spirits that kept landing him in one kind of fix or another. You see, my grandfather had shown no interest in the family business. He'd gone all the way to Yale to learn to be a dilettante and dabbler, a connoisseur of good times and good-time girls. None of this stopped him from worshipping the superior mind and morals of Henrietta Crake.

My Aunt Cassandra was conceived on their wedding night, spent across the river in Detroit, in one of the grand hotels. She was born exactly nine months later back in Windsor, in a house built for the newlyweds by Henrietta's parents. While George and his bride were touring the stately homes of England on their honeymoon, an imitation stately house was being built for them on the outskirts of Windsor. It might have been a whole lot smaller than the English originals, but it was decked out with all the conveniences, not to mention every Ye Olde feature the architect could cram in. Carved gables, herringbone-patterned brick, twisting chimneys, slate roof tiles, wrought-iron gates, a full set of stables, and a greenhouse as well as a rose garden.

Cassandra's conception was about the only moment of erotic shock in the whole twelve years of Henrietta Dunstan's marriage. By the time she was brought to bed of her first-born, she'd sworn never to share that bed with her husband again. You see, by the later months of her pregnancy, Henrietta had discovered that, after reading aloud to her from *The Ladies' Mirror* and kissing that part of her forehead not covered with an icepack, George would change his dinner jacket for a set of corduroys and a cloth cap. He'd sneak out of the house and walk south ten blocks, where he'd pick up the excursion steamer for the ten-minute ride across the river. From there, he'd hop another ferry to Sugar Island and dance with the factory girls all through the hot summer nights. If he missed the last ferry home, all George had to do was wave a lantern at the foot of Woodward Avenue. He knew Paddy O'Brien would answer the signal with a lantern of his own from the Windsor side of the river. For a cool quarter (you could ride the ferries all day for a dime) Paddy would row across to bring the truant home. Infidelity or irresponsibility? I'll bet if George had fessed up to one or the other, Henrietta would have taken him back into her stern good graces, bed included. But all her handsome husband would admit to was a rush of high spirits he had no intention of shutting off. What was so wrong about making a joyful noise from time to time on Sugar Island?

Windsor sits on an enormous salt bed. That salt is something of a natural treasure: it ends up shaken on Canada's tables, licked by Canada's cattle, scattered on Canada's winter roads. My grandfather's family made his money in the salt works at Sandwich, west of Windsor. Wivelsfield Manor was a house built on salt, not the most stable of minerals. My grandmother must have come to believe that the diamonds on her fingers were really salt, crystals of all the tears she'd refused to shed after slamming the door on George and joy. For Henrietta was no Mariana in the Moated Grange. Instead of wringing her hands over the crash of her marriage, she jumped into a regulation short skirt and sailor hat and hopped onto what became her crutch and her salvation—the machine that made her a bona fide member of the Windsor Ladies' Bicycle Club.

Bicycles were all the rage in those days, even in an automobile town like Windsor. Clubhouses sprang up in well-to-do neighbourhoods—there'd be evening parades down Ouellette Avenue, with cyclists fixing lanterns to their handlebars and wobbling away like monster glow-worms. Cycling guides were runaway bestsellers, mines of information on legal speed limits (no more than eight miles per hour) and how many cyclists could ride abreast in a single lane. Some of the guides warned the ladies against riding off with men on wheels—there seemed to be something about this particular mode of locomotion that exposed women to dangers unknown by hikers, for instance, or birdwatchers. But my grandmother's passion for cycling couldn't be doused by warnings from guidebooks. It ended only when a collision with an automobile caused her to fly off her bicycle, over her handlebars, and into a corrugated iron shed.

No bones were broken, but there was a wrenching of the spine no doctor could put right. The city's best physician ordered complete bedrest, and my grandfather gladly shared with twelve-year-old Cassandra the job of keeping Henrietta company. You could see George pushing his wife in a wicker wheelchair among the orchids in the conservatory, or playing Kings in the Corner with her at a marble table in the rose garden. Somewhere I still have his pack of Bicycle Brand playing cards that were one of Windsor's chief manufactures at the time, along with automobiles, tin buttons, and toilet seats. But there was something more interesting than card-playing going on. Anyone in his right mind could see that Henrietta was coasting downhill, but there must have been a moment when George's passion matched his pity and Henrietta had a relapse into the hopefulness of her wedding night. For in January of 1905, my mother, Delia, took her first gulp of air just as my grandmother shuddered out her last.

If George Dunstan inherited a kingdom of salt, liquor was my father's chosen territory. He didn't work for the sons of teetotalling, churchgoing Hiram Walker but for a more liberal organization, the "Free French," who made a killing running rum across the Detroit River in the 1920s, thanks to Prohibition. You see, while Canadians joined the American ban on booze, they proved to be enterprising in ways you might not have expected. It might have been against the law to have a drink in Canada, but it stayed legal to export liquor from Canada to just about anywhere except the United States. Funny, though, how the most direct route from Windsor to St. Pierre and Miquelon out in the Gulf of St. Lawrence lay straight across the Detroit River.

The summer of 1920, when Joseph Baby met my mother, was the start of the boom. Within four years there'd be an average of one factory a week moving into Windsor; real estate prices went through the roof. There was a fellow my grandfather sometimes played cards with, Jim Cooper, a great, tall man who built his own stately home with the proceeds from the booze he siphoned to the States. They even said he ran a tunnel under the river to pump the whisky through. My Aunt Cassandra thought Cooper's Court was vulgar compared with Wivelsfield—a pipe organ and a marble-lined swimming pool could buy the envy of the town, she always said, but never its respect. Big Jim Cooper used to send truckloads of orphans and foundlings to summer camps and expensive boarding schools, but somebody Up There had it in for him. He was drowned when he fell off the *Deutschland* somewhere in the mid Atlantic. Fell or was pushed, my aunt would say.

While Windsor millionaires were sailing off to Europe, immigrants from that crowded, smelly continent were pouring into Canada, to places like Montreal and Toronto, Winnipeg, and even Windsor. One of them was a Prince Volkonsky. He claimed to be a member of the Russian Imperial family as well as the world's premier swordsman. That was before a fencing coach from a local YMCA creamed him in a single round.

Aunt Cassandra always claimed that Delia was just the kind of girl to fall for a Prince Volkonsky. And since he had some social graces, foreign or not, he'd have been a hundred times better a match for Delia, she'd sniff, than that real foreigner on the grounds of Wivelsfield Manor, that French-speaking snake in the grass, Joseph Baby.

Many years later, my stepfather, Augustus Griffiths, tried to interest me in what he called my French blood. He explained that the Babys were an ancient French-Canadian family, and he suggested that they might even have been around when the French adventurer Cadillac founded Windsor in 1701. In 1812, Babys were among the British troops who chased home the Detroiters who'd crossed the river to capture Windsor. It was the Windsorites who ended up capturing Detroit, which may explain why Americans are so hazy about that little skirmish called the War of 1812. Anyway, there was a Baby manning the barricades in 1838 after the Mackenzie-Papineau uprisings had broken out north of the border. The folks in Detroit, you see, were of the opinion that Windsor should be liberated from the British. The British Crown gave Monsieur Baby a fine reward for his loyalty—a gift of land hundreds of miles to the northeast of Windsor, in what polite people called Muddy York. That land is now Baby Point Drive in the city I grew up calling Toronto the Good.

Goodness was beside the point, as far as Delia Dunstan was concerned. The summer of 1920, when she was just fifteen, George sent her in Cassandra's care to a place grandly called a Preventorium, though it was nothing more than a hobby farm in Sandwich West Township, near a place called Petite Côte. Petite Côte's only claim to fame was radishes, the soil there being pure, fine sand. Those radishes, millions of them, ended up crossing the river, along with vats of contraband rum, to Detroit. My grandfather must have thought radishes were the cure for whatever was ailing his youngest daughter. Cassandra admitted to me that Delia was paler and thinner then than she might have been, but she swore it was all due to wilfulness. You see, Delia had decided she was sick of Wivelsfield, sick of the wholesome meals Cassandra ordered from the cook, sick of walking between the rosebeds for exercise. So sick that she shut herself up in her room and refused to eat unless Cassandra let her join a schoolfriend who'd invited her to spend the summer with her family on Long Island. Cassandra had always been her sister's keeper, trying to thwart every plan George made to spoil his youngest daughter rotten. Those plans were legion. The result? Irritation and exhaustion for Cassandra, and for Delia, a talent for deceit, a put-on innocence, or stupidity that fooled Cassandra when it mattered most.

Cassandra, as you've probably guessed, had a talent for seeing the darker side of life. She was aware of the sacrifice she was making for her sister's sake. She'd been making those sacrifices ever since Delia had been conceived, with Henrietta coaching her first-born for a full nine months: "Make sure this baby grows up right!" Cassandra was twenty-seven and single that summer of 1920; honouring her mother's trust, she'd been refusing suitors for a good ten years. The most persistent of these was a certain Horace T. Plint, but we don't have to bother with him for a while. My aunt couldn't have believed she'd meet any eligible men at a Preventorium. She must have been thinking it should have been her, not Delia, invited to that summer home on Long Island. Cassandra was convinced she was George's worthiest concern, his one authentic offspring. Oh, Delia was George's daughter all right—she had his violet eyes and coal-black hair, just as she had all her mother's steel-strong will. But in some ways she was the cuckoo in the Wivelsfield nest. Henrietta was the soul of rectitude. George might have had the moral fibre of an overripe banana, but he wouldn't have hurt a fly. While Delia—but I'll leave you to come to your own conclusions.

TB killed enough people in those days for George to get alarmed at Delia's wasting away. It was one of the few times George crossed his youngest in anything when he listened to Cassandra and shipped Delia off to the Preventorium in her older sister's care. And it didn't matter that soon after Delia started her "cure," she showed drastic signs of improvement. Though her colour came back, and her bounce, she was told she had to stay the course. In fact, while Delia bloomed into the picture of health, poor Cassandra was struck down by migraines she'd never known before that summer at Petite Côte. On those many afternoons when Cassandra kept to her room with a cold cloth on her head and a sick-bowl near her lap, Delia would set off for walks through the fields, taking along a basketful of sandwiches and a jug of lemonade. Her long afternoon walks turned into evening rambles; as often as not she didn't return till the moon had come out. Cassandra was uneasy at her sister's disappearances but trusted to the wholesomeness of country life. How could Delia come to any harm among the radishes?

It wasn't till mid September, at the end of their stay, that the hot and heavy weather finally broke and Cassandra came to her senses. She did so while watching her sister stow away her usual breakfast of kippers and porridge and eggs and buttered toast and jam, while their hostess made a friendly remark about how nicely young Miss Dunstan was filling out.

At the breakfast table, over a cup of weak tea, Cassandra worked out the closest she could come to a master plan. Though for the first time in the fourteen weeks they'd spent at the farm she felt spry enough, she lay out on the verandah after breakfast while Delia flipped through fashion magazines. She refused any lunch, while Delia wolfed down enough for three, and she retired to her room, where she waited at the window to watch Delia set off with her picnic supper. Delia—so brazen, or hardened, or happy that she never bothered to look up at her sister's window to see if she was going to be followed.

It wasn't hard for Cassandra to catch up, or to keep out of sight. Delia was a slow, dreamy walker who sang to herself— tunelessly, Cassandra said—while she ambled. The route Delia took was a crooked one, naturally, leading away from and then circling back to the road from the old fish hatchery to Turkey Creek. For a while she followed the river, a pretty enough path. But then she struck out to shore, where it was much harder for Cassandra to hide. She ended up crouching behind a dune, waiting for what seemed like forever, while Delia sat cross-legged by the water, drawing patterns with a stick in the sand. Until all of a sudden she looked up in the opposite direction from where Cassandra was hiding. Until they both looked up, and there he was.

My aunt had expected some rosy-cheeked farmboy, some fisherman's teenaged son to show himself as her sister's ruin, but this man was in his thirties. He was old enough for Cassandra herself, though she'd never admit to thinking so. He wore a fisherman's sweater and corduroy trousers, but he didn't look as though he belonged in a boat. He was tall and big and powerfully built, and his nose had been broken in more than one fight. He had black curly hair and five o'clock shadow. That thought kept running through Cassandra's head as she watched him lumber over to her smiling sister: *he didn't even bother to shave!*

Delia's skin was creamy and delicate; she bruised easily, and when she cut herself, the scars were slow to heal. But Cassandra didn't have to worry about her sister's skin when Joseph Baby bent down beside her. His fingers were as light as a thief's, lifting the hem of Delia's dress and reaching up, not to the place where her thighs joined, not to her breasts, but to her round little belly.

This was the moment Cassandra swept down. Baby looked up at her, but didn't move his hand. Delia acted as though there was no one else on that beach but her. She just kept staring out at the slow milky water going by.

Before she even asked his name, Cassandra stated her terms:

"You have made my sister pregnant. You will have to marry her. She is only fifteen. You could be put in jail for what you've done. That would be far worse than marrying her. My father is a wealthy man."

"Wealthy men have tight fists," observed Joseph Baby.

"My father will want only one thing: for Delia to be happy. The way things stand now, she can only stay happy if she marries you."

Joseph withdrew his hand from Delia's belly and lightly stroked her head. And Delia? She caught his hand, held it against her cheek, and for the first time she turned to face her sister. "Don't be cross, Cassie," she said. "How else do you think we all come into the world?"

My aunt told me that this was one of the most irresponsible things she'd ever heard her sister say—and she had no illusions about Delia's sense of duty.

The wedding was held in the parlour of the Preventorium, George Dunstan giving the bride away, avoiding the groom, but smiling helplessly at shameless Delia who looked—Cassandra admitted it—a vision. The newlyweds stepped into a boat at the end of the ceremony and scooted off to a Detroit hotel for their honeymoon—who knows, maybe the very one patronized so many years before by George and Henrietta. George didn't speak to Cassandra for most of the ride home to Windsor. His long-suffering daughter took this as a poor reward for the way she'd saved the day by pulling off a shotgun wedding. But that was another of Cassandra's habits—misreading motives. Just as they drove past the gatehouse and up into the drive at Wivelsfield, George smiled an old sheep's smile and almost stuttered out the words: "You'll find a house guest at the Manor, Cass. Her name is Miss Barnes. You can call her Jeanette."

Cassandra did not take one step inside the manor house, though she'd been pining for it all summer. She did not return Miss Barnes's greeting. To the big-eyed, fluffy-haired, nervous Jeanette, who was hardly older than Cassandra herself, she just said: "I don't shake hands with whores." Her suitcases were still in the trunk of the car—she asked the chauffeur to take her straight to the Plints' house on Niagara Street. Luckily for her, they were all at home, Horace and his parents and hare-lipped sister, Geraldine. Cassandra gave no explanation for her actions, which were, in this order 1) accepting Horace's longstanding offer of marriage, and 2) accepting the Plints' offer of hospitality until the wedding could be arranged, with as little delay as possible. Horace, meanwhile, would board at a hotel downtown. No explanations were necessary. The Plints' house wasn't all that much bigger than the gatehouse at Wivelsfield Manor, but it was across the road and down the street. The neighbours knew about Jeanette Barnes being at the manor house before the staff clued in.

And that's how Cassandra Dunstan, oldest child of George Dunstan, millionaire salt-shaker-of-the-nation, and his upstanding cyclist wife, Henrietta, became Mrs. Horace Plint. It explains how she came to live in a gloomy chocolate-brick box with Tudor touches that must have been a constant reminder of the Olde English mansion she'd given her heart to. And it also gives you some clue as to how I ended up, in the fifteenth year of my life, living with my widowed Aunt Cassandra in this same gloomy pile at Victoria and Giles.

Where did I spend the first fourteen years of an existence provoked by the collision of two people who should never have become my parents or anyone else's? To answer that question, I have to tell you what happened after my parents' honeymoon in Detroit. I'll begin with a confession. I have no memory of ever setting eyes on Joseph Baby, radish-grower par excellence, rum-runner extraordinaire. Though I'm told he did set eyes on me at least once, at a stage when you couldn't call me anyone at all. If you've put your money on my parents' marriage getting dissolved as quickly as it got arranged, like a pinch of salt in a pot of soup, then you've hit the jackpot. My aunt would never tell me why Delia came back to her father's house three weeks after her wedding day. Maybe Cassandra didn't know for sure. She was having nothing to do any more with who and what went on there.

George welcomed his darling daughter home like the Prodigal Father of All Time. And Delia? Why, she greeted Jeanette Barnes with open arms. This wasn't any case of birds of a feather. You see, George hadn't met Jeanette at any house of ill repute but on the ferry boat to Sugar Island. She'd been sitting up top, reading a book, riding back and forth until she'd finished as much of the story as her eyes could stand. And if he hadn't run into difficulties after the marriage of his youngest child, he might have made an honest woman of her. Though, as far as I can see, Jeanette was the only honest one among us.

It's thanks to Miss Barnes that I got what mothering I did. Delia was mostly absent for my first four years of life, and my Aunt Cassandra (I'd been named for her in an act of crass revenge or cunning) kept away, as I said, from the house where I was such a happy prisoner. But let's go back to that grandstand event, my birth, on March 25, 1921. The doctor called in to attend my mother was in fact with my grandfather, who was having a stroke, when I came spurting out like a watermelon seed into Jeanette's arms. My mother was still woozy from chloroform while Jeanette washed me, wrapped me in a heated towel, and took me downstairs to the library—not the usual place to bring a newborn, unless that newborn's father has been waiting there for the past ten hours.

Now, there was more to Jeanette than big brown eyes and breasts like fresh loaves of bread. She had an incurably good heart, too. She'd got my father to promise he'd wait quietly in the library until, as she put it, there was something to see. More important, she'd made him promise to leave the house as soon as he'd seen this something. But she gave him the chance to hold me in his huge hands for the first and last time before disappearing for parts unknown, at least, to anyone but Jeanette.

As a rule, sixteen-year-old schoolgirls—for that's what Delia was at the time of my birth—couldn't give a damn for howling babies with ugly rashes and digestive troubles. Delia was no exception to this rule. You may find it hard to believe, but I hold no grudge against my mother for disappearing from my life when I was less than six weeks old. What was I supposed to resent? That instead of a bored, sulky girl taking care of me, or the kind of penitentiary nurse she would have hired in her place, I had Jeanette all to myself?

I have no clue if Jeanette was hoping to have kids of her own, one day. I was too selfish, maybe too scared, to want to ask her. She never doted on me, or spoiled me, but in her own way, Jeanette was the kind of nurse every foundling dreams about. I knew better than to give her any trouble, but why the hell would I want to? All the while my grandfather lay slowly fading in Wivelsfield's master bedroom, I had the run of the house and grounds. Jeanette taught me to read by the time I was three—she said she'd discovered me spelling out words from the *Windsor Star* and decided something should be done about my education. It was my one sign of having any gift, being anything even a bit out of the ordinary. I never did set any store by my being tall for my age and as solidly built as the manor itself.

While I was learning to read the *Windsor Star*, my mother was finishing her education at a Young Ladies' Academy in Connecticut and at various European establishments. During this time she was known as Delia Dunstan, with no one being any the wiser about the Baby or baby she'd left behind. My mother's divorce (on the grounds of desertion) came through as quietly as divorces could in those days. Some time around my ninth birthday she came back to live at Wivelsfield Manor, but she didn't seem in any hurry to play mother with me, or start all over by marrying again. Because no sooner had my mother come back to her father's house than disaster struck, a disaster worse than being deflowered by a radish-grower or bearing a rum-runner's child.

I'm speaking of the Great Crash of 1929, an event that means as little to you as Belshazzar's feast. Here's what it meant for the little world assembled at Wivelsfield Manor. The men who could have rescued my mother by marriage were all throwing themselves out of office buildings or sucking up to the few heiresses that were left. My grandfather's fortune disappeared overnight—so did the worldly goods of most other people. All he had left was Wivelsfield, and an annuity set up to maintain and improve the property. Now, that annuity was the untouchable portion of my grandmother's dowry, and it would cease whenever the house passed from the hands of Henrietta's heirs. Because of that annuity, George, Delia, Jeanette, and I were able to go on living at the manor, though not in the usual style. All but eight of the house's thirty rooms were closed up. The cook and maids all had to go; Jeanette agreed to take their place.

As for my Aunt Cassandra, she weathered the Crash thanks to her own shotgun wedding to Horace Plint. Marriage might spell *husband* and *children* to most women, but to Cassandra all it spelled was *house* and *home*. With a legacy from her mother, my aunt bought and furnished the house on Victoria Street outright, but it wasn't until the Crash, when housemaids could be hired for four bucks a week, from ads attracting maybe forty desperate women of all ages, that she could afford help to look after it. Horace was a lawyer, yes, but he specialized in the nickel-and-dime drudgery of family law—wills, house sales and purchases, and, ever so rarely, divorce. Namely Delia v. Joseph Baby, which he managed pretty well, you have to say that for him. He came from a family of short-lived men, and it's my hunch that Aunt

Cassandra was biding her time in that dark house on Victoria Street, until she could deck herself out in widow's weeds and return to the manor she considered hers by right.

And maybe she would have, except for the fact that the father she was aiming to forgive at his eleventh hour fell asleep one night and refused to wake up the next morning. When his will was read, didn't it give Cassandra all of George's now worthless stocks and bonds, as well as every book in the house. And didn't he give Wivelsfield Manor and all its contents, except those of the library, to Delia.

Now Wivelsfield, with its rusting iron fence and high-and-mighty gates, was still our little kingdom. None of us had to leave the property unless we wanted to—groceries were still delivered to the door, though the brands became less and less expensive. I should have been at school, but because I was growing like a giraffe, the doctor was afraid my heart wouldn't stand the strain. So Jeanette taught me at home, Delia deciding that anything she couldn't cover wasn't worth knowing.

Jeanette passed on to me her passion for books, and we spent most of our time together in my grandfather's library. Delia was happy enough with the way things worked out— she was less of a reader than Cassandra. And Delia was always away. She had the habit of paying long visits to friends she'd made at school, friends living in New York, Chicago, Miami. To pay for her tickets and the clothes she'd need, my mother would vanish for an afternoon to Detroit with a "little something" wrapped up in a silk shawl—a book from her father's library or some "collectible" she'd found in one of the rooms Jeanette shut up so carefully. It was after one of these visits to Detroit that my mother called her banker and lawyer and proceeded to sell Wivelsfield Manor from under our feet. Real estate was worth next to nothing now—there was no advantage to getting rid of the manor house just then.

I don't believe my mother had the will or the intellect to act from malice. Towards Jeanette, who'd be homeless once the manor was sold. Towards Cassandra, whose whole being was lodged in that house. Or towards her daughter, though Wivelsfield was the only home I'd ever known. My mother had a plan afoot, a plan that required a certain amount of cunning and a lot of capital.

Windsor was in a terrible state at the time. All the money that had been sloshing around in the 1920s—money made off bootlegging, gambling joints, bawdy houses—fell away like skin off a snake. Most of the people my aunt and mother knew were beaten hollow in the stock market crash. Most people most everywhere in the country didn't have the cash to buy the Fords and Chryslers the Windsor plants could have been making. And thousands of Windsor residents who used to go to work every day in Michigan were suddenly crossing a different kind of border. No work, no paycheque, their families eating at soup kitchens and living in shacks. Their cars, if they could afford to keep them, pulled by horses fit for the knacker's yard. The year the manor was sold off, over half of Windsor's population was on welfare. Builders stopped making houses. Doctors got paid in carrots, sugar beets, and wild ducks. Lawyers headed up north to the mining towns. With them went Horace Plint, who went for good. It wasn't a stroke that did him in but a nasty case of mumps.

No sooner had my aunt lost her childhood home, as well as her husband, than she was hit with a shameless appeal from the sister she'd given up on mothering. The appeal was this—would she take me in when no one else would touch me with a ten-foot pole? Delia, you see, was in a panic at the thought of turning thirty; she was gunning for a husband, the Right Kind, who'd undo the damage she'd suffered at the hands of the Wrong. Once she'd sold off the manor, she went to Chicago as a house guest of a Boston friend who'd married one of the Hog Kings. The man my mother was soon setting her sights on had nothing to do with slaughter-houses, though. He was wealthy, all right, and closer to her father's age than her own. He'd read for the bar but never practised law, and he devoted all his time to collecting documents and memorabilia dealing with the history of America, from French and British times to the War of Independence. Delia Dunstan had made his acquaintance at a party thrown by the Hog King. She'd furthered that acquaintance by volunteering to help Augustus Griffiths catalogue his collection. Though as far as any of us knew, Delia had no more knack for order than a cyclone.

So there we all were: Delia in Chicago, Jeanette banished to her sister's in Detroit, and me living with Aunt Cassandra in the mausoleum she called home. I wonder she took me in at all—I wasn't churning out the charm for anyone in those days. In fact, I was as sullen, moody, burdensome a child as you could hope to avoid. In looks I did not take after my black-haired, violet-eyed, beautiful mother, or her father, the handsomest man in Windsor. I didn't even bear a resemblance to my aunt, who was grimly handsome in her mother's way. By the time I was eight it was clear as crystal I was going to be the spitting image of the father I'd never known—raw-boned, hulking, with a face kindness could describe as unfortunate, though I've never suffered from a broken nose. And by the time I'd reached fifteen, that year I spent with my Aunt Cassandra, I'd grown to my full height of six-foot one.

It must have helped my aunt that I looked so little like Delia. She felt I could be trusted not to land in the kind of trouble that had led to my having been born in the first place. But she decided to make sure of me by pushing me into secretarial school and signing me up for music lessons with a local teacher. Every honest woman, she said, should have a technical skill she could use to earn her daily bread, if need be, and an accomplishment she could use to please herself. My aunt's accomplishment was needlework. The house on Victoria Street was chockablock with embroidered cushions, hassocks, benches. Her skill was bookkeeping, which she'd learned to help her husband when it was clear there weren't going to be any children. It turned out she had a head for numbers. She ended up working for an accountant in town, one of the few who still had any business. And that was why, saddled with a large house and a difficult niece, she sent to Detroit for Miss Jeanette Barnes.

As far as I know, my aunt never apologized for the words she'd said when she first met Jeanette. Likewise, Jeanette never offered a word of thanks for Cassandra's offer of room and board, all the books she could read, and a small wage in exchange for housework, cooking, and tending to me along with the vegetable garden. Somehow, they squared things between them. It helped that they shared a passion for Wivelsfield Manor. They seemed to know each oak floorboard and tiffany lamp by heart, they could recall the carvings on each fireplace, they knew just where the moss roses grew in the garden and the names of the different orchids in the greenhouse. They would talk the whole manor into life each day, over 6:00 a.m. cups of coffee or bedtime glasses of brandy.

I spent a year with Cassandra and Jeanette, taking music lessons and learning how to type. I wasn't brilliant at either, but I wasn't hopeless. My Aunt Cassandra let down her guard—she even laughed now and then, for the first time in my memory. She could never be described as a happy soul, but she stopped wearing lead in her shoes. Maybe it had to do with Delia finally growing up right, taking that burden, at least, off Cassandra's shoulders. There was her shameless little sister filing index cards for Augustus Griffiths, making herself indispensable for her competence and the sheer shine of her beauty. Cassandra wouldn't hold that beauty against her—she knew Delia couldn't stop it any more than a prism can keep light from falling through its walls.

When the news came of my mother's wedding, I didn't feel one way or another—what could that marriage have to do with me? It was later, when they came back from their honeymoon and moved into Mr. Griffiths's house in Lake Forest, that my mother's games began to matter. For some reason she'd told the bridegroom about my existence, or else he'd come across evidence of me that Delia couldn't talk him past or round. Or maybe my aunt had more than a little to do with it. Maybe the prospect of having me on her hands for the foreseeable future wasn't something she was going to stand for. All I know was that a letter came to her from Mr. Griffiths, saying how much he was looking forward to meeting me when I came to Lake Forest. Another letter arrived around the same time from Delia. This letter explained that Mr. Griffiths believed I was her adopted daughter, the child of the former housekeeper of Wivelsfield Manor, one Jeanette Barnes. This way, she declared, nobody would feel cheated and everyone would get what they wanted.

For the first time in my life, Jeanette was no help to me at all. Cassandra made it clear to both of us: my place was with my mother and her new husband, even if I was going to live there under false pretences. What mattered was that the husband of the new Mrs. Griffiths was a wealthy man who could find me respectable work that would pay me more than anything I could lay hold of in Windsor. I knew better than to appeal to Aunt Cassandra, but I thought Jeanette would put up a fight to keep me. I was wrong. Maybe she was tired of tidying up other people's lives. Maybe she wanted her life to herself, for a change. I would have run away, except all that I wanted was to stay put where I was.

But I couldn't stay, and so I left Windsor, swearing I'd never set foot in it again.

For all those females wanting to snag rich husbands, what better place to go than Chicago, the City of Millionaires? Stockyard or mail-order catalogue millionaires. Real estate or department store millionaires. Millionaires who invented Cracker Jack and oleomargarine. Sure, the number of Chicago millionaires dropped drastically after the Crash, but there were enough left who'd been smart enough to shift their assets to solid, unshakeable goods. Many of them were born fighters who'd made their bundles by working fifteen-hour days on bread and water.

And then there were the sons of the upstarts, like Augustus Griffiths. His father had been a clerk in a sporting goods shop before he'd thought of a scheme for manufacturing—and making a killing on—bicycle parts. Augustus Griffiths, refined, elderly, rich—he was the perfect match for the sweet, quiet girl of good family that Delia had managed to make-believe she was. It's funny, when you come to think of it; at the exact age at which her mother flew off her bicycle into a wicker wheelchair, Delia herself retired to a white clapboard mansion in Lake Forest. It was a humbler dwelling than the manor in its heyday, but it was a mansion all the same. Maybe she'd had enough by then of risk and pleasure. Maybe she'd used up all her careless youth by having a child when she was still a child herself, and then going on to hide the damage.

I don't want to give you the impression that Augustus was my saviour, the Father I Never Had. My mother started calling him a miser soon enough, but I thought it made good sense for him to spend his money on his collection of Americana instead of on chauffeurs and restaurants and tickets to the opera to please Delia, who wasn't supposed to care for that kind of thing, anyway. I liked Augustus Griffiths. For one thing, I saw right away that I didn't need to waste time or effort making Delia miserable—Augustus had seen to that already. As miserable, that is, as a woman with servants and antique china and fur coats had any right to be. If Augustus had tried to be a father to me, I would have hated him. Instead, he became my mentor. He saw I needed something practical to keep me occupied, so he put me to work as a typist at his Foundation. Of course, he skinned me on my wages, but the cash I earned was all my own. He drove me to work each day, and back at night. And he gave me some tips on what to do with my money—I wasn't about to blow it on lipstick and party dresses, now, was I?

It was Augustus who introduced me to the game of collecting. When he saw the kinds of books I read, he put me in touch with some local dealers who handled the manuscripts and letters of Katherine Mansfield. But don't get the wrong idea—it wasn't Augustus who gave me the money to feed my collecting bug. As Delia eventually discovered, his fortune went to the maintenance of the Augustus Griffiths Museum of Colonial America, except for a small allowance earmarked for his widow.

A couple of months before he died, Augustus traced my long-gone, presumed-dead father to the outskirts of Hastings, Nebraska—with help from Jeanette, I believe. I've often wondered whether Augustus saw through Delia's lie about having adopted me to help out a trusty servant. On balance, I'd say no. I don't think he could have believed Delia had been up to that kind of monkey business at such a tender age. I don't think he could have believed that the great big lump I was could ever have come out of Delia's delicate body. But when Augustus finally made contact with Joseph Baby, Delia's name wasn't mentioned any more than Jeanette's was. He just reacquainted my father with the fact of my existence, and from there it was a hop, skip, and jump to my being saved from any need to earn a living. You see, near the end of his life, my father made a fortune speculating on soybean futures during World War II. The whole of my collection—letters and notebooks and first drafts and other things you haven't a clue about—owes its existence to radishes, rum, and soybeans, and the good offices of my mother's second husband.

So there it is—my illustrious family line, the nest I sprang from, and my collection, too. In case you're one of those people who can't take loose ends, I can tell you that Augustus Griffiths died in 1949, at his home in Lake Forest. Delia died thirteen years later, trying to fish an English muffin out of a toaster with a paring knife. Aunt Cassandra, Jeanette—they're all dead and gone. As I told you before, I haven't a friend or relative left alive in the world—no creditors and no heirs, either, except for whoever gets my collection. So I figure I know what Katherine Mansfield meant in her will, when she said she had nothing to leave and no one to leave it to. Remember how she begged Murry to leave all fair, to destroy all traces of her camping ground? There's something clean, something decent, about an empty drawer, now, isn't there, Mr. Mills?

BEYOND THE BLUE MOUNTAINS

Hampstead, London, 1918

Jack comes to spend a week of holiday at Looe: to go boating; to eat strawberries and cream at the edge of a flower-strewn cliff; to debate the plans they've made for buying a home of their own. Jack gets sunburned and Katherine chokes down enough cream that the doctor, weighing her, pronounces her fit to return to London.

Soon after they leave Cornwall, the Murrys buy, furnish, and decorate the first real home Katherine has had since leaving her father's house on Fitzherbert Terrace. A place in Hampstead, near the Vale of Health, where Katherine will have her own room to write in, and Jack will have his own bedroom. It's impossible for him to sleep beside his wife, given her coughing fits and, worse, the jagged breath she scrapes from her lungs, each breath, just possibly, the last one she'll be able to tear free.

They call their house "The Elephant," and Katherine delights in its fitting-up. The kitchen walls are to be white, she instructs Jack, with the kitchen trimmed in hyacinth or

Wedgwood blue, to show off the crockery and painted plates from France and Italy. Soft dove grey for the stairway walls, with brass rods setting off a purple carpet, and gilded picture frames holding the originals that illustrated the ill-fated *Rhythm*. But the sketch of Maori girls with tattooed lips, the one she picked up at a flea market years ago, must hang in her writing room, she insists on that. Every cushion and bowl and piece of glass is to be placed just so, on furniture scavenged from junk or government surplus stores, and painted shining Brunswick black. Her own two rooms are to be cream and yellow—the whole house is to give off the feeling of spring. The other seasons will be accommodated in their turn, but for now it's to be all jonquils and crocuses, with their brusque saffron hearts; it is all to be about beginnings.

———

Not without regrets, Ida leaves her Putney aeroplane factory to take up the duties of housekeeper at The Elephant. She had been happier than she'd ever imagined possible in Putney, freer, more herself; she had made good friends with the other women living in the hostel. But she has come in spite of all this, Ida the Albatross, as the Murrys call her—the Albatross perched atop an Elephant.

Ida is neither efficient nor talented as a housekeeper, but she seems to get by. She can handle the various friends who come to call and who look right through her as though she is made of greased paper, but what she can't abide is the procession of doctors who glide in and out. The distinguished Dr. Sydney Beauchamp, for example, a cousin of Katherine's, who leans his head against her chest as she counts for him: "Ninety-nine, forty-four, one-two-three." He stays to lunch, and over veal cutlets looks up brightly at his patient, saying, "You do know you won't make old bones, my dear."

"Blast your eyes," she throws back at him. "I feel full of Fire and Buck—I'll outlive the lot of you!"

Then there's the TB specialist, who also lays his head on Mrs. Murry's chest and makes her count ninety-nine, forty-four, one-two-three. He advises her to enter a sanitorium immediately, and confides to Jack that if she doesn't, his wife has, at best, four years to live. "You must know, Mr. Murry, that if you continue as you are, you will be dealing day to day with a dying woman. She will often be in great pain, and she will respond to this pain with rage and even cruelty. You must prepare yourself."

Finally, a Dr. Victor Sorapure is sent to Katherine by her friend Anne. Dr. Sorapure is a former foundling from the streets of Paris, a fact that endears him to his doctor-hating patient. He makes her think of Chekhov, does Dr. Sorapure, though she can't know that he, too, will die of tuberculosis, ten years after her own death. He examines her thoroughly, takes a detailed medical history, and with the utmost gentleness explains to her that she is suffering not just from pulmonary tuberculosis, but also from advanced gonorrhea, which has given her those "rheumatic" pains in her hands and hips and in the small bones of her feet. And which has made it so difficult—though not impossible, he says—for her to conceive a child.

Unlike the other doctors, Sorapure does not command her to shut herself up in a sanatorium, where she will see no one, read nothing, write nothing, only lie in a narrow bed, exposed to sunny or to wintry air, eating eggs beaten up in cream. Unlike all the other doctors, he understands that not everyone means the same things by the words *life* and *death*. That the real threat to Katherine's life is not the bacilli eating caves and tunnels through her lungs, but the blinding of her passionately curious eyes by the white walls of a sanatorium.

On the desk in her study, where, on good days, she creeps

to work, is a copy of her first book since the German stories came out: *Prelude*, published by Leonard and Virginia Woolf. She inscribes a copy of it to Dr. Sorapure, telling him, as she puts it into his hands, that it is nothing like what she'd hoped it would be—that it hasn't the clarity, the openness, the light of true art. And yet it holds that possibility inside it; given the chance, she will write something real, something fully alive, one day. If she can only stay here, in her own home, with the people she loves close by her; if she can remain in reach of the peculiar, familiar things she knows herself by, she will have that chance.

But the only work she has energy for is the keeping of her journal, and the writing of reviews for Jack's magazine, *The Athenæum*: superb reviews of mostly ephemeral, insipid novels published by her healthy contemporaries. When she's not in so much pain that she cannot leave her bed, she attempts to lead the normal, ordinary life of a woman of thirty: for example, shopping on Oxford Street for shoes and the brilliantly coloured stockings she adores. It's along Oxford Street that a radiant woman with a violin case is walking when she's stopped by a voice she barely remembers, a beautifully musical voice attached to the body of a wraith: "Margaret! Oh, Margaret, don't you remember Kassie?"

Margaret Wishart—now Mrs. Woodhouse—shifts her violin case from one hand to the other. "Kassie?" she asks, as if afraid to admit such a change could occur to someone locked so safely in the bottom drawer of memory. And then she cries out, "Kassie!" She longs to throw her arms around her friend but is frightened by how brittle-looking Katherine's body has become. The two women stop on the pavement, oblivious of the shoppers jostling by; they talk of Beauchamp Lodge days, and how they used to eat boiled onions together out of little *bols de mariage* brought back from Paris. Neither of them mentions Garnet Trowell.

Margaret must come to see her, Katherine insists—she must come tomorrow, to tea at The Elephant. There is so much to remember together.

Because they are to see each other the next day, the two women don't embrace—there's Katherine's parcel and Margaret's violin to get in the way. They only kiss quickly and walk on. The next day, Mrs. Woodhouse receives a telegram from Mrs. Murry: "Too unwell" is all it says. Her husband asks Margaret what's upset her so. "Nothing," she answers, crumpling the telegram in her hand and going off to see to the baby, who has woken, wailing, in the next room. Holding her child with its head pressed in the space between her breast and collarbone, Margaret rocks gently on her heels, crooning *there there, there there,* her eyes prickling with tears.

That winter, and the next spring and summer, Katherine attempts a cure at home, at The Elephant. Sometimes she is strong enough to see friends, and even if she's confined to her room she takes care to dress as smartly as she can. In a purple wrapper with emerald green buttons and high-heeled mules on her feet, she makes tea for a young writer who can tell how thin Mrs. Murry has become from the way her rings slip up and down her fingers. Dr. Sorapure comes to give her injections to reduce the inflammation in her joints; he tests the sputum she coughs up, and cautions Ida and Jack that she's still actively infectious. He gives his patient pills and powders, but more importantly, he teaches her how to live with her disease and with a burden of pain only partly caused by the bacilli. The pain of loneliness, of feeling not just a room, or storey, but a planet away from those you love; the pain of finding yourself lashing out at those same people, at their concern for you, their patience, their very tenderness. The way hatred, like love, causes a physical ache; spikes with your fever or snakes through the wakefulness of your endless nights. They both know, Dr. Sorapure and his patient, that from now until the end, Katherine will be living on nothing but her extraordinary appetite for life, and on sheer concentrated will.

Appetite and will—they nourish her when Virginia Woolf comes to sit in Katherine's slowly darkening drawing room from early afternoon till the moment when Ida rattles in with a tray of tea things and lights the lamps. What do they talk about? Their mutual love of Chekhov; their mutual dislike of what Katherine describes as the "dark young men" who've inhaled the "decomposing vapours of poor Jules Laforgue." They are rivals in fiction, yet in some odd way their imaginations seem twinned, so that students of their work have found Katherine's best stories haunting Virginia's most important novels; have discovered, cloaked or stunningly naked, the same obsessions with death and life and solitariness, with beauty and corruption. Their priceless talk about their precious art, as Woolf described their conversations, must have been Katherine's substitute for the stories she was far too ill to write that long, hellish Hampstead winter.

———

Early September, too early for the day to be as cold, dark, rain-drenched as it is. The photographer's studio, again, the one off the Marloes Road. The same man who took the wedding photos is now helping Mrs. Murry off with her wet Burberry, posing her for a passport picture. He doesn't like to ask why she's leaving England—though the war's been over for a year now, travel can still be difficult, especially on the Continent. But then he doesn't need to ask: the sitter's face, under her small black hat, its lifted veil, speaks for itself. The eyes are exposed like an engraver's plate from which too many rubbings have been taken. The skin is pulled taut, a mask made of some perishable, easily stained material. And her mouth is small and sad. It's the face of someone, he realizes, who has made out her will. He remembers how she sat for her wedding portrait a year ago—how she coughed and coughed until he was afraid that she would choke on her own throat. The fact that she isn't coughing now seems, somehow, even worse, as if she's already dead.

Seeing her to the door, the photographer longs for her to say even the most commonplace words, as if language will cancel the extremity of her expression. "And where are you off to, Mrs. Murry?" he stammers, helping her on with her coat.

Katherine stares at him, the whites of her eyes startling against the blackness of iris and pupil. Finally she whispers, "San Remo. Just for the winter." And then, relenting, almost smiling, "The Mediterranean—the Italian Riviera."

"Ah, I see," he says, though of course he doesn't. The word *Riviera* means nothing to him, has still to be invented by Picasso and Diaghilev and American expatriates with bushels of money.

"Ah," he repeats, as if San Remo were a most delightful, a most enviable destination. He insists on going outside, hailing a cab for her as she looks on through the rain-blurred window. At which he replaces her, once she's vanished into the cab, and the cab drives off, leaving him staring at the unexpected absence she's left behind.

———

A train racketing through the night; two women in sleeping berths, one large, soft, snoring, the other wide awake, trying to stifle her cough, drifting off to sleep at last sometime towards dawn. When she wakes, it's nearly noon. Outside, it seems as if a fountain's started up, gushing and spraying day-light into the drab compartment. She's given a cup of tea; she drinks it as if it were her own life's blood she has to force back into her body. The curtains are drawn, unveiling the gentle slap of scene after scene of flowers crowning stone walls or crowding terra cotta pots; orchards bosomy with fruit; peasants in bright cotton clothes, getting the harvest in.

Wrapped in their thick travelling cloaks, the women check into one of the better hotels in San Remo. The desk clerk eyes them suspiciously, particularly the one with the bad heart, too weak to stand at the desk, needing a cane to walk the few steps from the chair to the lift. When the same thin, parched-looking woman breaks into a coughing fit in the hotel restaurant, the entire room of gleaming guests at their linen-covered tables falls silent, watching her. Her shoulders are like wings fastened on the wrong side, arching to protect the place in her chest where the air boils and seethes. Even the young waiter who'd been so gallant, pulling out their chairs, slipping the rolls onto their plates with his silver tongs, stands clutching a salver of grilled trout as though the lady's coughing could wrench it from his hands.

All of which forces the two women, muffled again in their travelling cloaks, to the front desk, where they are presented with a bill, not just for their three nights' stay, but for the fumi-gation of Mrs. Murry's room, as well. "It is the law," the hotel manager sternly declares, as if the state's criminalization of her disease should mollify his guest. Furious, ashamed—as if her lungs have been producing filth, not phlegm—Katherine pays the bill. Whereupon the manager relents; smiling slyly, he leans forward, whispering of a nearby villa they can rent, a pri-vate villa in the hills overlooking a sheltered bay.

To the Casetta Deerholm—sparsely furnished and extor-tionately priced, bereft of carpets, locks on the doors, and anything more than rudimentary heating—comes another procession of doctors. They fasten their stethoscopes to Katherine's chest while she repeats "ninety-nine, forty-four, one-two-three"; they shake their heads and prescribe restoratives she can't afford. Nearly mad with pain and loneliness, Katherine staggers through the day, writing fiery letters to tepid, passive Jack; railing at Ida for breaking plates, Ida who struggles bravely in the cramped kitchen to make simple meals. Unable to work, to think, to do anything but surrender to a cough echoed by the crash of waves and slash of the wind, Katherine curses winter on the Italian Riviera, a season of bleak cold and terrifying storms.

When the sun finally returns and the weather warms, Ida helps her into a deckchair in the garden, where Katherine sits with her journal open on her lap. She drags her pen across the paper: "Day spent in Hell." "Dark—no sky to be seen, livid sea, a noise of boiling in the air." Sometimes she summons just enough hope to record what's left of her heart's desire: "Work will win if only I can stick to it. It will win after all & through all."

But nothing wins out in this place whose name, Ospedaletti, sounds too much to Katherine's ear like *hospital*. Nothing but illness, cruelty, desolation. No letters arrive from Jack or anyone else. Their landlord shows up, not with a locksmith, but with a revolver they can use, he says, to protect themselves. Beggars come to the door, and when Ida goes to the kitchen to fetch them some bread, they steal Katherine's one warm cloak, hanging on a peg in the entrance hall. A malign-looking Englishman who lives at the opposite end of the bay calls on the women to boast of the roses he's able to grow right through the winter, and to frighten them away from the Casetta. They'll be shot in their beds, he declares, as if relishing the thought: shot by the striking workers, gangs of marauding thieves. Half of Italy's on strike, he tells them—didn't they know? Didn't they wonder why they weren't getting any mail?

That night, as Katherine lies awake, she hears voices, noises in the garden. She calls out to Ida, who runs for the revolver and leans timidly out of Katherine's bedroom window. Plump arms shaking, eyes shut tight, Ida fires into the dark.

———

Not a train, this time, but a private motor car, hired at great expense to take Ida and Katherine and their hastily packed trunks across the border into France, to the sunny town of Menton. From the upstairs windows of the villa she's rented for the rest of the winter, Katherine can look to the high forested hills behind, or out to the glassy waters of the Mediterranean. For whatever reason—the mildness of the weather, the warmth of the house, the high competence and style of the French maid who shops and cooks and arranges the household as poor Ida never could—the Villa Isola Bella turns out to be an enchanted place where Katherine's disease doesn't disappear but becomes something she can seal inside her, like the twists of colour in a glass paperweight. Look at her, now, in the garden, observing a lizard on a sun-cracked wall; putting her hands out to the datura plant, dragging herself from rose bush to rose bush, leaning on her parasol. Even when she's forced into bed, she struggles to sit up, reading Shakespeare, Dickens, Keats, Colette.

One morning in early December—nearly a year after she and Ida fled from Ospedaletti, a year in which, for the spring and summer, she returned to Jack and London only to be forced back to Menton by the autumn cold—Katherine sits down to work. She doesn't rise when Ida calls her for lunch or tea but eats absently from trays brought to her desk. By evening she's moved up to her bedroom, where, in pyjamas and a kimono, with a cigarette in one hand, a pen in the other, she fills page after page without stopping to cross out a single word. Ida fusses with the kettle and brings in trays of tea and toast, sitting on the stairs in between times, holding her breath. At two in the morning, Katherine shouts, "It's done!" and Ida rushes into the room, plunking herself on the edge of Katie's bed with its looped-up mosquito netting. Stubbing out her cigarette, Katherine takes the first sheet and starts to read aloud. Ida catches this and that paragraph, losing the thread in her relief, her staunch, staring wonder that Katherine has written, in spite of everything, her masterpiece:

> *The week after was one of the busiest weeks of their lives. Even when they went to bed it was only their bodies that lay down and rested; their minds went on thinking things out, talking things over, wondering, deciding, trying to remember . . .*
>
> *Josephine had had a moment of absolute terror at the cemetery, while the coffin was lowered, to think that she and Constantia had done this thing without asking his permission. What would father say when he found out? For he was bound to find out sooner or later. He always did. "Buried. You two girls had me buried!" She heard his stick thumping. Oh, what would they say? . . .*

Suddenly there's silence. Ida looks across at Katherine, realizing that the reading has finished, the story ended. "It's you, Lesley," Katherine sighs, leaning back in her chair, allowing her eyes to close. "It's you and your sister—and my little cousin Sylvia, and all the women terrorized by their fathers, terrorized until they didn't dare put a toe into a life of their own." She rubs her face with her hands; to Ida's anxious eyes, she looks as though she might stop breathing, there and then, have done with the whole business of catching, again and again, the iron ring of her breath.

Ida helps her into bed, and just as she's leaving the room, ventures, "It's good, Katie, isn't it?"

"It's the best thing I've ever done," Katherine replies. But after Ida has left the room and the latch has clicked on the door, Katherine starts shaking, as if she's just been dragged from a collapsing building. "It *is* good," she whispers, "it *is*— please God."

———

For the next year and a half of the two years she has left to live, Katherine writes as if it were her whole body and not just her hands moving the pen across the page; her lungs and gut as well as her head that pull the words from silence. She is writing to pay doctors' bills that the increased allowance her father sends doesn't cover. Some of the work is slick, the kind of thing Virginia Woolf will say makes you want to go and rinse your brains. But enough of the stories are strong, with a living root to them, a freshness of feeling and seeing; they're published not only in England but in America, and later France, Japan, and many other countries, never going out of print, and catching the attention of writers coming into their own voice and vision: Christopher Isherwood, Elizabeth Bowen, Patrick White, Mavis Gallant. But Katherine isn't writing for posterity; all that concerns her is the moment of writing, in which she struggles to make her stories as true as she can to what she knows and what she's guessed about the common mystery of being alive. And she is writing against other things besides time and the wreck of her body; she is writing against the loss of love, the illusion of personal happiness.

A scene is taking place in the garden of the Villa Isola Bella, a scene between Mr. and Mrs. Middleton Murry. They are leaning against a balustrade, side by side, but they are not looking at one another. Jack slopes against the stone, cigarette drooping from his lips, his hip stuck out at an awkward angle. Down to the waist, his body is adjacent to his wife's, but from there it pulls as far away from her flesh as it can. Behind them, through the gaps in the balustrade, carnations and bougainvillea bloom profusely, mocking Jack in his travelling clothes, fine for London weather but stifling, scratchy as a penitential shirt here on the Mediterranean. Katherine is holding a deep red sunshade over her head; her bare legs and sturdy black shoes make her look impossibly fragile. In his hands, Jack is holding a letter he's just read out at his wife's bidding, a letter written to her by a woman calling herself Jack's lover and berating Katherine for not setting him free. Jack's voice is tense, exhausted, as if he has walked every mile between Hampstead and Menton:

"She means nothing to me, nothing. No one who could have written you that letter—who could be as cruel as that— could ever mean anything to me. You're the one I'll always love, you must know that. You're the only woman in the world for me."

Katherine collapses the parasol; using it as a crutch she pushes away from the balustrade, making her way to a little metal chair perched on the terrace. She will need to sit down to reply.

"You've come all the way from London to tell me that? You've thrown up your work at the paper, you've rented out The Elephant, you've burned all your boats to come here and tell me *that*? And now you expect to stay on with me here?"

Katherine is sitting extremely straight: the dark fringe of hair cut high on her forehead makes her look much younger than her eyes, the skin below them inked by disease. She tilts her head forward in a way that seems painfully eager; she is doing so to relieve the pressure in her neck of a gland swollen by the toxins in her body, a gland needing to be punctured and drained in the clinic at Menton.

But she hasn't said what she needs to. That what has hurt her so badly has little to do with Jack's kissing stupid girls in taxicabs, and everything to do with his having to lie about it—to be furtive, deceitful. That, after all this time, he doesn't know her at all, and doesn't want to know her. That it's over, now, any belief in a living future they could make between them, a home, children, a life. She digs the point of her parasol into the fine gravel of the terrace. It's too late for them to start over, and too late to shake hands and part. Somehow, they are going to have to patch things up for however long she has left.

"God knows, Jack, I'm a miserable failure as a wife. You're only thirty-one, and as lonely in your prison as I am in mine. But here we are, together at last—we'll have to declare a truce." Jack has buried his face in his hands; his thin shoulders are shaking. Katherine calls him by his pet name, stretching out her hands, summoning the will to sustain this performance. "Look, Jag, once the winter's over you'll hate it here, you'll be sick of the jasmine, the lizards, the sea. And the doctor's been saying I mustn't stay any longer in Menton. He says I have to get to Switzerland. Shall we ask Lesley to pack up our things—shall we haul ourselves up by our bootstraps to a chalet on the top of a Swiss Alp?"

Katherine starts to laugh, as if she's forgotten it's a fiction she's sketching out for him. Somehow she finds the energy to rise from her chair and stretch her arms out to Jack, who comes to embrace her, nuzzling the top of her head with great gentleness. "We'll have a porcelain-tiled stove," Katherine goes on, "and an enormous picture window, and look out over the eternal crags and eternal cows. I shall stop coughing, and you will start the novel that's to make you famous, and at last we'll live happily, Jack Murry. Happily, and for ever and ever."

It's no fiction, this chalet—it's called the Chalet des Sapins and it lies on the edge of what's hardly a town, Montana-sur-Sierre. Winter is real, too: brutally cold and beautiful. You'd think everything outside their doors was coated in a sheath of ice, except for the birds that come to the balcony, diving at a suet ball Jack has hung for them there.

Katherine has not stopped coughing; much of the time she's confined to what she calls her "Wild West" bedroom, the walls smelling deliciously of pine, furs scattered over the blankets on her bed. Caruso is singing on the gramophone. A cat lounges on her lap; Katherine strokes his belly and gently pulls his ears as Ida brings in the mail. Sifting through her letters, Katherine reads out bits to Ida, who is tidying the room. "Charlie Chaplin's back in London—Brett say he's lovely. Anne's baby has come through the measles—she's painted a frieze of hippos over the nursery walls. Jeanne's fiancé is even more impossible in letters than in person. Mother would have gutted him on the spot, with just one look—poor Mother." Before she opens the last letter she lies back against the pillows; her eyes are feverish, but the expression on her face is serene. "You know, I shall like being dead if it makes me feel the way listening to music does. Caruso, singing Verdi—it makes me feel gloriously dead— wafted away, rejoicing. Oh, don't go all panicky and throw up your hands—you're not rid of me yet, Lesley."

As she opens the last letter, Jack comes inside; they hear him downstairs, whistling, banging the snow off his skis. Katherine is still reading, an eager, hungry look on her face, as Jack enters the room. Ida is sent off to fetch tea.

Jack draws a chair up to Katherine's bed; she reaches out for his hand, holds it, still reddened with cold, against her cheek, then lets it drop. She tells him about the letter she's received from their old friend Koteliansky. He's heard of a new cure for her disease, she says. There's a Russian refugee in Paris, a man named Manoukhin. He was a doctor in St. Petersburg. They say he's had remarkable success in curing tuberculosis by X-ray treatment—irradiation of the spleen.

Ida comes in with the tea things; Jack takes his cup and pulls back a little from the bed, as if he's afraid of spilling tea on the coverlet. "Sounds like a charlatan to me," he says, at last.

Katherine laces her hands round her cup. "Jag, listen, the cures are all documented. It's miraculous if it's true, and why shouldn't it be? Dr. Manoukhin is attached to the Pasteur Institute. His treatment's written up in *The Lancet*, see for yourself." She holds out a clipping to him; he takes it but makes no move to read it.

"There has to be a catch," Jack says. He's alarmed at his wife's enthusiasm; he can see her flinging herself into a cold, drafty train bound for France.

"It's expensive," Katherine adds, handing her untouched cup of tea to Ida. "It costs the earth," she continues, as Jack tries again to dissuade her:

"Look, Wig. I can't let you go. I'd be afraid that—"

Katherine cuts him off. "I *won't* be afraid. I won't let myself be afraid. Every mistake I've made in my life I've made out of fear. I mean to have this treatment, Jack. As soon as this terrible snow is gone—or even if it stays forever—I am going to Paris. I can write enough to cover the costs. *The Sphere* will take all the stories I can send them."

"But—" Jack begins, but doesn't finish. How can he say what he's thinking? That in the condition she's in, the journey to Paris would be enough to kill her. That she must keep on with the kind of stories she's been writing here, real stories, not the thin, breezy stuff *The Sphere* laps up. All that he can do is remind her of the good that Switzerland's done her. If she hasn't been cured, then at least she's no worse. They have just enough money to get by, to do their work, to live quietly, peaceably together.

Katherine lies quite still and calm in her bed, but the distance between them has become immense.

When they've left Katherine to sleep, Jack tells Ida that it must be the fever making her so volatile, so restless, now. Forgetting all those times before her illness when she'd flown off, run away from him: restless, volatile.

———

Three months later, in a very Parisian treatment room with a small wrought-iron balcony and young leaves pressing at the windows, Katherine lies on a metal examining table. A volley of X-rays shoots through her belly. Dr. Manoukhin, who is directing the treatment, tells her that at first she will feel nausea, extreme tiredness, bodily weakness, but that after a few weeks these symptoms will disappear, and there will be a radical improvement in her condition. His English is crisscrossed with heavy Russian and French accents; he looks, she thinks, like Turgenev—as if this is a guarantee that his treatment will cure her. And for a while it does. After three weeks of wretchedness, shut up in her hotel room, going out only to take a cab to her doctor's office at the Trocadéro and back again, she begins to feel well enough to sit in the Luxembourg Gardens, by the begonia-wreathed bust of Paul Verlaine. She even takes tea at her hotel with James Joyce, with whom she discusses *Ulysses*, Jack contradicting her now and then. He's finally joined her in Paris. He's come to escort her back to Switzerland, where Dr. Manoukhin has ordered her to spend the summer.

The train journey is a nightmare: it's a holiday weekend,

and Jack has failed to reserve seats, though they finally squeeze into a crowded carriage. On reaching Montreux, Jack manages to leave behind one of his wife's most important possessions, a travelling clock that's become her good-luck charm. Then, thanking the porter who helps them with their luggage, Jack gives the man a hundred-franc note instead of the ten-franc tip he can barely afford, an error he won't discover till later that evening. To top it off, they're caught in a vicious rainstorm on their drive from the station to the hotel; Katherine is soaked and chilled through by the time they arrive. She cannot, she pleads, go up to the chalet—her heart is pounding crazily, she's convinced the altitude will kill her. So Ida, who has come to the hotel to greet them, stays on with her there, while Jack jumps alone into the cart that jolts him up the mountain.

———

The Hôtel Château Belle-Vue in Montreux looks like a small, sober palace. The German poet Rilke is a guest here while he looks for a place to finish the elegies he's been struggling with throughout the war. One morning, on his way to view the Château Muzot, a photo of which he's seen in a local hairdresser's shop, Rilke passes an emaciated young woman sitting stiffly as a dowager in the lobby. He nods to her, but she doesn't seem to see him. She is preoccupied with trying to keep her bones and muscles and skin connected, with keeping herself from collapsing inward onto her small gilt chair while she waits to be driven to the doctor's.

It's been weeks since she arrived in the horror of that storm, yet all along her spine, and in the cavities of her lungs, she feels cold, brackish water. Ida has been plying her with morphine for her cough; Jack has come down every few days to take meals with her, the meals they pretend she eats, though she can't manage more than broth. Mostly she has sat out in the garden, close to the damson trees that remind her of the paddocks of her childhood. Swathed in rugs and woollen scarves, listening to the tinkling of bells round the necks of cows the colour of tarnished silver, she registers Ida's latest bon mot: "It's scandalous, Katie, what they charge here for a metre of milk."

This graceful gilt chair is far less comfortable than the deckchairs in the garden. Katherine bites her lip and holds on tightly to the purse on her lap. It contains an article she's cut out from one of the magazines strewn on tables in the lobby. Photographs of an old priory at Fontainebleau, near Paris, and a man with a bald domed head, a colossal moustache, and huge ringed eyes. He's an Armenian named Gurdjieff. The article explains how, with his program of mystical dances and manual labour, he has attracted followers as diverse as aristocratic ladies and hard-boiled men of letters: A. R. Orage, for example, the founder of *The New Age*.

When Ida arrives, her face flushed, crumbs from breakfast still clinging to her lips, Katherine takes her arm and lets herself be led, as if she were blind, through the entrance doors and down the steps to a waiting cab. Once they start moving, Katherine lays her hand on Ida's arm: "I need your help," she croaks, her beautiful voice coarsened by her illness. "I have to get back to France—not to Paris but to a place in the country, a *maison de santé*. I'm going to ask the doctor for enough morphine to keep my cough down while I'm on the train. I'll need you to get the tickets and arrange the paperwork, and I'll need you to travel with me. And then—listen to me, Lesley—once I'm there, I'll need you to let me go. The people at Fontainebleau, at the priory—they're the only ones who can help me, now."

Ida has clasped her hands so tightly in her lap that the skin of her fingers is gorged with blood. "Katie," she

finally stammers, "I couldn't leave you there—I couldn't."
Katherine looks away for a moment, then turns back to
Ida, taking her rough, large hands in her own little fans of
bone and skin. "Lesley," she whispers. "What a mess I've
made of your life. I would have died without your help.
And I've never, ever thanked you. I'll never be able to give
you anything but my love. You've always had it—you'll
have it always."

Ida shakes her head, smiles beautifully, foolishly. She has
never been happier or more miserable than she is now; she
wishes it could go on forever, this moment of riding in a
scrupulously clean Swiss cab, her hands held tight in Katie's
own, the word *love* on Katie's lips.

But Katherine lets go of Ida; she closes her eyes and
slumps back against the cushions. After a moment she
speaks again, still in a hoarse whisper. "Can I trust you? Will
you help me? Jack mustn't find out."

That night, Katherine writes a letter to be given to her husband on her death, a letter asking him to destroy all her
papers, letters, manuscripts, except for the very few things
worth keeping. Jack's a world away at the Chalet des Sapins,
reading at his desk. He hasn't bothered to draw the curtains;
his handsome face, still holding a trace of boyishness, is
caught in the lamplit window. It is very quiet in the chalet
and out on the balcony, where a hook hangs, the hook from
which a ball of suet was suspended months ago. It is as quiet,
he thinks, and as cold as snow.

MONTY

Chicago–Windsor, Ontario, October 1986

Monty lay on his unmade bed at the Dreiser Hotel, surrounded by the sheets of Miss Baby's *Rewards and Recollections*. What he'd read through was hardly a history, and if it was supposed to be a life story, it contained so many arabesques and complications that it approached the status of fiction. It was, of course, a parody, in scathing style, of Mrs. Edison Dick's sane and sunny *Recollections*. The only people who came out of it with any credit were Jeanette Barnes and Augustus Griffiths, both long dead. Of the obscure Miss Barnes there'd surely be no trace; Augustus Griffiths he'd already tracked down, for what that was worth. And Miss Baby herself could be in New Zealand for all he knew. No, there was nothing in this account of her life that could be of the slightest use to him, the smallest interest. Time to shut the book and go home again, tail between legs, begging bowl in hand.

And yet there was an image Monty couldn't get out of his head: the image of a tall, plain, moody schoolgirl, kept out of trouble with typing classes and music lessons. Music lessons always meant piano, didn't they? Abruptly, he sat up, looked at his watch, and started gathering Miss Baby's papers from the floor, shoving them into his briefcase. He packed his things, grabbed his coat, and sprinted down the hallway to the elevator. When it proved too slow, he ran for the stairs. The desk clerk looked up the bus schedule for him—if he hurried, he could catch an express to Detroit and then a local bus to Windsor. He'd get there just before morning.

Outside the Dreiser, a cab had just discharged a fare; he grabbed it and raced for the station, muttering under his breath, "Mr. Bullen, Mr. Bullen."

———

Eight hours later, Monty was relieved to find himself in a city by a river instead of an enormous lake, a city small enough that he could instantly get his bearings. He found himself a bed-and-breakfast by the river, then headed for the library of the University of Windsor.

The Special Collections were housed in the basement, the Rare Book Room, #304. The staff was all obliging kindness, though no one Monty talked to seemed to know very much about the Mansfield letters deposited there. As for the Trowells themselves, they might never have existed, though the parents of at least some of the students working in the library might have studied violin or piano at the studio on Ouellette Avenue.

Monty was asked to seat himself at a large square table under fluorescent lights; within minutes, the head librarian had brought him the binder in which Mansfield's letters were stored. Ingenuous, open-hearted letters, he'd always thought: lacy lies and quarter-truths, if Cassandra Baby were to be believed.

The envelopes in which the letters had been sent were

slotted into plastic holders. Some were addressed to Mr. Carrington Garnet—this one, for example, sent on September 17, 1908, to "Moody-Manners, Theatre Royal, New Street, Birmingham." The letters had been carefully folded and unfolded; the handwriting on them was strong and assured. Mansfield had underlined certain phrases with thick, hard strokes: "You are all I have in the world, and you are the whole world. I love you. I want you." When Monty came to the words "my hands tremble—I shake with passion," he saw that her handwriting, too, trembled and shook, but with the intensity of steel shaking in a high wind.

So there he sat, in a basement room, in a small, wintry city, reading letters he practically knew by heart, but reading them in a free and unaccustomed way. No longer texts scrutinized by scholars, transcribed, proofread, published, quoted, they'd changed back to words spilling across a page, words so fresh that the ink seemed wet. These stale papers with their living words. They'd travelled with Garnet from London to Durban to Windsor. They had been stored at dozens of addresses—boarding houses, hotel rooms, flats—before ending up in a drawer in the house on Ouellette Avenue. Where Garnet's wife would have discovered them, going through her husband's papers shortly after his death.

"I feel so curiously that you are the complement of me— that ours will be the Perfect Union." How did Marion Trowell, née Smith, read these letters? What did she make of the fact that, five years before she came to board in the Trowells' home in Carlton Hill, another bright, brave colonial girl had slept in the exact same bed and fallen madly in love with the same sweet, bookish Garnet? Reading Katherine's responses to the "beautiful, satisfying" letters Garnet wrote to her, did Marion feel bitter, resentful, envious that such letters had been written at all? Did she have in her possession similarly satisfying letters from Garnet? As far as Monty knew, she'd never left or been left by this lover, but had stood and slept beside him for a full quarter of a century.

There was a letter from Marion Trowell, dated November 26, 1958, addressed to the Chief Librarian:

> . . . The package was undisturbed for over forty years and only opened a few weeks before I presented them to the Library. Time had faded the ink somewhat, but the paper was intact, and I left the letters folded, in the original envelopes, to show the dates of mailing, since most of the letters were undated—some of them written in haste and all of them but one in a short period of time.
>
> I don't know what to think regarding photostatic copies of them, even taken after all personal connections have dissolved, because of their extremely private nature and the spontaneous carelessness in the writing. They add nothing to her great reputation and I feel my husband would not have wished them to appear in New Zealand. All these things I would like to talk to you about whenever you would be free.
>
> With kindest regards,
> sincerely yours,
>
> Marion Trowell
> (Mrs. G. C. Trowell)

A direct, intelligent letter from a sensitive, scrupulous woman. Not, Monty decided, the type who would bear fools gladly—fools or fools of biographers. She had been approached, he assumed, by the Turnbull, wanting copies of the letters for its own collection, and she had acted according to what she knew of her husband's mind and heart. If what she'd written were true, Garnet had never looked at the letters after the end of his affair with Kathleen: *The package was undisturbed for over forty years.* Why shouldn't it be true? But why, on the other hand, would Garnet have been so leery of the letters' being made available in New Zealand, a country where he had no family left, and which he'd last seen at the age of fourteen?

Why I feel, my darling, that together we could hold the world in the hollow of our hands, and watch it revolving—that from you, Garnet—as I am now, each separate thing in the world is a miracle, a revelation because I seem to see all with <u>double force</u>—you and I together—what will happen?

What did happen? Even now, after wrestling with Cassandra Baby's *Vindication*, working through the different versions of those ecstatic, disastrous eight months, Monty had no clear idea. Miss Baby's conviction, as solid as the bones in her body, that it was all Katherine's fault—how had she come by it? From this letter of Ida's, the odd man out in this collection of "spontaneously careless" words? A letter Ida wrote at Katherine's insistence? dictation? a year or more after the miscarriage. How stilted and upright Ida's lettering was, even her dashes like roadblocks:

2 LUXBOROUGH House,
Paddington St., 2:00 a.m. July 29, '10

Garnet—I am so sorry we have not met after all—especially as I have to go away next Tuesday. K came to see me today and asked me to send you this—and also to give you her address. She is living just now with some literary friends also on the staff of *The New Age*—and perhaps later will be able to take a small flat just by herself. She will never join G. Bowden again—she only did so at the beginning of the year because she thought it her duty for the sake of her mother and sister and brother. Now she is Katherine Mansfield, 39 Abingdon Mansions, Pater Street, Kensington. That is her writing name—*&* she is taking it almost entirely now.

I am so sorry—once more—we have not met. I shall be in a good deal of tomorrow, I think, especially the later part of the afternoon if you care to come up and chance it—or of course you can always phone to be sure—Ah well—if not perhaps late—I feel there is so much to hear *&* say.

Always, Ida ——

Always what? Katherine's willing slave, penning the letter Katherine couldn't trust herself to write? What was the "this" Katherine was sending back to Garnet through Ida's letter? Something small, something no longer precious, since it could be trusted to the mail—a lock of hair, a ring? It was a minuscule envelope, four inches by six, a little smaller than the ones in which Katherine had sent love letters to Garnet. This careful man had kept these letters for over forty years: why? What of the letters he wrote to Katherine? Were they part of the bonfire Ida was ordered to light in the garden of the house in St. John's Wood, five years after the break with Garnet? And why had Katherine asked Ida to send him her new name and her address: what was she expecting him to send or deliver?

Marion Trowell had specified that Katherine's letters to Garnet were not to be opened till after her own death. There was a newspaper clipping about a ceremony held on June 10, 1974, marking the occasion of the letters being made available to the public. And there was a note in another hand, explaining that Garnet Trowell and Marion

Smith had married in Durban in 1923—the year of Mansfield's death—and had honeymooned in the Ten Thousand Hills. Once in Windsor, Garnet had taught the violin until war broke out, whereupon he'd worked at the Ford motor plant in Windsor. In 1943 he and his wife had arranged for Wyndham Lewis, who was teaching at Assumption College and living on Sandwich Street, to draw a portrait of one of their sons; presumably Garnet and Lewis did not discuss Mansfield, who had met Lewis shortly before her death, and whose writing Lewis professed, in his usual abrasive way, to find "vulgar, dull and unpleasant." Apart from this, nothing noteworthy in literary terms appeared to have disturbed the Trowells' calm obscurity in Windsor. Garnet died of some type of cancer in 1949, and that was that.

Monty was in the process of shutting the black binder and returning it to the Chief Librarian when a badly mimeographed sheet of paper slipped out from the back, something you wouldn't expect to find in an archive of this sort. It was a letter from someone who had nothing to do with Katherine Mansfield, Garnet Trowell, or their families, and it was sent by a G. A. McIver, Chief Security Office, University of Windsor, to a Mr. W. F. Dollar, Librarian, on March 9, 1970:

The subject envelope containing the MANSFIELD letters, having previously been seen by Mr. W. F. Dollar, had been properly sealed (3 times) with the usual legal type of sealing wax. It could not be stated by Mr. DOLLAR if the said seal did in fact contain the imprint of a metal or other type of seal imprint.

The said letter had evidently been kept in an unlocked glass "watch display type" of cabinet in the "Rare Book" room, namely room 304 of the University of Windsor Library.

Upon perusal of the sealed obverse side of the subject envelope it was quite evident that the original sealing wax, parts of which had still adhered to the envelope, were mostly covered with a very poor and amateurish type of paraffin sealing wax.

The envelope in question now reposes in the vault located in Mr. DOLLAR'S office for its future security. Unfortunately, it was not initially given such security as a token of respect to its trust in accordance with the wishes of Mrs. TROWELL, namely that it not be opened until her demise.

Monty blinked hard and reread McIver's letter. It was a guarded way of saying that sometime between 1949 and 1970, someone had tampered with Mansfield's letters.

In simple fact, they'd been stolen, along with half a dozen other folders of sensitive material, as the Chief Librarian disclosed before Monty took his leave. It had happened long before his appointment there, of course; out of the blue, the library had received a phone call from the FBI, saying they'd come across material that belonged to the University of Windsor Library, material that had surfaced in a Michigan motel room, and which, from what they could tell, the thief had meant to be discovered.

———

Monty ate a late lunch at a hamburger place on Ouellette, then decided to take a walk down the street to an address listed in a 1930s phone directory he'd found in the library, along with Garnet's obituary and a few articles about concerts he and his wife had given in Windsor, over the years. Where the Trowell Music Studio had once stood, there was now a garage in between a few small shops.

Monty pulled up his collar and continued walking, this time in the direction of Wivelsfield Manor. It had been turned into a conference centre and reception hall, though its grounds were open to the public. He pushed through the gate of the iron fence and walked up to the house, looking into the greenhouse, trying to imagine it as Cassie Baby would have known it. He sat on a bench in the rose garden picturing George Dunstan wheeling his invalid wife between the floribundas and the rugosas. Until it struck him that he was as bad as Roger, an ocean away, tracking a vanished woman, sifting the world of wood and stone and glass for her traces. He rubbed his face with his hands; he'd barely got any sleep the night before. It was time to hail a cab back to his bed-and-breakfast.

Once there, he found he couldn't sleep. He kept thinking of an empty motel room in Detroit or Ann Arbor; someone entering that room, locking the door, drawing the curtains, sitting on the bed to read through a briefcase full of stolen papers. He thought of the Trowells' music studio on Ouellette Street, and the suspicions that had brought him to Windsor in the first place. At last he gave in, turned on the lamp, and reached for the collection of Mansfield's stories he'd brought with him from New Zealand.

He went to an early work, "The Wind Blows." Its plot is simple enough: Matilda, a young girl in colonial Wellington, at war with her conventional mother and provincial surroundings, curses and exults in the furious wind that comes to stand for the raw power of life—real, undomesticated life. While the wind shreds the laundry left on the lines and wrecks the chrysanthemums in the gardens, Matilda escapes from the prison of home to her piano lesson with kind Mr. Bullen, aesthetically advanced Mr. Bullen. He has a signed photo of Rubinstein over his mantelpiece and the same kind of flowers and pictures with which the young Kathleen Beauchamp once decorated her room in the philistine stronghold of her father's house on Fitzherbert Terrace.

Matilda is not one of those stupid girls who get flustered when the much older Mr. Bullen leans over their shoulders to correct the Beethoven they're butchering. And yet today, when her teacher sits down beside her at the keyboard, she feels her heart beating so hard it seems to lift her blouse up and down; it makes her hands shake so much she can hardly untie her satchel and pull out her sheet music. It's only when Mr. Bullen speaks to her "so awfully kindly—as though they had known each other for years and years and knew everything about each other" that Matilda begins to cry, to press her face against the spongy tweed of Mr. Bullen's jacket, as he takes her hands in his. "'Life is so dreadful,' she murmurs, but she does not feel it is dreadful at all." At least, not until the next pupil arrives, hours early, her hat blown off her head by the wind. Whereupon Matilda gathers up her music, slams it into her satchel, and runs home to her room, where her mother has heaped a coil of snakes on her quilt: socks needing darning.

Reading the story, Monty saw fifteen-year-old Cassie running into Mr. Trowell's studio, her sanctuary from her mother's neglect and her aunt's cold custody. He could see her face contort, the tears stuffing up her nose and blotching her skin as she tells her teacher she has to leave Windsor, leave her lessons, leave him, forever. Monty knows that Garnet would let her cry into his tweed jacket; would pull out a handkerchief and tenderly dry her face, then sit her down, take out his violin, and play for her—something sad, and sweet, and yet lilting, too, as if promising her that it wasn't, yet, the end of the world.

That volume of fiction with the title *Bliss*, containing the story of the girl and her music teacher and the wind: does it matter whether Cassie discovers it at the public library or on her grandfather's shelves? She has discovered her own story in Mansfield's imaginings; her true, her secret, self. Katherine consoles her for the loss of her music teacher and his studio, the one place where she can both find and forget herself and be completely happy. And when, some time later, reading those biographies she professed to despise, Cassie comes across Garnet Trowell's connection with Katherine Mansfield, her life changes forever. Had she remained in Windsor, seeing Garnet every day, seeing him grow older, grow ill and weak, her love for him would have altered into a mixture of pity and embarrassment. Instead, she locks his image inside her, like the fossil of a leaf: intricate, frozen, perfect. And years later, when she steals those letters from the Library of Assumption College, when she breaks the seal and reads them, the girl who'd once read herself into Mansfield's Matilda finally becomes Garnet's Kassie.

Fiction, speculation, no truer and no more false than the short story he'd just read. Were he by some miracle to find Miss Baby at this very moment and accuse her of the theft of Garnet Trowell's letters, she would laugh in his face. Anyone who could incriminate her, anyone who might have known of her actions, had died long ago—hadn't she told him that she was alone in the world, and delighted to be so?

All the same, Monty found himself creeping from his room into the hallway, where the telephone was kept. Someone was watching a game show in the living room, but no one came out to bother him as he searched through the Windsor telephone directory. There was nothing listed under Trowell, and no Dunstan or Plint to be found. Of Barnes there were many, several with the initial J. But only one of them lived on Victoria Street.

Windsor has been a relatively progressive place, by North American standards. Before the Civil War, the city was a regular stop on the Underground Railway; in the 1960s, Windsor's black community—2 percent of the city's total population—contributed a chairman to the Board of Education, as well as a solicitor and an alderman to the city government. Where Detroit was plagued by racial violence that led, well before the Civil Rights movement, to deaths and injuries (thirty-four fatalities, seven hundred casualties in the riots of 1943), Windsor celebrated a yearly Emancipation Day to mark the anniversary of the freeing of American slaves. The city even boasted a "Miss Sepia" beauty contest, which, Monty thought it fair to guess, Miss Barnes could easily have won in her day, had she cared to enter.

For the skin of Jeanette Barnes was a warm, dark, beautiful brown, something Cassandra Baby hadn't thought it necessary or important to mention in her *Rewards and Recollections*. Greeting him at the door of the sombre house on Victoria Street, Miss Barnes offered him a cup of coffee. He thanked her, and as she went off to the kitchen, Monty examined the shelves lining every wall of the sitting room. Not leather-bound show books, as at Miss Baby's, but a library comprehending almost every subject: geology and astronomy, history and philosophy, fine art and music, and shelf after shelf of poetry and fiction. There were some first editions, and many paperbacks that might have been picked up at secondhand stores and library sales. Had he known, he would have told Miss Barnes that he was a book dealer; instead he'd told her the truth, that he was a teacher. Not a writer, not a doctoral student, but a teacher. It had surprised him how easily the word had slipped out. It had also surprised him that she'd agreed to see him. But he figured she was as anxious for news of Cassie as he was.

"If it weren't for all those books, I'd have moved into an apartment years ago." Miss Barnes was back with the coffee; she handed him his cup and motioned him to sit down. "But I can't bear to part with even one of them. It's an expensive house to keep up, with the taxes and all. I'll have to sell it soon enough, move into one of those holding pens for shufflers-off. The books will go to the library, of course."

Monty must have looked confused, because she added, "I used to work there, until I retired. At Assumption College— only it's the University of Windsor now. But I expect you know that."

"Yes," Monty said, slowly. And then, "I think I know where in the library you used to work." He was remembering the inscription he'd found on the volume of *Bliss* at Crilly Court: *To Cassie from J. B., 1937* . . . He'd given her his name and confessed his profession: he might as well get on with the rest. "You worked in the Rare Books Collection, Miss Barnes. I don't know how or why, but you told Cassie about the Mansfield letters—you helped her get her hands on them."

Miss Barnes looked up at him, her head perched on one side like a small, wary bird. Behind the thick lenses of her glasses, her eyes were a cloudy blue. It was the only sign of failing powers he could detect; Miss Barnes, though she must have been in her eighties, was as bright as the crimson dress she wore. When she spoke at last, it was with a mixture of crispness and kindness.

"You must think you know a great deal, Mr. Mills. About Cassie, even about me. I expect she told you just about everything."

He nodded.

"Except maybe the truth? You know that Cassie grew up in this house—yes, of course you do. That her father worked, on and off—mostly off—for Hiram Walker's, and her mother was a housemaid here? They met at the movies or some such place—I'm sure I don't need to tell you the rest of that story. I was working for Mrs. Plint as a cook at the time. She was a decent woman, not many would have kept on a housemaid expecting a baby—or kept the baby when that housemaid ran off. Dilly disappeared about the same time as Joseph Baby left Windsor—no one ever heard from either of them again. The baby? Mrs. Plint raised her, educated her—treated her almost like a daughter."

Monty swallowed hard. "And Chicago? How did Cassie get to Chicago?"

"Through a cousin of Mrs. Plint's. He was a wealthy man, retired, with a hobby—I can't remember what he collected, but he needed someone to help him with cataloguing and correspondence. As soon as Cassie had finished her schooling, she was shipped off to work for him. She was just seventeen. There was no funny business, if that's what you're thinking. He was otherwise inclined, was Mr. Griffiths. But he took a liking to her, and she worked hard for him, and when he died he left her his apartment and a small pension. The way Cassandra left her house to me."

"Her house," Monty repeated, stupidly.

Miss Barnes ignored him. "She was a widow when I came to work for her. It was a good job—oh, it paid next to nothing, but I liked her, and I got along with Cassie, which was more than anyone else could do. When the war came, I got a factory job—wages were high enough that I could put myself through school on what I saved." She took his empty cup and placed it back on the tray. "When Cassandra got ill, I came back to nurse her—I took leave from my job at the library. She had no children and neither did I. It seemed the decent thing to do. And that's really all there is to know about us, Mr. Mills."

She was expecting him to rise from his chair and take his

leave, but he sat forward instead, his hands gripping his knees. "And Mr. Trowell?"

"Garnet Trowell." Miss Barnes sighed a little, shaking her head. "Cassie took music lessons from him for a while—violin. We thought it would take her out of herself. She was a terrible brooder, Cassie. She'd shut herself up in her room with a pile of books and a face like thunder. He was a lovely man, Mr. Trowell, a fine teacher. For that hour she spent each week in the studio on Ouellette he made her feel she was the most important person in the world. He was that kind of teacher.

"But you'll understand that, being a teacher yourself, Mr. Mills. I've always thought it a fine profession for a man—and women, too, of course. But it teaches a man patience, which is a virtue most men of my acquaintance are sorely lacking. Excuse me, I do ramble on, and you have far more important things to do than listen to an old woman's wool-gathering. When you next see Cassie, give her my best, will you? Now, I'll see you out and get back to my books."

Painfully, steadily, she rose to her feet; she stood waiting for Monty to rise as well. He did, but instead of thanking her and taking his leave he asked another question, speaking more loudly than he'd intended.

"Why did you tell her about the letters?"

Miss Barnes folded her arms against her chest and looked him straight in the eye. "Cassandra was dying. She was the closest thing to a mother Cassie ever had. It was time for some forgiveness, it was time for the two of them to speak face to face. As it turned out, it was too late for any of that—Cassandra died the day before Cassie showed up at her door. But what was done was done. How else could I get Cassie back to Windsor except by telling her about those letters?"

"You helped her steal them—"

"I told her where they were kept. It wasn't any secret to the people who worked there—the cabinet was never locked. Listen, Mr. Mills: the letters were taken, the letters were given back. It shouldn't have happened, but it did, and all in all there was no harm done."

He was shouting now. "How can you be so sure? How do you know that something didn't get taken but stolen, Miss Barnes, stolen and never returned?"

"Why dig up the past, why root around in other people's lives—in their hearts?" she threw back at him. "I've told you what you need to know, Mr. Mills. I've set you straight. Now I want you to go."

For the first time, Miss Barnes's voice sounded pleading, apprehensive. She'd taken the risk of seeing him, Monty realized, of letting him into her house, as a kindness to him— to tell him the truth of Cassie's story, to convince him to go quietly, and to go for good. None of this stopped him from crying out, "Where is she? You know, don't you?"

Before Miss Barnes could reply, another voice broke in, as crabbed as ever, but shakier than he remembered it.

"It's all right, Jeanette. If he's come all this way, I suppose I can spare him a minute of my time."

Cassie Baby was leaning on her cane, in the hallway. She took a few halting steps into the room, lowered herself into an armchair, and waved off Miss Barnes, who reminded her that she was supposed to be resting. Monty was shocked to see how ill Miss Baby looked. Miss Barnes's eyes must be worse than he thought; he whispered to her that they'd better get a doctor. She nodded and went off to phone. Cassie waited till she'd gone, then spoke, measuring her words, as if each one cost her more than she'd bargained for.

"You want to see what I stole from the library? You think you deserve to see it?"

He'd been about to say they could talk when she was feeling better, but she'd baited him, and he returned in kind:

"Much more than you do. At least I'm not a common thief."

She laughed, without smiling. "No more am I, Mr. Mills, no more am I." And then, clenching the head of her cane: "If I give you the letter, what'll you do with it?"

"Return it to the library."

"After you've read through it."

"Of course I'll read it—what difference can it make?"

She fumbled in the pocket of her cardigan, drawing out a small, thick envelope, four inches by six. And then she held it out to him, her hand shaking. He took the envelope as gingerly as if it had been a wafer, reading the address out loud: "Katherine Mansfield, 39 Abingdon Mansions, Pater Street, Kensington." It was postmarked August 1910. There was a return address: "10, Carlton Hill—G. C. Trowell."

So Garnet had sent it, grieving, bewildered Garnet, on receipt of Ida's stilted note. In this letter, if Miss Baby's instincts proved correct, Garnet had defended himself to the woman who'd run out on him, miscarried their child, and refused to have anything more to do with a man who wasn't ambitious or gifted or driven enough to matter.

Miss Baby held out her hand, and Monty gave the letter back to her. His hand was shaking, too: the letter he'd held had never been opened.

"No one's ever read it," she said. "Not even the person it's addressed to. Poor Garnet—he poured out his heart to her, and she didn't even get her feet wet. She must have sent it back with Ida, got her to deliver it to Carlton Hill, put it straight into his hands. And Garnet could never throw it away."

Monty stared at the letter in his adversary's hand. It seemed to him that, for the first time, he could read everything clearly. Cassie had stolen the letter only to keep it sealed up, to hold Garnet's secret safe in her keeping. Why?

In case, just in case, the contents of that envelope addressed to Abingdon Mansions should show what she couldn't stand to see. A Garnet who was just as the biographers described him: dreamy, immature, weak-willed; a coward whose refusal to stand by his lover had set off that chain of medical disasters—miscarriage, gonorrhea, pleurisy, tuberculosis—that had led to Mansfield's early death at Fontainebleau. And yet the temptation to believe in him must have been so strong—to open that letter and hear Garnet speaking to her, not as a teacher this time, but as the lover from whom she'd been forced to part. Garnet's Cassie.

Miss Baby lay back in her chair, her eyes closed, her breathing suddenly rough and shallow. Monty bent down beside her. The next thing he knew, ambulance attendants were pushing him aside, and Miss Barnes was whispering something in Cassie's ear. No one paid the slightest attention to Monty as he left the house, Garnet's letter in his pocket.

BEYOND THE BLUE MOUNTAINS

Fontainebleau, 1922

Katherine and Ida arrive at Gurdjieff's commune at Le Prieuré des Basses Loges, near Fontainebleau, a little more than a week after Katherine's thirty-fourth birthday. They have driven in a cab from the station at Avon; the priory's sagging gates are open, and they ride down the drive between rows of huge chestnut trees, their few remaining leaves a soft, burning yellow. The cab stops by the entrance, near a stone fountain into which Katherine dips her hand, then raises it, as if to taste the water on her fingertips. Ida tries hard not to look alarmed; the fountain is cracked and dry. All through the day's long journey Katherine has seemed more dead than alive; now she is holding out her arms to the flower beds brimming with orange and scarlet nasturtiums, her face alight with a joy Ida fears will go straight to her heart.

But Katherine fails to collapse; she walks up the steps and into the priory hall looking stronger than she has for weeks. Ida follows with the luggage, which a young man immediately takes in hand, disappearing down a long, bare hallway that reminds her of an orphanage. She is offered a room for the night, but she shakes her head and returns to the cab, keeping her promise to Katie. Ida fixes her eyes on the back of the driver's head as the car pulls away; it's only once they've passed through the gates that she turns to look back. What she sees is what is plainly not there: Katie running towards her with arms outstretched, her feet kicking up clouds of golden leaves that reach to the black branches of the chestnut trees.

Le Prieuré has been falling apart for a century at least. The windowsills have lost their paint—grey wood comes away from them in soft splinters. The wallpaper is discoloured with smoke from guttering candles; the floor tiles are cracked, and some have been gouged away. But there's a fire burning blue and orange in the room where Katherine is led by a pretty girl of seventeen who comes from Lithuania and speaks a mixture of English and Russian. A tray of mulled wine and cakes is waiting for her, and once the girl has helped Katherine change from her travelling clothes, Gurdjieff himself appears. He's taller than she expected, and heavier, but he moves gracefully in his flowing trousers, wearing an equally flowing shirt beneath an embroidered vest. Anyone less like the thin-shouldered, tweed-jacketed, eternally anxious-looking Jack Murry can't be imagined. Gurdjieff sits down across from her; he speaks with great authority but with kindness, too, as he asks this obviously dying woman what she wants of him.

"Health," Katherine answers.

Gurdjieff says nothing. His silence frightens her; she rushes to stitch over its nakedness.

"There is no line, no split, between body and spirit—that's what you teach here, isn't it, Mr. Gurdjieff? I've been ill for such a long time, I have been dying for four years now, but no doctor has ever tried to heal the whole of me. I want to change my life, completely. I want to become one true person, not just a shuffle of selves and masks, each one falser than the one before. It's death already, living as I've lived, always playing a part, thinking sometimes I've become that part, my true self lost or stolen or thrown away. I know how late it is to want anything, but all I want now is to live as simply as I can, to do nothing but the work you give me, however unimportant. I don't even want to write—not until I've stopped being such a poor excuse for a human being."

Gurdjieff has not taken his eyes off her all this time. With his enormous moustaches, he reminds her of the sandy-whiskered god of her childhood. Yet this is no Harold Beauchamp before her, folding his arms, speaking at last.

"If you wish to stay with us, Mrs. Murry, you may do so. You may live among us, trying to find your feet and your hands for the first time, the way a baby does. You must share whatever of the daily work you feel strong enough to do. And you must also spend time resting in the cow barn." For the first time, he smiles—not just his eyes, but his whole face curves into a grin. "In my country, Mrs. Murry, the best treatment for your complaint is to inhale the warm, moist breath of cows—this is good for the spirit and the body."

Gurdjieff takes his leave, and the girl, whose name is Adèle, asks Mrs. Murry if she would like to be helped into bed. Katherine, who has spent so many months of the past two years confined to her bed, says no, she is happy just to sit on the couch, wrapped in her shawl. But would Adèle mind very much staying with her, not speaking, but just sitting there, looking at the fire? Adèle settles down on cushions piled by Katherine's feet; the women's shadows stagger against the walls as the flames leap up.

———

For the next two months, Katherine takes part in the life of the commune. In her fur coat she cheerfully ruins her hands, scraping carrots and peeling onions in the damp, cold kitchen. She lies on Persian carpets above the cow byre; walks in the flower and vegetable gardens, admiring the basic forms of stalk and leaf. Though she insists in her letters to Ida that her life with Gurdjieff is the opposite of hardship, the fire in her room is one that doesn't roar but flickers, and the room itself is now in the servants' quarters, an affair of bare scrubbed boards, a jug and basin, and a bed that is more like a packing crate. Icy winds whistle down the corridors; meals at the communal table are plain and prescriptive. And yet she hasn't spent a single day in bed since coming to the Prieuré: what better sign of a miracle could there be?

Ida has found work at a farm in Lisieux, where she milks cows and churns butter, all to be close to Katie. The letters she receives from Le Prieuré are a mass of contradictions. Letters forbidding her to trespass on Katherine's freedom, to treat her as a helpless invalid. Letters complaining that if Ida doesn't sew her some new knickers, Katherine will have to go about with paper ham frills on her legs. Letters confessing that, without her, Katherine cannot live—quite literally. Letters insisting that Katherine is no "grateful angel" but as much the "old Adam" as ever. And that Ida is to believe, without any signs of encouragement, that Katherine loves her always; wants her for her wife.

And so the wifely albatross takes the train to Paris, where she purchases toothpaste and mouthwash, coats and shawls, and nightdresses made of the softest fabrics, all to send to

Katherine. She spends a small fortune of her own on a bottle of Genêt Fleuri, that bittersweet scent made of muguet and heliotrope and wild yellow broom. She retrieves, from the concierge of some hotel or other, Katherine's blue velvet coat with the black rabbit collar; she seeks out the brilliantly coloured stockings for which Katherine has a passion. Craving to do the one good thing that can still be done for a body falling to pieces from inside. To swathe it in beautiful, sumptuous cloth, as if it were a doll whose cloth limbs have split and turned to powder.

With Adèle, Katherine practises Russian, learning how to say: "I am cold, please bring me wood for a fire" and "Could you please take this letter to the post?" She sits one evening with her former mentor, Orage, watching the dancing in the great hall, listening to the singing and the thump of tambourines. When he asks her if she's been able to write anything since coming to Le Prieuré, she tells him she has finished with stories. When she is well again, she will begin something larger, something much more generous, something that doesn't just squint or snap at the world, but sees. Orage can't tell whether she is speaking truthfully when she tells him how small and false everything she's written seems to her now. But she looks so frail—not ill so much as insubstantial—that he has no heart to press her on the matter, as he would have years ago.

As Christmas approaches, Mrs. Murry helps the children make paper stars and snowflakes; she writes to her husband telling him of the enormous plum pudding being prepared in the kitchen—enough for sixty people. Mr. Gurdjieff, she says, wants a true English Christmas. Jack may not have any use for an English Christmas spent among Russians in France, but would he consider coming to stay for a few days afterwards—would he come for the New Year? There are things she must talk to him about, important things concerning them both that she can't trust to paper. She has been so happy here—she is so much stronger. But perhaps she has learned all she can at Le Prieuré; perhaps it is time for her to leave, for them to pick up their life together.

Adèle takes the letter to the post for her; Adèle, who has fallen in love with Mrs. Murry, with her exquisite clothes and beautiful manners and the black, brilliant eyes that turn her thin face into a lantern.

ROGER

Avon, France, October 1986

It's far too wild outside to visit your grave. Rain is slamming down and the wind moans as if it had a body and could know that body's pain. I have had to take shelter here in the conservatory of a dull, comfortable hotel in an equally dull and comfortable town. This is a fine room to read in; no one comes here, no radios or voices drift in to disturb me. What am I reading? Your *Collected Stories*, which I've brought with me from Looe, and which I shall leave behind in yet another hotel, the morning I board the plane back to New Zealand. So that someone else may experience that joy you knew in discovering those rare books that come, you said, from a far country, giving us "something never dreamed of, something new, marvellous, dazzling—changing the whole of life."

Which of all your stories dazzles me here, now, with the wind tearing leaves from the trees and the sun small as a coin? "The Daughters of the Late Colonel"—your masterpiece, they say. And "The Canary," the last piece you ever wrote: slight, sentimental, they also say. What speaks to me in these stories, now, is what the people in them sense but cannot express. What Constantia longs for when she lies outstretched in the chill moonlight; what she can't explain to her sister, what she forgets to say, just as it seems she is about to speak herself into life, her own life, at long last. And what the old woman in "The Canary" understands to be at the core of life, "something which is like longing, and yet is not longing." "What is it?" she asks, and then gives the only truthful reply: "One can never know." The only bearable answer, for what you'd learned by then: that the mystery we sense at the heart of life is nothing but emptiness.

All the pages and pages given over to explicating, analyzing, theorizing about your hundreds of thousands of words, Katherine. Not altogether useless, those pages, so long as one understands that they are nothing but the mesh through which the story slips, a sieve cupping water. Not gold or jewels, but water, what we are, after all, mostly made of. Ida was right to fault your biographers for failing to catch the opalescence, the always shifting milk and fire of you. Signals of your "real inmost self"—signals that only lovers can send to one another; signals at once similar and contradictory.

If purity of heart is to will one thing, Katherine, then your heart was as spotted as a pair of dice. Ambivalence, and a metaphysical, not just moral, ambiguity: these were your heart's truth. I am not speaking of duplicity, mind you, but of meaning two opposing things at once, the confluence of Imagination—what could be—and Wisdom—what must be. Thus you meant your body to be cured by Gurdjieff, so that you could become invisible instead of invalid, so that no friend or stranger, appalled at the fragility of your face and body, should feel compelled to offer you an arm, a chair. And thus, at the very moment of willing yourself cured, you made clear your desire to die in Gurdjieff's hands, with your soul, at least, whole and healed.

Your death was like so much of your handwriting—illegible, or, at the most, offering multiple interpretations. The girl Adèle said that you danced up the stairs that last night at Le Prieuré; Jack declared you climbed those same stairs, slowly and carefully, starting to haemorrhage halfway up. Two different stories from two witnesses in the same place at the same time. And from a friend who was not there, we hear that you met your death while talking to Jack, that you turned your head too quickly, so that your lungs tore like a scrap of silk.

No one disputes that blood gushed from your lips: true to form, Jack merely mentions the fact, while Adèle tells how she grabbed a towel to press against your mouth to try to stop the bleeding. In which case you could not have uttered those last words your husband gives to you: "I believe . . . I am going . . . to die." Is Adèle, young but capable, telling the truth, or Jack, who came to dream of you sitting up and smiling at him from a flower-filled coffin? Who am I to trust, what am I to write—how am I to end your story?

Not as your husband did. Two months after he buried you at Avon, he proposed matrimony to a school chum whom you'd once feared capable of blackmailing you. He was on the verge of consoling himself with pillowy Frieda Lawrence when he was carried off by Violet Lemaistre, a slip of a girl who set herself to copy you in every way: the cut of your hair, the style of your prose, the very slant of your handwriting. They were married a year and four months after he buried you. They might still have been honeymooning when the sexton had to dig you up and toss you into a *fosse commune* in the paupers' section of the cemetery (Jack had forgotten to pay for the upkeep of your grave). Violet was dying of tuberculosis by the time you were dug up again and restored to solitude. Five years underground and your body, the sexton swore, was perfectly preserved. There's no report as to how

Violet fared; she did, however, succeed in giving Jack his children: a daughter and a son. Twice a widower, he waited only a month before he took another wife, a harridan who, by all accounts, made his life—and his children's—a living hell.

Yet Murry's children loved him, it appears: "Beloved Quixote" his daughter called him, the daughter to whom he gave your name. What would you have made of that marriage, those children—you who wrote, so airily and bitterly, that Jack ought to marry some really healthy young thing and have children to whom you'd gladly stand godmother? Tell me, Katherine, I badly need to know. I have a child of my own, a son I love more dearly than my life—or yours, though I have never been able to tell him so. I am much less than a Quixote in his eyes—and as for being loved by him, how can I answer? Perhaps all that ties him to me, still, is the fiction of a bloodline: were he to know the truth, he might walk away from me as if I were nothing more than the stranger he has made of me. And I of him, yes. I confess my stupidity, the blunder I've never been able to undo, sending him away from me. As I was sent by my parents, to a school I loathed, to cure me of my shyness, when all it gave me was a hunger for silence, for painless obscurity.

Why do we force upon others—the ones we most love—the mistakes others have forced on us? By repeating the error, or swinging so fully to its opposite that different but equal damage is done? I sent my son away from me because it was, I believed, "the right thing to do, under the circumstances." Because it was either send him away to school, or marry again to give him what's called a normal family life. I had done well enough, I was told, in raising a child; to "make a man" was a far more difficult task. What Estelle meant by this was a successful breadwinner, a trusty husband, a forceful father. What I understood the term to mean was this: a man able to live and love fully, at home in a community, on speaking terms with happiness.

Tell me, Katherine, is there such a thing? Not success, but happiness? You promised Ida you'd return to her as a coffin worm in a matchbox, confiding the secrets of the grave. Surely this is the greatest of those secrets, the one that most concerns the living. Ida says you broke your promise—poor, dim, clumsy Ida. Your monster, your albatross—why should I wring my hands over Ida? While you lived, she had the life she wanted, serving you with her love, making you the gift of her life, as innumerable wives have done forever for their husbands. When you died, Ida mourned, but her grief was no monstrosity; she looked after Jack till he wanted her gone. She moved to a shambles of a cottage in the New Forest and became Our Lady of Good Intentions and Heartfelt Deeds, showering others with her worldly goods but giving to no one else that clumsy devotion saved for you alone.

You were right, Ida did recover from your death. There really was something rock-like in her under "all that passion for helplessness." Ida gave all and received in turn—what? Herself made beautiful through the beauty you conjured up by placing flowers in a vase, just so, or wakening a room by tossing a shawl here, a cushion there. In life and in death, you were Ida's Black Opal, flashing out light and opening seams of dark. Of all those who loved you, was it Ida who glimpsed the truth you found? That this life of ours that we think of as a journey, with a marked road to follow and a destination to achieve, is really a random leaping back and forth. Between what we have and what we want, what we are and what we would become, what we can't help but know and what we can only imagine. An opal thrown like a skipping stone, light to light across the dark.

There have been worse deaths than yours. For example, that of Mrs. Patrick Campbell—Shaw's Eliza—alone, in a cheap French hotel. It was three days before anyone noticed she hadn't come down to breakfast. She wasn't entirely alone: her Pekingese, Moonbeam, was with her, lying on the foot of the bed. Just what did that elderly, ill-tempered dog do for three whole days, shut up with a dead actress who'd once been beautiful as a summer night, they say, and with a voice like a cello?

Or Frederick Goodyear's. Out of sheer boredom—or boredom bitten by despair—Goodyear left his cushy job at the Meteorological Records Office and rushed to France just in time for the Battle of the Somme. You know this, of course; you had all those letters from him wishing you blossoming breasts and navel. You knew that, like your young brother, he died in France, but did you know that first he'd had both legs blown off for his trouble? Or that, while waiting to be shipped back to England, he'd lain in a makeshift ward, among the not-yet-corpses, reading Joyce's *Dubliners*? Before he'd had a chance to finish the book, his heart caught up with his shattered legs. He died reading "The Dead"; he disappeared, along with the handful of poems he'd written: "Slow and sweet Decomposition . . . / Time for Silence and the Worm!" His literary remains were left to the British Library, where they lodged undisturbed for decades. Until one of your biographers found them, read them, and turned their author into yet another footnote in the life of someone vastly more important.

Garnet Trowell, Floryan Sobieniowski, Frederick Goodyear, Francis Carco, John Middleton Murry, and the others: footnotes, all. None of them gave you what I offered you, unasked. My whole life, my whole heart, my chances for some small measure of success, my possibilities of happiness. Sometimes it seems to me that happiness is the greatest theft of all. The moments or hours—years, if we're very lucky—that we manage to steal from loneliness, boredom, grief. From understanding too well what and where we really are and what's going to become of us. The Grand Larceny of Happiness.

Larceny, and lies. I have said it's been too dark and wild today to go to your grave, but why should the weather have stopped me? Unlike the room where you died, the little cemetery at Avon still stands firm. I can thank the manager of my hotel for saving me the trouble of visiting Le Prieuré. The whole building is under demolition, he says, its stones carted away to prop up someone's garden wall. What a pass we've come to when even stones can find no resting place. As for the stone over your grave—who knows how long it will stand there, spelling out your name and dates?

It is not so very remarkable, of course, having a fear of death; it's one of the things, they say, that make us human. What's worse, unthinkably worse, is to face death believing that it would have been better never to have lived at all. My terror has little to do with the body, but everything to do with the end of possibility, of the chance, however small, of change and difference. Of desire, Katherine. In place of blue mountains, a stone. It's not that I fear how seeing your grave, touching that stone with my hand, will kill a woman who's been dead, now, these sixty years. What I fear, of course, is that it will kill me—kill everything I've been, everything I've longed for, leaving me even less than I am. I want so badly to believe it could still happen as you've imagined it: that secret self, pushing its sealed bud, its green spear, through the leaves and mould, "until, one day, the light discovers it and sets the flower free and—we are alive—we are flowering for our moment upon the earth."

I want this flowering, I want it badly—not just for myself, but for my son. It is time, high time, that we sat down together and unpacked our hearts to make room for it. I had meant to make a beginning on this journey, in a place neither of us knew—it would be easier, I thought. I want him to believe it possible, however mysterious and even absurd, that we can come into ourselves, uncover ourselves, real at last in our vision of what and how we might be. Real, not true—I don't want truth, I don't want that crystal you held up at the end of your life, calling it finer, more precious, than happiness.

Perhaps for the extraordinary ones, those whose bodies are composed more of fire than water, truth is the sole desire. But I, in my wateriness, choose love, love over everything. Love for my dead wife and my living child. Love for the small space of time that is all we are given to desire in.

And love for you, again and always, Katherine—you.

MONTY

It was late afternoon; Monty was walking along the river. He'd called the hospital for news of Miss Baby and had spoken to Jeanette: Cassie was in intensive care, she said; it didn't look good. There was no reproach in her voice, but no great warmth, either. Why should there be? He'd been more than a bully, barging into her house, shouting accusations. He'd been a hypocrite, too. For if Cassie Baby was a thief, what in the world was he? Two letters in his possession that didn't belong to him—two letters he'd not just intercepted, but stolen.

But who did it belong to, this letter hiding in his coat pocket? To the dead or the living? Garnet's widow hadn't been able to make up her mind. She might have sold some of the papers found with Garnet's belongings to Mrs. Dick, but this envelope, addressed in her husband's handwriting, she hadn't been able to open, any more than Cassie had, or Katherine herself. Did Marion Trowell suspect all the pain and confusion she'd open if she broke the seal? Or did she simply refuse to take what didn't belong to her?

When he reached the Dieppe Gardens, Monty sat down on a bench to watch the freighters passing by. The lights of skyscrapers across the water seemed to be ripening in the dusk. How many times during his life in Windsor had Garnet sat on a bench like this and looked out over the river? At the spectacular facade of the Penobscot Building, which may have come to symbolize to him all the brave and splendid things he'd meant to do with his life, or perhaps just the all too visible line between success and failure. What did he feel, taking in the Ambassador Bridge and its invisible twin, the Tunnel, which had made it doubly easy to cross the river at the very moment the Trowells had arrived in Windsor? Had Garnet and Marion crossed to Detroit on Saturday nights to listen to the symphony for twenty-five cents at the Orchestra Hall, stopping for a ginger ale on the way home? Or would it have been too painful to take such temporary flight to the land where they were supposed to have made their fortunes? Did Garnet long for the kind of orchestral position he'd had in Durban; had Marion been aiming for a concert career in the States? Did the Trowells consider Windsor a haven or prison?

Garnet, dying of cancer, sitting on a park bench on the wrong side of the Detroit River. In many ways, his life had been lucky, perhaps even happy—wouldn't you agree? He'd escaped the hell of both world wars, his lungs being too weak for the first and his age keeping him out of the second. He'd nearly lived out his three score and ten; he'd been a valued member of the musical community of Windsor, a respected performer, a cherished teacher. Marriage, children, a profession—all the things we're supposed to want, all the things that are supposed to make up a full life.

And yet, and yet—Garnet hadn't had anything like that glorious career the phrenologist had predicted, feeling the lumps and bumps of a small boy's skull all those years ago in

Wellington. When he was a child, he'd been kidnapped by Maoris, or had dreamed such a break from the jail of being his father's son, a none too prodigious prodigy. Did he sit by this river in the last months of his life, dreaming himself back to being a child of the Sun God? What would Tui have made of that story, Tui whose ancestors had been working the gumfields through which the Trowells would have travelled on their way to give concerts in the bush towns of the North? During the long depression of the 1880s, the decade of Garnet's and Katherine's births, Maori had been joined in the gumfields by the unemployed and by minor criminals, sent there by judges who decreed that wasteland of shanties and rotten roads, swamp and scrub, a fit and proper punishment for thieves.

Monty reached into his pocket and took out Garnet's letter. Holding it in his gloved hands, he looked at it as if he were trying to memorize not just the writing on the envelope but the precise slant of ink against paper. A private collector would pay a small fortune for this letter; scholars would fight for the chance to light up one of the murkier hallways of Mansfield's life. If he were to publish the contents of this envelope, it would be a coup that could launch him, make his name. Did it matter what the letter would reveal about Garnet or Kassie? Didn't people have the right to know what was true and what false in Mansfield's life—wasn't that the work of a biographer? And if Garnet came off as the hero of the piece, Monty could do exactly what Miss Baby had wanted—publish her *Vindication*. Hadn't he worked on it hard enough to make it, at least in part, his own? He could work out some explanation for how he'd come by the letter; he could hop a plane to New Zealand tomorrow with everything he'd hoped for from this journey safe in his pocket.

Do you remember my telling you about the curved glass walls Monty looked at so long on Wacker Drive? The lighted windows of the skyscrapers across the river brought those glass walls back to him. Only this time what he saw there was the face of the child who'd been Cassie Baby, as she'd described herself in her *Recollections*, and as Miss Barnes had revealed her to be. He saw the young girl Matilda, running off to her music lesson, yelling, "To hell with my mother!" He saw, too, the child in a sketch of a story Mansfield never finished, a child dragged between a quarrelling couple walking down a dirt road. "Obstinate, ugly & heavy—their only child, the child of their love. The only thing that held them together & kept them alive to each other."

Once again, the face of Cassie Baby merged, in his mind's eye, with another face. But this time it wasn't Roger's. It was his own. Love and hate, misery and the rarest flash of happiness: running away to a music lesson; jumping in and out of the waves with a bunch of Maori kids. In Cassie's story, her father held her in his arms before leaving her forever, spoke to her, in his own way, before dying. In Roger's story, Tui adored her child and husband, never meant to steal away or take from them anything they might have loved.

Carefully, Monty slipped the letter into his pocket. He shivered, as much from fear as from cold. Of course he had nothing in common with Cassie Baby; of course his life, his work, his prospects for success, would be nothing like hers. Impatiently, he got up from the bench and started walking, almost running, back to his bed-and-breakfast. It was time to have done with this messy, troubling, disruptive journey. It was time, at last, to go home.

Come, my unseen, my unknown, let us talk together. To whom have I spoken, writing out this story? Who, if anyone, will answer me? A girl who asked me to write to her, to give her my address, and, along with it, some sense of who I am, of what my story is and where it might take me.

Or have I been speaking, at last, with my real self, the one I've kept so carefully hidden, letting my other self deal with everything ugly or painful, deal with it in a way that has cost me nothing? Until this unreal self, "greedy and jealous of the real one . . . took more and stayed longer," the most masterful thief of all, the self who robs the self. Until I was always acting a part, the part of a distant, detached, addictively dishonest man, who didn't know or care whether any real self was left at all. That "radiant being who wasn't either spiteful or malicious" but honest and open, the self Montgomery Mills would give anything to merge with, but is terrified to become.

It's a common response, the saying goes, to welcome a gift and resent a theft. I've always thought of thefts and gifts as opposites, but I've come to see that they can be one and the same. My mother's death, and Roger's inexhaustible love; all the work I've lost, the book I can never write, and the chance, the barest chance, now, for some simple, honest kind of happiness. Learning to talk with my father, a task so difficult for both of us that learning sign language would be simpler. And yet we go on trying, groping towards something, giving something, refusing to believe that something, however small or awkward or unsure, is nothing. Perhaps the only way to happiness is hope. The way I hope that you might, one day, ring up from the bus station in Invercargill, asking for directions to the school where you'll find me teaching once term begins again after the summer holidays. Teaching boys as miserable as I was in their place; giving them something—knowledge, language, even just stories—to push the misery away.

You see, I didn't, as you may have feared, publish Garnet's letter along with my own version of Cassie's *Vindication*. And though the letter is no longer in my possession, I didn't destroy it unread, either, but gave it to the one person I could trust to honour it. But before I explain, before I finish this story I've been telling you, I want to correct something I said earlier—something about how sadly mistaken a name my mother's was. There's something I've come across while preparing a history lesson for my class of twelve-year-olds, an observation of Captain Cook's, no less, on the tuis he encountered while navigating Dusky Sound two hundred years ago:

> Under its throat hang two little tufts of snow-white feathers, called poies, which being the Otaheitean word for ear-rings, occasioned our giving that name to the bird, which is not more remarkable for the beauty of its plumage than the sweetness of its note.

I've gone on to find out as much as I can about the tui. I've learned that it's a largely solitary bird, and partly nomadic; that when it cannot find the nectar it needs, it will jump about in the bush in order to attract large insects—cicadas and walking sticks. That Maori kept tuis in cages and taught them to speak. That the highest notes of the tui's song—perhaps the most beautiful notes—are pitched beyond the range of human hearing.

———

Two men are walking down a gravel path in a small square cemetery on the outskirts of Avon, near Fontainebleau. On one side of them stands the wall of a modest factory; on another, a railway line. Katherine Mansfield hated noise and loved flowers; in this, the only "abiding place" she ever found, she is hounded by the one and bereft of the other, except for what pilgrims like these bring to her grave.

One of the men, the older one, is carrying a bouquet of marigolds—not what you know as marigolds, Edna, those crumpled-looking plants meant to keep slugs away, but the golden daisy-like flowers Mansfield loved above all others. The other man has brought nothing, it seems. He is listening carefully to his companion, who is telling him about the monuments erected to Mansfield's memory in her native Wellington. Her father commissioned a rest house and a bird bath in his daughter's name. This rest house, or bus shelter, was constructed opposite a former Beauchamp home on Fitzherbert Terrace; the bird bath was installed at the writer's old school in Karori. And just after Christmas 1934, the Wellington County Council decided to bestow the name of "Katherine" on a newly dug street. The younger man nods—he knows all this already, but he understands that what he's listening to is not meant as a lesson but as a ceremony of sorts, a protective ritual.

Perhaps because so many Wellingtonians compared the rest house to a public convenience, Sir Harold (he was knighted the year his daughter died) defended it staunchly in his *Reminiscences and Recollections.* In any case, the rest house was demolished in 1960 and replaced by another memorial shelter, in which certain of the capital's citizens are to be found to this day with bottles of cheap wine. Perhaps, Roger continues, it would have been better for Harold Beauchamp to have established a fund for the provision of decent drink to the indigent. As for the other monument, the one at Karori Public School, it, too, has gone. In 1933 *The Dominion* praised "the bird bath which is the memorial to the distinguished authoress." Sir Harold and a niece of his came out to remove the bunting with which the monument had been veiled, and to hear a Mr. Wright speak on Katherine Mansfield's life and accomplishments. Sir Harold professed himself to be deeply touched by this speech, which, he said, unlike some things written of his daughter, had the merit of being accurate.

A bird bath might have been a flighty choice for a memorial, but, Roger observes, the building of a rest house or tram shelter is no inappropriate way to mark the life of one afflicted by "wandering fits." Monty nods his agreement, then calls out to a workman leaning on a spade; the man directs them to a far corner of the cemetery. Roger stumbles, approaching the grave, and steadies himself by putting his hand on his son's arm. They are still standing arm in arm as they look down at the stone on which two names are carved: *Katherine Mansfield, Wife of John Middleton Murry*. Names, dates, and that rash speech of Hotspur's which Katherine chose for her epitaph: the speech about plucking, from danger's nettlepatch, the flower of safety.

Roger says something about having expected more—if not some quotation from Mansfield's own work, then a list of her various names and aliases: Kassie, Kezia, Katie, Kass, Kissienka, Käthe, Sally, Julian Mark, Matilda Berry, Elizabeth Stanley, Lili Heron . . . And then, having nothing left to say, he bends down to leave his flowers at the base of her grave, touching the stone as he does so. It's strange, he says, that there isn't even a pocket of earth, nothing in which flowers or even weeds might bloom. I bend down and pick up a handful of gravel, sketching out a flower on the base of the headstone, a flower simple as the ones children are taught to draw at school. And then I reach into my pocket and draw out an envelope, which I hand to my father. He stares at it for a moment, looks up at me, then slits it open with the penknife he always carries.

It's not a long letter. He reads it out as we stand in the cool, still sunlight falling over Mansfield's grave.

Dearest Kassie,

Forgive me for not using the name you wish to be known by now, but for me, it's the name of a stranger. I know it will be a famous name one day, and I wish you all the success in the world with your writing. I wish this with my whole heart.

I have thought long and hard about how to write this letter; its brevity bears no relation to the time it has taken to compose it. I have gone over and over all that happened between us, Kassie, all the joy and pain and anger. What good can it do, now, to accuse or assign blame? We might as well blame the breath in our bodies, the air we breathed together.

Perhaps you will think me foolish, dear Kassie, but what I wish for you, even more than success with your writing, is happiness. It goes without saying that I mean true happiness, the kind that isn't made or arranged, but comes as a gift, and requires a gift to embrace it.

I know no one else like you. I never shall know anyone with your passion for life, your quickness and joy, your way of becoming what you see and whom you love. May you have much love, and a long life, and may you know happiness, in spite of everything.

Ever your devoted
Garnie

BEYOND THE BLUE MOUNTAINS

Dancers are performing in the great hall to steps Gurdjieff has devised, music he's composed. Christmas—a Dickensian extravaganza—has come and gone. It's an evening early in the new year, the end of the first week of 1923. Katherine and Jack are sitting on a sofa, watching the dancers. Jack looks embarrassed at the bodies weaving and swaying before him, but Katherine's eyes are huge with pleasure. She's wearing a brilliantly embroidered shawl over her black dress, and turquoise stockings that Adèle admires, a little sadly, from across the room. She helped Mrs. Murry put on those stockings—pure silk, sent all the way from Milan. She fastened her dress for her, and pinned up her hair, which is growing long now, the fringe combed back to show the whole of her face.

Adèle is sad because she knows that Mrs. Murry is planning to leave Le Prieuré; she will ask her tonight, or when she comes to help Mrs. Murry dress in the morning, if she may come along to take care of her. Adèle has forgotten the large unhappy lady who brought Mrs. Murry to them barely three months ago. As for the husband, with his dark-rimmed glasses, his thinning hair, the anxious expression on his face, it's clear he's incapable of looking after himself, never mind a sick wife.

But Katherine has shown no signs of sickness today other than the ones Jack has seen for so long that they've lost their power to startle him. She is thin, yes, terribly thin and pale, and her face is all eyes, but she walks without a cane and has not coughed, she swears, for days. She has taken her husband all over the grounds of Le Prieuré, showing him the workrooms, the stables and mangers. They stayed to help paint the walls of the children's classrooms: fanciful animals and paradisal flowers—real flowers, Katherine insisted, the kind that bloom without any fuss in New Zealand. He was glad to pitch in; it made him think of the times they set up house when they were still the Two Tigers, painting the kitchen chairs black and the wardrobes yellow. But sitting here in the cold, drafty hall, the rigours of the voyage catching up with him, his wife expecting him to match her ardour for the strange nasal music, the heavy movements of the dancers, he feels as out of place as poor Ida did.

"It's extraordinary, don't you think?" Katherine is pressing his arm in hers. A shawl embroidered with fuchsias and peonies and birds of paradise—a long-ago gift from Ottoline—drops from her shoulders. He has to lean towards her to catch the words she's whispering now: how, even if only for a moment, she longs to join the dancers; how she can imagine no greater happiness than to be dancing.

Jack is no longer looking apprehensive, but alarmed. He can't tell how much of this talk of dancing is a performance his wife is putting on, an imitation of health and high spirits meant to convince him that it will be the easiest thing in the world for her to go back with him to London in a few days' time. It's been years since she attempted to spend a winter in

London—the few weeks she spent on her last visit there were disastrous. Take that afternoon when Anne Drey phoned to express her panic after Katherine had come to visit. She'd insisted on seeing the nursery, the frieze Anne had painted over the baby's cot. Seeing the nursery meant climbing a flight of stairs, and each of the twelve steps had torn out a piece of Katherine's lungs. She'd refused to stop climbing; even in her terror, Anne hadn't been able to make her stop.

The performance finishes, and the fire burns down to almost nothing. People are leaving the room, but Katherine sits on, wrapped in the shawl that Jack has put back around her. Through the silk of her dress, he felt the bones of her shoulders; it's been so long since he's touched her body—he's been afraid of hurting her, except that there is almost no flesh left to bruise. Glancing at Katherine's face now, he sees her watching him as if through a mask. She isn't his wife any more, she isn't his confidante, or even the writer he's published in all those small magazines and journals. She is a doll made out of porcelain and silk, and the black stones of her eyes.

But then she smiles, her eyes radiant, her whole face unbearably bright. In one fluid movement, she rises, her shawl falling to the ground. She isn't dragging herself, or creeping, now; she is running, her stockings flashing. Jack stumbles after her, shouting for her to stop, but he can barely keep up with her. By the time he reaches the hall, she is already on the stairs, holding out her arms as she's seen the Russian dancers do, glancing back but not at her husband, nor at the darkness behind him.

Ahead of her is a room with a narrow bed, where she will sit pressing her hands over her mouth, trying to keep the blood from spurting out between her fingers. Ahead of her is terror and noise and confusion; doctors pushing people from the room, more and more blood drenching her dress, the bedclothes, the doctors' hands. But this moment she is flying up the stairs, her legs brilliant as the birds embroidered on the shawl Jack holds out helplessly, below.

For this last, brief moment on the stairway, she is not arriving or departing. She is dancing.

ACKNOWLEDGMENTS

As readers of Katherine Mansfield will know, there are many echoes in this novel—especially in Roger Mills' *Beyond the Blue Mountains*—of episodes in Mansfield's life, and abundant quotations from or paraphrases of passages in her oeuvre. I am most grateful to the Society of Authors as the Literary Representative of the Estate of Katherine Mansfield for permission to reproduce copyright extracts from this author's work.

To Mansfield's biographers, in particular Antony Alpers ("The Mansfield Man") and Claire Tomalin, I am greatly beholden for superb accounts of the life and times of an extraordinary woman. Claire Tomalin's *Katherine Mansfield: A Secret Life* first alerted me to the importance—and poignancy—of Garnet Trowell's role in Katherine's story, especially vis-à-vis Ms. Tomalin's account of the chain of events leading to Mansfield's chronic invalidism and early death, a chain begun by the brief affair between these two young people. And I have found Ida Baker's *Katherine Mansfield: The Memories of L.M.* an intriguing source of information about a remarkably enduring friendship.

As do all students of Katherine Mansfield, I owe a tremendous debt to Vincent O'Sullivan and Margaret Scott, the co-editors of Mansfield's *Collected Letters*.

Margaret Scott's two-volume edition of *The Notebooks of Katherine Mansfield* has been invaluable to me; her deciphering of Mansfield's often-elusive handwriting counts as a major feat of detection. In this context, however, I should admit to authorship of Garnet Trowell's farewell letter to Kassie, at the novel's end.

I am grateful to Mansfield scholars in general, and to Gillian Boddy, Mary Burgan, Vincent O'Sullivan, and Angela Smith in particular, for their richly informed and perceptive accounts and interpretations of Mansfield's work and the contexts in which it was written. While Monty and Roger Mills and Cassandra Baby owe many of their insights into Mansfield's life and work to these critics, they do have me to thank for a number of their speculations and analyses.

I owe a lasting debt to the late Jacqueline Bardolph; it is to a short story conference organized by Dr. Bardolph during Mansfield's centenary that I owe the genesis of *Thieves*.

For their kind hospitality and fine conversation, I would like to thank Val Ashford, Catherine Byron and David Greenfield, Jan and Antony Cleminson, Judith and Robin Fairlie, Catherine and George Goodyear, Jaimy Gordon, Avril and John Harvey, Kathleen Jones and Neil Ferber, Fiona and Ian Kidman, Vincent O'Sullivan, Margaret Scott, Angela and Graham Smith, Conny Steenman-Marcusse, and Pat and Brian Wills. Claire Tomalin generously gave me time, tea, and access to papers in her possession, including the letter of Dorothy Richards to Ida Baker referred to by Miss Baby.

For their expert and cheerful help, I would like to thank the librarians of the Alexander Turnbull collection at the National Library of New Zealand, Wellington, in which I found, *inter alia*, Lady Ottoline Morrell's reminiscences of

Katherine Mansfield, and to the librarians at Queen's University, Kingston, the Newberry Library, Chicago, the Mitchell Library, Glasgow, and the British Library, London. I am grateful for the kind assistance of Brian Owens, at the University of Windsor Archives, in dealing with the Garnet Trowell Collection, Accession Number 02-013.

Constance Rooke, Eva Stachniak, and Rhea Tregebov all read earlier drafts of this novel, providing invaluable critique and encouragement. My agent, Dean Cooke, has been both generous and astute in his frequent readings of the work-in-progress; my editor, Iris Tupholme, has shown exemplary patience with and insight into the numerous forms this novel has taken. Many thanks to Siobhan Blessing, Ian Murray, and Becky Vogan for their thoughtful and painstaking assistance in the preparation of *Thieves* for publication.

In their different ways, Natalka Husar and Mary Jensen have helped enormously in sustaining me over the years I've worked on this novel. To Michael, Thomas, and Christopher Keefer I owe thanks beyond words.

I have taken the liberty of changing the publication date of Jane Dick's *Recollections* from 1993 to 1986. And, as residents of New Zealand will know, I have played fast and loose with Somes Island, turning it into a publicly accessible park long before the government did so.

Except for the initial quotation from Tolstoy, all epigraphs are drawn from Mansfield's work.

The quotation from the *New Zealand Freelance*, with its bogus account of Maori "worship," is from an actual article published there on April 27, 1907; the quotation from the New Zealand Mail has been slightly altered from the original article published there on October 29, 1902.

Miss Baby formed her knowledge of the Moody-Manners company from "The Moody-Manners Partnership," an article by Perceval Graves, Opera 9:9 (September 1958); from an article published in the *Limerick Chronicle* on July 9, 1966; and from research carried out by Godfrey Harding between 1963 and 1969, deposited at the Mitchell Library, Glasgow.

Miss Baby's summary of Windsor history is indebted to an article by Ian Sclanders in *Maclean's* magazine (August 25, 1953), "The Salty Capital of Southern Canada."

———

Those interested in the "true" identity of the thief responsible for purloining Mansfield's letters, as well as other materials, from the library of the University of Windsor may wish to consult Nicholas A. Basbane's *A Gentle Madness: Bibliophiles, Bibliomanes and the Eternal Passion for Books*, for an account of the career of Stephen C. Blumberg, who was tried and convicted for the theft of 28,000 books and documents—worth some 20 million dollars—from 154 college libraries and museums in forty-five American states and in Canada.

For an informative discussion of the Chekhov-Mansfield plagiarism debate, see Claire Tomalin's *Katherine Mansfield: A Secret Life*.

The plant which Roger finds growing on a Cornish wall is ivy-leaved toadflax.

———

Every effort has been made to trace copyright holders. The publishers would be interested to hear from any copyright holders not here acknowledged.

P.S.

Ideas,
interviews
& features

Meet Janice Kulyk Keefer

Janice Kulyk Keefer was born in Toronto in 1952 to immigrant parents of Ukrainian background. She was educated at the University of Toronto and at the University of Sussex, England, where she obtained a doctorate in English literature. She has lived in England, France, Spain, and in Nova Scotia as well as Ontario, where she currently makes her home. She teaches English Literature and Creative Writing at the University of Guelph. She and her husband, Michael Keefer, have two grown sons, Thomas and Christopher.

Janice Kulyk Keefer has been widely praised for her writing, which includes fiction, poetry, memoir, scholarly non-fiction, and children's literature. She has twice been nominated for a Governor General's Award: for *The Green Library* in the fiction category; and for *Under Eastern Eyes: A Critical Reading of Maritime Fiction* in the non-fiction category. She is a two-time winner of the CBC Radio Literary Competition and has won several National Magazine Awards for poetry, travel writing, and essays.

Kulyk Keefer has lectured throughout Canada, Europe, New Zealand and Australia, Japan, and the United States. Her writing has been translated into Spanish, Dutch, Italian, and German.

Novels and Short Fiction

Thieves: A Novel of Katherine Mansfield.
  Toronto: HarperFlamingo, 2004.
The Green Library. Toronto: HarperCollins, 1996.
Rest Harrow. Toronto: HarperCollins, 1992.
Travelling Ladies. Toronto: HarperCollins, 1992.
Constellations. Toronto: Random House, 1987.
Transfigurations. Charlottetown: Ragweed
  Press, 1987.
The Paris-Napoli Express. Ottawa: Oberon Press,
  1986.

Memoir

Honey and Ashes: A Story of Family. Toronto:
  HarperCollins, 1998.

Poetry

White of the Lesser Angels. Charlottetown:
  Ragweed Press, 1986.
Marrying the Sea. London, Ont.: Brick Books,
  1998.

Critical Works

*Two Lands: New Visions, an anthology of short
  fiction from Ukraine and Canada.* Co-edited
  with Solemea Pavlychko. Regina: Coteau
  Books, 1998.
Reading Mavis Gallant. Toronto: Oxford
  University Press, 1989.
*Under Eastern Eyes: A Critical Reading of
  Maritime Fiction.* Toronto: University of
  Toronto Press, 1987.

Meet Janice Kulyk Keefer (continued)

Awards

2004 National Magazine Award, essay, first prize.

1999 The Marian Engel Award, presented to a female Canadian writer in mid-career for her body of work.

1999 Canadian Authors Association Award for Poetry, *Marrying the Sea*.

1996 Shortlisted for the Governor General's Award for Fiction, *The Green Library*.

1994 National Magazine Award, poetry, first prize.

1991 Shortlisted for the Commonwealth Writers' Prize, Canada and the Caribbean Region, *Travelling Ladies*.

1991 Malahat Long Poem Prize, *Isle of Demons*.

1990 National Magazine Award, poetry, first prize.

1987 Shortlisted for the Governor General's Award for Non-fiction, *Under Eastern Eyes: A Critical Reading of Maritime Fiction*.

1987 British Airways Commonwealth Poetry Prize, Regional Winner, Canada and the Caribbean.

1986 CBC Radio Literary Competition: first prize, fiction.

1985 CBC Radio Literary Competition: first prize, fiction.

What the critics have said . . .

. . . about *Thieves*
"A subtle work of art that repays close reading, and Janice Kulyk Keefer deserves all the recognition at home and abroad this book is likely to gain her." —*The Globe and Mail*

"A compelling novel." —*The Vancouver Sun*

"[*Thieves*] brings us one step closer to understanding a great writer and, for that matter, great writing." —*Edmonton Journal*

. . . about *Honey and Ashes*
"To trace the legacy of five generations of a family through world wars and social upheaval is a feat. When that family is your own . . . it's an act of courage." —*Chatelaine*

"*Honey and Ashes* is filled with passion and intelligence, and it is gorgeously written."
—*Edmonton Journal*

. . . about *The Green Library*
"Janice Kulyk Keefer's new work delights and disturbs. . . . She weaves a tale of love and betrayal as intricate as the embroidery on a Slavic shawl." —*Maclean's*

"Luminous, lyrical writing."
—*The Globe and Mail*

The Inspiration

I've always been fascinated by brief, brave, and brilliant lives.

When I happened to read the journals of Katherine Mansfield, I was captivated by the voice that emerged from them, a voice that expressed more powerfully than I'd ever thought possible both the rawness of pain and a dazzling delight in being alive in the world. I'd always admired Mansfield's short stories, the way she portrayed in them the richness of childhood and the risky lives of women alone ("la dame seule") but when I learned how adventurous her own life had been, and how high a price she had paid for living freely—even recklessly—in an age when women had none of the safety nets we depend on today—for example—contraception, awareness of and cures for sexually transmitted disease—I knew I had to write about her.

The fact that she was a born performer, wearer of masks, inventor of selves and keeper of secrets, and that she had written so openly and honestly in her journals of her conflicting emotions and desires, made her irresistible. As importantly, the fact that she had destroyed journals recording some of the most painful and puzzling events and periods in her life created a blank that, as a creative writer, I could mark-up to my heart's content.

Katherine Mansfield's consuming desire to be a writer who mattered, and to live a writer's life, even when she was reeling with loneliness and crippled by illness, raised crucial questions for

"I'd always admired Mansfield's short stories."

me, questions that resonate as strongly today as they did in the first two decades of the twentieth century: is personal happiness the price we must pay for public success? Are the greatest artists—especially women—the ones who pay most dearly for their gifts—Virginia Woolf's madness, Mansfield's illness and early death? Finally, how fair is our demand that the writers who mean most to us, for whom we develop a passion, should be outstanding human beings as well as extraordinary artists?

I've mentioned Virginia Woolf—on whom I wrote a master's thesis back in the boom years of Bloomsbury, and who figures prominently in my novel *Rest Harrow*. I think of it now as a time bomb ticking away: my early knowledge of Woolf's jealousy of Mansfield's literary achievement and success, as well as of Woolf's sense of solidarity with Mansfield (in a man's jealously guarded literary world, they were attempting to radically alter the nature and function of the art of fiction by writing as women, of women's perceptions and experience of the real world).

Over the last five years I was able to acquire the time and understanding to push this knowledge further and to start exploring the brave new world Woolf and Mansfield shared—a world shattered by the first truly global war, by startling advances in communications, media, and technology, by the struggles and successes of feminism. Finally, I was able to undertake "field-research"—one of the most rewarding elements of a writer's life—travelling to New Zealand, across Europe, through the British

> *"Are the greatest artists—especially women—the ones who pay most dearly for their gifts?"*

The Inspiration (continued)

Isles, and to one of the great American cities—
Chicago—to flesh out my sense of the journey
Katherine Mansfield, and the characters I had
invented to accompany her, had taken. ❧

Behind the Scenes

I highly recommend becoming a "literary tourist": my enjoyment of the splendours of New Zealand, Cornwall, Scotland, Switzerland and the Riviera, and the excitement of cities like London and Paris was greatly intensified by the knowledge that I was following in Katherine's footsteps, trying to find traces of her passage in a Swiss hotel, a Glasgow tenement, a garden on the outskirts of Wellington, New Zealand.

One of the most arresting moments I experienced was in the Turnbull Library in Wellington, when I was allowed to unwrap, with my white-gloved hands, a parcel of tissue paper in which lay carefully folded a lock of Katherine's chestnut-coloured hair. It felt electric, it was so alive! And to be able to hold in my own hands one of Kathleen Beauchamp's letters to the young Garnet Trowell, in the library of the University of Windsor, Ontario, was more than an act of voyeurism—if it was that at all. There is a shock of reality as well as romance in realizing that what you are holding, poring over, is something utterly unique.

Mansfield's handwriting was as alive as that lock of her hair—the sense of her presence in the slant and dash of the letters was overwhelming. It wasn't the sensation of being haunted, or of seeing a ghost, but rather that of feeling, at your side—as you read—the lively mind and quick heart of the writer herself.

Fact, Fiction,
and the Invisible Line

There seems to be a new literary genre emerging in which the lives of writers, real or imagined, are investigated by characters who are passionate, not to say obsessed readers. Novels such as Byatt's *Possession*, Cunningham's *The Hours*, and Toibin's *The Master* are well-known examples. One of the challenges this genre poses to both writer and reader is the old struggle of fact vs. fiction. If you are writing of a writer who actually lived, who left behind journals and diaries as well as literary texts, what license do you have to invent episodes or dialogues or even meditations and then ascribe them to, say, Mansfield or Sylvia Plath?

My own rule of thumb in writing *Thieves* has been to respect, scrupulously, the facts and known limits of the writer's life—there is nothing in the "Beyond the Blue Mountains" sections of *Thieves* that hasn't been documented in or that can't be verified by any of the biographies of Mansfield or the journals she left behind.

On the other hand, I have happily experimented with the possibilities that the blanks in that life have created. Hence, Miss Baby's aggressive "Vindication" of Katherine's lover, Garnet Trowell—at Katherine's expense. It is, however, presented as a hypothesis—and a highly tendentious one at that!

"One of the challenges this genre poses to both writer and reader is the old struggle of fact vs. fiction."

Favourite Works
by Katherine Mansfield

Which are Mansfield's most arresting, most
rewarding stories? For her sensuous evocation
of childhood and the dynamics of (extended)
family life, her long stories, "Prelude" and "At
the Bay" are key. Her most shimmering,
enchanting prose is to be found in these fictions.
Her masterpiece is almost certainly "The
Daughters of the Late Colonel," which treats
the lives of two tyrannized spinster sisters with
an intricate mix of high comedy and subtle
pathos. "The Doll's House" is a superb treatment of class snobbery and schoolyard bullying
that also manages to be luminously healing. And
"The Garden Party," with its interweaving of
festivity and tragedy, and its investigation of the
mystery at the heart of human life, is a classic.

More on Mansfield

Katherine Mansfield is widely regarded as one
of the masters of the short story.

She was born Kathleen Mansfield Beauchamp
in 1888 in Wellington, New Zealand, into a
middle-class colonial family. Her father,
Harold Beauchamp, was a banker and her
mother, Annie Burnell Dyer, the granddaughter
of a pub owner, was both beautiful and socially
ambitious. Mansfield lived for six years in the
rural village of Karori. She attended Queen's
College in London in 1903, then returned to
New Zealand in 1906, where she read vora-
ciously, became an accomplished cellist, and
resisted her family's attempts to marry her off
safely and respectably. She also published her
first pieces of prose in local journals.

Katherine eventually persuaded her father to
allow her to move back to England, with an
allowance of £100 a year. There she devoted
herself to writing. Mansfield never visited New
Zealand again.

Her first volume of short stories, *In a German
Pension* (1911), received little notice, but the stories in *Bliss* (1920) and *The Garden Party* (1922)
established her as a major writer. Later volumes
of stories include *The Dove's Nest* (1923) and
Something Childish (1924; published in the U.S.
as *The Little Girl*). *Novels and Novelists* (1930) is
a compilation of critical essays. Her collected
stories appeared in 1937.

After a brief first marriage, she married John
Middleton Murry, an editor and critic, in 1918.

During the last five years of her life she suffered from tuberculosis; she died of a pulmonary hemorrhage on January 9, 1923, in a commune founded by Gurdjieff near Fontainebleau, France.

After Mansfield's death, Murry culled a number of books from her literary remains, editing her poems (1923, new ed. 1930) and publishing extracts from her journals (1927), her letters (1928), and a collection of unfinished pieces from her notebooks (1939).

More recently, her letters were published in a two-volume edition (1984–87), edited by Vincent O'Sullivan and Margaret Scott. Her notebooks were edited and published by Margaret Scott in 2003. The major biographies are by Antony Alpers (1980) and Claire Tomalin (1988).

If you loved *Thieves*, You'll Enjoy . . .

Clara Callan, by Richard B. Wright
Paperback 0-00-639212-1 $21.95

The Poisonwood Bible, by Barbara Kingsolver
Paperback 0-06-093053-5 $22.95

Enemy Women, by Paulette Jiles
Paperback 0-00-639172-9 $19.95

Garden of Venus, by Eva Stachniak
Original trade paperback 0-00-200578-6 $24.95
(Available in July 2005)